The Complete Strategy & War Collection (Vol. 8)

War, Morality & Power — Fear and Trembling, Genealogy of Morals & Twilight of the Idols

A Modern Translation

Adapted for the Contemporary Reader

Søren Kierkegaard | Frederick the Great

Translated by Tim Zengerink

Table of Contents

Preface - Message to the Reader

What If You Could Help Rebuild the Greatest Library in Human History?

Thousands of years ago, the Library of Alexandria stood as the crown jewel of human achievement — a sanctuary where the collected wisdom of every known civilization was gathered, preserved, and shared freely.

And then, it was lost.

Through fire, conquest, and the slow erosion of time, humanity lost not just books — but ideas, dreams, discoveries, and stories that could have changed the world forever.

Today, the Library of Alexandria lives again — and you are invited to be a part of its restoration.

Our mission is simple yet profound:

To rebuild the greatest library the world has ever known, and to translate all timeless works into every language and dialect, so that no seeker of knowledge is ever left behind again.

By joining our movement to rebuild the modern Library of Alexandria, you become part of an unprecedented mission:

- **Unlimited Access to the Greatest Audiobooks & eBooks Ever Written:**

  Instantly explore thousands of legendary works—Plato, Shakespeare, Jane Austen, Leo Tolstoy, and countless more. All instantly available to read or listen, placing a complete literary universe at your fingertips.

- **Beautiful Paperback & Deluxe Editions at Printing Cost**

  Own any title as an elegant paperback, deluxe hardcover, or stunning collectible boxset—offered to you at true printing cost, delivered straight to your door. Build your personal Library of Alexandria, crafted for beauty, built for durability, and worthy of proud display.

- **Fresh Translations for Modern Readers—in Every Language & Dialect**

  Enjoy timeless masterpieces reimagined in clear, contemporary language—no more outdated phrases or obscure references. Alongside the original versions, we're tirelessly translating these classics into every language and dialect imaginable, ensuring accessibility and understanding across cultures and generations.

- **Join a Global Renaissance of Literature & Knowledge**

  You directly support expanding our library, publishing deluxe editions at true cost, translating works into all global languages, and bringing humanity's greatest stories to people everywhere. By joining today, you're not just preserving a legacy of masterpieces; you set in motion a powerful wave of literary accessibility.

Become a Torchbearer of Knowledge.

Join us for free now at **LibraryofAlexandria.com**

Together, we will ensure that the light of human wisdom never fades again.

With gratitude and a shared love of knowledge,
The Modern Library of Alexandria Team

Visit:

www.libraryofalexandria.com

Or scan the code below:

Introduction

Empire Maintained:
Intelligence, Subterfuge, and Strategic Statecraft

In the aftermath of conquest, a different kind of struggle begins—the struggle to govern, to hold power, to prevent collapse, and to sustain a legacy. The stability of empires depends not only on battlefield victories, but on what follows: diplomacy, intelligence, communication, and the invisible machinery of control. In The Complete Strategy & War Collection (Vol. 7), we turn our attention to the finer mechanisms of imperial management and elite strategy through the appendices, fragments, and codas from three of history's most formidable minds: Julius Caesar, Kautilya, and Frederick the Great.

This volume features three distinct yet harmonizing texts: the appendices to Caesar's Commentaries, Kautilya's Book XIV: Secret Campaigns from the Arthashastra, and the Addenda to Instructions written by Frederick the Great. Each provides rare insight into the backstage of empire—how rulers think when the wars are supposedly over, and how power must be preserved not only with strength, but with subtlety.

These writings are smaller in scale than the sweeping narratives or philosophical treatises of their primary works, but their intimacy makes them more revealing. They reflect the realities of leadership behind closed doors: decisions made in quiet, operations carried out in the shadows, and strategies refined not for grand audiences, but for trusted agents and successors.

This introduction explores the common threads that unite these pieces: a belief in preemption, a reliance on secrecy, and a deep understanding that politics and warfare are not distinct but continuous fields of contest. The tools of empire—when diplomacy

4

fails and the sword is sheathed—are shown here in their rawest form: espionage, targeted assassination, surveillance, manipulation, and the manipulation of public narrative. These are not tales of conquest. They are instructions for control.

Caesar's Addenda:
Political Warfare and the Endgame of Civil Conflict

The Commentaries of Julius Caesar, especially those recounting the Gallic and Civil Wars, are famous for their clarity, restraint, and rhetorical mastery. But in the appendices and addenda—often overlooked—Caesar reveals something subtler: a leader's obsessive concern with justification, perception, and legacy.

The fragments attributed to Caesar's later campaigns, letters, and marginalia function as after-action reports, internal memos, and justifications for controversial decisions. They reveal a mind preoccupied with consolidating control after the swords have fallen still. These writings do not describe battles; they manage memory.

In them, we find strategies of information control, tactical leniency for political effect, and the systematic neutralization of internal threats. Caesar carefully constructs a narrative of reluctant war, of moderation in victory, and of clemency toward enemies. This was not only magnanimity—it was policy. By shaping the story of the war, Caesar shaped the legitimacy of his rule.

He also shows how the end of war does not end conflict. Instead, it shifts the terrain from the field to the forum, from military victory to political reconstruction. Caesar's treatment of pardoned senators, his dealings with foreign client states, and his reorganization of Rome's administrative order reflect a consistent doctrine: suppress rebellion before it forms, reward loyalty in public, and eliminate rivals with plausible legality.

In this way, Caesar's appendices become a masterclass in postwar statecraft. They reveal how a general becomes a ruler not just by force, but by foresight. In them, the sword becomes a pen—and that pen becomes the most enduring weapon of all.

Kautilya's Secret Campaigns: The Machinery of Preemptive Strategy

Book XIV of the Arthashastra, titled "Secret Conduct," is the climax of Kautilya's long treatise on statecraft. Where earlier books establish administration, diplomacy, law, and economics, this final book drops all pretense of civility. Here, we enter the world of spies, poisoners, staged betrayals, disinformation campaigns, and deep-state intrigue.

Kautilya does not flinch from harsh methods. He advocates the use of secret agents to foment rebellions in neighboring states, assassinate disloyal ministers, corrupt enemy commanders, and manipulate popular opinion. For him, secrecy is not the absence of visibility—it is a strategic force. The ruler must maintain two faces: one for the public and one for survival.

He outlines various types of agents—wandering ascetics, merchants, beggars, prostitutes—all of whom serve as instruments of information gathering and influence. His model of intelligence is decentralized, embedded, and psychologically acute. He warns that even allies may turn enemy, and so counsels constant surveillance.

Kautilya's "secret campaigns" are as much psychological as physical. He speaks of inducing fear in rival courts, spreading panic among commanders, or staging the appearance of divine omens to manipulate religious sentiment. His tools include not only force, but myth and perception.

This book has often been compared to The Prince for its realism and ruthlessness, but it goes even further. Where Machiavelli focuses on princely behavior, Kautilya builds an entire institutional framework for subversion and counter-subversion. He shows how covert war runs parallel to formal diplomacy, and how the most effective campaigns are those the enemy never detects.

In modern terms, Book XIV reads like a manual of asymmetric warfare, counterintelligence, and regime change. Yet at its core is a consistent ethical logic: the preservation of the state, by any means necessary. In this doctrine, knowledge is security—and secrecy is power.

Frederick's Legacy:
Prudence, Order, and the Imperial Mind

Frederick the Great, King of Prussia, was known for his campaigns of maneuver, his Enlightenment patronage, and his tight administrative control. His original Instructions to His Generals offered rules of conduct, command principles, and moral expectations. But the Addenda to Instructions—compiled near the end of his reign—reveal a more nuanced, reflective tone. Here, we find a king not at war, but planning for succession.

These addenda focus on continuity. Frederick emphasizes the importance of judgment over rules, flexibility over dogma. He reiterates that generals must know the character of the enemy commander as much as their troops. He warns against predictability, advocates selective disobedience, and calls for logistical foresight above all.

One theme that emerges strongly is Frederick's concern for moderation. He understood that empires can die not only from weakness, but from overreach. He stresses that victories must be consolidated with restraint, that repression must not produce revolt, and that the economy of violence is preferable to its excess.

His reflections also touch on civil-military relations. He cautions against generals becoming politicians, and politicians meddling too deeply in field command. He urges the preservation of military discipline not just through force, but through shared honor and clarity of purpose.

Unlike Caesar's ambition or Kautilya's total control, Frederick's addenda reflect a sovereign managing the long life of an institution.

His style is methodical, cool, and deeply rational. He views statecraft as continuity over charisma, systems over personalities.

In this way, Frederick's final writings serve as a bridge between classical strategy and modern doctrine. They model an imperial ethos that is not expansionist, but preservative. His goal was not to conquer more—but to keep what had been won.

Between Silence and Sovereignty: The Deep Mechanics of Rule

Together, these texts form a unique triptych. They are not treatises of war, but of what follows: how power, once seized, must be managed, defended, and hidden in plain sight.

- Caesar teaches how narrative and magnanimity mask ambition.
- Kautilya demonstrates how subversion and surveillance are baked into state security.
- Frederick models a sober, systems-based approach to strategic governance.

They reveal that the most enduring empires are not those that win battles, but those that manage risk, deflect threats, and embed their control in structures, symbols, and systems invisible to their enemies.

These texts are especially relevant today in a world of cyberwar, political theater, misinformation, and the erosion of visible front lines. They remind us that the logic of empire has always been layered—some of it announced, but much of it concealed. And that behind every throne is not just a soldier or a general, but a strategist who thinks in years, not days; in shadows, not declarations.

Welcome to The Complete Strategy & War Collection (Vol. 7). May these blueprints for imperial maintenance challenge your assumptions, sharpen your foresight, and reveal the quiet, often unseen, mechanisms by which power endures.

Fear And Trembling

Søren Kierkegaard

Preface

Not merely in the realm of commerce but in the world of ideas as well our age is organizing a regular clearance sale. Everything is to be had at such a bargain that it is questionable whether in the end there is anybody who will want to bid. Every speculative price-fixer who conscientiously directs attention to the significant march of modern philosophy, every Privatdocent, tutor, and student, every crofter and cottar in philosophy, is not content with doubting everything but goes further. Perhaps it would be untimely and ill-timed to ask them where they are going, but surely it is courteous and unobtrusive to regard it as certain that they have doubted everything, since otherwise it would be a queer thing for them to be going further. This preliminary movement they have therefore all of them made, and presumably with such ease that they do not find it necessary to let drop a word about the how; for not even he who anxiously and with deep concern sought a little enlightenment was able to find any such thing, any guiding sign, any little dietetic prescription, as to how one was to comport oneself in supporting this prodigious task. "But Descartes3 did it." Descartes, a venerable, humble and honest thinker, whose writings surely no one can read without the deepest emotion, did what he said and said what he did. Alas, alack, that is a great rarity in our times! Descartes, as he repeatedly affirmed, did not doubt in matters of faith.

What those ancient Greeks (who also had some understanding of philosophy) regarded as a task for a whole lifetime, seeing that dexterity in doubting is not acquired in a few days or weeks, what the veteran combatant attained when he had preserved the equilibrium of doubt through all the pitfalls he encountered, who intrepidly denied the certainty of sense-perception and the certainty of the processes of thought, incorruptibly defied the apprehensions of self-love and the insinuations of sympathy—that is where everybody begins in our time. In our time nobody is content to stop with faith but wants to go further. It would perhaps be rash to ask where these people are going, but it is surely a sign of breeding and culture for me to assume that

everybody has faith, for otherwise it would be queer for them to be ...
going further. In those old days it was different, then faith was a task
for a whole lifetime, because it was assumed that dexterity in faith is
not acquired in a few days or weeks. When the tried oldster drew near
to his last hour, having fought the good fight and kept the faith, his
heart was still young enough not to have forgotten that fear and
trembling which chastened the youth, which the man indeed held in
check, but which no man quite outgrows ... except as he might
succeed at the earliest opportunity in going further. Where these
revered figures arrived, that is the point where everybody in our day
begins to go further. The present writer is nothing of a philosopher,
he has not understood the System, does not know whether it actually
exists, whether it is completed; already he has enough for his weak
head in the thought of what a prodigious head everybody in our day
must have, since everybody has such a prodigious thought. Even
though one were capable of converting the whole content of faith into
the form of a concept, it does not follow that one has adequately
conceived faith and understands how one got into it, or how it got
into one. The present writer is nothing of a philosopher; he is, poetice
et eleganter, an amateur writer who neither writes the System nor
promises6 of the System, who neither subscribes to the System nor
ascribes anything to it. He writes because for him it is a luxury which
becomes the more agreeable and more evident, the fewer there are
who buy and read what he writes. He can easily foresee his fate in an
age when passion has been obliterated in favor of learning, in an age
when an author who wants to have readers must take care to write in
such a way that the book can easily be perused during the afternoon
nap, and take care to fashion his outward deportment in likeness to
the picture of that polite young gardener in the advertisement sheet,7
who with hat in hand, and with a good certificate from the place
where he last served, recommends himself to the esteemed public. He
foresees his fate—that he will be entirely ignored. He has a
presentiment of the dreadful event, that a jealous criticism will many
a time let him feel the birch; he trembles at the still more dreadful
thought that one or another enterprising scribe, a gulper of

paragraphs, who to rescue learning is always willing to do with other peoples' writings what Trop8 "to preserve good taste" magnanimously resolved to do with a book called The Destruction of the Human Race—that is, he will slice the author into paragraphs, and will do it with the same inflexibility as the man who in the interest of the science of punctuation divided his discourse by counting the words, so that there were fifty words for a period and thirty-five for a semicolon. I prostrate myself with the profoundest deference before every systematic "bag-peerer" at the custom house, protesting, "This is not the System, it has nothing whatever to do with the System." I call down every blessing upon the System and upon the Danish shareholders in this omnibus9—for a tower it is hardly likely to become. I wish them all and sundry good luck and all prosperity.

Respectfully,

Johannes DE SILENTIO

Fear and Trembling

PRELUDE10 Once upon a time there was a man who as a child had heard the beautiful story11 about how God tempted Abraham, and how he endured temptation, kept the faith, and a second time received again a son contrary to expectation. When the child became older he read the same story with even greater admiration, for life had separated what was united in the pious simplicity of the child. The older he became, the more frequently his mind reverted to that story, his enthusiasm became greater and greater, and yet he was less and less able to understand the story. At last in his interest for that he forgot everything else; his soul had only one wish, to see Abraham, one longing, to have been witness to that event. His desire was not to behold the beautiful countries of the Orient, or the earthly glory of the Promised Land, or that godfearing couple whose old age God had blessed, or the venerable figure of the aged patriarch, or the vigorous young manhood of Isaac whom God had bestowed upon Abraham— he saw no reason why the same thing might not have taken place on a barren heath in Denmark. His yearning was to accompany them on the three days' journey when Abraham rode with sorrow before him and with Isaac by his side. His only wish was to be present at the time when Abraham lifted up his eyes and saw Mount Moriah afar off, at the time when he left the asses behind and went alone with Isaac up unto the mountain; for what his mind was intent upon was not the ingenious web of imagination but the shudder of thought. That man was not a thinker, he felt no need of getting beyond faith; he deemed it the most glorious thing to be remembered as the father of it, an enviable lot to possess it, even though no one else were to know it. That man was not a learned exegete, he didn't know Hebrew, if he had known Hebrew, he perhaps would easily have understood the story and Abraham. I "And God tempted Abraham and said unto him, Take Isaac, shine only son, whom thou lovest, and get thee into the land of Moriah, and offer him there for a burnt offering upon the mountain which I will show thee." It was early in the morning, Abraham arose betimes, he had the asses saddled, left his tent, and Isaac with him, but Sarah looked out of the window after them until they had passed down the valley and she could see them no more.12 They rode in silence for three days. On the morning of the fourth day Abraham said never a word, but he lifted up his eyes and saw Mount Moriah afar off. He left the young men behind and went on alone with Isaac beside him up to the mountain. But Abraham said to himself, "I will not conceal from Isaac whither this course leads him." He stood still, he laid his hand upon the head of Isaac in benediction, and Isaac bowed to receive the blessing. And Abraham's face was fatherliness, his look was mild, his speech encouraging. But Isaac was unable to understand him, his soul could not be exalted; he embraced Abraham's knees, he fell at his feet imploringly, he begged for his young life, for the fair hope of his future, he called to mind the joy in Abraham's house, he called to mind the sorrow and loneliness. Then Abraham lifted up the boy, he walked with him by his side, and his talk was full of comfort and exhortation. But Isaac could not understand him. He climbed Mount Moriah, but Isaac understood him not. Then for an instant he turned away from him, and when

Isaac again saw Abraham's face it was changed, his glance was wild, his form was horror. He seized Isaac by the throat, threw him to the ground, and said, "Stupid boy, dost thou then suppose that I am thy father? I am an idolater. Dost thou suppose that this is God's bidding? No, it is my desire." Then Isaac trembled and cried out in his terror, "O God in heaven, have compassion upon me. God of Abraham, have compassion upon me. If I have no father upon earth, be Thou my father!" But Abraham in a low voice said to himself, "O Lord in heaven, I thank Thee. After all it is better for him to believe that I am a monster, rather than that he should lose faith in Thee." When the child must be weaned, the mother blackens her breast, it would indeed be a shame that the breast should look delicious when the child must not have it. So the child believes that the breast has changed, but the mother is the same, her glance is as loving and tender as ever. Happy the person who had no need of more dreadful expedients for weaning the child! II It was early in the morning, Abraham arose betimes, he embraced Sarah, the bride of his old age, and Sarah kissed Isaac, who had taken away her reproach, who was her pride, her hope for all time. So they rode on in silence along the way, and Abraham's glance was fixed upon the ground until the fourth day when he lifted up his eyes and saw afar off Mount Moriah, but his glance turned again to the ground. Silently he laid the wood in order, he bound Isaac, in silence he drew the knife—then he saw the ram which God had prepared. Then he offered that and returned home. ... From that time on Abraham became old, he could not forget that God had required this of him. Isaac throve as before, but Abraham's eyes were darkened, and he knew joy no more. When the child has grown big and must be weaned, the mother virginally hides her breast, so the child has no more a mother. Happy the child which did not in another way lose its mother. III It was early in the morning, Abraham arose betimes, he kissed Sarah, the young mother, and Sarah kissed Isaac, her delight, her joy at all times. And Abraham rode pensively along the way, he thought of Hagar and of the son whom he drove out into the wilderness, he climbed Mount Moriah, he drew the knife. It was a quiet evening when Abraham rode out alone, and he rode to Mount

Moriah; he threw himself upon his face, he prayed God to forgive him his sin, that he had been willing to offer Isaac, that the father had forgotten his duty toward the son. Often he rode his lonely way, but he found no rest. He could not comprehend that it was a sin to be willing to offer to God the best thing he possessed, that for which he would many times have given his life; and if it was a sin, if he had not loved Isaac as he did, then he could not understand that it might be forgiven. For what sin could be more dreadful? When the child must be weaned, the mother too is not without sorrow at the thought that she and the child are separated more and more, that the child which first lay under her heart and later reposed upon her breast will be so near to her no more. So they mourn together for the brief period of mourning. Happy the person who has kept the child as near and needed not to sorrow any more! IV It was early in the morning, everything was prepared for the journey in Abraham's house. He bade Sarah farewell, and Eleazar, the faithful servant, followed him along the way, until he turned back. They rode together in harmony, Abraham and Isaac, until they came to Mount Moriah. But Abraham prepared everything for the sacrifice, calmly and quietly; but when he turned and drew the knife, Isaac saw that his left hand was clenched in despair, that a tremor passed through his body—but Abraham drew the knife. Then they returned again home, and Sarah hastened to meet them, but Isaac had lost his faith. No word of this had ever been spoken in the world, and Isaac never talked to anyone about what he had seen, and Abraham did not suspect that anyone had seen it. When the child must be weaned, the mother has stronger food in readiness, lest the child should perish. Happy the person who has stronger food in readiness! Thus and in many like ways that man of whom we are speaking thought concerning this event. Every time he returned home after wandering to Mount Moriah, he sank down with weariness, he folded his hands and said, "No one is so great as Abraham! Who is capable of understanding him?" A PANEGYRIC UPON ABRAHAM If there were no eternal consciousness in a man, if at the foundation of all there lay only a wildly seething power which writhing with obscure passions produced everything that is great and everything that is insignificant, if a bottomless void never satiated lay hidden beneath all– what then would life be but despair? If such were the case, if there were no sacred bond which united mankind, if one generation arose after another like the leafage in the forest, if the one generation replaced the other like the song of birds in the forest, if the human race passed through the world as the ship goes through the sea, like the wind through the desert, a thoughtless and fruitless activity, if an eternal oblivion were always lurking hungrily for its prey and there was no power strong enough to wrest it from its maw–how empty then and comfortless life would be! But therefore it is not thus, but as God created man and woman, so too He fashioned the hero and the poet or orator. The poet cannot do what that other does, he can only admire, love and rejoice in the hero. Yet he too is happy, and not less so, for the hero is as it were his better nature, with which he is in love, rejoicing in the fact that this after all is not himself, that his love can be admiration. He is the genius of recollection, can do nothing except call to mind what has been done, do nothing but admire what has been done; he contributes nothing of his own, but is jealous of the intrusted treasure. He follows the option of his heart, but when he has found what he sought, he wanders before every man's door with his song and with his oration, that all may admire the hero as he does, be proud of the hero as he is. This is his achievement, his humble work, this is his faithful service in the house of the hero. If he thus remains true to his love, he strives day and night against the cunning of oblivion which would trick him out of his hero, then he has completed his work, then he is gathered to the hero, who has loved him just as faithfully, for the poet is as it were the hero's better nature, powerless it may be as a memory is, but also transfigured as a memory is. Hence no one shall be forgotten who was great, and though time tarries long, though a cloud13 of misunderstanding takes the hero away, his lover comes nevertheless, and the longer the time that has passed, the more faithfully will he cling to him. No, not one shall be forgotten who was great in the world. But each was great in his own way, and each in proportion to the greatness of that which he loved. For he who loved himself became great by himself, and he who loved other men became great by his selfless devotion, but he who loved God became greater than all. Everyone shall be remembered, but each became great in proportion to his expectation. One became great by expecting the possible, another by expecting the eternal, but he who expected the impossible became greater than all. Everyone shall be remembered, but each was great in proportion to the greatness of that with which he strove. For he who strove with the world became great by overcoming the world, and he who strove with himself became great by overcoming himself, but he who strove with God became greater than all. So there was strife in the world, man against man, one against a thousand, but he who strove with God was greater than all. So there was strife upon earth: there was one who overcame all by his power, and there was one who overcame God by his impotence. There was one who relied upon himself and gained all, there was one who secure in his strength sacrificed all, but he who believed God was greater than all. There was one who was great by reason of his power, and one who was great by reason of his wisdom, and one who was great by reason of his hope, and one who was great by reason of his love; but Abraham was greater than all, great by reason of his power whose strength is impotence, great by reason of his wisdom whose secret is foolishness, great by reason of his hope whose form is madness, great by reason of the love which is hatred of oneself. By faith Abraham went out from the land of his fathers and became a sojourner in the land of promise. He left one thing behind, took one thing with him: he left his earthly understanding behind and took faith with him— otherwise he would not have wandered forth but would have thought this unreasonable. By faith he was a stranger in the land of promise, and there was nothing to recall what was dear to him, but by its novelty everything tempted his soul to melancholy yearning—and yet he was God's elect, in whom the Lord was well pleased! Yea, if he had been disowned, cast off from God's grace, he could have comprehended it better; but now it was like a mockery of him and of his faith. There was in the world one too who lived in banishment14 from the fatherland he loved. He is not forgotten, nor his Lamentations when he sorrowfully sought and found what he had lost. There is no song of Lamentations by Abraham. It is human to lament, human to weep with them that weep, but it is greater to believe, more blessed to contemplate the believer. By faith Abraham received the promise that in his seed all races of the world would be blessed. Time passed, the possibility was there, Abraham believed; time passed, it became unreasonable, Abraham believed. There was in the world one who had an expectation, time passed, the evening drew nigh, he was not paltry enough to have forgotten his expectation, therefore he too shall not be forgotten. Then he sorrowed, and sorrow did not deceive him as life had done, it did for him all it could, in the sweetness of sorrow he possessed his delusive expectation. It is human to sorrow, human to sorrow with them that sorrow, but it is greater to believe, more blessed to contemplate the believer. There is no song of Lamentations by Abraham. He did not mournfully count the days while time passed, he did not look at Sarah with a suspicious glance, wondering whether she were growing old, he did not arrest the course of the sun, that Sarah might not grow old, and his expectation with her. He did not sing lullingly before Sarah his mournful lay. Abraham became old, Sarah became a laughingstock in the land, and yet he was God's elect and inheritor of the promise that in his seed all the races of the world would be blessed. So were it not better if he had not been God's elect? What is it to be God's elect? It is to be denied in youth the wishes of youth, so as with great pains to get them fulfilled in old age. But Abraham believed and held fast the expectation. If Abraham had wavered, he would have given it up. If he had said to God, "Then perhaps it is not after all Thy will that it should come to pass, so I will give up the wish. It was my only wish, it was my bliss. My soul is sincere, I hide no secret malice because Thou didst deny it to me"–he would not have been forgotten, he would have saved many by his example, yet he would not be the father of faith. For it is great to give up one's wish, but it is greater to hold it fast after having given it up, it is great to grasp the eternal, but it is greater to hold fast to the temporal after having given it up.15 Then came the fulness of time. If Abraham had not believed, Sarah surely would have been dead of sorrow, and Abraham, dulled by grief, would not have understood the fulfilment but would have smiled at it as at a dream of youth. But Abraham believed, therefore he was young; for he who always hopes for the best becomes old, and he who is always prepared for the worst grows old early, but he who believes preserves an eternal youth. Praise therefore to that story! For Sarah, though stricken in years, was young enough to desire the pleasure of motherhood, and Abraham, though gray-haired, was young enough to wish to be a father. In an outward respect the marvel consists in the fact that it came to pass according to their expectation, in a deeper sense the miracle of faith consists in the fact that Abraham and Sarah were young enough to wish, and that faith had preserved their wish and therewith their youth. He accepted the fulfilment of the promise, he accepted it by faith, and it came to pass according to the promise and according to his faith—for Moses smote the rock with his rod, but he did not believe. Then there was joy in Abraham's house, when Sarah became a bride on the day of their golden wedding. But it was not to remain thus. Still once more Abraham was to be tried. He had fought with that cunning power which invents everything, with that alert enemy which never slumbers, with that old man who outlives all things—he had fought with Time and preserved his faith. Now all the terror of the strife was concentrated in one instant. "And God tempted Abraham and said unto him, Take Isaac, thine only son, whom thou lovest, and get thee into the land of Moriah, and offer him there for a burnt offering upon the mountain which I will show thee." So all was lost—more dreadfully than if it had never come to pass! So the Lord was only making sport of Abraham! He made miraculously the preposterous actual, and now in turn He would annihilate it. It was indeed foolishness, but Abraham did not laugh at it like Sarah when the promise was announced. All was lost! Seventy years of faithful expectation, the brief joy at the fulfilment of faith. Who then is he that plucks away the old man's staff, who is it that requires that he himself shall break it? Who is he that would make a man's gray hairs comfortless, who is it that requires that he himself shall do it? Is there no compassion for the venerable oldling, none for the innocent child? And yet Abraham was God's elect, and it was the Lord who imposed the trial. All would now be lost. The glorious memory to be preserved by the human race, the promise in Abraham's seed–this was only a whim, a fleeting thought which the Lord had had, which Abraham should now obliterate. That glorious treasure which was just as old as faith in Abraham's heart, many, many years older than Isaac, the fruit of Abraham's life, sanctified by prayers, matured in conflict–the blessing upon Abraham's lips, this fruit was now to be plucked prematurely and remain without significance. For what significance had it when Isaac was to be sacrificed? That sad and yet blissful hour when Abraham was to take leave of all that was dear to him, when yet once more he was to lift up his head, when his countenance would shine like that of the Lord, when he would concentrate his whole soul in a blessing which was potent to make Isaac blessed all his days–this time would not come! For he would indeed take leave of Isaac, but in such a way that he himself would remain behind; death would separate them, but in such a way that Isaac remained its prey. The old man would not be joyful in death as he laid his hands in blessing upon Isaac, but he would be weary of life as he laid violent hands upon Isaac. And it was God who tried him. Yea, woe, woe unto the messenger who had come before Abraham with such tidings! Who would have ventured to be the emissary of this srrow? But it was God who tried Abraham. Yet Abraham believed, and believed for this life. Yea, if his faith had been only for a future life, he surely would have cast everything away in order to hasten out of this world to which he did not belong. But Abraham's faith was not of this sort, if there be such a faith; for really this is not faith but the furthest possibility of faith which has a presentiment of its object at the extremest limit of the horizon, yet is separated from it by a yawning abyss within which despair carries on its game. But Abraham believed precisely for this life, that he was to grow old in the land, honored by the people, blessed in his generation, remembered forever in Isaac, his dearest thing in life, whom he embraced with a love for which it would be a poor expression to say that he loyally fulfilled the father's duty of loving the son, as indeed is evinced in the words of the summons, "the son whom thou lovest."

Jacob had twelve sons, and one of them he loved; Abraham had only one, the son whom he loved. Yet Abraham believed and did not doubt, he believed the preposterous. If Abraham had doubted–then he would have done something else, something glorious; for how could Abraham do anything but what is great and glorious! He would have marched up to Mount Moriah, he would have cleft the fire-wood, lit the pyre, drawn the knife–he would have cried out to God, "Despise not this sacrifice, it is not the best thing I possess, that I know well, for what is an old man in comparison with the child of promise; but it is the best I am able to give Thee. Let Isaac never come to know this, that he may console himself with his youth." He would have plunged the knife into his own breast. He would have been admired in the world, and his name would not have been forgotten; but it is one thing to be admired, and another to be the guiding star which saves the anguished. But Abraham believed. He did not pray for himself, with the hope of moving the Lord–it was only when the righteous punishment was decreed upon Sodom and Gomorrha that Abraham came forward with his prayers. We read in those holy books: "And God tempted Abraham, and said unto him, Abraham, Abraham, where art thou? And he said, Here am I." Thou to whom my speech is addressed, was such the case with thee? When afar off thou didst see the heavy dispensation of providence approaching thee, didst thou not say to the mountains, Fall on me, and to the hills, Cover me? Or if thou wast stronger, did not thy foot move slowly along the way, longing as it were for the old path? When a call was issued to thee, didst thou answer, or didst thou not answer perhaps in a low voice, whisperingly? Not so Abraham: joyfully, buoyantly, confidently, with a loud voice, he answered, "Here am I." We read further: "And Abraham rose early in the morning"–as though it were to a festival, so he hastened, and early in the morning he had come to the place spoken of, to Mount Moriah. He said nothing to Sarah, nothing to Eleazar. Indeed who could understand him? Had not the temptation by its very nature exacted of him an oath of silence? He cleft the wood, he bound Isaac, he lit the pyre, he drew the knife. My hearer, there was many a father who believed that with his son he lost everything that was dearest to him in the world, that he was deprived of every hope for the future, but yet there was none that was the child of promise in the sense that Isaac was for Abraham. There was many a father who lost his child; but then it was God, it was the unalterable, the unsearchable will of the Almighty, it was His hand took the child. Not so with Abraham. For him was reserved a harder trial, and Isaac's fate was laid along with the knife in Abraham's hand. And there he stood, the old man, with his only hope! But he did not doubt, he did not look anxiously to the right or to the left, he did not challenge heaven with his prayers. He knew that it was God the Almighty who was trying him, he knew that it was the hardest sacrifice that could be required of him; but he knew also that no sacrifice was too hard when God required it–and he drew the knife. Who gave strength to Abraham's arm? Who held his right hand up so that it did not fall limp at his side? He who gazes at this becomes paralyzed. Who gave strength to Abraham's soul, so that his eyes did not grow dim, so that he saw neither Isaac nor the ram? He who gazes at this becomes blind.–And yet rare enough perhaps is the man who becomes paralyzed and blind, still more rare one who worthily recounts what happened. We all know it–it was only a trial. If Abraham when he stood upon Mount Moriah had doubted, if he had gazed about him irresolutely, if before he drew the knife he had by chance discovered the ram, if God had permitted him to offer it instead of Isaac– then he would have betaken himself home, everything would have been the same, he has Sarah, he retained Isaac, and yet how changed! For his retreat would have been a flight, his salvation an accident, his reward dishonor, his future perhaps perdition. Then he would have borne witness neither to his faith nor to God's grace, but would have teshfied only how dreadful it is to march out to Mount Moriah. Then Abraham would not have been forgotten, nor would Mount Moriah, this mountain would then be mentioned, not like Ararat where the Ark landed, but would be spoken of as a consternation, because it was here that Abraham doubted. Venerable Father Abraham! In marching home from Mount Moriah thou hadst no need of a panegyric which might console thee for thy loss; for thou didst gain all and didst retain

Isaac. Was it not so? Never again did the Lord take him from thee, but thou didst sit at table joyfully with him in thy tent, as thou cost in the beyond to all eternity. Venerable Father Abraham! Thousands of years have run their course since those days, but thou hast need of no tardy lover to snatch the memorial of thee from the power of oblivion, for every language calls thee to remembrance–and yet thou cost reward thy lover more gloriously than does any other; hereafter thou cost make him blessed in thy bosom; here thou cost enthral his eyes and his heart by the marvel of thy deed. Venerable Father Abraham! Second Father of the human race! Thou who first wast sensible of and didst first bear witness to that prodigious passion which disdains the dreadful conflict with the rage of the elements and with the powers of creation in order to strive with God; thou who first didst know that highest passion, the holy, pure and humble expression of the divine madness16 which the pagans admired–forgive him who would speak in praise of thee, if he does not do it fittingly. He spoke humbly, as if it were the desire of his own heart, he spoke briefly, as it becomes him to do, but he will never forget that thou hadst need of a hundred years to obtain a son of old age against expectation, that thou didst have to draw the knife before retaining Isaac; he will never forget that in a hundred and thirty years thou didst not get further than to faith. PROBLEMATA: PRELIMINARY EXPECTORATION An old proverb fetched from the outward and visible world says: "Only the man that works gets the bread." Strangely enough this proverb does not aptly apply in that world to which it expressly belongs. For the outward world is subjected to the law of imperfection, and again and again the experience is repeated that he too who does not work gets the bread, and that he who sleeps gets it more abundantly than the man who works. In the outward world everything is made payable to the bearer, this world is in bondage to the law of indifference, and to him who has the ring, the spirit of the ring is obedient, whether he be Noureddin or Aladdin,17 and he who has the world's treasure, has it, however he got it. It is different in the world of spirit. Here an eternal divine order prevails, here it does not rain both upon the just and upon the unjust, here the sun does not shine both upon the good and upon the evil, here it holds good that only he who works gets the bread, only he who was in anguish finds repose, only he who descends into the underworld rescues the beloved, only he who draws the knife gets Isaac. He who will not work does not get the bread but remains deluded, as the gods deluded Orpheus with an airy figure in place of the loved one, deluded him because he was effeminate, not courageous, because he was a cithara-player, not a man. Here it is of no use to have Abraham for one's father, nor to have seventeen ancestors—he who will not work must take note of what is written about the maidens of Israel,18 for he gives birth to wind, but he who is willing to work gives birth to his own father. There is a knowledge which would presumptuously introduce into the world of spirit the same law of indifference under which the external world sighs. It counts it enough to think the great— other work is not necessary. But therefore it doesn't get the bread, it perishes of hunger, while everything is transformed into gold. And what does it really know? There were many thousands of Greek contemporaries, and countless numbers in subsequent generations, who knew all the triumphs of Miltiades, but only one19 was made sleepless by them. There were countless generations which knew by rote, word for word, the story of Abraham—how many were made sleepless by it? Now the story of Abraham has the remarkable property that it is always glorious, however poorly one may understand it; yet here again the proverb applies, that all depends upon whether one is willing to labor and be heavy laden. But they will not labor, and yet they would understand the story. They exalt Abraham—but how? They express the whole thing in perfectly general terms: "The great thing was that he loved God so much that he was willing to sacrifice to Him the best." That is very true, but "the best" is an indefinite expression. In the course of thought, as the tongue wags on, Isaac and "the best" are confidently identified, and he who meditates can very well smoke his pipe during the meditation, and the auditor can very well stretch out his legs in comfort. In case that rich young man whom Christ encountered on the road had sold all his goods and given to the poor, we should extol him, as we do all that is great, though without labor we would not understand him—and yet he would not have become an Abraham, in spite of the fact that he offered his best. What they leave out of Abraham's history is dread;20 for to money I have no ethical obligation, but to the son the father has the highest and most sacred obligation. Dread, however, is a perilous thing for effeminate natures, hence they forget it, and in spite of that they want to talk about Abraham. So they talk—in the course of the oration they use indifferently the two terms, Isaac and "the best." All goes famously. However, if it chanced that among the auditors there was one who suffered from insomnia—then the most dreadful, the profoundest tragic and comic misunderstanding lies very close. He went home, he would do as Abraham did, for the son is indeed "the best." If the orator got to know of it, he perhaps went to him, he summoned all his clerical dignity, he shouted, "O abominable man, offscouring of society, what devil possessed thee to want to murder thy son?" And the parson, who had not been conscious of warmth or perspiration in preaching about Abraham, is astonished at himself, at the earnest wrath which he thundered down upon that poor man. He was delighted with himself, for he had never spoken with such verve and unction. He said to himself and to his wife, "I am an orator. What I lacked was the occasion. When I talked about Abraham on Sunday I did not feel moved in the least." In case the same orator had a little superabundance of reason which might be lost, I think he would have lost it if the sinner were to say calmly and with dignity, "That in fact is what you yourself preached on Sunday." How could the parson be able to get into his head such a consequence? And yet it was so, and the mistake was merely that he didn't know what he was saying. Would there were a poet who might resolve to prefer such situations, rather than the stuff and nonsense with which comedies and novels are filled! The comic and the tragic here touch one another at the absolute point of infinity. The parson's speech was perhaps in itself ludicrous enough, but it became infinitely ludicrous by its effect, and yet this consequence was quite natural. Or if the sinner, without raising any objection, were to be converted by the parson's severe lecture, if the zealous clergyman were to go joyfully home, rejoicing in the consciousness that he not only was effective in the pulpit, but above all by his irresistible power as a pastor of souls, who on Sunday roused the congregation to enthusiasm, and on Monday like a cherub with a flaming sword placed himself before the man who by his action wanted to put to shame the old proverb, that "things don't go on in the world as the parson preaches."* *In the old days they said, "What a pity things don't go on in the world as the parson preaches"–perhaps the time is coming, especially with the help of philosophy, when they will say, "Fortunately things don't go on as the parson preaches; for after all there is some sense in life, but none at all in his preaching." If on the other hand the sinner was not convinced, his situation is pretty tragic. Presumably he would be executed or sent to the lunatic asylum, in short, he would have become unhappy in relation to so-called reality–in another sense I can well think that Abraham made him happy, for he that labors does not perish. How is one to explain the contradichon illustrated by that orator? Is it because Abraham had a prescriptive right to be a great man, so that what he did is great, and when another does the same it is sin, a heinous sin? In that case I do not wish to participate in such thoughtless eulogy. If faith does not make it a holy act to be willing to murder one's son, then let the same condemnation be pronounced upon Abraham as upon every other man. If a man perhaps lacks courage to carry his thought through, and to say that Abraham was a murderer, then it is surely better to acquire this courage, rather than waste time upon undeserved eulogies. The ethical expression for what Abraham did is, that he would murder Isaac; the religious expression is, that he would sacrifice Isaac; but precisely in this contradiction consists the dread which can well make a man sleepless, and yet Abraham is not what he is without this dread. Or perhaps he did not do at all what is related, but something altogether different, which is accounted for by the circumstances of his times–then let us forget him, for it is not worth while to remember that past which cannot become a present. Or had perhaps that orator forgotten something which corresponds to the ethical forgetfulness of the fact that Isaac was the son? For when faith is eliminated by becoming null or nothing, then there only remains the crude fact that Abraham wanted to murder Isaac—which is easy enough for anyone to imitate who has not faith, the faith, that is to say, which makes it hard for him. For my part I do not lack the courage to think a thought whole. Hitherto there has been no thought I have been afraid of; if I should run across such a thought, I hope that I have at least the sincerity to say, "I am afraid of this thought, it stirs up something else in me, and therefore I will not think it. If in this I do wrong, the punishment will not fail to follow." If I had recognized that it was the verdict of truth that Abraham was a murderer, I do not know whether I would have been able to silence my pious veneration for him. However, if I had thought that, I presumably would have kept silent about it, for one should not initiate others into such thoughts. But Abraham is no dazzling illusion, he did not sleep into renown, it was not a whim of fate. Can one then speak plainly about Abraham without incurring the danger that an individual might in bewilderment go ahead and do likewise? If I do not dare to speak freely, I will be completely silent about Abraham, above all I will not disparage him in such a way that precisely thereby he becomes a pitfall for the weak. For if one makes faith everything, that is, makes it what it is, then, according to my way of thinking, one may speak of it without danger in our age, which hardly extravagates in the matter of faith, and it is only by faith one attains likeness to Abraham, not by murder. If one makes love a transitory mood, a voluptuous emotion in a man, then one only lays pitfalls for the weak when one would talk about the exploits of love. Transient emotions every man surely has, but if as a consequence of such emotions one would do the terrible thing which love has sanctified as an immortal exploit, then all is lost, including the exploit and the bewildered doer of it. So one surely can talk about Abraham, for the great can never do harm when it is apprehended in its greatness; it is like a two-edged sword which slays and saves. If it should fall to my lot to talk on the subject, I would begin by showing what a pious and God-fearing man Abraham was, worthy to be called God's elect. Only upon such a man is imposed such a test. But where is there such a man? Next I would describe how Abraham loved Isaac.

To this end I would pray all good spirits to come to my aid, that my speech might be as glowing as paternal love is. I hope that I should be able to describe it in such a way that there would not be many a father in the realms and territories of the King who would dare to affirm that he loved his son in such a way. But if he does not love like Abraham, then every thought of offering Isaac would be not a trial but a base temptation [Anfechtung]. On this theme one could talk for several Sundays, one need be in no haste. The consequence would be that, if one spoke rightly, some few of the fathers would not require to hear more, but for the time being they would be joyful if they really succeeded in loving their sons as Abraham loved. If there was one who, after having heard about the greatness, but also about the dreadfulness of Abraham's deed, ventured to go forth upon that road, I would saddle my horse and ride with him. At every stopping place till we came to Mount Moriah I would explain to him that he still could turn back, could repent the misunderstanding that he was called to be tried in such a conflict, that he could confess his lack of courage, so that God Himself must take Isaac, if He would have him. It is my conviction that such a man is not repudiated but may become blessed like all the others. But in time he does not become blessed. Would they not, even in the great ages of faith, have passed this judgment upon such a man? I knew a person who on one occasion could have saved my life if he21 had been magnanimous. He said, "I see well enough what I could do, but I do not dare to. I am afraid that later I might lack strength and that I should regret it." He was not magnanimous, but who for this cause would not continue to love him? Having spoken thus and moved the audience so that at least they had sensed the dialectical conflict of faith and its gigantic passion, I would not give rise to the error on the part of the audience that "he then has faith in such a high degree that it is enough for us to hold on to his skirts." For I would add, "I have no faith at all, I am by nature a shrewd pate, and every such person always has great difficulty in making the movements of faith– not that I attach, however, in and for itself, any value to this difficulty which through the overcoming of it brought the clever head further than the point which the simplest and most ordinary man reaches more easily." After all, in the poets love has its priests, and sometimes one hears a voice which knows how to defend it; but of faith one hears never a word. Who speaks in honor of this passion? Philosophy goes further. Theology sits rouged at the window and courts its favor, offering to sell her charms to philosophy. It is supposed to be difficult to understand Hegel, but to understand Abraham is a trifle. To go beyond Hegel22 is a miracle, but to get beyond Abraham is the easiest thing of all. I for my part have devoted a good deal of time to the understanding of the Hegelian philosophy, I believe also that I understand it tolerably well, but when in spite of the trouble I have taken there are certain passages I cannot understand, I am foolhardy enough to think that he himself has not been quite clear. All this I do easily and naturally, my head does not suffer from it. But on the other hand when I have to think of Abraham, I am as though annihilated. I catch sight every moment of that enormous paradox which is the substance of Abraham's life, every moment I am repelled, and my thought in spite of all its passion cannot get a hairs-breadth further. I strain every muscle to get a view of it–that very instant I am paralyzed. I am not unacquainted with what has been admired as great and noble in the world, my soul feels affinity with it, being convinced in all humility that it was in my cause the hero contended, and the instant I contemplate his deed I cry out to myself, jam tua res agitur. 23 I think myself into the hero, but into Abraham I cannot think myself; when I reach the height I fall down, for what I encounter there is the paradox. I do not however mean in any sense to say that faith is something lowly, but on the contrary that it is the highest thing, and that it is dishonest of philosophy to give something else instead of it and to make light of faith. Philosophy cannot and should not give faith, but it should understand itself and know what it has to offer and take nothing away, and least of all should fool people out of something as if it were nothing. I am not unacquainted with the perplexities and dangers of life, I do not fear them, and I encounter them buoyantly. I am not unacquainted with the dreadful, my memory is a faithful wife, and my imagination is (as I myself am not) a diligent little maiden who all day sits quietly at her work, and in the evening knows how to chat to me about it so prettily that I must look at it, though not always, I must say, is it landscapes, or flowers, or pastoral idyls she paints. I have seen the dreadful before my own eyes, I do not flee from it timorously, but I know very well that, although I advance to meet it, my courage is not the courage of faith, nor anything comparable to it. I am unable to make the movements of faith, I cannot shut my eyes and plunge confidently into the absurd, for me that is an impossibility ... but I do not boast of it. I am convinced that God is love,24 this thought has for me a primitive lyrical validity. When it is present to me, I am unspeakably blissful, when it is absent, I long for it more vehemently than does the lover for his object; but I do not believe, this courage I lack. For me the love of God is, both in a direct and in an inverse sense, incommensurable with the whole of reality. I am not cowardly enough to whimper and complain, but neither am I deceitful enough to deny that faith is something much higher. I can well endure living in my way, I am joyful and content, but my joy is not that of faith, and in comparison with that it is unhappy. I do not trouble God with my petty sorrows, the particular does not trouble me, I gaze only at my love, and I keep its virginal flame pure and clear. Faith is convinced that God is concerned about the least things. I am content in this life with being married to the left hand, faith is humble enough to demand the right hand–for that this is humility I do not deny and shall never deny. But really is everyone in my generation capable of making the movements of faith, I wonder? Unless I am very much mistaken, this generation is rather inclined to be proud of making what they do not even believe I am capable of making, viz. incomplete movements. It is repugnant to me to do as so often is done, namely, to speak inhumanly about a great deed, as though some thousands of years were an immense distance; I would rather speak humanly about it, as though it had occurred yesterday, letting only the greatness be the distance, which either exalts or condemns. So if (in the quality of a tragic hero, for I can get no higher) I had been summoned to undertake such a royal progress to Mount Moriah, I know well what I would have done. I would not have been cowardly enough to stay at home, neither would I have laid down or sauntered along the way, nor have forgotten the knife, so that there might be a little delay–I am pretty well convinced that I would have been there on the stroke of the clock and would have had everything in order, perhaps I would have arrived too early in order to get through with it sooner. But I also know what else I would have done. The very instant I mounted the horse I would have said to myself, "Now all is lost. God requires Isaac, I sacrifice him, and with him my joy–yet God is love and continues to be that for me; for in the temporal world God and I cannot talk together, we have no language in common." Perhaps one or another in our age will be foolish enough, or envious enough of the great, to want to make himself and me believe that if I really had done this, I would have done even a greater deed than Abraham; for my prodigious resignation was far more ideal and poetic than Abraham's narrow-mindedness. And yet this is the greatest falsehood, for my prodigious resignation was the surrogate for faith, nor could I do more than make the infinite movement, in order to find myself and again repose in myself. In that case I would not have loved Isaac as Abraham loved. That I was resolute in making the movement might prove my courage, humanly speaking; that I loved him with all my soul is the presumption apart from which the whole thing becomes a crime, but yet I did not love like Abraham, for in that case I would have held back even at the last minute, though not for this would I have arrived too late at Mount Moriah. Besides, by my behavior I would have spoiled the whole story; for if I had got Isaac back again, I would have been in embarrassment. What Abraham found easiest, I would have found hard, namely to be joyful again with Isaac; for he who with all the infinity of his soul, propio motu et propiis auspiciis [by his own power and on his own responsibility], has performed the infinite movement [of resignation] and cannot do more, only retains Isaac with pain. But what did Abraham do? He arrived neither too soon nor too late. He mounted the ass, he rode slowly along the way. All that time he believed– he believed that God would not require Isaac of him, whereas he was willing nevertheless to sacrifice him if it was required. He believed by virtue of the absurd;

for there could be no question of human calculation, and it was indeed the absurd that God who required it of him should the next instant recall the requirement. He climbed the mountain, even at the instant when the knife glittered he believed … that God would not require Isaac. He was indeed astonished at the outcome, but by a doublemovement he had reached his first position, and therefore he received Isaac more gladly than the first time. Let us go further. We let Isaac be really sacrificed. Abraham believed. He did not believe that some day he would be blessed in the beyond, but that he would be happy here in the world. God could give him a new Isaac, could recall to life him who had been sacrificed. He believed by virtue of the absurd; for all human reckoning had long since ceased to function. That sorrow can derange a man's mind, that we see, and it is sad enough. That there is such a thing as strength of will which is able to haul up so exceedingly close to the wind that it saves a man's reason, even though he remains a little queer,25 that too one sees. I have no intention of disparaging this; but to be able to lose one's reason, and therefore the whole of finiteness of which reason is the broker, and then by virtue of the absurd to gain precisely the same finiteness–that appalls my soul, but I do not for this cause say that it is something lowly, since on the contrary it is the only prodigy. Generally people are of the opinion that what faith produces is not a work of art, that it is coarse and common work, only for the more clumsy natures; but in fact this is far from the truth. The dialectic of faith is the finest and most remarkable of all; it possesses an elevation, of which indeed I can form a conception, but nothing more. I am able to make from the springboard the great leap whereby I pass into infinity, my back is like that of a tight-rope dancer, having been twisted in my childhood,26 hence I find this easy; with a one-two-three! I can walk about existence on my head; but the next thing I cannot do, for I cannot perform the miraculous, but can only be astonished by it. Yes, if Abraham the instant he swung his leg over the ass's back had said to himself, "Now, since Isaac is lost, I might just as well sacrifice him here at home, rather than ride the long way to Moriah"– then I should have no need of Abraham, whereas now I bow seven times before his name and seventy times before his deed. For this indeed he did not do, as I can prove by the fact that he was glad at receiving Isaac, heartily glad, that he needed no preparation, no time to concentrate upon the finite and its joy. If this had not been the case with Abraham, then perhaps he might have loved God but not believed; for he who loves God without faith reflects upon himself, he who loves God believingly reflects upon God. Upon this pinnacle stands Abraham. The last stage he loses sight of is the infinite resignation. He really goes further, and reaches faith; for all these caricatures of faith, the miserable lukewarm indolence which thinks, "There surely is no instant need, it is not worth while sorrowing before the time," the pitiful hope which says, "One cannot know what is going to happen … it might possibly be after all"–these caricatures of faith are part and parcel of life's wretchedness, and the infinite resignation has already consigned them to infinite contempt. Abraham I cannot understand,27 in a certain sense there is nothing I can learn from him but astonishment. If people fancy that by considering the outcome of this story they might let themselves be moved to believe, they deceive themselves and want to swindle God out of the first movement of faith, the infinite resignation. They would suck worldly wisdom out of the paradox. Perhaps one or another may succeed in that, for our age is not willing to stop with faith, with its miracle of turning water into wine, it goes further, it turns wine into water. Would it not be better to stop with faith, and is it not revolting that everybody wants to go further? When in our age (as indeed is proclaimed in various ways) they will not stop with love, where then are they going? To earthy wisdom, to petty calculation, to paltriness and wretchedness, to everything which can make man's divine origin doubtful. Would it not be better that they should stand still at faith, and that he who stands should take heed lest he fall? For the movements of faith must constantly be made by virtue of the absurd, yet in such a way, be it observed, that one does not lose the finite but gains it every inch. For my part I can well describe the movements of faith, but I cannot make them. When one would learn to make the motions of swimming one can let oneself be hung by a swimming-belt from the ceiling and go through the motions (describe them, so to speak, as we speak of describing a circle), but one is not swimming. In that way I can describe the movements of faith, but when I am thrown into the water, I swim, it is true (for I don't belong to the beach-waders), but I make other movements, I make the movements of infinity, whereas faith does the opposite: after having made the movements of infinity, it makes those of finiteness. Hail to him who can make those movements, he performs the marvellous, and I shall never grow tired of admiring him, whether he be Abraham or a slave in Abraham's house; whether he be a professor of philosophy or a servantgirl, I look only at the movements. But at them I do look, and do not let myself be fooled, either by myself or by any other man. The knights of the infinite resignation are easily recognized: their gait is gliding and assured. Those on the other hand who carry the jewel of faith are likely to be delusive, because their outward appearance bears a striking resemblance to that which both the infinite resignation and faith profoundly despise ... to Philistinism. I candidly admit that in my practice I have not found any reliable example of the knight of faith, though I would not therefore deny that every second man may be such an example. I have been trying, however, for several years to get on the track of this, and all in vain. People commonly travel around the world to see rivers and mountains, new stars, birds of rare plumage, queerly deformed fishes, ridiculous breeds of men—they abandon themselves to the bestial stupor which gapes at existence, and they think they have seen something. This does not interest me. But if I knew where there was such a knight of faith, I would make a pilgrimage to him on foot, for this prodigy interests me absolutely. I would not let go of him for an instant, every moment I would watch to see how he managed to make the movements, I would regard myself as secured for life, and would divide my time between looking at him and practicing the exercises myself, and thus would spend all my time admiring him. As was said, I have not found any such person, but I can well think him. Here he is. Acquaintance made, I am introduced to him. The moment I set eyes on him I instantly push him from me, I myself leap backwards, I clasp my hands and say half aloud, "Good Lord, is this the man? Is it really he? Why, he looks like a taxcollector!" However, it is the man after all. I draw closer to him, watching his least movements to see whether there might not be visible a little heterogeneous fractional telegraphic message from the infinite, a glance, a look, a gesture, a note of sadness, a smile, which betrayed the infinite in its heterogeneity with the finite. No! I examine his figure from tip to toe to see if there might not be a cranny through which the infinite was peeping. No! He is solid through and through. His tread? It is vigorous, belongingentirely to finiteness; no smartly dressed townsman who walksout to Fresberg on a Sunday afternoon treads the ground more firmly, he belongs entirely to the world, no Philistine more so. One can discover nothing of that aloof and superior nature whereby one recognizes the knight of the infinite. He takes delight in everything, and whenever one sees him taking part in a particular pleasure, he does it with the persistence which is the mark of the earthly man whose soul is absorbed in such things. He tends to his work. So when one looks at him one might suppose that he was a clerk who had lost his soul in an intricate system of book-keeping, so precise is he. He takes a holiday on Sunday. He goes to church. No heavenly glance or any other token of the incommensurable betrays him; if one did not know him, it would be impossible to distinguish him from the rest of the congregation, for his healthy and vigorous hymnsinging proves at the most that he has a good chest. In the afternoon he walks to the forest. He takes delight in everything he sees, in the human swarm, in the new omnibuses,25 in the water of the Sound; when one meets him on the Beach Road one might suppose he was a shopkeeper taking his fling, that's just the way he disports himself, for he is not a poet, and I have sought in vain to detect in him the poetic incommensurability. Toward evening he walks home, his gait is as indefatigable as that of the postman. On his way he reflects that his wife has surely a special little warm dish prepared for him, e.g. a calf's head roasted, garnished with vegetables. If he were to meet a man like-minded, he could continue as far as East Gate to discourse with him about that dish, with a passion befitting a hotel chef. As it happens, he hasn't four pence to his name, and yet he fully and firmly believes that his wife has that dainty dish for him. If she had it, it would then be an invidious sight for superior people and an inspiring one for the plain man, to see him eat; for his appetite is greater than Esau's. His wife hasn't it—strangely enough, it is quite the same to him. On the way he comes past a building site and runs across another man. They talk together for a moment. In the twinkling of an eye he erects a new building, he has at his disposition all the powers necessary for it. The stranger leaves him with the thought that he certainly was a capitalist, while my admired knight thinks, "Yes, if the money were needed, I dare say I could get it." He lounges at an open window and looks out on the square on which he lives; he is interested in everything that goes on, in a rat which slips under the curb, in the children's play, and this with the nonchalance of a girl of sixteen. And yet he is no genius, for in vain I have sought in him the incommensurability of genius. In the evening he smokes his pipe; to look at him one would swear that it was the grocer over the way vegetating in the twilight. He lives as carefree as a ne'er-do-well, and yet he buys up the acceptable time at the dearest price, for he does not do the least thing except by virtue of the absurd. And yet, and yet—actually I could become furious over it, for envy if for no other reason—this man has made and every instant is making the movements of infinity. With infinite resignation he has drained the cup of life's profound sadness, he knows the bliss of the infinite, he senses the pain of renouncing everything, the dearest things he possesses in the world, and yet finiteness tastes to him just as good as to one who never knew anything higher, for his continuance in the finite did not bear a trace of the cowed and fearful spirit produced by the process of training; and yet he has this sense of security in enjoying it, as though the finite life were the surest thing of all. And yet, and yet the whole earthly form he exhibits is a new creation by virtue of the absurd. He resigned everything infinitely, and then he grasped everything again by virtue of the absurd. He constantly makes the movements of infinity, but he does this with such correctness and assurance that he constantly gets the finite out of it, and there is not a second when one has a notion of anything else. It is supposed to be

the most difficult task for a dancer to leap into a definite posture in such a way that there is not a second when he is grasping after the posture, but by the leap itself he stands fixed in that posture. Perhaps no dancer can do it–that is what this knight does. Most people live dejectedly in worldly sorrow and joy; they are the ones who sit along the wall and do not join in the dance. The knights of infinity are dancers and possess elevation. They make the movements upward, and fall down again; and this too is no mean pastime, nor ungraceful to behold. But whenever they fall down they are not able at once to assume the posture, they vacillate an instant, and this vacillation shows that after all they are strangers in the world. This is more or less strikingly evident in proportion to the art they possess, but even the most artistic knights cannot altogether conceal this vacillation. One need not look at them when they are up in the air, but only the instant they touch or have touched the ground–then one recognizes them. But to be able to fall down in such a way that the same second it looks as if one were standing and walking, to transform the leap of life into a walk, absolutely to express the sublime in the pedestrian– that only the knight of faith can do–and this is the one and only prodigy. But since the prodigy is so likely to be delusive, I will describe the movements in a definite instance which will serve to illustrate their relation to reality, for upon this everything turns. A young swain falls in love with a princess,29 and the whole content of his life consists in this love, and yet the situation is such that it is impossible for it to be realized, impossible for it to be translated from ideality into reality.*
*Of course any other instance whatsoever in which the individual finds that for him the whole reality of actual existence is concentrated, may, when it is seen to be unrealizable, be an occasion for the movement of resignation. However, I have chosen a love experience to make the movement visible, because this interest is doubtless easier to understand, and so relieves me from the necessity of making preliminary observations which in a deeper sense could be of interest only to a few. The slaves of paltriness, the frogs in life's swamp, will naturally cry out, "Such a love is foolishness. The rich brewer's widow is a match fully as good and respectable." Let them croak in the

swamp undisturbed. It is not so with the knight of infinite resignation, he does not give up his love, not for all the glory of the world. He is no fool. First he makes sure that this really is the content of his life, and his soul is too healthy and too proud to squander the least thing upon an inebriation. He is not cowardly, he is not afraid of letting love creep into his most secret, his most hidden thoughts, to let it twine in innumerable coils about every ligament of his consciousness—if the love becomes an unhappy love, he will never be able to tear himself loose from it. He feels a blissful rapture in letting love tingle through every nerve, and yet his soul is as solemn as that of the man who has drained the poisoned goblet and feels how the juice permeates every drop of blood—for this instant is life and death.30 So when he has thus sucked into himself the whole of love and absorbed himself in it, he does not lack courage to make trial of everything and to venture everything. He surveys the situation of his life, he convokes the swift thoughts, which like tame doves obey his every bidding, he waves his wand over them, and they dart off in all directions. But when they all return, all as messengers of sorrow, and declare to him that it is an impossibility, then he becomes quiet, he dismisses them, he remains alone, and then he performs the movements. If what I am saying is to have any significance, it is requisite that the movement come about normally.* *To this end passion is necessary. Every movement of infinity comes about by passion, and no reflection can bring a movement about. This is the continual leap in existence which explains the movement, whereas mediation is a chimera which according to Hegel is supposed to explain everything, and at the same time this is the only thing he has never tried to explain. Even to make the well-known Socratic distinction between what one understands and what one does not understand, passion is required, and of course even more to make the characteristic Socratic movement, the movement, namely, of ignorance. What our age lacks, however, is not reflection but passion. Hence in a sense our age is too tenacious of life to die, for dying is one of the most remarkable leaps, and a little verse of a poet has always attracted me much, because, after having expressed prettily and simply in five or six preceding lines his wish for good things in life, he concludes thus:31 Ein seliger Sprung in die Ewigkeit. So for the first thing, the knight will have power to concentrate the whole content of life and the whole significance of reality in one single wish. If a man lacks this concentration, this intensity, if his soul from the beginning is dispersed in the multifarious, he never comes to the point of making the movement, he will deal shrewdly in life like the capitalists who invest their money in all sorts of securities, so as to gain on the one what they lose on the other–in short, he is not a knight. In the next place the knight will have the power to concentrate the whole result of the operations of thought in one act of consciousness. If he lacks this intensity, if his soul from the beginning is dispersed in the multifarious, he will never get time to make the movements, he will be constantly running errands in life, never enter into eternity, for even at the instant when he is closest to it he will suddenly discover that he has forgotten something for which he must go back. He will think that to enter eternity is possible the next instant, and that also is perfectly true, but by such considerations one never reaches the point of making the movements, but by their aid one sinks deeper and deeper into the mire. So the knight makes the movement–but what movement? Will he forget the whole thing? (For in this too there is indeed a kind of concentration.) No! For the knight does not contradict himself, and it is a contradiction to forget the whole content of one's life and yet remain the same man. To become another man he feels no inclination, nor does he by any means regard this as greatness. Only the lower natures forget themselves and become something new. Thus the butterfly has entirely forgotten that it was a caterpillar, perhaps it may in turn so entirely forget it was a butterfly that it becomes a fish. The deeper natures never forget themselves and never become anything else than what they were. So the knight remembers everything, but precisely this remembrance is pain, and yet by the infinite resignation he is reconciled with existence. Love for that princess became for him the expression for an eternal love, assumed a religious character, was transfigured into a love for the Eternal Being, which did to be sure deny him the fulfilment of his love, yet reconciled him again by the eternal consciousness of its validity in the form of eternity, which no reality can take from him. Fools and young men prate about everything being possible for a man. That, however, is a great error. Spiritually speaking, everything is possible, but in the world of the finite there is much which is not possible. This impossible, however, the knight makes possible by expressing it spiritually, but he expresses it spiritually by waiving his claim to it. The wish which would carry him out into reality, but was wrecked upon the impossibility, is now bent inward, but it is not therefore lost, neither is it forgotten. At one moment it is the obscure emotion of the wish within him which awakens recollections, at another moment he awakens them himself; for he is too proud to be willing that what was the whole content of his life should be the thing of a fleeting moment. He keeps this love young, and along with him it increases in years and in beauty. On the other hand, he has no need of the intervention of the finite for the further growth of his love. From the instant he made the movement the princess is lost to him. He has no need of those erotic tinglings in the nerves at the sight of the beloved etc., nor does he need to be constantly taking leave of her in a finite sense, because he recollects her in an eternal sense,32 and he knows very well that the lovers who are so bent upon seeing "her" yet once again, to say farefell for the last time, are right in being bent upon it, are right in thinking that it is the last time, for they forget one another the soonest. He has comprehended the deep secret that also in loving another person one must be sufficicut unto oneself. He no longer takes a finite interest in what the princess is doing, and precisely this is proof that he has made the movement infinitely. Here one may have an opportunity to see whether the movement on the part of a particular person is true or fictitious. There was one who also believed that he had made the movement; but lo, time passed, the princess did something else, she married33—a prince, let us say—then his soul lost the elasticity of resignation. Thereby he knew that he had not made the movement rightly; for he who has made the act of resignation infinitely is sufficient unto himself. The knight does not annul his resignation, he preserves his love just as young as it was in its first moment, he never lets it go from him, precisely because he makes the movements infinitely. What the princess does, cannot disturb him, it is only the lower natures which find in other people the law for their actions, which find the premises for their actions outside themselves. If on the other hand the princess is like-minded, the beautiful consequence will be apparent. She will introduce herself into that order of knighthood into which one is not received by balloting, but of which everyone is a member who has courage to introduce himself, that order of knighthood which proves its immortality by the fact that it makes no distinction between man and woman. The two will preserve their love young and sound, she also will have triumphed over her pains, even though she does not, as it is said in the ballad, "lie every night beside her lord." These two will to all eternity remain in agreement with one another, with a well-timed harmonia praestabilita, 34 so that if ever the moment were to come, the moment which does not, however, concern them finitely (for then they would be growing older), if ever the moment were to come which offered to give love its expression in time, then they will be capable of beginning precisely at the point where they would have begun if originally they had been united. He who understands this, be he man or woman, can never be deceived, for it is only the lower natures which imagine they were deceived. No girl who is not so proud really knows how to love; but if she is so proud, then the cunning and shrewdness of all the world cannot deceive her. In the infinite resignation there is peace and rest; every man who wills it, who has not abased himself by scorning himself (which is still more dreadful than being proud), can train himself to make this movement which in its pain reconciles one with existence. Infinite resignation is that shirt we read about in the old fable.35 The thread is spun under tears, the cloth bleached with tears, the shirt sewn with tears; but then too it is a better protection than iron and steel. The imperfection in the fable is that a third party can manufacture this shirt. The secret in life is that everyone must sew it for himself, and the astonishing thing is that a man can sew it fully as well as a woman. In the infinite resignation there is peace and rest and comfort in sorrow—that is, if the movement is made normally. It would not be difficult for me, however, to write a whole book, were I to examine the various misunderstandings, the preposterous attitudes, the deceptive movements, which I have encountered in my brief practice. People believe very little in spirit, and yet making this movement depends upon spirit, it depends upon whether this is or is not a one-sided result of a dira necessitas, and if this is present, the more dubious it always is whether the movement is normal. If one means by this that the cold, unfruitful necessity must necessarily be present, one thereby affirms that no one can experience death before he actually dies, and that appears to me a crass materialism. However, in our time people concern themselves rather little about making pure movements. In case one who was about to learn to dance were to say, "For centuries now one generation after another has been learning positions, it is high time I drew some advantage out of this and began straightway with the French dances"–then people would laugh at him; but in the world of spirit they find this exceedingly plausible. What is education? I should suppose that education was the curriculum one had to run through in order to catch up with oneself, and he who will not pass through this curriculum is helped very little by the fact that he was born in the most enlightened age. The infinite resignation is the last stage prior to faith, so that one who has not made this movement has not faith; for only in the infinite resignation do I become clear to myself with respect to my eternal validity, and only then can there be any question of grasping existence by virtue of faith. Now we will let the knight of faith appear in the role just described. He makes exactly the same movements as the other knight, infinitely renounces claim to the love which is the content of his life, he is reconciled in pain; but then occurs the prodigy, he makes still another movement more wonderful than all, for he says, "I believe nevertheless that I shall get her, in virtue, that is, of the absurd, in virtue of the fact that with God all things are possible."36 The absurd is not one of the factors which can be discriminated within the proper compass of the understanding: it is not identical with the improbable, the unexpected, the unforeseen. At the moment when the knight made the act of resignation37 he was convinced, humanly speaking, of the impossibility. This was the result reached by the understanding, and he had sufficient energy to think it. On the other hand, in an infinite sense it was possible, namely, by renouncing it; but this sort of possessing is at the same time a relinquishing, and yet there is no absurdity in this for the understanding, for the understanding continued to be in the right in affirming that in the world of the finite where it holds sway this was and remained an impossibility. This is quite as clear to the knight of faith, so the only thing that can save him is the absurd, and this he grasps by faith. So he recognizes the impossibility, and that very instant he believes the absurd; for, if without recognizing the impossibility with all the passion of his soul and with all his heart, he should wish to imagine that he has faith, he deceives himself, and his testimony has no bearing, since he has not even reached the infinite resignation. Faith therefore is not an aesthetic emotion but something far higher, precisely because it has resignation as its presupposition; it is not an immediate instinct of the heart, but is the paradox of life and existence. So when in spite of all difficulties a young girl still remains convinced that her wish will surely be fulfilled, this conviction is not the assurance of faith, even if she was brought up by Christian parents, and for a whole year perhaps has been catechized by the parson. She is convinced in all her childish naïveté and innocence, this conviction also ennobles her nature and imparts to her a preternatural greatness, so that like a thaumaturge she is able to conjure the finite powers of existence and make the very stones weep, while on the other hand in her flurry she may just as well run to Herod as to Pilate and move the whole world by her tears. Her convichon is very lovable, and one can learn much from her, but one thing is not to be learned from her, one does not learn the movements, for her conviction does not dare in the pain of resignation to face the impossibility. So I can perceive that it requires strength and energy and freedom of spirit to make the infinite movement of resignation, I can also perceive that it is feasible. But the next thing astonishes me, it makes my head swim, for after having made the movement of resignation, then by virtue of the absurd to get everything, to get the wish whole and uncurtailed—that is beyond human power, it is a prodigy. But this I can perceive, that the young girl's conviction is mere levity in comparison with the firmness faith displays notwithstanding it has perceived the impossibility. Whenever I essay to make this movement, I turn giddy, the very instant I am admiring it absolutely a prodigious dread grips my soul—for what is it to tempt God? And yet this movement is the movement of faith and remains such, even though philosophy, in order to confuse the concepts, would make us believe that it has faith, and even though theology would sell out faith at a bargain price. For the act of resignation faith is not required, for what I gain by resignation is my eternal consciousness, and this is a purely philosophical movement which I dare say I am able to make if it is required, and which I can train myself to make, for whenever any finiteness would get the mastery over me, I starve myself until I can make the movement, for my eternal consciousness is my love to God, and for me this is higher than everything. For the act of resignation faith is not required, but it is needed when it is the case of acquiring the very least thing more than my eternal consciousness, for this is the paradoxical. The movements are frequently confounded, for it is said that one needs faith to renounce the claim to everything, yea, a stranger thing than this may be heard, when a man laments the loss of his faith, and when one looks at the scale to see where he is, one sees, strangely enough, that he has only reached the point where he should make the infinite movement of resignation. In resignation I make renunciation of everything, this movement I make by myself, and if I do not make it, it is because I am cowardly and effeminate and without enthusiasm and do not feel the significance of the lofty dignity which is assigned to every man, that of being his own censor, which is a far prouder title than that of Censor General to the whole Roman Republic. This movement I make by myself, and what I gain is myself in my eternal consciousness, in blissful agreement with my love for the Eternal Being. By faith I make renunciation of nothing, on the contrary, by faith I acquire everything, precisely in the sense in which it is said that he who has faith like a grain of mustard can remove mountains. A purely human courage is required to renounce the whole of the temporal to gain the eternal; but this I gain, and to all eternity I cannot renounce it–that is a selfcontradiction. But a paradoxical and humble courage is required to grasp the whole of the temporal by virtue of the absurd, and this is the courage of faith. By faith Abraham did not renounce his claim upon Isaac, but by faith he got Isaac. By virtue of resignation that rich young man should have given away everything, but then when he had done that, the knight of faith should have said to him, "By virtue of the absurd thou shalt get every penny back again. Canst thou believe that?" And this speech ought by no means to have been indifferent to the aforesaid rich young man, for in case he gave away his goods because he was tired of them, his resignation was not much to boast of. It is about the temporal, the finite, everything turns in this case. I am able by my own strength to renounce everything, and then to find peace and repose in pain. I can stand everything– even though that horrible demon, more dreadful than death, the king of terrors, even though madness were to hold up before my eyes the motley of the fool, and I understood by its look that it was I who must put it on, I still am able to save my soul, if only it is more to me than my earthly happiness that my love to God should triumph in me. A man may still be able at the last instant to concentrate his whole soul in a single glance toward that heaven from which cometh every good gift, and his glance will be intelligible to himself and also to Him whom it seeks as a sign that he nevertheless remained true to his love. Then he will calmly put on the motley garb. He whose soul has not this romantic enthusiasm has sold his soul, whether he got a kingdom for it or a paltry piece of silver. But by my own strength I am not able to get the least of the things which belong to finiteness, for I am constantly using my strength to renounce everything. By my own strength I am able to give up the princess, and I shall not become a grumbler, but shall find joy and repose in my pain; but by my own strength I am not able to get her again, for I am employing all my strength to be resigned. But by faith, says that marvellous knight, by faith I shall get her in virtue of the absurd. So this movement I am unable to make. As soon as I would begin to make it everything turns around dizzily, and I flee back to the pain of resignation. I can swim in existence, but for this mystical soaring I am too heavy. To exist in such a way that my opposition to existence is expressed as the most beautiful and assured harmony with it, is something I cannot do. And yet it must be glorious to get the princess, that is what I say every instant, and the knight of resignation who does not say it is a deceiver, he has not had one only wish, and he has not kept the wish young by his pain. Perhaps there was one who thought it fitting enough that the wish was no longer vivid, that the barb of pain was dulled, but such a man is no knight. A free-born soul who caught himself entertaining such thoughts would despise himself and begin over again, above all he would not permit his soul to be deceived by itself. And yet it must be glorious to get the princess, and yet the knight of faith is the only happy one, the heir apparent to the finite, whereas the knight of resignation is a stranger and a foreigner. Thus to get the princess, to live with her joyfully and happily day in and day out (for it is also conceivable that the knight of resignation might get the princess, but that his soul had discerned the impossibility of their future happiness), thus to live joyfully and happily every instant by virtue of the absurd, every instant to see the sword hanging over the head of the beloved, and yet not to find repose in the pain of resignation, but joy by virtue of the absurd–this is marvellous. He who does it is great, the only great man. The thought of it stirs my soul, which never was niggardly in the admiration of greatness. In case then everyone in my generation who will not stop at faith is really a man who has comprehended life's horror, who has understood what Daub38 means when he says that a soldier who stands alone at his post with a loaded gun in a stormy night beside a powder-magazine ... will get strange thoughts into his head–in case then everyone who will not stop at faith is a man who had strength of soul to comprehend that the wish was an impossibility, and thereupon gave himself time to remain alone with this thought, in case everyone who will not stop at faith is a man who is reconciled in pain and is reconciled to pain, in case everyone who will not stop at faith is a man who in the next place (and if he has not done all the foregoing, there is no need of his troubling himself about faith)–in the next place did the marvellous thing, grasped the whole of existence by virtue of the absurd ... then what I write is the highest eulogy of my contemporaries by one of the lowliest among them, who was able only to make the movement of resignation. But why will they not stop at faith, why does one sometimes hear that people are ashamed to acknowledge that they have faith? This I cannot comprehend. If ever I contrive to be able to make this movement, I shall in the future ride in a coach and four. If it is really true that all the Philistinism I behold in life (which I do not permit my word but my actions to condemn) is not what it seems to be–is it the miracle? That is conceivable, for the hero of faith had in fact a striking resemblance to it–for that hero of faith was not so much an ironist or a humorist, but something far higher. Much is said in our age about irony and humor, especially by people who have never been capable of engaging in the practice of these arts, but who neverthless know how to explain everything. I am not entirely unacquainted with these two passions,39 I know a little more about them than what is to be found in German and German-Danish compendiums. I know therefore that these two passions are essentially different from the passion of faith. Irony and humor reflect also upon themselves, and therefore belong within the sphere of the infinite resignation, their elasticity is due to the fact that the individual is incommensurable with reality. The last movement, the paradoxical movement of faith, I cannot make (be that a duty or whatever it may be), in spite of the fact that I would do it more than gladly. Whether a man has a right to make this affirmation, must be left to him, it is a question between him and the Eternal Being who is the object of faith whether in this respect he can hit upon an amicable compromise. What every man can do is to make the movement of infinite resignation, and I for my part would not hesitate to pronounce everyone cowardly who wishes to make himself believe he can not do it. With faith it is a different matter. But what every man has not a right to do, is to make others believe that faith is something lowly, or that it is an easy thing, whereas it is the greatest and the hardest. People construe the story of Abraham in another way. They extol God's grace in bestowing Isaac upon him again–the whole thing was only a trial. A trial–that word may say much or little, and yet the whole thing is over as quickly as it is said. One mounts a winged horse, the same instant one is at Mount Moriah, the same instant one sees the ram; one forgets that Abraham rode only upon an ass, which walks slowly along the road, that he had a journey of three days, that he needed some time to cleave the wood, to bind Isaac, and to sharpen the knife. And yet they extol Abraham. He who is to deliver the discourse can very well sleep till a quarter of an hour before he has to preach, the auditor can well take a nap during the discourse, for all goes smoothly, without the least trouble from any quarter. If there was a man present who suffered from insomnia, perhaps he then went home and sat in a corner and thought: "It's an affair of a moment, this whole thing; if only you wait a minute, you see the ram, and the trial is over." If the orator were to encounter him in this condition, he would, I think, confront him with all his dignity and say, "Wretched man, that thou couldst let thy soul sink into such foolishness! No miracle occurs. The whole of life is a trial." In proportion as the orator proceeds with his outpouring, he would get more and more excited, would become more and more delighted with himself, and whereas he had noticed no congestion of the blood while he talked about Abraham, he now felt how the vein swelled in his forehead. Perhaps he would have lost his breath as well as his tongue if the sinner had answered calmly and with dignity, "But it was about this you preached last Sunday." Let us then either consign Abraham to oblivion, or let us learn to be dismayed by the tremendous paradox which constitutes the significance of Abraham's life, that we may understand that our age, like every age, can be joyful if it has faith. In case Abraham is not a nullity, a phantom, a show one employs for a pastime, then the fault can never consist in the fact that the sinner wants to do likewise, but the point is to see how great a thing it was that Abraham did, in order that man may judge for himself whether he has the call and the courage to be subjected to such a test. The comic contradiction in the behavior of the orator is that he reduced Abraham to an insignificance, and yet would admonish the other to behave in the same way. Should not one dare then to talk about Abraham? I think one should. If I were to talk about him, I would first depict the pain of his trial. To that end I would like a leech suck all the dread and distress and torture out of a father's sufferings, so that I might describe what Abraham suffered, whereas all the while he nevertheless believed. I would remind the audience that the journey lasted three days and a good part of the fourth, yea, that these three and a half days were infinitely longer than the few thousand years which separate me from Abraham. Then I would remind them that, in my opinion, every man dare still turn around ere he begins such an undertaking, and every instant he can repentantly turn back. If one does this, I fear no danger, nor am I afraid of awakening in people an inclination to be tried like Abraham. But if one would dispose of a cheap edition of Abraham, and yet admonish everyone to do likewise, then it is ludicrous. It is now my intention to draw out from the story of Abraham the dialectical consequences inherent in it, expressing them in the form of problemata, in order to see what a tremendous paradox faith is, a paradox which is capable of transforming a murder into a holy act well-pleasing to God, a paradox which gives Isaac back to Abraham, which no thought can master, because faith begins precisely there where thinking leaves off. PROBLEM I Is there such a thing as a teleological suspension of the ethical? The ethical as such is the universal, and as the universal it applies to everyone, which may be expressed from another point of view by saying that it applies every instant. It reposes immanently in itself, it has nothing without itself which is its telos, 40 but is itself telos for everything outside it, and when this has been incorporated by the ethical it can go no further. Conceived immediately as physical and psychical, the particular individual is the individual who has his telos in the universal, and his ethical task is to express himself constantly in it, to abolish his particularity in order to become the universal. As soon as the individual would assert himself in his particularity over against the universal he sins, and only by recognizing this can he again reconcile himself with the universal. Whenever the individual after he has entered the universal feels an impulse to assert himself as the particular, he is in temptation (Anfechtung), and he can labor himself out of this only by penitently abandoning himself as the particular in the universal. If this be the highest thing that can be said of man and of his existence, then the ethical has the same character as man's eternal blessedness, which to all eternity and at every instant is his telos, since it would be a contradiction to say that this might be abandoned (i.e. teleologically suspended), inasmuch as this is no sooner suspended than it is forfeited, whereas in other cases what is suspended is not forfeited but is preserved precisely in that higher thing which is its telos. 41 If such be the case, then Hegel is right when in his chapter on "The Good and the Conscience," 42 he characterizes man merely as the particular and regards this character as "a moral form of evil" which is to be annulled in the teleology of the moral, so that the individual who remains in this stage is either sinning or subjected to temptation (Anfechtung). On the other hand, Hegel is wrong in talking of faith, wrong in not protesting loudly and clearly against the fact that Abraham enjoys honor and glory as the father of faith, whereas he ought to be prosecuted and convicted of murder. For faith is this paradox, that the particular is higher than the universal– yet in such a way, be it observed, that the movement repeats itself, and that consequently the individual, after having been in the universal, now as the particular isolates himself as higher than the universal. If this be not faith, then Abraham is lost, then faith has never existed in the world … because it has always existed. For if the ethical (i.e. the moral) is the highest thing, and if nothing incommensurable remains in man in any other way but as the evil (i.e. the particular which has to be expressed in the universal), then one needs no other categories besides those which the Greeks possessed or which by consistent thinking can be derived from them. This fact Hegel ought not to have concealed, for after all he was acquainted with Greek thought. One not infrequently hears it said by men who for lack of losing themselves in studies are absorbed in phrases that a light shines upon the Christian world whereas a darkness broods over paganism. This utterance has always seemed strange to me, inasmuch as every profound thinker and every serious artist is even in our day rejuvenated by the eternal youth of the Greek race. Such an utterance may be explained by the consideration that people do not know what they ought to say but only that they must say something. It is quite right for one to say that paganism did not possess faith, but if with this one is to have said something, one must be a little clearer about what one understands by faith, since otherwise one falls back into such phrases. To explain the whole of existence and faith along with it, without having a conception of what faith is, is easy, and that man does not make the poorest calculation in life who reckons upon admiration when he possesses such an explanation; for, as Boileau says, "un sot trouve toujours un plus sot qui l'admire." Faith is precisely this paradox, that the individual as the particular is higher than the universal, is justified over against it, is not subordinate but superior—yet in such a way, be it observed, that it is the particular individual who, after he has been subordinated as the particular to the universal, now through the universal becomes the individual who as the particular is superior to the universal, for the fact that the individual as the particular stands in an absolute relation to the absolute. This position cannot be mediated, for all mediation comes about precisely by virtue of the universal; it is and remains to all eternity a paradox, inaccessible to thought. And yet faith is this paradox—or else (these are the logical deductions which I would beg the reader to have in mente at every point, though it would be too prolix for me to reiterate them on every occasion)— or else there never has been faith ... precisely because it always has been. In other words, Abraham is lost. That for the particular individual this paradox may easily be mistaken for a temptation (Anfechtung) is indeed true, but one ought not for this reason to conceal it. That the whole constitution of many persons may be such that this paradox repels them is indeed true, but one ought not for this reason to make faith something different in order to be able to possess it, but ought rather to admit that one does not possess it, whereas those who possess faith should take care to set up certain criteria so that one might distinguish the paradox from a temptation (Anfechtung). Now the story of Abraham contains such a teleological suspension of the ethical. There have not been lacking clever pates and profound investigators who have found analogies to it. Their wisdom is derived from the pretty proposition that at bottom everything is the same. If one will look a little more closely, I have not much doubt that in the whole world one will not find a single analogy (except a later instance which proves nothing), if it stands fast that Abraham is the representative of faith, and that faith is normally expressed in him whose life is not merely the most paradoxical that can be thought but so paradoxical that it cannot be thought at all. He acts by virtue of the absurd, for it is precisely absurd that he as the particular is higher than the universal. This paradox cannot be mediated; for as soon as he begins to do this he has to admit that he was in temptation (Anfechtung), and if such was the case, he never gets to the point of sacrificing Isaac, or, if he has sacrificed Isaac, he must turn back repentantly to the universal. By virtue of the absurd he gets Isaac again. Abraham is therefore at no instant a tragic hero but something quite different, either a murderer or a believer. The middle term which saves the tragic hero, Abraham has not. Hence it is that I can understand the tragic hero but cannot understand Abraham, though in a certain crazy sense I admire him more than all other men. Abraham's relation to Isaac, ethically speaking, is quite simply expressed by saying that a father shall love his son more dearly than himself. Yet within its own compass the ethical has various gradations. Let us see whether in this story there is to be found any higher expression for the ethical such as would ethically explain his conduct, ethically justify him in suspending the ethical obligation toward his son, without in this search going beyond the teleology of the ethical. When an undertaking in which a whole nation is concerned is hindered,43 when such an enterprise is brought to a standshll by the disfavor of heaven, when the angry deity sends a calm which mocks all efforts, when the seer performs his heavy task and proclaims that the deity demands a young maiden as a sacrifice—then will the father heroically make the sacrifice. He will magnanimously conceal his pain, even though he might wish that he were "the lowly man who dares to weep," 44 not the king who must act royally. And though solitary pain forces its way into his breast, he has only three confidants among the people, yet soon the whole nation will be cognizant of his pain, but also cognizant of his exploit, that for the welfare of the whole he was willing to sacrifice her, his daughter, the lovely young maiden. O charming bosom! O beautiful cheeks! O bright golden hair! (v. 687). And the daughter will affect him by her tears, and the father will turn his face away, but the hero will raise the knife.—When the report of this reaches the ancestral home, then will the beautiful maidens of Greece blush with enthusiasm, and if the daughter was betrothed, her true love will not be angry but be proud of sharing in the father's deed, because the maiden belonged to him more feelingly than to the father. When the intrepid judge45 who saved Israel in the hour of need in one breath binds himself and God by the same vow, then heroically the young maiden's jubilation, the beloved daughter's joy, he will turn to sorrow, and with her all Israel will lament her maiden youth; but every free-born man will understand, and every stout-hearted woman will admire Jephtha, and every maiden in Israel will wish to act as did his daughter. For what good would it do if Jephtha were victorious by reason of his vow if he did not keep it? Would not the victory again be taken from the nation? When a son is forgetful of his duty,46 when the state entrusts the father with the sword of justice, when the laws require punishment at the hand of the father, then will the father heroically forget that the guilty one is his son, he will magnanimously conceal his pain, but there will not be a single one among the people, not even the son, who will not admire the father, and whenever the law of Rome is interpreted, it will be remembered that many interpreted it more learnedly, but none so gloriously as Brutus. If, on the other hand, while a favorable wind bore the fleet on with swelling sails to its goal, Agamemnon had sent that messenger who fetched Iphigenia in order to be sacrificed; if Jephtha, without being bound by any vow which decided the fate of the nahon, had said to his daughter, "Bewail now thy virginity for the space of two months, for I will sacrifice thee"; if Brutus had had a righteous son and yet would have ordered the lictors to execute him—who would have understood them? If these three men had replied to the query why they did it by saying, "It is a trial in which we are tested," would people have understood them better? When Agamemnon, Jephtha, Brutus at the decisive moment heroically overcome their pain, have heroically lost the beloved and have merely to accomplish the outward sacrifice, then there never will be a noble soul in the world who will not shed tears of compassion for their pain and of admiration for their exploit. If, on the other hand, these three men at the decisive moment were to adjoin to their heroic conduct this little word, "But for all that it will not come to pass," who then would understand them? If as an explanation they added, "This we believe by virtue of the absurd," who would understand them better? For who would not easily understand that it was absurd, but who would understand that one could then believe it? The difference between the tragic hero and Abraham is clearly evident. The tragic hero still remains within the ethical. He lets one expression of the ethical find its telos in a higher expression of the ethical; the ethical relation between father and son, or daughter and father, he reduces to a sentiment which has its dialectic in its relation to the idea of morality. Here there can be no question of a teleological suspension of the ethical itself. With Abraham the situation was different. By his act he overstepped the ethical entirely and possessed a higher telos outside of it, in relation to which he suspended the former. For I should very much like to know how one would bring Abraham's act into relation with the universal, and whether it is possible to discover any connection whatever between what Abraham did and the universal ... except the fact that he transgressed it. It was not for the sake of saving a people, not to maintain the idea of the state, that Abraham did this, and not in order to reconcile angry deities. If there could be a question of the deity being angry, he was angry only with Abraham, and Abraham's whole action stands in no relation to the universal, is a purely private undertaking. Therefore, whereas the tragic hero is great by reason of his moral virtue, Abraham is great by reason of a purely personal virtue. In Abraham's life there is no higher expression for the ethical than this, that the father shall love his son. Of the ethical in the sense of morality there can be no question in this instance. In so far as the universal was present, it was indeed cryptically present in Isaac, hidden as it were in Isaac's loins, and must therefore cry out with Isaac's mouth, "Do it not! Thou art bringing everything to naught." Why then did Abraham do it? For God's sake, and (in complete identity with this) for his own sake. He did it for God's sake because God required this proof of his faith; for his own sake he did it in order that he might furnish the proof. The unity of these two points of view is perfectly expressed by the word which has always been used to characterize this situation: it is a trial, a temptation (Fristelse).47 A temptation—but what does that mean? What ordinarily tempts a man is that which would keep him from doing his duty, but in this case the temptation is itself the ethical ... which would keep him from doing God's will. But what then is duty? Duty is precisely the expression for God's will. Here is evident the necessity of a new category if one would understand Abraham. Such a relationship to the deity paganism did not know. The tragic hero does not enter into any private relationship with the deity, but for him the ethical is the divine, hence the paradox implied in his situation can be mediated in the universal. Abraham cannot be mediated, and the same thing can be expressed also by saying that he cannot talk. So soon as I talk I express the universal, and if I do not do so, no one can understand me. Therefore if Abraham would express himself in terms of the universal, he must say that his situation is a temptation (Anfechtung), for he has no higher expression for that universal which stands above the universal which he transgresses. Therefore, though Abraham arouses my admiration, he at the same time appalls me. He who denies himself and sacrifices himself for duty gives up the finite in order to grasp the infinite, and that man is secure enough. The tragic hero gives up the certain for the still more certain, and the eye of the beholder rests upon him confidently. But he who gives up the universal in order to grasp something still higher which is not the universal—what is he doing? Is it possible that this can be anything else but a temptation (Anfechtung)? And if it be possible ... but the individual was mistaken—what can save him? He suffers all the pain of the tragic hero, he brings to naught his joy in the world, he renounces everything ... and perhaps at the same instant debars himself from the sublime joy which to him was so precious that he would purchase it at any price. Him the beholder cannot understand nor let his eye rest confidently upon him. Perhaps it is not possible to do what the believer proposes, since it is indeed unthinkable. Or if it could be done, but if the individual had misunderstood the deity– what can save him? The tragic hero has need of tears and claims them, and where is the envious eye which would be so barren that it could not weep with Agamemnon; but where is the man with a soul so bewildered that he would have the presumption to weep for Abraham? The tragic hero accomplishes his act at a definite instant in time, but in the course of time he does something not less significant, he visits the man whose soul is beset with sorrow, whose breast for stifled sobs cannot draw breath, whose thoughts pregnant with tears weigh heavily upon him, to him he makes his appearance, dissolves the sorcery of sorrow, loosens his corslet, coaxes forth his tears by the fact that in his sufferings the sufferer forgets his own. One cannot weep over Abraham. One approaches him with a horror religiosus, as Israel approached Mount Sinai.–If then the solitary man who ascends Mount Moriah, which with its peak rises heaven-high above the plain of Aulis, if he be not a somnambulist who walks securely above the abyss while he who is stationed at the foot of the mountain and is looking on trembles with fear and out of reverence and dread dare not even call to him–if this man is disordered in his mind, if he had made a mistake! Thanks and thanks again to him who proffers to the man whom the sorrows of life have assaulted and left naked–proffers to him the figleaf of the word with which he can cover his wretchedness. Thanks be to thee, great Shakespeare, who art able to express everything, absolutely everything, precisely as it is–and yet why didst thou never pronounce this pang? Didst thou perhaps reserve it to thyself–like the loved one whose name one cannot endure that the world should mention? For the poet purchases the power of words, the power of uttering all the dread secrets of others, at the price of a little secret he is unable to utter … and a poet is not an apostle, he casts out devils only by the power of the devil. But now when the ethical is thus teleologically suspended, how does the individual exist in whom it is suspended? He exists as the particular in opposition to the universal. Does he then sin? For this is the form of sin, as seen in the idea. Just as the infant, though it does not sin, because it is not as such yet conscious of its existence, yet its existence is sin, as seen in the idea, and the ethical makes its demands upon it every instant. If one denies that this form can be repeated [in the adult] in such a way that it is not sin, then the sentence of condemnation is pronounced upon Abraham. How then did Abraham exist? He believed. This is the paradox which keeps him upon the sheer edge and which he cannot make clear to any other man, for the paradox is that he as the individual puts himself in an absolute relation to the absolute. Is he justified in doing this? His justification is once more the paradox; for if he is justified, it is not by virtue of anything universal, but by virtue of being the particular individual. How then does the individual assure himself that he is justified? It is easy enough to level down the whole of existence to the idea of the state or the idea of society. If one does this, one can also mediate easily enough, for then one does not encounter at all the paradox that the individual as the individual is higher than the universal—which I can aptly express also by the thesis of Pythagoras, that the uneven numbers are more perfect than the even. If in our age one occasionally hears a rejoinder which is pertinent to the paradox, it is likely to be to the following effect: "It is to be judged by the result." A hero who has become a skándalon48 to his contemporaries because they are conscious that he is a paradox who cannot make himself intelligible, will cry out defiantly to his generation, "The result will surely prove that I am justified." In our age we hear this cry rather seldom, for as our age, to its disadvantage, does not produce heroes, it has also the advantage of producing few caricatures. When in our age one hears this saying, "It is to be judged according to the result," a man is at once clear as to who it is he has the honor of talking with. Those who talk thus are a numerous tribe, whom I will denominate by the common name of Docents. 49 In their thoughts they live secure in existence, they have a solid position and sure prospects in a well-ordered state, they have centuries and even millenniums between them and the concussions of existence, they do not fear that such things could recur—for what would the police say to that! and the newspapers! Their lifework is to judge the great, and to judge them according to the result. Such behavior toward the great betrays a strange mixture of arrogance and misery: of arrogance because they think they are called to be judges; of misery because they do not feel that their lives are even in the remotest degree akin to the great. Surely a man who possesses even a little erectioris ingenii [of the higher way of thinking] has not become entirely a cold and clammy mollusk, and when he approaches what is great it can never escape his mind that from the creation of the world it has been customary for the result to come last, and that, if one would truly learn anything from great actions, one must pay attention precisely to the beginning. In case he who should act were to judge himself according to the result, he would never get to the point of beginning. Even though the result may give joy to the whole world, it cannot help the hero, for he would get to know the result only when the whole thing was over, and it was not by this he became a hero, but he was such for the fact that he began. Moreover, the result (inasmuch as it is the answer of finiteness to the infinite query) is in its dialectic entirely heterogeneous with the existence of the hero. Or is it possible to prove that Abraham was justified in assuming the position of the individual with relation to the universal ... for the fact that he got Isaac by miracle? If Abraham had actually sacrificed Isaac, would he then have been less justified? But people are curious about the result, as they are about the result in a book—they want to know nothing about dread, distress, the paradox. They flirt aesthetically with the result, it comes just as unexpectedly but also just as easily as a prize in the lottery; and when they have heard the result they are edified. And yet no robber of temples condemned to hard labor behind iron bars, is so base a criminal as the man who pillages the holy, and even Judas who sold his Master for thirty pieces of silver is not more despicable than the man who sells greatness. It is abhorrent to my soul to talk inhumanly about greatness, to let it loom darkly at a distance in an indefinite form, to make out that it is great without making the human character of it evident—wherewith it ceases to be great. For it is not what happens to me that makes me great, but it is what I do, and there is surely no one who thinks that a man became great because he won the great prize in the lottery. Even if a man were born in humble circumstances, I would require of him nevertheless that he should not be so inhuman toward himself as not to be able to think of the King's castle except at a remote distance, dreaming vaguely of its greatness and wanting at the same time to exalt it and also to abolish it by the fact that he exalted it meanly. I require of him that he should be man enough to step forward confidently and worthily even in that place. He should not be unmanly enough to desire impudently to offend everybody by rushing straight from the street into the King's hall. By that he loses more than the King. On the contrary, he should find joy in observing every rule of propriety with a glad and confident enthusiasm which will make him frank and fearless. This is only a symbol, for the difference here remarked upon is only a very imperfect expression for spiritual distance. I require of every man that he should not think so inhumanly of himself as not to dare to enter those palaces where not merely the memory of the elect abides but where the elect themselves abide. He should not press forward impudently and impute to them kinship with himself; on the contrary, he should be blissful every time he bows before them, but he should be frank and confident and always be something more than a charwoman, for if he will not be more, he will never gain entrance. And what will help him is precisely the dread and distress by which the great are tried, for otherwise, if he has a bit of pith in him, they will merely arouse his justified envy. And what distance alone makes great, what people would make great by empty and hollow phrases, that they themselves reduce to naught. Who was ever so great as that blessed woman, the Mother of God, the Virgin Mary? And yet how do we speak of her? We say that she was highly favored among women. And if it did not happen strangely that those who hear are able to think as inhumanly as those who talk, every young girl might well ask, "Why was not I too the highly favored?" And if I had nothing else to say, I would not dismiss such a question as stupid, for when it is a matter of favor, abstractly considered, everyone is equally entitled to it. What they leave out is the distress, the dread, the paradox. My thought is as pure as that of anyone, and the thought of the man who is able to think such things will surely become pure–and if this be not so, he may expect the dreadful; for he who once has evoked these images cannot be rid of them again, and if he sins against them, they avenge themselves with quiet wrath, more terrible than the vociferousness of ten ferocious reviewers. To be sure, Mary bore the child miraculously, but it came to pass with her after the manner of women, and that season is one of dread, distress and paradox. To be sure, the angel was a ministering spirit, but it was not a servile spirit which obliged her by saying to the other young maidens of Israel, "Despise not Mary. What befalls her is the extraordinary." But the Angel came only to Mary, and no one could understand her. After all, what woman was so mortified as Mary? And is it not true in this instance also that one whom God blesses He curses in the same breath? This is the spirit's interpretation of Mary, and she is not (as it shocks me to say, but shocks me still more to think that they have thoughtlessly and coquettishly interpreted her thus)–she is not a fine lady who sits in state and plays with an infant god. Nevertheless, when she says, "Behold the handmaid of the Lord"–then she is great, and I think it will not be found difficult to explain why she became the Mother of God. She has no need of worldly admiration, any more than Abraham has need of tears, for she was not a heroine, and he was not a hero, but both of them became greater than such, not at all because they were exempted from distress and torment and paradox, but they became great through these.50 It is great when the poet, presenting his tragic hero before the admiration of men, dares to say, "Weep for him, for he deserves it." For it is great to deserve the tears of those who are worthy to shed tears. It is great that the poet dares to hold the crowd in check, dares to castigate men, requiring that every man examine himself whether he be worthy to weep for the hero. For the waste-water of blubberers is a degradation of the holy.– But greater than all this it is that the knight of faith dares to say even to the noble man who would weep for him, "Weep not for me, but weep for thyself." One is deeply moved, one longs to be back in those beautiful times, a sweet yearning conducts one to the desired goal, to see Christ wandering in the promised land. One forgets the dread, the distress, the paradox. Was it so easy a matter not to be mistaken? Was it not dreadful that this man who walks among the others—was it not dreadful that He was God? Was it not dreadful to sit at table with Him? Was it so easy a matter to become an Apostle? But the result, eighteen hundred years—that is a help, it helps to the shabby deceit wherewith one deceives oneself and others. I do not feel the courage to wish to be contemporary with such events, but hence I do not judge severely those who were mistaken, nor think meanly of those who saw aright. I return, however, to Abraham. Before the result, either Abraham was every minute a murderer, or we are confronted by a paradox which is higher than all mediation. The story of Abraham contains therefore a teleological suspension of the ethical. As the individual he became higher than the universal. This is the paradox which does not permit of mediation. It is just as inexplicable how he got into it as it is inexplicable how he remained in it. If such is not the position of Abraham, then he is not even a tragic hero but a murderer. To want to continue to call him the father of faith, to talk of this to people who do not concern themselves with anything but words, is thoughtless. A man can become a tragic hero by his own powers—but not a knight of faith. When a man enters upon the way, in a certain sense the hard way of the tragic hero, many will be able to give him counsel; to him who follows the narrow way of faith no one can give counsel, him no one can understand. Faith is a miracle, and yet no man is excluded from it; for that in which all human life is unified is passion,* and faith is a passion. *Lessing has somewhere given expression to a similar thought from a purely aesthetic point of view. What he would show expressly in this passage is that sorrow too can find a witty expression. To this end he quotes a rejoinder of the unhappy English king, Edward II. In contrast to this he quotes from Diderot a story of a peasant woman and a rejoinder of hers. Then he continues: "That too was wit, and the wit of a peasant at that; but the situation made it inevitable. Consequently one must not seek to kind the excuse for the witty expressions of pain and of sorrow in the fact that the person who uttered them was a superior person, well educated, intelligent, and witty withal, for the passions make all men again equal–but the explanation is to be found in the fact that in all probability everyone would have said the same thing in the same situation. The thought of a peasant woman a queen could have had and must have had, just as what the king said in that instance a peasant too would have been able to say and doubtless would have said." Cf. Sämtliche Werke, XXX. p. 223.51 PROBLEM II Is there such a thing as an absolute duty toward God? The ethical is the universal, and as such it is again the divine. One has therefore a right to say that fundamentally every duty is a duty toward God; but if one cannot say more, then one affirms at the same time that properly I have no duty toward God. Duty becomes duty by being referred to God, but in duty itself I do not come into relation with God. Thus it is a duty to love one's neighbor, but in performing this duty I do not come into relation with God but with the neighbor whom I love. If I say then in this connection that it is my duty to love God, I am really uttering only a tautology, inasmuch as "God" is in this instance used in an entirely abstract sense as the divine, i.e. the universal, i.e. duty. So the whole existence of the human race is rounded off completely like a sphere, and the ethical is at once its limit and its content. God becomes an invisible vanishing point, a powerless thought, His power being only in the ethical which is the content of existence. If in any way it might occur to any man to want to love God in any other sense than that here indicated, he is romantic, he loves a phantom which, if it had merely the power of being able to speak, would say to him, "I do not require your love. Stay where you belong." If in any way it might occur to a man to want to love God otherwise, this love would be open to suspicion, like that of which Rousseau speaks, referring to people who love the Kaffirs instead of their neighbors. So in case what has been expounded here is correct, in case there is no incommensurability in a human life, and what there is of the incommensurable is only such by an accident from which no consequences can be drawn, in so far as existence is regarded in terms of the idea, Hegel is right; but he is not right in talking about faith or in allowing Abraham to be regarded as the father of it; for by the latter he has pronounced judgment both upon Abraham and upon faith. In the Hegelian philosophy52 das Äussere (die Entäusserung) is higher than das Innere. This is frequently illustrated by an example. The child is das Innere, the man das Äussere. Hence it is that the child is defined by the outward, and conversely, the man, as das Äussere, is defined precisely by das Innere. Faith, on the contrary, is the paradox that inwardness is higher than outwardness—or, to recall an expression used above, the uneven number is higher than the even. In the ethical way of regarding life it is therefore the task of the individual to divest himself of the inward determinants and express them in an outward way. Whenever he shrinks from this, whenever he is inclined to persist in or to slip back again into the inward determinants of feeling, mood, etc., he sins, he is in a temptation (Anfechtung). The paradox of faith is this, that there is an inwardness which is incommensurable for the outward, an inwardness, be it observed, which is not identical with the first but is a new inwardness. This must not be overlooked. Modern philosophy53 has permitted itself without further ado to substitute in place of "faith" the immediate. When one does that it is ridiculous to deny that faith has existed in all ages. In that way faith comes into rather simple company along with feeling, mood, idiosyncrasy, vapors, etc. To this extent philosophy may be right in saying that one ought not to stop there. But there is nothing to justify philosophy in using this phrase with regard to faith. Before faith there goes a movement of infinity, and only then, necopinate, 54 by virtue of the absurd, faith enters upon the scene. This I can well understand without maintaining on that account that I have faith. If faith is nothing but what philosophy makes it out to be, then Socrates already went further, much further, whereas the contrary is true, that he never reached it. In an intellectual respect he made the movement of infinity. His ignorance is infinite resignation. This task in itself is a match for human powers, even though people in our time disdain it; but only after it is done, only when the individual has evacuated himself in the infinite, only then is the point attained where faith can break forth. The paradox of faith is this, that the individual is higher than the universal, that the individual (to recall a dogmatic distinction now rather seldom heard) determines his relation to the universal by his relation to the absolute, not his relation to the absolute by his relation to the universal. The paradox can also be expressed by saying that there is an absolute duty toward God; for in this relationship of duty the individual as an individual stands related absolutely to the absolute. So when in this connection it is said that it is a duty to love God, something different is said from that in the foregoing; for if this duty is absolute, the ethical is reduced to a position of relativity. From this, however, it does not follow that the ethical is to be abolished, but it acquires an entirely different expression, the paradoxical expression— that, for example, love to God may cause the knight of faith to give his love to his neighbor the opposite expression to that which, ethically speaking, is required by duty. If such is not the case, then faith has no proper place in existence, then faith is a temptation (Anfechtung), and Abraham is lost, since he gave in to it. This paradox does not permit of mediation, for it is founded precisely upon the fact that the individual is only the individual. As soon as this individual [who is aware of a direct command from God] wishes to express his absolute duty in [terms of] the universal [i.e. the ethical, and] is sure of his duty in that [i.e. the universal or ethical precept], he recognizes that he is in temptation [i.e. a trial of faith], and, if in fact he resists [the direct indication of God's will], he ends by not fulfilling the absolute duty so called [i.e. what here has been called the absolute duty]; and, if he doesn't do this, [i.e. doesn't put up a resistance to the direct intimation of God's will], he sins, even though realiter his deed were that which it was his absolute duty to do.* *The translator has ventured to render this muddy sentence very liberally (though he has bracketed his explanatory additions), in order to bring out the meaning this sentence must have if it is to express the anguishing paradox of a "teleological suspension of the ethical." This is the meaning Niels Thulstrup gets out of it, and he tells me that this is the translation of Emanuel Hirsch. As S.K.'s sentence stands, without explanatory additions, it reminds me of a rigmarole 1 have often recited to the mystification of my hearers: "If a man were to signify, which he were not, if he had the power, which being denied him, he were to endeavor anyhow—merely because he don't, would you?"

Much as I love Kierkegaard, I sometimes hate him for keeping me awake at night. Only between sleeping and waking am I able to unravel some of his most complicated sentences. So what should Abraham do? If he would say to another person, "Isaac I love more dearly than everything in the world, and hence it is so hard for me to sacrifice him"; then surely the other would have shaken his head and said, "Why will you sacrifice him then?"—or if the other had been a sly fellow, he surely would have seen through Abraham and perceived that he was making a show of feelings which were in strident contradiction to his act. In the story of Abraham we find such a paradox. His relation to Isaac, ethically expressed, is this, that the father should love the son. This ethical relation is reduced to a relative position in contrast with the absolute relation to God. To the question, "Why?" Abraham has no answer except that it is a trial, a temptation (Fristelse)—terms which, as was remarked above, express the unity of the two points of view: that it is for God's sake and for his own sake. In common usage these two ways of regarding the matter are mutually exclusive. Thus when we see a man do something which does not comport with the universal, we say that he scarcely can be doing it for God's sake, and by that we imply that he does it for his own sake. The paradox of faith has lost the intermediate term, i.e. the universal. On the one side it has the expression for the extremest egoism (doing the dreadful thing it does for one's own sake); on the other side the expression for the most absolute self-sacrifice (doing it for God's sake). Faith itself cannot be mediated into the universal, for it would thereby be destroyed. Faith is this paradox, and the individual absolutely cannot make himself intelligible to anybody. People imagine maybe that the individual can make himself intelligible to another individual in the same case. Such a notion would be unthinkable if in our time people did not in so many ways seek to creep slyly into greatness. The one knight of faith can render no aid to the other. Either the individual becomes a knight of faith by assuming the burden of the paradox, or he never becomes one. In these regions partnership is unthinkable. Every more precise explication of what is to be understood by Isaac the individual can give only to himself. And even if one were able, generally speaking,55 to define ever so precisely what should be intended by Isaac (which moreover would be the most ludicrous self-contradiction, i.e. that the particular individual who definitely stands outside the universal is subsumed under universal categories precisely when he has to act as the individual who stands outside the universal), the individual nevertheless will never be able to assure himself by the aid of others that this application is appropriate, but he can do so only by himself as the individual. Hence even if a man were cowardly and paltry enough to wish to become a knight of faith on the responsibility of an outsider, he will never become one; for only the individual becomes a knight of faith as the particular individual, and this is the greatness of this knighthood, as I can well understand without entering the order, since I lack courage; but this is also its terror, as I can comprehend even better. In Luke 14:26, as everybody knows, there is a striking doctrine taught about the absolute duty toward God: "If any man cometh unto me and hateth not his own father and mother and wife and children and brethren and sisters, yea, and his own life also, he cannot be my disciple." This is a hard saying, who can bear to hear it? For this reason it is heard very seldom. This silence, however, is only an evasion which is of no avail. Nevertheless, the student of theology learns to know that these words occur in the New Testament, and in one or another exegetical aid56 he finds the explanation that miseîn in this passage and a few others is used in the sense of meísein, signifying minus diligo, posthabeo, non colo, nihili facio. However, the context in which these words occur does not seem to strengthen this tasteful explanation. In the verse immediately following there is a story about a man who desired to build a tower but first sat down to calculate whether he was capable of doing it, lest people might laugh at him afterwards. The close connection of this story with the verse here cited seems precisely to indicate that the words are to be taken in as terrible a sense as possible, to the end that everyone may examine himself as to whether he is able to erect the building. In case this pious and kindly exegete, who by abating the price thought he could smuggle Christianity into the world, were fortunate enough to convince a man that grammatically, linguistically and kat' a'nalogían [analogically] this was the meaning of that passage, it is to be hoped that the same moment he will be fortunate enough to convince the same man that Christianity is one of the most pitiable things in the world. For the doctrine which in one of its most lyrical outbursts, where the consciousness of its eternal validity swells in it most strongly, has nothing else to say but a noisy word which means nothing but only signifies that one is to be less kindly, less attentive, more indifferent; the doctrine which at the moment when it makes as if it would give utterance to the terrible ends by driveling instead of terrifying–that doctrine is not worth taking off my hat to. The words are terrible, yet I fully believe that one can understand them without implying that he who understands them has courage to do them. One must at all events be honest enough to acknowledge what stands written and to admit that it is great, even though one has not the courage for it. He who behaves thus will not find himself excluded from having part in that beautiful story which follows, for after all it contains consolation of a sort for the man who had not courage to begin the tower. But we must be honest, and not interpret this lack of courage as humility, since it is really pride, whereas the courage of faith is the only humble courage. One can easily perceive that if there is to be any sense in this passage, it must be understood literally. God it is who requires absolute love. But he who in demanding a person's love thinks that this love should be proved also by becoming lukewarm to everything which hitherto was dear–that man is not only an egoist but stupid as well, and he who would demand such love signs at the same moment his own death-warrant, supposing that his life was bound up with this coveted love. Thus a husband demands that his wife shall leave father and mother, but if he were to regard it as a proof of her extraordinary love for him that she for his sake became an indolent, lukewarm daughter etc., then he is the stupidest of the stupid. If he had any notion of what love is, he would wish to discover that as daughter and sister she was perfect in love, and would see therein the proof that she would love him more than anyone else in the realm. What therefore in the case of a man one would regard as a sign of egoism and stupidity, that one is to regard by the help of an exegete as a worthy conception of the Deity. But how hate them? I will not recall here the human distinction between loving and hating—not because I have much to object to in it (for after all it is passionate), but because it is egoistic and is not in place here. However, if I regard the problem as a paradox, then I understand it, that is, I understand it in such a way as one can understand a paradox. The absolute duty may cause one to do what ethics would forbid, but by no means can it cause the knight of faith to cease to love. This is shown by Abraham. The instant he is ready to sacrifice Isaac the ethical expression for what he does is this: he hates Isaac. But if he really hates Isaac, he can be sure that God does not require this, for Cain and Abraham are not identical. Isaac he must love with his whole soul; when God requires Isaac he must love him if possible even more dearly, and only on this condition can he sacrifice him; for in fact it is this love for Isaac which, by its paradoxical opposition to his love for God, makes his act a sacrifice. But the distress and dread in this paradox is that, humanly speaking, he is entirely unable to make himself intelligible. Only at the moment when his act is in absolute contradiction to his feeling is his act a sacrifice, but the reality of his act is the factor by which he belongs to the universal, and in that aspect he is and remains a murderer. Moreover, the passage in Luke must be understood in such a way as to make it clearly evident that the knight of faith has no higher expression of the universal (i.e. the ethical) by which he can save himself. Thus, for example, if we suppose that the Church requires such a sacrifice of one of its members, we have in this case only a tragic hero. For the idea of the Church is not qualitatively different from that of the State, in so far as the individual comes into it by a simple mediation, and in so far as the individual comes into the paradox he does not reach the idea of the Church; he does not come out of the paradox, but in it he must find either his blessedness or his perdition. Such an ecclesiastical hero expresses in his act the universal, and there will be no one in the Church—not even his father and mother etc.—who fails to understand him. On the other hand, he is not a knight of faith, and he has also a different answer from that of Abraham: he does not say that it is a trial or a temptation in which he is tested. People commonly refrain from quoting such a text as this in Luke. They are afraid of giving men a free rein, are afraid that the worst will happen as soon as the individual takes it into his head to comport himself as the individual. Moreover, they think that to exist as the individual is the easiest thing of all, and that therefore people have to be compelled to become the universal. I cannot share either this fear or this opinion, and both for the same reason. He who has learned that to exist as the individual is the most terrible thing of all will not be fearful of saying that it is great, but then too he will say this in such a way that his words will scarcely be a snare for the bewildered man, but rather will help him into the universal, even though his words do to some extent make room for the great. The man who does not dare to mention such texts will not dare to mention Abraham either, and his notion that it is easy enough to exist as the individual implies a very suspicious admission with regard to himself; for he who has a real respect for himself and concern for his soul is convinced that the man who lives under his own supervision, alone in the whole world, lives more strictly and more secluded than a maiden in her lady's bower. That there may be some who need compulsion, some who, if they were free-footed, would riot in selfish pleasures like unruly beasts, is doubtless true; but a man must prove precisely that he is not of this number by the fact that he knows how to speak with dread and trembling; and out of reverence for the great one is bound to speak, lest it be forgotten for fear of the ill effect, which surely will fail to eventuate when a man talks in such a way that one knows it for the great, knows its terror—and apart from the terror one does not know the great at all. Let us consider a little more closely the distress and dread in the paradox of faith. The tragic hero renounces himself in order to express the universal, the knight of faith renounces the universal in order to become the individual. As has been said, everything depends upon how one is placed. He who believes that it is easy enough to be the individual can always be sure that he is not a knight of faith, for vagabonds and roving geniuses are not men of faith. The knight of faith knows, on the other hand, that it is glorious to belong to the universal. He knows that it is beautiful and salutary to be the individual who translates himself into the universal, who edits as it were a pure and elegant edition of himself, as free from errors as possible and which everyone can read. He knows that it is refreshing to become intelligible to oneself in the universal so that he understands it and so that every individual who understands him understands through him in turn the universal, and both rejoice in the security of the universal. He knows that it is beautiful to be born as the individual who has the universal as his home, his friendly abiding-place, which at once welcomes him with open arms when he would tarry in it. But he knows also that higher than this there winds a solitary path, narrow and steep; he knows that it is terrible to be born outside the universal, to walk without meeting a single traveller. He knows very well where he is and how he is related to men. Humanly speaking, he is crazy and cannot make himself intelligible to anyone. And yet it is the mildest expression, to say that he is crazy. If he is not supposed to be that, then he is a hypocrite, and the higher he climbs on this path, the more dreadful a hypocrite he is. The knight of faith knows that to give up oneself for the universal inspires enthusiasm, and that it requires courage, but he also knows that security is to be found in this, precisely because it is for the universal. He knows that it is glorious to be understood by every noble mind, so glorious that the beholder is ennobled by it, and he feels as if he were bound; he could wish it were this task that had been allotted to him. Thus Abraham could surely have wished now and then that the task were to love Isaac as becomes a father, in a way intelligible to all, memorable throughout all ages; he could wish that the task were to sacrifice Isaac for the universal, that he might incite the fathers to illustrious deeds—and he is almost terrified by the thought that for him such wishes are only temptations and must be dealt with as such, for he knows that it is a solitary path he treads and that he accomplishes nothing for the universal but only himself is tried and examined. Or what did Abraham accomplish for the universal? Let me speak humanly about it, quite humanly. He spent seventy years in getting a son of his old age. What other men get quickly enough and enjoy for a long time he spent seventy years in accomplishing. And why? Because he was tried and put to the test. Is not that crazy? But Abraham believed, and Sarah wavered and got him to take Hagar as a concubine–but therefore he also had to drive her away. He gets Isaac, then he has to be tried again. He knew that it is glorious to express the universal, glorious to live with Isaac. But this is not the task. He knew that it is a kingly thing to sacrifice such a son for the universal, he himself would have found repose in that, and all would have reposed in the commendation of his deed, as a vowel reposes in its consonant,57 but that is not the task–he is tried. That Roman general who is celebrated by his name of Cunctator58 checked the foe by procrastination–but what a procrastinator Abraham is in comparison with him! ... yet he did not save the state. This is the content of one hundred and thirty years. Who can bear it? Would not his contemporary age, if we can speak of such a thing, have said of him, "Abraham is eternally procrastinating. Finally he gets a son. That took long enough. Now he wants to sacrifice him. So is he not mad? And if at least he could explain why he wants to do it–but he always says that it is a trial." Nor could Abraham explain more, for his life is like a book placed under a divine attachment and which never becomes publici juris. 59 This is the terrible thing. He who does not see it can always be sure that he is no knight of faith, but he who sees it will not deny that even the most tried of tragic heroes walks with a dancing step compared with the knight of faith, who comes slowly creeping forward. And if he has perceived this and assured himself that he has not courage to understand it, he will at least have a presentiment of the marvellous glory this knight attains in the fact that he becomes God's intimate acquaintance, the Lord's friend, and (to speak quite humanly) that he says "Thou" to God in heaven, whereas even the tragic hero only addresses Him in the third person. The tragic hero is soon ready and has soon finished the fight, he makes the infinite movement and then is secure in the universal. The knight of faith, on the other hand, is kept sleepless, for he is constantly tried, and every instant there is the possibility of being able to return repentantly to the universal, and this possibility can just as well be a temptation as the truth. He can derive evidence from no man which it is, for with that query he is outside the paradox. So the knight of faith has first and foremost the requisite passion to concentrate upon a single factor the whole of the ethical which he transgresses, so that he can give himself the assurance that he really loves Isaac with his whole soul.*

I would elucidate yet once more the difference between the collisions which are encountered by the tragic hero and by the knight of faith. The tragic hero assures himself that the ethical obligation [i.e., the lower ethical obligation, which he puts aside for the higher in the present case, accorclingly, it is the obligation to spare his daughter's life] is totally present in him by the fact that he transforms it into a wish. Thus Agamemnon can say, "The proof that I do not offend against my parental duty is that my duty is my only wish." So here we have wish and duty face to face with one another. The fortunate chance in life is that the two correspond, that my wish is my duty and vice versa, and the task of most men in life is precisely to remain within their duty and by their enthusiasm to transform it into their wish. The tragic hero gives up his wish in order to accomplish his duty. For the knight of faith wish and duty are also identical, but he is required to give up both. Therefore when he would resign himself to giving up his wish he does not find repose, for that is after all his duty. If he would remain within his duty and his wish he is not a knight of faith, for the absolute duty requires precisely that he should give them up. The tragic hero apprehended a higher expression of duty but not an absolute duty. If he cannot do that, he is in temptation (Anfechtung). In the next place, he has enough passion to make this assurance available in the twinkling of an eye and in such a way that it is as completely valid as it was in the first instance. If he is unable to do this, he can never budge from the spot, for he constantly has to begin all over again. The tragic hero also concentrated in one factor the ethical which he teleologically surpassed, but in this respect he had support in the universal. The knight of faith has only himself alone, and this constitutes the dreadfulness of the situation. Most men live in such a way under an ethical obligation that they can let the sorrow be sufficient for the day, but they never reach this passionate concentration, this energetic consciousness. The universal may in a certain sense help the tragic hero to attain this, but the knight of faith is left all to himself. The hero does the deed and finds repose in the universal, the knight of faith is kept in constant tension. Agamemnon gives up Iphigenia and thereby has found repose in the universal, then he takes the step of sacrificing her. If Agamemnon does not make the infinite movement, if his soul at the decisive instant, instead of having passionate concentration, is absorbed by the common twaddle that he had several daughters and vielleicht [perhaps] the Ausserordentliche [extraordinary] might occur– then he is of course not a hero but a hospital-case. The hero's concentration Abraham also has, even though in his case it is far more difficult, since he has no support in the universal; but he makes one more movement by which he concentrates his soul upon the miracle. If Abraham did not do that, he is only an Agamemnon–if in any way it is possible to explain how he can be justified in sacrificing Isaac when thereby no profit accrues to the universal. Whether the individual is in temptation (Anfechtung) or is a knight of faith only the individual can decide. Nevertheless it is possible to construct from the paradox several criteria which he too can understand who is not within the paradox. The true knight of faith is always absolute isolation, the false knight is sectarian. This sectarianism is an attempt to leap away from the narrow path of the paradox and become a tragic hero at a cheap price. The tragic hero expresses the universal and sacrifices himself for it. The sectarian punchinello, instead of that, has a private theatre, i.e. several good friends and comrades who represent the universal just about as well as the beadles in The Golden Snuffbox60 represent justice. The knight of faith, on the contrary, is the paradox, is the individual, absolutely nothing but the individual, without connections or pretensions. This is the terrible thing which the sectarian manikin cannot endure. For instead of learning from this terror that he is not capable of performing the great deed and then plainly admitting it (an act which I cannot but approve, because it is what I do) the manikin thinks that by uniting with several other manikins he will be able to do it. But that is quite out of the question. In the world of spirit no swindling is tolerated. A dozen sectaries join arms with one another, they know nothing whatever of the lonely temptations which await the knight of faith and which he dares not shun precisely because it would be still more dreadful if he were to press forward presumptuously. The sectaries deafen one another by their noise and racket, hold the dread off by their shrieks, and such a hallooing company of sportsmen think they are storming heaven and think they are on the same path as the kight of faith who in the solitude of the universe never hears any human voice but walks alone with his dreadful responsibility. The knight of faith is obliged to rely upon himself alone, he feels the pain of not being able to make himself intelligible to others, but he feels no vain desire to guide others. The pain is his assurance that he is in the right way, this vain desire he does not know, he is too serious for that. The false knight of faith readily betrays himself by this proficiency in guiding which he has acquired in an instant. He does not comprehend what it is all about, that if another individual is to take the same path, he must become entirely in the same way the individual and have no need of any man's guidance, least of all the guidance of a man who would obtrude himself. At this point men leap aside, they cannot bear the martyrdom of being uncomprehended, and instead of this they choose conveniently enough the worldly admiration of their proficiency. The true knight of faith is a witness, never a teacher, and therein lies his deep humanity, which is worth a good deal more than this silly participation in others' weal and woe which is honored by the name of sympathy, whereas in fact it is nothing but vanity. He who would only be a witness thereby avows that no man, not even the lowliest, needs another man's sympathy or should be abased that another may be exalted. But since he did not win what he won at a cheap price, neither does he sell it out at a cheap price, he is not petty enough to take men's admiration and give them in return his silent contempt, he knows that what is truly great is equally accessible to all. Either there is an absolute duty toward God, and if so it is the paradox here described, that the individual as the individual is higher than the universal and as the individual stands in an absolute relation to the absolute/or else faith never existed, because it has always existed, or, to put it differently, Abraham is lost, or one must explain the passage in the fourteenth chapter of Luke as did that tasteful exegete, and explain in the same way the corresponding passages and similar ones.61 PROBLEM III Was Abraham ethically defensible in keeping silent about his purpose before Sarah, before Eleazar, before Isaac? The ethical as such is the universal, again, as the universal it is the manifest, the revealed. The individual regarded as he is immediately, that is, as a physical and psychical being, is the hidden, the concealed. So his ethical task is to develop out of this concealment and to reveal himself in the universal. Hence whenever he wills to remain in concealment he sins and lies in temptation (Anfechtung), out of which he can come only by revealing himself. With this we are back again at the same point. If there is not a concealment which has its ground in the fact that the individual as the individual is higher than the universal, then Abraham's conduct is indefensible, for he paid no heed to the intermediate ethical determinants. If on the other hand there is such a concealment, we are in the presence of the paradox which cannot be mediated inasmuch as it rests upon the consideration that the individual as the individual is higher than the universal, but it is the universal precisely which is mediation. The Hegelian philosophy holds that there is no justified concealment, no justified incommensurability. So it is self-consistent when it requires revelation, but it is not warranted in regarding Abraham as the father of faith and in talking about faith. For faith is not the first immediacy but a subsequent immediacy. The first immediacy is the aesthetical, and about this the Hegelian philosophy may be in the right. But faith is not the aesthetical–or else faith has never existed because it has always existed. It will be best to regard the whole matter from a purely aesthetical point of view, and with that intent to embark upon an aesthetic deliberation, to which I beg the reader to abandon himself completely for the moment, while I, to contribute my share, will modify my presentation in conformity with the subject. The category I would consider a little more closely is the interesting, a category which especially in our age (precisely because our age lives in discrimine rerum) [at a turning point in history] has acquired great importance, for it is properly the category of the turning-point. Therefore we, after having loved this category pro virili [with all our power], should not scorn it as some do because we have outgrown it, but neither should we be too greedy to attain it, for certain it is that to be interesting or to have an interesting life is not a task for industrial art but a fateful privilege, which like every privilege in the world of spirit is bought only by deep pain. Thus, for example, Socrates was the most interesting man that ever lived, his life the most interesting that has been recorded, but this existence was alloted to him by the Deity, and in so far as he himself had to acquire it he was not unacquainted with trouble and pain. To take such a life in vain does not beseem a man who takes life seriously, and yet it is not rare to see in our age examples of such an endeavor. Moreover the interesting is a border-category, a boundary between aesthetics and ethics. For this reason our deliberation must constantly glance over into the field of ethics, while in order to be able to acquire significance it must grasp the problem with aesthetic intensity and concupiscence. With such matters ethics seldom deals in our age. The reason is supposed to be that there is no appropriate place for it in the System. Then surely one might do it in a monograph, and moreover, if one would not do it prolixly, one might do it briefly and yet attain the same end—if, that is to say, a man has the predicate in his power, for one or two predicates can betray a whole world. Might there not be some place in the System for a little word like the predicate? In his immortal Poetics (Chapter 11) Aristotle says,62 dúo mèn oûn toû múqou mérh perì taût' e'stí, peripéteia kaì a'nagnw'risiv. I am of course concerned here only with the second factor, a'nagnw'risiv, recognition. Where there can be question of a recognition there is implied eo ipso a previous concealment. So just as recognition is the relieving, the relaxing factor in the dramatic life, so is concealment the factor of tension. What Aristotle has to say in the same chapter about the merits of tragedy which are variously appraised in proportion as peripéteia and a'nagnw'risiv impinge63 upon one another, and also what he says about the "individual" and the "double recognition," I cannot take into consideration here, although by its inwardness and quiet concentration what he says is peculiarly tempting to one who is weary of the superficial omniscience of encyclopedic scholars. A more general observation may be appropriate here. In Greek tragedy concealment (and consequently recognition) is an epic survival grounded upon a fate in which the dramatic action disappears from view and from which it derives its obscure and enigmatic origin. Hence it is that the effect produced by a Greek tragedy is like the impression of a marble statue which lacks the power of the eye. Greek tragedy is blind. Hence a certain abstraction is necessary in order to appreciate it properly. A son64 murders his father, but only afterwards does he learn that it was his father. A sister65 wants to sacrifice her brother, but at the decisive moment she learns who he is. This dramatic motive is not so apt to interest our reflective age. Modern drama has given up fate, has emancipated itself dramatically, sees with its eyes, scrutinizes itself, resolves fate in its dramatic consciousness. Concealment and revelation are in this case the hero's free act for which he is responsible. Recognition and concealment are also present as an essential element in modern drama. To adduce examples of this would be too prolix. I am courteous enough to assume that everybody in our age, which is so aesthetically wanton, so potent and so enflamed that the act of conception comes as easy to it as to the partridge hen, which, according to Aristotle's affirmation,66 needs only to hear the voice of the cock or the sound of its flight overhead—I assume that everyone, merely upon hearing the word "concealment" will be able to shake half a score of romances and comedies out of his sleeve. Wherefore I express myself briefly and so will throw out at once a general observation. In case one who plays hide and seek (and thereby introduces into the play the dramatic ferment) hides something nonsensical, we get a comedy; if on the other hand he stands in relation to the idea, he may come near being a tragic hero. I give here merely an example of the comic. A man rouges his face and wears a periwig. The same man is eager to try his fortune with the fair sex, he is perfectly sure of conquering by the aid of the rouge and the periwig which make him absolutely irresistible. He captures a girl and is at the acme of happiness. Now comes the gist of the matter: if he is able to admit this embellishment, he does not lose all of his infatuating power; when he reveals himself as a plain ordinary man, and bald at that, he does not thereby lose the loved one.–Concealment is his free act, for which aesthetics also holds him responsible. This science is no friend of bald hypocrites, it abandons him to the mercy of laughter. This must suffice as a mere hint of what I mean–the comical cannot be a subject of interest for this investigation. It is incumbent upon me to examine dialectically the part played by concealment in aesthetics and ethics, for the point is to show the absolute difference between the aesthetic concealment and the paradox. A couple of examples. A girl is secretly in love with a man, although they have not definitely avowed their love to one another. Her parents compel her to marry another (there may be moreover a consideration of filial piety which determines her), she obeys her parents, she conceals her love, "so as not to make the other unhappy, and no one will ever know what she suffers."–A young man is able by a single word to get possession of the object of his longings and his restless dreams. This little word, however, will compromise, yea, perhaps (who knows?) bring to ruin a whole family, he resolves magnanimously to remain in his concealment, "the girl shall never get to know it, so that she may perhaps become happy by giving her hand to another." What a pity that these two persons, both of whom were concealed from their respective beloveds, were also concealed from one another, otherwise a remarkable higher unity might have been brought about.–Their concealment is a free act, for which they are responsible also to aesthetics. Aesthetics, however, is a courteous and sentimental science which knows of more expedients than a pawnbroker. So what does it do? It makes everything possible for the lovers. By the help of a chance the partners to the projected marriage get a hint of the magnanimous resolution of the other part, it comes to an explanation, they get one another and at the same time attain rank with real heroes. For in spite of the fact that they did not even get time to sleep over their resolution, aesthetics treats them nevertheless as if they had courageously fought for their resolution during many years. For aesthetics does not trouble itself greatly about time, whether in jest or seriousness time flies equally fast for it. But ethics knows nothing about that chance or about that sentimentality, nor has it so speedy a concept of time. Thereby the matter receives a different aspect. It is no good arguing with ethics for it has pure categories. It does not appeal to experience, which of all ludicrous things is the most ludicrous, and which so far from making a man wise rather makes him mad if he knows nothing higher than this. Ethics has in its possession no chance, and so matters do not come to an explanation, it does not jest with dignities, it lays a prodigious responsibility upon the shoulders of the puny hero, it denounces as presumption his wanting to play providence by his actions, but it also denounces him for wanting to do it by his suffering. It bids a man believe in reality and have courage to fight against all the afflictions of reality, and still more against the bloodless sufferings he has assumed on his own responsibility. It warns against believing the calculations of the understanding, which are more perfidious than the oracles of ancient times. It warns agtunst every untimely magnanimity. Let reality decide–then is the time to show courage, but then ethics itself offers all possible assistance. If, however, there was something deeper which moved in these two, if there was seriousness to see the task, seriousness to commence it, then something will come of them; but ethics cannot help, it is offended, for they keep a secret from it, a secret they hold at their own peril. So aesthetics required concealment and rewarded it, ethics required revelation and punished concealment. At times, however, even aesthetics requires revelation. When the hero ensnared in the aesthetic illusion thinks by his silence to save another man, then it requires silence and rewards it. On the other hand, when the hero by his action intervenes disturbingly in another man's life, then it requires revelation. I am now on the subject of the tragic hero. I would consider for a moment Euripides' Iphigenia in Aulis. Agamemnon must sacrifice Iphigenia. Now aesthetics requires silence of Agamemnon inasmuch as it would be unworthy of the hero to seek comfort from any other man, and out of solicitude for the women too he ought to conceal this from them as long as possible. On the other hand, the hero, precisely in order to be a hero, must be tried by dreadful temptations which the tears of Clytemnestra and Iphigenia provide for him. What does aesthetics do? It has an expedient, it has in readiness an old servant who reveals everything to Clytemnestra. Then all is as it should be. Ethics, however, has at hand no chance and no old servant. The aesthetical idea contradicts itself as soon as it must be carried out in reality. Hence ethics requires revelation. The tragic hero displays his ethical courage precisely by the fact that it is he who, without being ensnared in any aesthetic illusion, himself announces to Iphigenia her fate. If the tragic hero does this, then he is the beloved son of ethics in whom it is well pleased. If he keeps silent, it may be because he thinks thereby to make it easier for others, but it may also be because thereby he makes it easier for himself. However, he knows that he is not influenced by this latter motive. If he keeps silent, he assumes as the individual a serious responsibility inasmuch as he ignores an argument which may come from without. As a tragic hero he cannot do this, for ethics loves him precisely because he constantly expresses the universal. His heroic action demands courage, but it belongs to this courage that he shall shun no argumentation. Now it is certain that tears are a dreadful argumentum ad hominem, and doubtless there are those who are moved by nothing yet are touched by tears. In the play Iphigenia had leave to weep, really she ought to have been allowed like Jephthah's daughter two months for weeping, not in solitude but at her father's feet, allowed to employ all her art "which is but tears," and to twine about his knees instead of presenting the olive branch of the suppliant. Aesthetics required revelation but helped itself out by a chance; ethics required revelation and found in the tragic hero its satisfaction. In spite of the severity with which ethics requires revelation, it cannot be denied that secrecy and silence really make a man great precisely because they are characteristics of inwardness. When Amor leaves Psyche he says to her, "Thou shalt give birth to a child which will be a divine infant if thou dost keep silence, but a human being if thou dost reveal the secret." The tragic hero who is the favorite of ethics is the purely human, and him I can understand, and all he does is in the light of the revealed. If I go further, then I stumble upon the paradox, either the divine or the demoniac, for silence is both. Silence is the snare of the demon, and the more one keeps silent, the more terrifying the demon becomes; but silence is also the mutual understanding between the Deity and the individual. Before going on to the story of Abraham, however, I would call before the curtain several poetic personages. By the power of dialectic I keep them upon tiptoe, and by wielding over them the scourge of despair I shall surely keep them from standing still, in order that in their dread they may reveal one thing and another. *These movements and attitudes might well be a subject for further aesthetic treatment. However, I leave it undecided to what extent faith and the whole life of faith might be a fit subject for such treatment. Only, because it is always a joy to me to thank him to whom I am indebted, I would thank Lessing for some hints of a Christian drama which is found in his Hamburgische Dramaturgie. 69 He, however, fixed his glance upon the purely divine side of the Christian life (the consummated victory) and hence he had misgivings; perhaps he would have expressed a different judgment if he had paid more attention to the purely human side (theologia viatorum).70 Doubtless what he says is very brief, in part evasive, but since I am always glad to have the company of Lessing, I seize it at once. Lessing was not merely one of the most comprehensive minds Germany has had, he not only was possessed of rare exactitude in his learning (for which reason one can securely rely upon him and upon his autopsy without fear of being duped by inaccurate quotations which can be traced nowhere, by half-understood phrases which are drawn from untrustworthy compendiums, or to be disoriented by a foolish trumpeting of novelties which the ancients have expounded far better) but he possessed at the same time an exceedingly uncommon gift of explaining what he himself had understood. There he stopped. In our age people go further and explain more than they have understood. In his Poetics67 Aristotle relates a story of a political disturbance at Delphi which was provoked by a question of marriage. The bridegroom, when the augurs68 foretell to him that a misfortune would follow his marriage, suddenly changes his plan at the decisive moment when he comes to fetch the bride–he will not celebrate the wedding. I have no need of more.* *According to Aristotle the historic catastrophe was as follows. To avenge themselves the family of the bride introduced a temple-vessel among his household goods, and he is sentenced as a temple-robber. This, however, is of no consequence, for the question is not whether the family is shrewd or stupid in taking revenge. The family has an ideal significance only in so far as it is drawn into the dialectic of the hero. Besides it is fateful enough that he, when he would shun danger by not marrying, plunges into it, and also that his life comes into contact with the divine in a double way: first by the saying of the augurs, and then by being condemned for sacrilege. In Delphi this event hardly passed without tears; if a poet were to have adopted it as his theme, he might have dared to count very surely upon sympathy. Is it not dreadful that love, which in human life often enough was cast into exile, is now deprived of the support of heaven? Is not the old proverb that "marriages are made in heaven" here put to shame? Usually it is all the afflictions and difficulties of the finite which like evil spirits separate the lovers, but love has heaven on its side, and therefore this holy alliance overcomes all enemies. In this case it is heaven itself which separates what heaven itself has joined together. And who would have guessed such a thing? The young bride least of all. Only a moment before she was sitting in her chamber in all her beauty, and the lovely maidens had conscientiously adorned her so that they could justify before all the world what they had done, so that they not merely derived joy from it but envy, yea, joy for the fact that it was not possible for them to become more envious, because it was not possible for her to become more beautiful. She sat alone in her chamber and was transformed from beauty unto beauty, for every means was employed that feminine art was capable of to adorn worthily the worthy. But there still was lacking something which the young maidens had not dreamed of: a veil finer, lighter and yet more impenetrable than that in which the young maidens had enveloped her, a bridal dress which no young maiden knew of or could help her to obtain, yea, even the bride herself did not know how to obtain it. It was an invisible, a friendly power, taking pleasure in adorning a bride, which enveloped her in it without her knowledge; for she saw only how the bridegroom passed by and went up to the temple. She saw the door shut behind him, and she became even more calm and blissful, for she only knew that he now belonged to her more than ever. The door of the temple opened, he stepped out, but maidenly she cast down her eyes and therefore did not see that his countenance was troubled, but he saw that heaven was jealous of the bride's loveliness and of his good fortune. The door of the temple opened, and the young maidens saw the bridegroom step out, but they did not see that his countenance was troubled, they were busy fetching the bride. Then forth she stepped in all her maidenly modesty and yet like a queen surrounded by her maids of honor, who bowed before her as the young maiden always bows before a bride. Thus she stood at the head of her lovely band and waited—it was only an instant, for the temple was near at hand—and the bridegroom came ... but he passed by her door. But here I break off—I am not a poet, I go about things only dialectically. It must be remembered first of all that it is at the decisive instant the hero gets this elucidation, so he is pure and blameless, has not light-mindedly tied himself to the fiancée. In the next place, he has a divine utterance for him, or rather against him,71 he is therefore not guided like those puny lovers by his own conceit. Moreover, it goes without saying that this utterance makes him just as unhappy as the bride, yea, a little more so, since he after all is the occasion of her unhappiness. It is true enough that the augurs only foretold a misfortune to him, but the question is whether this misfortune is not of such a sort that in injuring him it would also affect injuriously their conjugal happiness. What then is he to do? (1) Shall he preserve silence and celebrate the wedding?—with the thought that "perhaps the misfortune will not come at once, at any rate I have upheld love and have not feared to make myself unhappy. But keep silent I must, for otherwise even the short moment is wasted." This seems plausible, but it is not so by any means, for in doing this he has insulted the girl. He has in a way made the girl guilty by his silence, for in case she had known the truth she never would have consented to such a union. So in the hour of need he would not only have to bear the misfortune but also the responsibility for having kept silent and her justified indignation that he had kept silent. Or (2) shall he keep silent and give up celebrating the wedding? In this case he must embroil himself in a mystifictition by which he reduces himself to naught in relation to her. Aesthetics would perhaps approve of this. The catastrophe might then be fashioned like that of the real story, except that at the last instant an explanation would be forthcoming—however, that would be after it was all over, since aesthetically viewed it is a necessity to let him die … unless this science should see its way to annul the fateful prophecy. Still, this behavior, magnanimous as it is, implies an offense against the girl and against the reality of her love. Or (3) shall he speak? One of course must not forget that our hero is a little too poetical for us to suppose that to sign away his love might not have for him a significance very different from the result of an unsuccessful business speculation. If he speaks, the whole thing becomes a story of unhappy love in the style of Axel and Valborg.* *Moreover, from this point one might conduct the dialectical movements in another direction. Heaven foretells a misfortune consequent upon his marriage, so in fact he might give up the wedding but not for this reason give up the girl, rather live with her in a romantic union which for the lovers would be more than satisfactory. This implies, however, an offense against the girl because in his love for her he does not express the universal. However, this would be a theme both for a poet and for an ethicist who would defend marriage. On the whole, if poetry were to pay attention to the religious and to the inwardness of personalities, it would find themes of far greater importance than those with which it now busies itself. In poetry one hears again and again this story: a man is bound to a girl whom he once loved—or perhaps never sincerely loved, for now he has seen another girl who is the ideal. A man makes a mistake in life, it was in the right street but it was in the wrong house, for opposite, on the second floor, dwells the ideal—this people think a theme for poetry. A lover has made a mistake, he saw his fiancée by lamplight and thought she had dark hair, but, lo, on closer inspection she is blonde–but her sister, she is the ideal! This they think is a theme for poetry! My opinion is that every such man is a lout who may be intolerable enough in real life but ought instantly to be hissed off the stage when he would give himself airs in poetry. Only passion against passion provides a poetic collision, not the rumpus of these particulars within the same passion. If, for example, a girl in the Middle Ages, after having fallen in love, convinces herself that all earthly love is a sin and prefers a heavenly, here is a poetic collision, and the girl is poetic, for her life is in the idea. This is a pair which heaven itself separates.72 However, in the present case the separation is to be conceived somewhat differently since it results at the same time from the free act of the individuals. What is so very difficult in the dialectic of this case is that the misfortune is to fall only upon him. So the two lovers do not find like Axel and Valborg a common expression for their suffering, inasmuch as heaven levels its decree equally against Axel and Valborg because they are equally near of kin to one another. If this were the case here, a way out would be thinkable. For since heaven does not employ any visible power to separate them but leaves this to them, it is thinkable that they might resolve between them to defy heaven and its misfortune too. Ethics, however, will require him to speak. His heroism then is essentially to be found in the fact that he gives up aesthetic magnanimity, which in this case, however, could not easily be thought to have any admixture of the vanity which consists in being hidden, for it must indeed be clear to him that he makes the girl unhappy. The reality of this heroism depends, however, upon the fact that he had had his opportunity [for a genuine love] and annulled it; for if such heroism could be acquired without this, we should have plenty of heroes in our age, in our age which has attained an unparalleled proficiency in forgery and does the highest things by leaping over the intermediate steps. But then why this sketch, since I get no further after all than the tragic hero? Well, because it is at least possible that it might throw light upon the paradox. Everything depends upon how this man stands related to the utterance of the augurs which is in one way or another decisive for his life. Is this utterance publici juris, or is it a privatissimum? The scene is laid in Greece, the utterance of the augur is intelligible to all. I do not mean merely that the ordinary man is able to understand its content lexically, but that the ordinary man can understand that an augur announces to the individual the decision of heaven. So the utterance of the augur is not intelligible only to the hero but to all, and no private relationship to the deity results from it. Do what he will, that which is foretold will come to pass, and neither by doing nor by leaving undone does he come into closer relationship with the deity, or become either the object of its grace or of its wrath. The result foretold is a thing which any ordinary man will be just as well able as the hero to understand, and there is no secret writing which is legible to the hero only. Inasmuch as he would speak, he can do so perfectly well, for he is able to make himself intelligible; inasmuch as he would keep silent, it is because by virtue of being the individual he would be higher than the universal, would delude himself with all sorts of fantastic notions about how she will soon forget the sorrow, etc. On the other hand, in case the will of heaven had not been announced to him by an augur, in case it had come to his knowledge in an entirely private way, in case it had put itself into an entirely private relationship with him, then we encounter the paradox (supposing there is such a thing–for my reflection takes the form of a dilemma), then he could not speak, however much he might wish to.73 He did not then enjoy himself in the silence but suffered pain–but this precisely was to him the assurance that he was justified. So the reason for his silence is not that he as the individual would place himself in an absolute relation to the universal, but that he as the individual was placed in an absolute relation to the absolute. In this then he would also be able to find repose (as well as I am able to figure it to myself), whereas his magnanimous silence would constantly have been disquieted by the requirements of the ethical. It is very much to be desired that aesthetics would for once essay to begin at the point where for so many years it has ended, with the illusory magnanimity. Once it were to do this it would work directly in the interest of the religious, for religion is the only power which can deliver the aesthetical out of its conflict with the ethical. Queen

Elizabeth74 sacrificed to the State her love for Essex by signing his death-warrant. This was a heroic act, even if there was involved a little personal grievance for the fact that he had not sent her the ring. He had in fact sent it, as we know, but it was kept back by the malice of a lady of the court. Elizabeth received intelligence of this (so it is related, ni fallor), thereupon she sat for ten days with one finger in her mouth and bit it without saying a word, and thereupon she died. This would be a theme for a poet who knew how to wrench the mouth open–without this condition it is at the most serviceable to a conductor of the ballet, with whom in our time the poet too often confuses himself. I will follow this with a sketch which involves the demoniacal. The legend of Agnes and the Merman will serve my purpose. The merman is a seducer who shoots up from his hiding-place in the abyss, with wild lust grasps and breaks the innocent flower which stood in all its grace on the seashore and pensively inclined its head to listen to the howling of the ocean. This is what the poets hitherto have meant by it. Let us make an alteration. The merman was a seducer. He had called to Agnes, had by his smooth speech enticed from her the hidden sentiments, she has found in the merman what she sought, what she was gazing after down at the bottom of the sea. Agnes would like to follow him. The merman has lifted her up in his arms, Agnes twines about his neck, with her whole soul she trustingly abandons herself to the stronger one; he already stands upon the brink, he leans over the sea, about to plunge into it with his prey–then Agnes looks at him once more, not timidly, not doubtingly, not proud of her good fortune, not intoxicated by pleasure, but with absolute faith in him, with absolute humility, like the lowly flower she conceived herself to be; by this look she entrusts to him with absolute confidence her whole fate.75 And, behold, the sea roars no more, its voice is mute, nature's passion which is the merman's strength leaves him in the lurch, a dead calm ensues–and still Agnes continues to look at him thus. Then the merman collapses, he is not able to resist the power of innocence, his native element is unfaithful to him, he cannot seduce Agnes. He leads her back again, he explains to her that he only wanted to show her how beautiful the sea is when it is calm, and

Agnes believes him.–Then he turns back alone and the sea rages, but despair in the merman rages more wildly. He is able to seduce Agnes, he is able to seduce a hundred Agneses, he is able to infatuate every girl–but Agnes has conquered, and the merman has lost her. Only as a prey can she become his, he cannot belong faithfully to any girl, for in fact he is only a merman. Here I have taken the liberty of making a little alteration* in the merman; substantially I have also altered Agnes a little, for in the legend Agnes is not entirely without fault–and generally speaking it is nonsense and coquetry and an insult to the feminine sex to imagine a case of seduction where the girl is not the least bit to blame. *One might also treat this legend in another way. The merman does not want to seduce Agnes, although previously he had seduced many. He is no longer a merman, or, if one so will, he is a miserable merman who already has long been sitting on the floor of the sea and sorrowing. However, he knows (as the legend in fact teaches),76 that he can be delivered by the love of an innocent girl. But he has a bad conscience with respect to girls and does not dare to approach them. Then he sees Agnes. Already many a time when he was hidden in the reeds he had seen her walking on the shore.77 Her beauty, her quiet occupation with herself, fixes his attention upon her; but only sadness prevails in his soul, no wild desire stirs in it. And so when the merman mingles his sighs with the soughing of the reeds she turns her ear thither, and then stands still and falls to dreaming, more charming than any woman and yet beautiful as a liberating angel which inspires the merman with confidence. The merman plucks up courage, he approaches Agnes, he wins her love, he hopes for his deliverance. But Agnes was no quiet maiden, she was fond of the roar of the sea, and the sad sighing beside the inland lake pleased her only because then she seethed more strongly within. She would be off and away, she would rush wildly out into the infinite with the merman whom she loved–so she incites the memman. She disdained his humility, now pride awakens. And the sea roars and the waves foam and the merman embraces Agnes and plunges with her into the deep. Never had he been so wild, never so full of desire, for he had hoped by this girl to find deliverance. He soon became tired of Agnes, yet no one ever found her corpse, for she became a mermaid who tempted men by her songs. In the legend Agnes is (to modernize my expression a little) a woman who craves "the interesting," and every such woman can always be sure that there is a merman in the offing, for with half an eye mermen discover the like of that and steer for it like a shark after its prey. It is therefore very stupid to suppose (or is it a rumor which a merman has spread abroad?) that the so-called culture protects a girl against seduction. No, existence is more righteous and fair: there is only one protection, and that is innocence. We will now bestow upon the merman a human consciousness and suppose that the fact of his being a merman indicates a human preexistence in the consequences of which his life is entangled. There is nothing to prevent him from becoming a hero, for the step he now takes is one of reconciliation. He is saved by Agnes, the seducer is crushed, he has bowed to the power of innocence, he can never seduce again. But at the same instant two powers are striving for possession of him: repentance; and Agnes and repentance. If repentance alone takes possession of him, then he is hidden; if Agnes and repentance take possession of him, then he is revealed. Now in case repentance grips the merman and he remains concealed, he has clearly made Agnes unhappy, for Agnes loved him in all her innocence, she believed that at the instant when even to her he seemed changed, however well he hid it, he was telling the truth in saying that he only wanted to show her the beautiful calmness of the sea. However, with respect to passion the merman himself becomes still more unhappy, for he loved Agnes with a multiplicity of passions and had besides a new guilt to bear. The demoniacal element in repentance will now explain to him that this is precisely his punishment [for the faults of his pre-existent state], and that the more it tortures him the better. If he abandons himself to this demoniacal influence, he then perhaps makes still another attempt to save Agnes, in such a way as one can, in a certain sense, save a person by means of the evil. He knows that Agnes loves him. If he could wrest from Agnes this love, then in a way she is saved. But how? The merman has too much sense to depend upon the notion that an open-hearted confession would awaken her disgust. He will therefore try perhaps to incite in her all dark passions, will scorn her, mock her, hold up her love to ridicule, if possible he will stir up her pride. He will not spare himself any torment; for this is the profound contradiction in the demoniacal, and in a certain sense there dwells infinitely more good in a demoniac than in a trivial person. The more selfish Agnes is, the easier the deceit will prove for him (for it is only very inexperienced people who suppose that it is easy to deceive innocence; existence is very profound, and it is in fact the easiest thing for the shrewd to fool the shrewd)—but all the more terrible will be the merman's sufferings. The more cunningly his deceit is planned, the less will Agnes bashfully hide from him her suffering; she will resort to every means, nor will they be without effect—not to shake his resolution, I mean, but to torture him. So by help of the demoniacal the merman desires to be the individual who as the individual is higher than the universal. The demoniacal has the same characteristic as the divine inasmuch as the individual can enter into an absolute relation to it. This is the analogy, the counterpart, to that paradox of which we are talking. It has therefore a certain resemblance which may deceive one. Thus the merman has apparently the proof that his silence is justified for the fact that by it he suffers all his pain. However, there is no doubt that he can talk. He can thus become a tragic hero, to my mind a grandiose tragic hero, if he talks. Some, perhaps, will only understand wherein this is grandiose.* *Aesthetics sometimes treats a similar subject with its customary coquetry. The merman is saved by Agnes, and the whole thing ends in a happy marriage. A happy marriage! That's easy enough. On the other hand, if ethics were to deliver the address at the wedding service, it would be quite another thing, I imagine. Aesthetics throws the cloak of love over the merman, and so everything is forgotten. It is also careless enough to suppose that at a wedding things go as they do at an auction where everything is sold in the state it is in when the hammer falls. All it cares for is that the lovers get one another, it doesn't trouble about the rest. If only it could see what happens afterwards—but for that it has no time, it is at once in full swing with the business of clapping together a new pair of lovers. Aesthetics is the most faithless of all sciences. Everyone who has deeply loved it becomes in a certain sense unhappy, but he who has never loved it is and remains a pecus. He will then be able to wrest from his mind every self-deceit about his being able to make Agnes happy by his trick, he will have courage, humanly speaking, to crush Agnes. Here I would make in conclusion only one psychological observation. The more selfishly Agnes has been developed, the more dazzling will the self-deception be, indeed it is not inconceivable that in reality it might come to pass that a merman by his demoniac shrewdness has, humanly speaking, not only saved an Agnes but brought something extraordinary out of her; for a demon knows how to torture powers out of even the weakest person, and in his way he may have the best intentions toward a human being. The merman stands at the dialectical turning-point. If he is delivered out of the demoniacal into repentance there are two paths open to him. He may hold back, remain in his concealment, but not rely upon his shrewdness. He does not come as the individual into an absolute relationship with the demoniacal but finds repose in the counter-paradox that the deity will save Agnes. (So it is the Middle Ages would perform the movement, for according to its conception the merman is absolutely dedicated to the cloister.) Or else he may be saved along with Agnes. Now this is not to be understood to mean that by the love of Agnes for him he might be saved from being henceforth a deceiver (this is the aesthetic way of performing a rescue, which always goes around the main point, which is the continuity of the merman's life); for so far as that goes he is already saved, he is saved inasmuch as he becomes revealed. Then he marries Agnes. But still he must have recourse to the paradox. For when the individual by his guilt has gone outside the universal he can return to it only by virtue of having come as the individual into an absolute relationship with the absolute. Here I will make an observation by which I say more than was said at any point in the foregoing discussion.* *In the foregoing discussion I have intentionally refrained from any consideration of sin and its reality. The whole discussion points to Abraham, and him I can still approach by immediate categories—in so far, that is to say, as I am able to understand him. As soon as sin makes its appearance ethics comes to grief precisely upon repentance; for repentance is the highest ethical expression, but precisely as such it is the deepest ethical selfcontradiction. Sin is not the first immediacy, sin is a later immediacy. By sin the individual is already higher (in the direction of the demoniacal paradox) than the universal, because it is a contradiction on the part of the universal to impose itself upon a man who lacks the conditio sine qua non. If philosophy among other vagaries were also to have the notion that it could occur to a man to act in accordance with its teaching, one might make out of that a queer comedy. An ethics which disregards sin is a perfectly idle science; but if it asserts sin, it is eo ipso well beyond itself. Philosophy teaches that the immediate must be annulled (aufgehoben). That is true enough; but what is not true in this is that sin is as a matter of course the immediate, for that is no more true than that faith as a matter of course is the immediate. As long as I move in these spheres everything goes smoothly, but what is said here does not by any means explain Abraham; for it was not by sin Abraham became the individual, on the contrary, he was a righteous man, he is God's elect. So the analogy to Abraham will not appear until after the individual has been brought to the point of being able to accomplish the universal, and then the paradox repeats itself. The movements of the merman I can understand, whereas I cannot understand Abraham; for it is precisely through the paradox that the merman comes to the point of realizing the universal. For if he remains hidden and initiates himself into all the torments of repentance, then he becomes a demon and as such is brought to naught. If he remains concealed but does not think cunningly that being himself tormented in the bondage of repentance he could work Agnes loose, then he finds peace indeed but is lost for this world. If he becomes revealed and allows himself to be saved by Agnes, then he is the greatest man I can picture to myself; for it is only the aesthetic writer who thinks lightmindedly that he extols the power of love by letting the lost man be loved by an innocent girl and thereby saved, it is only the aesthetic writer who sees amiss and believes that the girl is the heroine, instead of the man being the hero.

So the merman cannot belong to Agnes unless, after having made the infinite movement, the movement of repentance, he makes still one more movement by virtue of the absurd. By his own strength he can make the movement of repentance, but for that he uses up absolutely all his strength and hence he cannot by his own strength return and grasp reality. If a man has not enough passion to make either the one movement or the other, if he loiters through life, repenting a little, and thinks that the rest will take care of itself, he has once for all renounced the effort to live in the idea—and then he can very easily reach and help others to reach the highest attainments, i.e. delude himself and others with the notion that in the world of spirit everything goes as in a well-known game of cards where everything depends on haphazard. One can therefore divert oneself by reflecting how strange it is that precisely in our age when everyone is able to accomplish the highest things doubt about the immortality of the soul could be so widespread, for the man who has really made even so much as the movement of infinity is hardly a doubter. The conclusions of passion are the only reliable ones, that is, the only convincing conclusions. Fortunately existence is in this instance more kindly and more faithful than the wise maintain, for it excludes no man, not even the lowliest, it fools no one, for in the world of spirit only he is fooled who fools himself. It is the opinion of all, and so far as I dare permit myself to pass judgment it is also my opinion, that it is not the highest thing to enter the monastery; but for all that it is by no means my opinion that in our age when nobody enters the monastery everybody is greater than the deep and earnest souls who found repose in a monastery. How many are there in our age who have passion enough to think this thought and then to judge themselves honestly? This mere thought of taking time upon one's conscience, of giving it time to explore with its sleepless vigilance every secret thought, with such effect that, if even, instant one does not make the movement by virtue of the highest and holiest there is in a man, one is able with dread and horror to discover* and by dread itself, if in no other way, to lure forth the obscure libido78 which is concealed after all in even, human life, whereas on the contrary, when one lives in society with others one so easily forgets, is let off so easily, is sustained in so many ways, gets opportunity to start afresh–this mere thought, conceived with proper re spect, I would suppose, must chasten many an individual in our age which imagines it has already reached the highest attainment. *People do not believe this in our serious age, and yet it is remarkable that even in paganism, more easy-going and less given to redection, the two outstanding representatives of the Greek gnôqi sautón [know thyself] as a conception of existence intimated each in his way that by delving deep into oneself one would first of all discover the disposition to evil. I surely do not need to say that I am thinking of Pythagoras and Socrates. But about this people concern themselves very little in our age which has reached the highest attainment, whereas in truth no age has so fallen victim to the comic as this has, and it is incomprehensible that this age has not already by a generatio acquivoca [breeding without mating] given birth to its hero, the demon who would remorselessly produce the dreadful spectacle of making the whole age laugh and making it forget that it was laughing at itself. Or what is existence for but to be laughed at if men in their twenties have already attained the utmost? And for all that, what loftier emotion has the age found since men gave up entering the monastery? Is it not a pitiable prudence, shrewdness, faintheartedness, it has found, which sits in high places and cravenly makes men believe they have accomplished the greatest things and insidiously withholds them from attempting to do even the lesser things? The man who has performed the cloister-movement has only one movement more to make, that is, the movement of the absurd. How many in our age understand what the absurd is? How many of our contemporaries so live that they have renounced all or have gained all? How many are even so honest with themselves that they know what they can do and what they cannot? And is it not true that in so far as one finds such people one finds them rather among the less cultured and in part among women? The age in a kind of clairvoyance reveals its weak point, as a demoniac always reveals himself without understanding himself, for over and over again it is demanding the comic. If it really were this the age needed, the theater might perhaps need a new play in which it was made a subject of laughter that a person died of love—or would it not rather be salutary for this age if such a thing were to happen among us, if the age were to witness such an occurrence, in order that for once it might acquire courage to believe in the power of spirit, courage to stop quenching cravenly the better impulses in oneself and quenching enviously the better impulses in others … by laughter? Does the age really need a ridiculous exhibition by a religious enthusiast in order to get something to laugh at, or does it not need rather that such an enthusiastic figure should remind it of that which has been forgotten? If one would like to have a story written on a similar theme but more touching for the fact that the passion of repentance was not awakened, one might use to this effect a tale which is narrated in the book of Tobit. The young Tobias wanted to marry Sarah the daughter of Raguel and Edna. But a sad fatality hung over this young girl. She had been given to seven husbands, all of whom had perished in the bride-chamber. With a view to my plan this feature is a blemish in the narrative, for almost irresistibly a comic effect is produced by the thought of seven fruitless attempts to get married notwithstanding she was very near to it—just as near as a student who seven times failed to get his diploma. In the book of Tobit the accent falls on a different spot, therefore the high figure is significant and in a certain sense is contributary to the tragic effect, for it enhances the courage of Tobias, which was the more notable because he was the only son of his parents (6:14) and because the deterrent was so striking. So this feature must be left out. Sarah is a maiden who has never been in love, who treasures still a young maiden's bliss, her enormous first mortgage upon life, her Vollmachtbrief zum Glücke, 79 the privilege of loving a man with her whole heart. And yet she is the most unhappy maiden, for she knows that the evil demon who loves her will kill the bridegroom the night of the wedding. I have read of many a sorrow, but I doubt if there is anywhere to be found so deep a sorrow as that which we discover in the life of this girl. However, if the misfortune comes from without, there is some consolation to be found after all. Although existence did not bring one that which might have made one happy, there is still consolation in the thought that one would have been able to receive it. But the unfathomable sorrow which time can never divert, which time can never heal: To be aware that it was of no avail though existence were to do everything! A Greek writer conceals so infinitely much by his simple naïveté when he says: pántov gàr ou'deís erota efugen h feúxetai, mécriv an kállov h kaì o'fqalmoì bléposin (cf. Longi Pastoralia).80 There has been many a girl who became unhappy in love, but after all she became so, Sarah was so before she became so. It is hard not to find the man to whom one can surrender oneself devotedly, but it is unspeakably hard not to be able to surrender oneself. A young girl surrenders herself, and then they say, "Now she is no longer free"; but Sarah was never free, and yet she had never surrendered herself. It is hard if a girl surrendered herself and then was cheated,81 but Sarah was cheated before she surrendered herself. What a world of sorrow is implied in what follows, when finally Tobias wishes to marry Sarah! What wedding ceremonies! What preparations! No maiden has ever been so cheated as Sarah, for she was cheated out of the most sacred thing of all, the absolute wealth which even the poorest girl possesses, cheated out of the secure, boundless, unrestrained, unbridled devotion of surrender— for first there had to be a fumigation by laying the heart of the fish and its liver upon glowing coals. And think of how the mother had to take leave of her daughter, who having herself been cheated out of all, in continuity with this must cheat the mother out of her most beautiful possession. Just read the narrative. "Edna prepared the chamber and brought Sarah thither and wept and received the tears of her daughter. And she said unto her, Be of good comfort, my child, the Lord of heaven and earth give thee joy for this thy sorrow! Be of good courage, my daughter." And then the moment of the nuptials! Let one read it if one can for tears. "But after they were both shut in together Tobias rose up from the bed and said, Sister, arise, and let us pray that the Lord may have mercy upon us" (8:4). In case a poet were to read this narrative, in case he were to make use of it, I wager a hundred to one that he would lay all the emphasis upcn the young Tobias. His heroic courage in being willing to risk his life in such evident danger—which the narrative recalls once again, for the morning after the nuptials Raguel says to Edna, "Send one of the maidservants and let her see whether he be alive; but if not, that we may bury him and no man know of it" (8:12)—this heroic courage would be the poet's theme. I take the liberty of proposing another. Tobias acted bravely, stoutheartedly and chivalrously, but any man who has not the courage for this is a mollycoddle who does not know what love is, or what it is to be a man, or what is worth living for; he had not even comprehended the little mystery, that it is better to give than to receive, and has no inkling of the great one, that it is far more difficult to receive than to give—that is, if one has had courage to do without and in the hour of need did not become cowardly. No, it is Sarah that is the heroine. I desire to draw near to her as I never have drawn near to any girl or felt tempted in thought to draw near to any girl I have read about. For what love to God it requires to be willing to let oneself be healed when from the beginning one has been thus bungled without one's fault, from the beginning has been an abortive specimen of humanity!82 What ethical maturity was required for assuming the responsibility of allowing the loved one to do such a daring deed! What humility before the face of another person! What faith in God to believe that the next instant she would not hate the husband to whom she owed everything! Let Sarah be a man, and with that the demoniacal is close at hand. The proud and noble nature can endure everything, but one thing it cannot endure, it cannot endure pity. In that there is implied an indignity which can only be inflicted upon one by a higher power, for by oneself one can never become an object of pity. If a man has sinned, he can bear the punishment for it without despairing; but without blame to be singled out from his mother's womb as a sacrifice to pity, as a sweet-smelling savor in its nostrils, that he cannot put up with. Pity has a strange dialectic, at one moment it requires guilt, the next moment it will not have it, and so it is that to be predestinated to pity is more and more dreadful the more the individual's misfortune is in the direction of the spiritual. But Sarah had no blame attaching to her, she is cast forth as a prey to every suffering and in addition to this has to endure the torture of pity—for even I who admire her more than Tobias loved her, even I cannot mention her name without saying, "Poor girl." Put a man in Sarah's place, let him know that in case he were to love a girl a spirit of hell would come and murder his loved one—it might well be possible that he would choose the demoniacal part, that he would shut himself up within himself and say in the way a demoniacal nature talks in secret, "Many thanks, I am no friend of courteous and prolix phrases, I do not absolutely need the pleasure of love, I can become a Blue Beard, finding my delight in seeing maidens perish during the night of their nuptials." Commonly one hears little about the demoniacal, notwithstanding that this field, particularly in our time, has a valid claim to be explored, and notwithstanding that the observer, in case he knows how to get a little in rapport with the demon, can, at least occasionally, make use of almost every man for this purpose. As such an explorer Shakespeare is and constantly remains a hero. That horrible demon, the most demoniacal figure Shakespeare has depicted and depicted incomparably, the Duke of Gloucester (afterwards to become Richard III)—what made him a demon? Evidently the fact that he could not bear the pity he had been subjected to since childhood. His monologue in the first act of Richard III is worth more than all the moral systems which have no inkling of the terrors of existence or of the explanation of them. I, that am rudely stamped, and want love's majesty To strut before a wanton ambling nymph; I, that am curtail'd of this fair proportion, Cheated of feature by dissembling nature, Deformed, unfinished, sent before my time Into this breathing world, scarse half made up, And that so lamely and unfashionable That dogs bark at me as I halt by them. Such natures as that of Gloucester one cannot save by mediating them into an idea of society. Ethics in fact only makes game of them, just as it would be a mockery of Sarah if ethics were to say to her, "Why dost thou not express the universal and get married?" Essentially such natures are in the paradox and are no more imperfect than other men, but are either lost in the demoniacal paradox or saved in the divine. Now from time out of mind people have been pleased to think that witches, hobgoblins, gnomes etc. were deformed, and undeniably every man on seeing a deformed person has at once an inclination to associate this with the notion of moral depravity. What a monstrous injustice! For the situation must rather be inverted, in the sense that existence itself has corrupted them, in the same way that a stepmother makes the children wicked. The fact of being originally set outside of the universal, by nature or by a historical circumstance, is the beginning of the demoniacal, for which the individual himself however is not to blame. Thus Cumberland's Jew83 is also a demon notwithstanding he does what is good. Thus too the demoniacal may express itself as contempt for men—a contempt, be it observed, which does not cause a man to behave contemptibly, since on the contrary he counts it his forte that he is better than all who condemn him.–In view of such cases the poets ought to lose no time in sounding the alarm. God knows what books are read now by the younger generation of verse makers! Their study likely consists in learning rhymes by rote. God knows what significance in existence these men have! At this moment I do not know what use they are except to furnish an edifying proof of the immortality of the soul, for the fact that one can say of them as Baggesen says84 of the poet of our town, Kildevalle, "If he is immortal, then we all are."–What has here been said about Sarah, almost as a sort of poetic production and therefore with a fantastic presupposition, acquires its full significance if one with psychological interest will delve deep into the meaning of the old saying: Nullum unquam exstitit magnum ingenium sine aliqua dementia. 85 For this dementia is the suffering allotted to genius in existence, it is the expression, if I may say so, of the divine jealousy, whereas the gift of genius is the expression of the divine favor. So from the start the genius is disoriented in relation to the universal and is brought into relation with the paradox—whether it be that in despair at his limitation (which in his eyes transforms his omnipotence into impotence) he seeks a demoniacal reassurance and therefore will not admit such limitation either before God or men, or whether he reassures himself religiously by love to the Deity. Here are implied psychological topics to which, it seems to me, one might gladly sacrifice a whole life–and yet one so seldom hears a word about them.86 What relation has madness to genius? Can we construct the one out of the other? In what sense and how far is the genius master of his madness? For it goes without saying that to a certain degree he is master of it, since otherwise he would be actually a madman. For such observations, however, ingenuity in a high degree is requisite, and love; for to make observation upon a superior mind is very difficult. If with due attention to this difficulty one were to read through the works of particular authors most celebrated for their genius, it might in barely a single instance perhaps be possible, though with much pains, to discover a little. I would consider skill another case, that of an individual who by being hidden and by his silence would save the universal. To this end I make use of the legend of Faust.87 Faust is a doubter,* an apostate against the spirit, who takes the path of the flesh. *If one would prefer not to make use of a doubter, one might choose a similar figure, an ironist, for example, whose sharp sight has discovered fundamentally the ludicrousness of existence, who by a secret understanding with the forces of life ascertains what the patient wishes. He knows that he possesses the power of laughter if he would use it, he is sure of his victory, yea, also of his good fortune. He knows that an individual voice will be raised in resistance, but he knows that he is stronger, he knows that for an instant one still can cause men to seem serious, but he knows also that privately they long to laugh with him; he knows that for an instant one can still cause a woman to hold a fan before her eyes when he talks, but he knows that she is laughing behind the fan, that the fan is not absolutely impervious to vision, he knows that one can write on it an invisible inscription, he knows that when a woman strikes at him with her fan it is because she has understood him, he knows without the least danger of deception how laughter sneaks in, and how when once it has taken up its lodging it lies in ambush and waits. Let us imagine such an Aristophanes, such a Voltaire, a little altered, for he is at the same time a sympathetic nature, he loves existence, he loves men, and he knows that even though the reproof of laughter will perhaps educate a saved young race, yet in the contemporary generation a multitude of men will be ruined. So he keeps silent and as far as possible forgets how to laugh. But dare he keep silent? Perhaps there are sundry persons who do not in the least understand the difficulty I have in mind. They are likely of the opinion that it is an admirable act of magnanimity to keep silent. That is not at all my opinion, for I think that every such character, if he has not had the magnanimity to keep silent, is a traitor against existence. So I require of him this magnanimity, but when he possesses it, dare he then keep silent? Ethics is a dangerous science and it might be possible that Aristophanes was determined by purely ethical considerations in resolving to reprove by laughter his misguided age. Aesthetical magnanimity does not help [to solve the question whether one ought to keep silent], for on the credit of that one does not take such a risk. If he is to keep silent, then into the paradox he must go.–I will suggest still another plan for a story. Suppose e.g. that a man possessed a explanation of a heroic life which explained it in a sorry way, and yet a whole generation reposes securely in an absolute belief in this hero, without suspecting anything of the sort. This is what the poets mean by it, and whereas again and again it is repeated that every age has its Faust, yet one poet after another follows indefatigably the same beaten track. Let us make a little alteration. Faust is the doubter par excellence, but he is a sympathetic nature. Even in Goethe's interpretation of Faust I sense the lack of a deeper psychological insight into the secret conversations of doubt with itself. In our age, when indeed all have experienced doubt, no poet has yet made a step in this direction. So I think I might well offer them Royal Securities88 to write on, so that they could write down all they have experienced in this respect– they would hardly write more than there is room for on the left hand margin. Only when one thus deflects Faust back into himself, only then can doubt appear poetic, only then too does he himself discover in reality all its sufferings. He knows that it is spirit which sustains existence, but he knows then too that the security and joy in which men live is not founded upon the power of spirit but is easily explicable as an unreflected happiness. As a doubter, as the doubter, he is higher than all this, and if anyone would deceive him by making him believe that he has passed through a course of training in doubt, he readily sees through the deception; for the man who has made a movement in the world of spirit, hence an infinite movement, can at once hear through the spoken word whether it is a tried and experienced man who is speaking or a Münchhausen. What a Tamberlane is able to accomplish by means of his Huns, that Faust is able to accomplish by means of his doubt: to frighten men up in dismay, to cause existence to quake beneath their feet, to disperse men abroad, to cause the shriek of dread to be heard on all sides. And if he does it, he is nevertheless no Tamberlane, he is in a certain sense warranted and has the warranty of thought. But Faust is a sympathetic nature, he loves existence, his soul is acquainted with no envy, he perceives that he is unable to check the raging he is well able to arouse, he desires no Herostratic honor89—he keeps silent, he hides the doubt in his soul more carefully than the girl who hides under her heart the fruit of a sinful love, he endeavors as well as he can to walk in step with other men, but what goes on within him he consumes within himself, and thus he offers himself a sacrifice for the universal. When an eccentric pate raises a whirlwind of doubt one may sometimes hear people say, "Would that he had kept silent." Faust realizes this idea. He who has a conception of what it means to live upon spirit knows also what the hunger of doubt is, and that the doubter hungers just as much for the daily bread of life as for the nutriment of the spirit. Although all the pain Faust suffers may be a fairly good argument that is was not pride possessed him, yet to test this further I will employ a little precautionary expedient which I invent with great ease. For as Gregory of Rimini was called tortor infantium90 because he espoused the view of the damnation of infants, so I might be tempted to call myself tortor heroum; for I am very inventive when it is a question of putting heroes to the torture. Faust sees Marguerite—not after he had made the choice of pleasure, for my Faust does not choose pleasure— he sees Marguerite, not in the concave mirror of Mephistopheles but in all her lovable innocence, and as his soul has preserved love for mankind he can perfectly well fall in love with her. But he is a doubter, his doubt has annihilated reality for him; for so ideal is my Faust that he does not belong to these scientific doubters who doubt one hour every semester in the professorial chair, but at other times are able to do everything else, as indeed they do this, without the support of spirit or by virtue of spirit. He is a doubter, and the doubter hungers just as much for the daily bread of joy as for the food of the spirit. He remains, however, true to his resolution and keeps silent, and he talks to no man of his doubt, nor to Marguerite of his love. It goes without saying that Faust is too ideal a figure to be content with the tattle that if he were to talk he would give occasion to an ordinary discussion and the whole thing would pass off without any consequences– or perhaps, and perhaps. ... (Here, as every poet will easily see, the comic is latent in the plan, threatening to bring Faust into an ironical relation to these fools of low comedy who in our age run after doubt, produce an external argument, e.g. a doctor's diploma, to prove that they really have doubted, or take their oath that they have doubted everything, or prove it by the fact that on a journey they met a doubter–these expressmessengers and foot-racers in the world of spirit, who in the greatest haste get from one man a little hint of doubt, from another a little hint of faith, and then turn it to account as best they can, according as the congregation wants to have fine sand or coarse sand.)91 Faust is too ideal a figure to go about in carpet-slippers. He who has not an infinite passion is not the ideal, and he who has an infinite passion has long ago saved his soul out of such nonsense. He keeps silent and sacrifices himself/or he talks with the consciousness that he will confound everything. If he keeps silent, ethics condemns him, for it says, "Thou shalt acknowledge the universal, and it is precisely by speaking thou dost acknowledge it, and thou must not have compassion upon the universal." One ought not to forget this consideration when sometimes one judges a doubter severely for talking. I am not inclined to judge such conduct leniently, but in this case as everywhere all depends upon whether the movements occur normally. If worse comes to worst, a doubter, even though by talking he were to bring down all possible misfortune upon the world, is much to be preferred to these miserable sweet-tooths who taste a little of everything, and who would heal doubt without being acquainted with it, and who are therefore usually the proximate cause of it when doubt breaks out wildly and with ungovernable rage.–If he speaks, then he confounds everything–for though this does not actually occur, he does not get to know it till afterwards, and the upshot cannot help a man either at the moment of action or with regard to his responsibility. If he keeps silent on his own responsibility, he may indeed be acting magnanimously, but to his other pains he adds a little temptation (Anfechtung), for the universal will constantly torture him and say, "You ought to have talked. Where will you find the certainty that it was not after all a hidden pride which governed your resolution?" If on the other hand the doubter is able to become the particular individual who as the individual stands in an absolute relation to the absolute, then he can get a warrant for his silence. In this case he must transform his doubt into guilt. In this case he is within the paradox, but in this case his doubt is cured, even though he may get another doubt. Even the New Testament would approve of such a silence. There are even passages in the New Testament which commend irony–if only it is used to conceal something good. This movement, however, is as properly a movement of irony as is any other which has its ground in the fact that subjectivity is higher than reality. In our age people want to hear nothing about this, generally they want to know no more about irony than Hegel has said about it92–who strangely enough had not much understanding of it, and bore a grudge against it, which our age has good reason not to give up, for it had better beware of irony. In the Sermon on the Mount it is said, "When thou fastest, anoint thy head and wash thy face, that thou be not seen of men to fast." This passage bears witness directly to the truth that subjectivity is incommensurable with reality, yea, that it has leave to deceive. If only the people who in our age go gadding about with vague talk about the congregational idea93 were to read the New Testament, they would perhaps get other ideas into their heads. But now as for Abraham–how did he act? For I have not forgotten, and the reader will perhaps be kind enough to remember, that it was with the aim of reaching this point I entered into the whole foregoing discussion–not as though Abraham would thereby become more intelligible, but in order that the unintelligibility might become more desultory.94 For, as I have said, Abraham I cannot understand, I can only admire him. It was also observed that the stages I have described do none of them contain an analogy to Abraham. The examples were simply educed in order that while they were shown in their own proper sphere they might at the moment of variation [from Abraham's case] indicate as it were the boundary of the unknown land. If there might be any analogy, this must be found in the paradox of sin, but this again lies in another sphere and cannot explain Abraham and is itself far easier to explain than Abraham. So then, Abraham did not speak, he did not speak to Sarah, nor to Eleazar, nor to Isaac, he passed over three ethical authorities; for the ethical had for Abraham no higher expression than the family life. Aesthetics permitted, yea, required of the individual silence, when he knew that by keeping silent he could save another. This is already sufficient proof that Abraham does not lie within the circumference of aesthetics. His silence has by no means the intention of saving Isaac, and in general his whole task of sacrificing Isaac for his own sake and for God's sake is an offense to aesthetics, for aesthetics can well understand that I sacrifice myself, but not that I sacrifice another for my own sake. The aesthetic hero was silent. Ethics condemned him, however, because he was silent by virtue of his accidental particularity. His human foreknowledge was what determined him to keep silent. This ethics cannot forgive, every such human knowledge is only an illusion, ethics requires an infinite movement, it requires revelation. So the aesthetic hero can speak but will not. The genuine tragic hero sacrifices himself and all that is his for the universal, his deed and every emotion with him belong to the universal, he is revealed, and in this self-revelation he is the beloved son of ethics. This does not fit the case of Abraham: he does nothing for the universal, and he is concealed. Now we reach the paradox. Either the individual as the individual is able to stand in an absolute relation to the absolute (and then the ethical is not the highest)/or Abraham is lost–he is neither a tragic hero, nor an aesthetic hero. Here again it may seem as if the paradox were the easiest and most convenient thing of all. However, I must repeat that he who counts himself convinced of this is not a knight of faith, for distress and anguish are the only legitimations that can be thought of, and they cannot be thought in general terms, for with that the paradox is annulled. Abraham keeps silent—but he cannot speak. Therein lies the distress and anguish. For if I when I speak am unable to make myself intelligible, then I am not speaking—even though I were to talk uninterruptedly day and night. Such is the case with Abraham. He is able to utter everything, but one thing he cannot say, i.e. say it in such a way that another understands it, and so he is not speaking. The relief of speech is that it translates me into the universal. Now Abraham is able to say the most beautiful things any language can express about how he loves Isaac. But it is not this he has at heart to say, it is the profounder thought that he would sacrifice him because it is a trial. This latter thought no one can understand, and hence everyone can only misunderstand the former. This distress the tragic hero does not know. He has first of all the comfort that every counter-argument has received due consideration, that he has been able to give to Clytemnestra, to Iphigenia, to Achilles, to the chorus, to every living being, to every voice from the heart of humanity, to every cunning, every alarming, every accusing, every compassionate thought, opportunity to stand up against him. He can be sure that everything that can be said against him has been said, unsparingly, mercilessly— and to strive against the whole world is a comfort, to strive with oneself is dreadful. He has no reason to fear that he has overlooked anything, so that afterwards he must cry out as did King Edward the Fourth at the news of the death of Clarence:95 Who su'd to me for him? who, in my wrath, Kneel'd at my feet and bade me be advised? Who spoke of brotherhood? who spoke of love? The tragic hero does not know the terrible responsibility of solitude. In the next place he has the comfort that he can weep and lament with Clytemnestra and Iphigenia—and tears and cries are assuaging, but unutterable sighs are torture. Agamemnon can quickly collect his soul into the certainty that he will act, and then he still has time to comfort and exhort. This Abraham is unable to do. When his heart is moved, when his words would contain a blessed comfort for the whole world, he does not dare to offer comfort, for would not Sarah, would not Eleazar, would not Isaac say, "Why wilt thou do it? Thou canst refrain?" And if in his distress he would give vent to his feelings and would embrace all his dear ones before taking the final step, this might perhaps bring about the dreadful consequence that Sarah, that Eleazar, that Isaac would be offended in him and would believe he was a hypocrite. He is unable to speak, he speaks no human language. Though he himself understood all the tongues of the world, though his loved ones also understood them, he nevertheless cannot speak–he speaks a divine language ... he "speaks with tongues." This distress I can well understand, I can admire Abraham, I am not afraid that anyone might be tempted by this narrative light-heartedly to want to be the individual, but I admit also that I have not the courage for it, and that I renounce gladly any prospect of getting further–if only it were possible that in any way, however late, I might get so far. Every instant Abraham is able to break off, he can repent the whole thing as a temptation (Anfechtung), then he can speak, then all could understand him–but then he is no longer Abraham. Abraham cannot speak, for he cannot utter the word which explains all (that is, not so that it is intelligible), he cannot say that it is a test, and a test of such a sort, be it noted, that the ethical is the temptation (Versuchung). He who is so situated is an emigrant from the sphere of the universal. But the next word he is still less able to utter. For, as was sufficiently set forth earlier, Abraham makes two movements: he makes the infinite movement of resignahon and gives up Isaac (this no one can understand because it is a private venture); but in the next place, he makes the movement of faith every instant. This is his comfort, for he says: "But yet this will not come to pass, or, if it does come to pass, then the Lord will give me a new Isaac, by virtue viz. of the absurd." The tragic hero does at last get to the end of the story. Iphigenia bows to her father's resolution, she herself makes the infinite movement of resignation, and now they are on good terms with one another. She can understand Agamemnon because his undertaking expresses the universal. If on the other hand Agamemnon were to say to her, "In spite of the fact that the deity demands thee as a sacrifice, it might yet be possible that he did not demand it–by virtue viz. of the absurd," he would that very instant become unintelligible to Iphigenia. If he could say this by virtue of human calculation, Iphigenia would surely understand him, but from that it would follow that Agamemnon had not made the infinite movement of resignation, and so he is not a hero, and so the utterance of the seer is a sea-captain's tale and the whole occurrence a vaudeville. Abraham did not speak. Only one word of his has been preserved, the only reply to Isaac, which also is sufficient proof that he had not spoken previously. Isaac asks Abraham where the lamb is for the burnt offering. "And Abraham said, God will provide Himself the lamb for the burnt offering, my son." This last word of Abraham I shall consider a little more closely. If there were not this word, the whole event would have lacked something; if it were to another effect, everything perhaps would be resolved into confusion. I have often reflected upon the question whether a tragic hero, be the culmination of his tragedy a suffering or an action, ought to have a last rejoicer. In my opinion it depends upon the life-sphere to which he belongs, whether his life has intellectual significance, whether his suffering or his action stands in relation to spirit. It goes without saying that the tragic hero, like every other man who is not deprived of the power of speech, can at the instant of his culmination utter a few words, perhaps a few appropriate words, but the question is whether it is appropriate for him to utter them. If the significance of his life consists in an outward act, then he has nothing to say, since all he says is essentially chatter whereby he only weakens the impression he makes, whereas the ceremonial of tragedy requires that he perform his task in silence, whether this consists in action or in suffering. Not to go too far afield, I will take an example which lies nearest to our discussion. If Agamemnon himself and not Calchas had had to draw the knife against Iphigenia, then he would have only demeaned himself by wanting at the last moment to say a few words, for the significance of his act was notorious, the juridical procedure of piety, of compassion, of emotion, of tears was completed, and moreover his life had no relation to spirit, he was not a teacher or a witness to the spirit. On the other hand, if the significance of a hero's life is in the direction of spirit, then the lack of a rejoinder would weaken the impression he makes. What he has to say is not a few appropriate words, a little piece of declamation, but the significance of his rejoinder is that in the decisive moment he carries himself through. Such an intellectual tragic hero ought to have what in other circumstances is too often striven for in ludicrous ways, he ought to have and he ought to keep the last word. One requires of him the same exalted bearing which is seemly in every tragic hero, but in addition to this there is required of him one word. So when such an intellectual tragic hero has his culmination in suffering (in death), then by his last word he becomes immortal before he dies, whereas the ordinary tragic hero on the other hand does not become immortal till after his death. One may take Socrates as an example. He was an intellectual tragic hero. His death sentence was announced to him. That instant he dies—for one who does not understand that the whole power of the spirit is required for dying, and that the hero always dies before he dies, that man will not get so very far with his conception of life. So as a hero it is required of Socrates that he repose tranquilly in himself, but as an intellectual tragic hero it is required of him that he at the last moment have spiritual strength sufficient to carry himself through. So he cannot like the ordinary tragic hero concentrate upon keeping himself face to face with death, but he must make this movement so quickly that at the same instant he is consciously well over and beyond this strife and asserts himself. If Socrates had been silent in the crisis of death, he would have weakened the effect of his life and aroused the suspicion that in him the elasticity of irony was not an elemental power but a game, the flexibility of which he had to employ at the decisive moment to sustain him emotionally.* *Opinions may be divided as to which rejoinder of Socrates is to be regarded as the decisive one, inasmuch as Socrates has been in so many ways volatilized by Plato. I propose the following. The sentence of death is announced to him, the same instant he dies, the same instant he overcomes death and carries himself through in the famous reply which expresses surprise that he had been condemned by a majority of three votes.96 With no vague and idle talk in the marketplace, with no foolish remark of an idiot, could he have jested more ironically than with the sentence which condemned him to death. What is briefly suggested here has to be sure no application to Abraham in case one might think it possible to find out by analogy an appropriate word for Abraham to end with, but it does apply to this extent, that one thereby perceives how necessary it is that Abraham at the last moment must carry himself through, must not silently draw the knife, but must have a word to say, since as the father of faith he has absolute significance in a spiritual sense. As to what he must say, I can form no conception beforehand; after he has said it I can maybe understand it, maybe in a certain sense can understand Abraham in what he says, though without getting any closer to him than I have been in the foregoing discussion. In case no last rejoinder of Socrates had existed, I should have been able to think myself into him and formulate such a word; if I were unable to do it, a poet could, but no poet can catch up with Abraham. Before I go on to consider Abraham's last word more closely I would call attention to the difficulty Abraham had in saying anything at all. The distress and anguish in the paradox consisted (as was set forth above) in silence—Abraham cannot speak.* *If there can be any question of an analogy, the circumstance of the death of Pythagoras furnishes it, for the silence which he had always maintained he had to carry through in his last moment, and therefore [being compelled to speak] he said, "It is better to be put to death than to speak" (cf. Diogenes Laertius, viii. 39). So in view of this fact it is a contradiction to require him to speak, unless one would have him out of the paradox again, in such a sense that at the last moment he suspends it, whereby he ceases to be Abraham and annuls all that went before. So then if Abraham at the last moment were to say to Isaac, "To thee it applies," this would only have been a weakness. For if he could speak at all, he ought to have spoken long before, and the weakness in this case would consist in the fact that he did not possess the maturity of spirit and the concentration to think in advance the whole pain but had thrust something away from him, so that the actual pain contained a plus over and above the thought pain. Moreover, by such a speech he would fall out of the role of the paradox, and if he really wanted to speak to Isaac, he must transform his situation into a temptation (Anfechtung), for otherwise he could say nothing, and if he were to do that, then he is not even so much as a tragic hero. However, a last word of Abraham has been preserved, and in so far as I can understand the paradox I can also apprehend the total presence of Abraham in this word. First and foremost, he does not say anything, and it is in this form he says what he has to say. His reply to Isaac has the form of irony, for it always is irony when I say something and do not say anything. Isaac interrogates Abraham on the supposition that Abraham knows. So then if Abraham were to have replied, "I know nothing," he would have uttered an untruth. He cannot say anything, for what he knows he cannot say. So he replies, "God will provide Himself the lamb for the burnt offering, my son." Here the double movement in Abraham's soul is evident, as it was described in the foregoing discussion. If Abraham had merely renounced his claim to Isaac and had done no more, he would in this last word be saying an untruth, for he knows that God demands Isaac as a sacrifice, and he knows that he himself at that instant precisely is ready to sacrifice him. We see then that after making this movement he made every instant the next movement, the movement of faith by virtue of the absurd. Because of this he utters no falsehood, for in virtue of the absurd it is of course possible that God could do something entirely different. Hence he is speaking no untruth, but neither is he saying anything, for he speaks a foreign language. This becomes still more evident when we consider that it was Abraham himself who must perform the sacrifice of Isaac. Had the task been a different one, had the Lord commanded Abraham to bring Isaac out to Mount Moriah and then would Himself have Isaac struck by lightning and in this way receive him as a sacrifice, then, taking his words in a plain sense, Abraham might have been right in speaking enigmatically as he did, for he could not himself know what would occur. But in the way the task was prescribed to Abraham he himself had to act, and at the decisive moment he must know what he himself would do, he must know that Isaac will be sacrificed. In case he did not know this definitely, then he has not made the infinite movement of resignation, then, though his word is not indeed an untruth, he is very far from being Abraham, he has less significance than the tragic hero, yea, he is an irresolute man who is unable to resolve either on one thing or another, and for this reason will always be uttering riddles. But such a hesitator is a sheer parody of a knight of faith. Here again it appears that one may have an understanding of Abraham, but can understand him only in the same way as one understands the paradox. For my part I can in a way understand Abraham, but at the same time I apprehend that I have not the courage to speak, and still less to act as he did—but by this I do not by any means intend to say that what he did was insignificant, for on the contrary it is the one only marvel. And what did the contemporary age think of the tragic hero? They thought that he was great, and they admired him. And that honorable assembly of nobles, the jury which every generation impanels to pass judgment upon the foregoing generation, passed the same judgment upon him. But as for Abraham there was no one who could understand him. And yet think what he attained! He remained true to his love. But he who loves God has no need of tears, no need of admiration, in his love he forgets his suffering, yea, so completely has he forgotten it that afterwards there would not even be the least inkling of his pain if God Himself did not recall it, for God sees in secret and knows the distress and counts the tears and forgets nothing. So either there is a paradox, that the individual as the individual stands in an absolute relation to the absolute/or Abraham is lost.

EPILOGUE One time in Holland when the market was rather dull for spices the merchants had several cargoes dumped into the sea to peg up prices. This was a pardonable, perhaps a necessary device for deluding people. Is it something like that we need now in the world of spirit? Are we so thoroughly convinced that we have attained the highest point that there is nothing left for us but to make ourselves believe piously that we have not got so far—just for the sake of having something left to occupy our time? Is it such a self-deception the present generation has need of, does it need to be trained to virtuosity in self-deception, or is it not rather sufficiently perfected already in the art of deceiving itself? Or rather is not the thing most needed an honest seriousness which dauntlessly and incorruptibly points to the tasks, an honest seriousness which lovingly watches over the tasks, which does not frighten men into being over hasty in getting the highest tasks accomplished, but keeps the tasks young and beautiful and charming to look upon and yet difficult withal and appealing to noble minds. For the enthusiasm of noble natures is aroused only by difficulties. Whatever the one generation may learn from the other, that which is genuinely human no generation learns from the foregoing. In this respect every generation begins primitively, has no different task from that of every previous generation, nor does it get further, except in so far as the preceding generation shirked its task and deluded itself. This authentically human factor is passion, in which also the one generation perfectly understands the other and understands itself. Thus no generation has learned from another to love, no generation begins at any other point than at the beginning, no generation has a shorter task assigned to it than had the preceding generation, and if here one is not willing like the previous generations to stop with love but would go further, this is but idle and foolish talk. But the highest passion in a man is faith, and here no generation begins at any other point than did the preceding generation, every generation begins all over again, the subsequent generation gets no further than the foregoing—in so far as this remained faithful to its task and did not leave it in the lurch. That this should be wearisome is of course something the generation cannot say, for the generation has in fact the task to perform and has nothing to do with the consideration that the foregoing generation had the same task—unless the particular generation or the particular individuals within it were presumptuous enough to assume the place which belongs by right only to the Spirit which governs the world and has patience enough not to grow weary. If the generation begins that sort of thing, it is upside down, and what wonder then that the whole of existence seems to it upside down, for there surely is no one who has found the world so upside down as did the tailor in the fairy tale97 who went up in his lifetime to heaven and from that standpoint contemplated the world. If the generation would only concern itself about its task, which is the highest thing it can do, it cannot grow weary, for the task is always sufficient for a human life. When the children on a holiday have already got through playing all their games before the clock strikes twelve and say impatiently, "Is there nobody can think of a new game?" does this prove that these children are more developed and more advanced than the children of the same generation or of a previous one who could stretch out the familiar games, to last the whole day long? Or does it not prove rather that these children lack what I would call the lovable seriousness which belongs essentially to play? Faith is the highest passion in a man. There are perhaps many in every generation who do not even reach it, but no one gets further. Whether there be many in our age who do not discover it, I will not decide, I dare only appeal to myself as a witness who makes no secret that the prospects for him are not the best, without for all that wanting to delude himself and to betray the great thing which is faith by reducing it to an insignificance, to an ailment of childhood which one must wish to get over as soon as possible. But for the man also who does not so much as reach faith life has tasks enough, and if one loves them sincerely, life will by no means be wasted, even though it never is comparable to the life of those who sensed and grasped the highest. But he who reached faith (it makes no difference whether he be a man of distinguished talents or a simple man) does not remain standing at faith, yea, he would be offended if anyone were to say this of him, just as the lover would be indignant if one said that he remained standing at love, for he would reply, "I do not remain standing by any means, my whole life is in this." Nevertheless he does not get further, does not reach anything different, for if he discovers this, he has a different explanation for it. "One must go further, one must go further." This impulse to go further is an ancient thing in the world. Heraclitus the obscure, who deposited his thoughts in his writings and his writings in the Temple of Diana (for his thoughts had been his armor during his life, and therefore he hung them up in the temple of the goddess),98 Heraclitus the obscure said, "One cannot pass twice through the same stream." [Plato's Cratyllus, §402.] Heraclitus the obscure had a disciple who did not stop with that, he went further and added, "One cannot do it even once." [Cf. Tennemann, Geschichte der Philosophie, I, p. 220.] Poor Heraclitus, to have such a disciple! By this amendment the thesis of Heraclitus was so improved that it became an Eleatic thesis which denies movement, and yet that disciple desired only to be a disciple of Heraclitus … and to go further—not back to the position Heraclitus had abandoned

The Genealogy of Morals

Friedrich Nietzsche

Prologue

We don't truly know ourselves—we who try to understand so much. And there's a good reason for that. We've never really looked for ourselves, so how could we possibly expect to find ourselves? It's been wisely said, "Where your treasure is, there your heart will be also." Our treasure lies in the things we strive to understand. It's like a beehive for us, filled with the knowledge we're always working to gather. As creatures of the air, born to roam, we're like bees gathering honey for our hive. Deep down, we care about one thing: bringing something valuable back home to that hive.

When it comes to the rest of life—what people call "experiences"— how many of us really care about them deeply? Who even has the time or the focus? We rarely engage seriously with those moments. To be honest, our hearts aren't truly in it, and neither are our ears. It's like someone lost in a dream, so absorbed in their thoughts that they don't even notice the loud tolling of the clock. Then, when the clock has finished striking twelve, they suddenly snap out of it and wonder, "Wait, what just happened?" That's how we often feel. We rub our ears afterward, confused, and ask ourselves in complete surprise, "What exactly have we just been through? Who are we, really?"

When we try to make sense of our experiences—those twelve striking moments of our life and being—we always miscount. We get it wrong every time. We remain strangers to ourselves, unable to truly understand who we are. For us, the saying is eternally true: "Each of us is furthest from knowing ourselves." When it comes to understanding ourselves, we are not "knowers."

The thoughts I have about the origins of our moral beliefs— because that's what this argument is all about—were first put into words in my book Human,

All- Too- Human: A Book for Free Spirits. I began writing it in Sorrento during the winter of 1876-77, a time when I could look back on the wide and challenging journey my mind had traveled up to that point. But these ideas aren't new; they're older.

The thoughts I share here are essentially the same as those I explored in that earlier book. Over the years, I hope they've become sharper, clearer, stronger, and more complete. The fact that I still hold onto them today—that they've grown and evolved together—gives me confidence. It makes me believe that these ideas didn't come about by accident or in isolation. Instead, they must have a common source, rooted in a deep and fundamental desire for knowledge. That desire has grown stronger and more focused over time, becoming clearer in its demands. For a philosopher, that's exactly how things should be.

We have no right to be disconnected. Our thoughts must not err separately, nor should we stumble upon truth by chance or in isolation. Like the fruit that a tree bears out of necessity, our thoughts, values, affirmations, denials, questions, and doubts must grow in connection with one another. They are all interrelated, bearing witness to one will, one health, one unity, one guiding light. As for whether you, the observer, find these fruits pleasing to your taste—does that matter to the tree? Should it matter to us, the philosophers?

I must reluctantly admit to a peculiar and deeply ingrained scrupulousness within myself, one that revolves around morality. This trait, evident in me from an early age, appeared so naturally, so persistently, and with such strong resistance to the influences of my environment, time, traditions, and ancestry that I might almost call it my a priori. From a young age, my curiosity and skepticism forced me to confront the question of the true origin of our ideas of "Good" and "Evil." At just thirteen years old, when most children are divided between playing games and contemplating God, I was already haunted by the problem of the origin of Evil. It was at that age that I wrote my first philosophical essay, a naïve and childlike attempt to tackle the question. My solution, as you might expect, attributed the creation of evil to God Himself— I named Him its father. Was that conclusion driven by my own a prior i? That new, immoral—or at least "amoral"—instinct, that inner imperative so far removed from Kant's ideals and yet so full of its own challenges? This imperative has since become the focus of not just my attention but something far greater.

Fortunately, I soon learned to separate theological prejudices from moral ones. I gave up the search for a supernatural origin of evil. Through a combination of historical and philological study—and an innate talent for psychological insight—I was able to shift my original question into a new and more precise form: under what conditions did humanity create these value judgments of "Good" and "Evil"? What inherent worth do they possess? Have these values up to now helped or hindered human flourishing? Are they signs of humanity's suffering, decline, and impoverishment? Or are they, instead, manifestations of life's fullness, strength, and determination—its courage, its self-assurance, its will to face the future?

To these questions, I entertained a variety of answers. I explored distinctions across different periods, cultures, and social classes. I became a specialist in my chosen problem, and each answer led to further questions, deeper investigations, new theories, and fresh possibilities. Gradually, I found myself with my own domain, my own fertile ground, a hidden world filled with growing and blooming ideas—secret gardens that no one could have suspected existed. How happy we are, we seekers of knowledge, as long as we know how to remain silent for long enough!

My initial urge to publish some of my ideas about the origins of morality came from a small, clear, well-written book— precocious even—in which a twisted and flawed kind of moral philosophy (a quintessentially English kind) was laid out plainly for the first time. This book intrigued me, pulling me in with that irresistible attraction that comes from encountering something fundamentally opposed to one's own beliefs. The book was titled The Origin of the Moral Emotions, authored by Dr. Paul Rée, and it was published in 1877.

I can almost say that I've never read anything where every argument and conclusion inspired such a strong, unequivocal rejection from me as this book did. Yet my rejection was free of irritation or intolerance. In fact, I often referred to its arguments in my own writings of that time—not to refute them (for I see no point in mere refutations), but rather to replace improbable theories with ones I found more plausible. Occasionally, of course, I might have substituted one philosophical error with another.

It was during that early phase that I began publicly expressing the theories of origin that these essays now explore, though I did so with a clumsiness I could not ignore. I lacked a specialized language for these particular topics and often found myself vacillating or falling back into old patterns.

For specific examples, one might compare what I wrote in Human, All- Too- Human, Part I, Aphorism 45, about the parallel early histories of Good and Evil—how they originated from the castes of aristocrats and slaves. Or Aphorisms 136 and following, on the birth and value of ascetic morality. Similarly, Aphorisms 96 and 99 in Volume II, and Aphorism 89, regarding the Morality of Custom—a much older and more fundamental form of morality, completely distinct from the altruistic ethics that Dr. Rée and other English moral philosophers mistake for the "essence" of ethics. Finally, see Aphorism 92.

Likewise, consider Aphorism 26 in Human, All- Too- Human, Part II, or Aphorism 112 in The Dawn of Day, where I discuss the origin of Justice as a balance of power between individuals of roughly equal strength. This equilibrium serves as the foundation for all agreements and thus for all law. Similarly, my thoughts on the origin of Punishment in Human, All- Too- Human, Part II, Aphorisms 22 and 23, challenge Dr. Rée's view. Contrary to his belief that the primary purpose of punishment is deterrence, I argue that this purpose is neither original nor essential but is instead a secondary addition that arises under specific conditions.

At that time, my focus was not so much on the theories—my own or others'—about the origins of morality. The real purpose of those theories, in my view, was to serve as a means to a greater end. My true concern was the value of morality itself. To approach this question, I had to place myself in a state of detachment, almost as though I were entirely alone with my great teacher, Schopenhauer. It was to him that my work, with all its passion and inherent contradictions (for it, too, was a polemic), turned for guidance, as if he were still alive.

The issue I grappled with was, oddly enough, the value of "unegoistic" instincts—the instincts of pity, self-denial, and self-sacrifice. Schopenhauer had persistently celebrated these instincts, portraying them in golden hues, exalting and idealizing them until they appeared to him as ultimate, intrinsic values. It was on the basis of these instincts that he pronounced his negation of both Life and himself. Yet, within me, a deep and growing mistrust arose toward these very instincts. My skepticism dug deeper and deeper, and I came to see in these instincts a profound danger to humanity. They seemed to me humanity's most sublime temptation, its greatest seduction. But seduction to what? To nothingness?

In these unegoistic instincts, I saw the seeds of humanity's decline—the beginning of its end. I saw stagnation, exhaustion, a longing to retreat, and the will turning against Life itself. These instincts appeared to me as the heralds of humanity's last illness, signaling their arrival with a delicate, sorrowful melancholy. I realized that the morality of pity, spreading ever wider and infecting even philosophers with its sickness, was the darkest symptom of modern European civilization. It was the path along which this civilization was sliding—toward what? A new Buddhism? A European Buddhism? Nihilism?

This overvaluation of pity by modern philosophers is a completely new phenomenon. Until then, philosophers were unanimous in their disdain for pity. I need only mention Plato, Spinoza, La Rochefoucauld, and Kant—four thinkers as vastly different as one could imagine, yet united on this one point: their contempt for pity.

This question about the value of pity and the morality it represents (I am deeply opposed to the modern, disgraceful softening of our emotions) might at first seem like an isolated issue—a problem standing on its own. But anyone who pauses to examine it, as I did, and learns to ask the right questions will experience what I experienced: a vast and immense new perspective unfolds before them. A sense of limitless possibilities overtakes them, almost like vertigo. Doubts, mistrust, and fears spring up everywhere. Belief in morality—indeed, in all morality—begins to waver. Finally, a new demand makes itself heard.

Let us state this demand clearly: we need a critique of moral values. The worth of these values themselves must, for the first time, be called into question. To do this, we need to understand the conditions and circumstances under which these values arose, evolved, and were distorted. Morality must be examined as both a result and a symptom, as a mask, as hypocrisy, as disease, and as misunderstanding—but also as a cause, as a remedy, as a stimulant, as a restraint, and as a drug. Such an investigation has never existed before, nor has it even been desired. Up until now, the value of these "values" has been taken as self-evident, beyond any question. No one has ever doubted or hesitated in judging the "good man" to be of higher worth than the "evil man," particularly regarding human progress, utility, and general well-being, including the future.

But what if the opposite were true? What if the "good man" turned out to be a symptom of decline—a danger, a temptation, a poison, a narcotic that allows the present to feed off the future? What if this morality is more comfortable and less risky than its opposite, but also smaller, meaner? What if morality itself is to blame for preventing humanity from reaching its highest potential for power and greatness? What if morality is, in fact, the greatest danger of all dangers?

Once this perspective opened up to me, I had every reason to search for colleagues—scholarly, bold, and diligent companions to help explore this immense, distant, and entirely uncharted territory of morality. This search continues even today. To question morality with such fresh and pressing inquiries, to see it with entirely new eyes, is practically equivalent to discovering morality for the first time. This is a morality that has actually existed, one that has been lived! And isn't discovering it for the first time like uncovering a new land?

When I thought of Dr. Paul Rée in this context, it was because I believed that his questions would eventually force him to adopt a more accurate method to arrive at his answers. Was I wrong to think so? In any case, I wanted to guide his sharp and impartial vision toward a better path. I wanted to point him toward the real history of morality and to warn him, while there was still time, against the world of English theories, which lead ultimately to the empty blue vacuum of heaven. Other colors, more grounded and powerful than blue, are far better suited for the genealogy of morals. Grey, for example, represents hard, provable facts, things that truly happened. It stands for that long, intricate script—the history of human morality—which is so difficult to decipher.

This script was unknown to Dr. Rée. What he had read was Darwin. And so, in his philosophy, the Darwinian beast and the refined, modern weakling— the polite dilettante who "bites no longer"—join hands in a way that, at least, provides an interesting lesson. The latter wears an expression of refined laziness, good-natured indifference, tinged with pessimism and exhaustion, as though it were hardly worth taking moral problems seriously.

I, on the other hand, believe there is no subject more deserving of serious attention. One of the rewards for taking these issues seriously is that, eventually, they may allow us to approach them with a light heart. This light-heartedness— or, to use my own term, this joyful wisdom—is a reward for long, courageous, and painstaking effort, a reward for digging deep. Such effort, of course, is the province of only a few. But the day will come when we can say, with full hearts, "Forward! Even our old morality is fit for comedy!" Then we will have discovered a new plot, a new possibility for the Dionysian drama of The Soul's Fate. And who better to make use of it than the ancient, eternal playwright of the grand comedy of existence?

If anyone finds this writing unclear or discordant, I do not believe the fault necessarily lies with me. My assumption is that the reader has already gone through my earlier works and has invested the effort required to grasp their essence—an effort that is far from simple. Take, for example, my Zar athustra. I do not consider anyone to truly understand that book unless every word in it has, at some point, deeply wounded them and, at another point, profoundly enchanted them. Only then can they earn the privilege of partaking reverently in the tranquil, radiant realm from which that work emerged—a realm of sunlight, vast horizons, clarity, and certainty.

In many cases, difficulty arises from the aphoristic form itself, though this is often because it is approached too superficially. A well-crafted aphorism, carefully formed and cast into its final shape, is far from being "understood" merely upon reading. On the contrary, it is only after being read that it demands interpretation and explanation—and this requires a true art of exposition. An example of what I mean by this can be found in the third essay of this book. That essay begins with an aphorism, and the essay itself serves as its commentary.

There is, however, one quality that has been largely forgotten in our time— a quality necessary to practice reading as an art. It is, in fact, why my writings will require time before they become widely readable. This quality demands, above all else, the patience of a cow— an ability completely foreign to the modern man. That quality is rumination.

Sils-Maria, Upper Engadine,

July, 1887.

Chapter 1
Good and Evil, Good and Bad

The English psychologists, who so far are the only philosophers to have made any real attempt at tracing the history of morality's origins, present us with an intriguing puzzle—not a minor one, either. To be completely honest, their personalities as living riddles are often more fascinating than their books.

They themselves are interesting! But what do these English psychologists truly aim to achieve?

We find them, consciously or unconsciously, always engaged in the same endeavor: bringing to the forefront the partie honteuse—the "shameful part"—of our inner world. They seek the driving, governing, and decisive principles of human behavior in precisely the places where intellectual pride would least want to look. They point to things like the inertia of habit, forgetfulness, blind chance, mechanical associations of ideas, or passive, reflexive, molecular, and fundamentally senseless processes. Why do these psychologists feel compelled to search in such degrading and uncomfortable corners?

Is it a dark instinct for disparagement—a sinister, vulgar, and malicious impulse, perhaps not even understood by themselves?

Or is it a residue of pessimistic jealousy, the bitterness of disillusioned idealists who have become grim and poisoned? Could it be an unspoken, subconscious grudge against Christianity (and perhaps Plato), never fully acknowledged in their minds? Or might it simply reflect a strange fascination with the grotesque, the painfully paradoxical, the mystical, and the illogical elements of life? Perhaps the answer lies in a mix of all these motives—a little vulgarity, a touch of gloominess, a sprinkle of anti-Christian sentiment, and a craving for the bizarre and provocative.

Some would say these psychologists are nothing more than cold, tiresome frogs, hopping and crawling inside people as if they were as much at home in human minds as they are in a swamp. But I reject this idea; I cannot believe it. If, in the absence of certain knowledge, one is permitted to wish, then I sincerely hope the opposite is true.

I hope that these analysts with their psychological microscopes are, at their core, brave, proud, and magnanimous beings. I wish they are individuals who know how to restrain both their hearts and their pains and have trained themselves to sacrifice what is desirable for the sake of what is true. Any truth— even the bitter, ugly, unpleasant, unchristian, and immoral truths—for such truths do exist.

All honor, then, to the noble minds who strive to surpass these historians of morality. Yet it is truly unfortunate that they lack a historical sense themselves, that they are utterly abandoned by the guiding spirits of history. Their entire mode of thinking follows the pattern of old-fashioned philosophers: thoroughly unhistorical. There can be no doubt about this. The glaring inadequacy of their genealogy of morals becomes evident the moment they try to determine the origin of the concept and judgment of "good."

Their theory declares, "Originally, humans praised and called 'good' those altruistic acts that benefited others, specifically those who received the acts' advantages. Over time, people forgot the origin of this praise, and altruistic acts came to be regarded as good in themselves, as if they contained an inherent goodness." This explanation is typical of English psychologists and contains all their signature elements: "utility," "forgetting," "habit," and finally "error." These elements combine to form a foundation for a system of values—a system upon which higher humanity has prided itself as if it were a unique and universal privilege of humankind. But this pride must be humbled; this system of values must be dismantled. Does their theory achieve that?

The first objection that comes to mind is that they have sought and located the true home of the concept of "good" in entirely the wrong place. The idea of "good" did not originate among those to whom goodness was shown. Rather, it was the good themselves—

the aristocratic, the powerful, the high-ranking, and the noble-minded—who felt that they themselves wer e good, along with their actions. Their "goodness" was of the first rank, standing in stark contrast to everything low, common, vulgar, and plebeian. From this sense of superiority—the pathos of distance—they claimed for themselves the right to define values, to name them, and to create a moral hierarchy that served their own nature. What concern did they have for utility?

The perspective of utility is utterly foreign and irrelevant when we consider such an explosive outpouring of supreme values— values that create and delineate their own hierarchies. This creative force stands in stark contrast to the lukewarm conditions that underpin worldly wisdom and calculations of practical expediency, conditions that are not just occasional but perpetual. The pathos of nobility and distance, as I have said—the persistent and commanding esprit de corps of a dominant higher race in contact with a subordinate or lower race—this is the true origin of the contrast between "good" and "bad."

(The masters' right to name things extends so far that language itself can be viewed as an expression of their power: they declare, "This is this," and "That is that," sealing every object and event with a sound, and in doing so, they claim possession of it.) Because of this origin, the word "good" has no necessary connection to altruistic acts, despite the superstitious assumptions of moral philosophers. On the contrary, it is only during the decline of aristocratic values that the contrast between "egoistic" and "altruistic" begins to weigh heavily on the human conscience. To use my own terminology, this contrast is an expression of the herd instinct, which eventually embeds itself in many forms of morality. Even then, it takes considerable time for this instinct to dominate so thoroughly that moral valuations become inseparable from this contrast, as we see in contemporary Europe. Today, the prejudice persists—obsessive and ingrained, like a mental affliction—that equates "moral," "altruistic," and désintéressé (selfless) as interchangeable concepts.

In addition to the historical inaccuracy of this hypothesis about the origin of "good," it suffers from a fundamental psychological

ontradiction. The theory suggests that the utility of altruistic acts led to their being praised and that this origin was subsequently forgotten. But how, exactly, could such forgetting occur? Did the utility of altruistic acts suddenly vanish at some point? Clearly not. Quite the opposite: their utility is experienced constantly, every day, and is therefore continually reinforced. This utility does not fade from memory; instead, it becomes ever more deeply imprinted on human consciousness. Far from being forgotten, it should, by all logic, grow increasingly prominent and undeniable with time.

A more coherent—though not necessarily more correct—theory is that proposed by Herbert Spencer, who equates the concept of "good" with "useful" or "purposeful." According to this perspective, judgments of "good" and "bad" are humanity's way of summarizing and formalizing its unforgettable and continually reinforced experiences of what is "useful-purposeful" and "harmful- non-purposeful." In this view, "good" is attributed to whatever has repeatedly proven to be useful and, therefore, comes to be regarded as "valuable in the highest degree," even "valuable in itself."

While I maintain that this explanation is also flawed, it at least has the merit of being internally consistent and psychologically plausible.

The key insight that set me on the right path came from asking this question: What is the true etymological meaning of the symbols for the concept of "good" across different languages? I discovered that they all traced back to the same evolution of an idea: universally, the root meaning of "good" is tied to "aristocrat" or "noble" (in the social sense). From this root developed the meanings of "good" as "possessing an aristocratic soul," "noble" as "possessing a high-caliber soul," or "having a privileged soul." This evolution consistently parallels another: the transformation of terms like "vulgar," "plebeian," or "low" into their eventual meaning of "bad."

One of the most striking examples of this is the German word schlecht. Originally, schlecht was identical in meaning to schlicht—(consider expressions like schlechtweg and schlechterdings)—which, at first, carried no negative connotation. It simply referred to someone of plebeian origin, as opposed to someone of aristocratic standing. It was only much later, around the time of the Thirty Years' War, that schlecht came to mean what it does today.

From the perspective of the Genealogy of Mor als, this discovery is significant. The delay in recognizing it can be attributed to the influence of democratic prejudice, which has long distorted questions of origin in the modern era. This bias, as I will soon demonstrate, extends even into fields like natural science and physiology, which are ostensibly the most objective of disciplines. The harm caused by this prejudice—particularly in the fields of ethics and history—is considerable once it breaks free from constraints and acts purely out of malice.

The notorious example of Buckle illustrates this point. In Buckle, the plebeianism of the modern spirit—rooted in English culture—erupted once again from its foul soil, as violent and uncontrolled as a slimy volcano. This eruption came with the same coarse, overblown, and vulgar rhetoric that has always accompanied such phenomena, mirroring the crude eloquence with which all volcanoes seem to speak.

Regarding our subject, which is undoubtedly an intimate one and appeals only to a select few, it is significant to note that in the words and roots associated with "good," we glimpse the defining traits by which aristocrats perceive themselves as beings of a higher order. Often, they name themselves based on their power and superiority, referring to themselves as "the powerful," "the lords," or "the commanders." Similarly, they might draw upon visible markers of their status, such as wealth, naming themselves "the rich" or "the possessors"—a meaning reflected in words like arya in Sanskrit, as well as parallels in Iranian and Slavic languages.

But they also name themselves according to their unique qualities, which is particularly relevant to our inquiry. For instance, they call themselves "the truthful," a designation originating with the Greek nobility, voiced through Theognis, the poet of Megara. The Greek word ἐσθλός, crafted for this purpose, etymologically means "one who is," someone real, someone true. Later, it takes on a more subjective sense as "truthful." At this stage, the concept evolves into the motto and rallying cry of the nobility, distinguishing them from the "lying," vulgar man, as Theognis describes. Over time, as the nobility decays, the term ἐσθλός comes to represent a psychological nobility, maturing into a more abstract notion of "noble."

On the other hand, words like κακ ός and δειλ ός (contrasting with ἀγαθός, the noble) emphasize cowardice. This provides a clue about the etymological origin of the ambiguous ἀγαθός, which likely developed along similar lines. The Latin word malus (possibly related to μέλας, meaning "black") reflects a similar distinction: the vulgar man was often characterized as dark-complexioned or black-haired, in contrast to the lighter- haired Aryan conquerors who subjugated them. The pre-Aryan inhabitants of Italy, marked by their darker features, became the visual antithesis of the blonde ruling class. Gaelic offers a striking parallel, with the word Fin—as in Fin- Gal—being a term of nobility that originally denoted blonde-haired individuals as opposed to dark-haired aboriginals.

The Celts, I should note, were largely a blonde-haired people. It is a mistake, as Virchow and others have suggested, to associate the dark-haired populations mapped in certain regions of Germany with Celtic ancestry. Instead, these populations are remnants of the pre-Aryan inhabitants of Europe. This phenomenon is not limited to Germany; throughout Europe, the characteristics of the older subject races—darker complexions, shorter skulls—have resurfaced, even becoming dominant. One might speculate whether modern democracy, anarchism, or the widespread socialist push for communal structures— primitive societal forms—represents a regression to this earlier state. Could it signify that the once-dominant Aryan "master race" is now in physiological decline?

As for the Latin word bonus, I propose that it originally meant "the warrior." My hypothesis derives bonus from an earlier form, duonus, as seen in the word duellum (an older form of bellum, "war"), where duonus seems embedded. Bonus, then, would signify "the man of discord," "one who divides" (duo), the warrior. This sheds light on what "the good" meant in ancient Rome: a man of battle.

Finally, consider our German word gut. Could it mean "the godlike," referring to "a man of godlike race"? Might it even share origins with the national name of the Goths, originally a noble designation? The evidence for this hypothesis lies outside the scope of this work.

Above all, there are no exceptions—though there are opportunities for exceptions—to the rule that the idea of political superiority ultimately transforms into the idea of psychological superiority. This is particularly evident when the highest caste also serves as the priestly caste, and in line with its defining traits, claims titles that specifically refer to its priestly role. In such cases, the concepts of "clean" and "unclean" emerge as markers of class distinction for the first time. Here, the notions of "good" and "bad" take on meanings that go beyond mere social distinctions.

It is important, however, not to interpret these concepts of "clean" and "unclean" too broadly, seriously, or symbolically. On the contrary, the ideas of ancient humanity must be understood in their most rudimentary and literal sense—crude, coarse, physical, and narrowly practical, without symbolic undertones. The "clean man," at the start, is simply someone who washes himself, avoids foods that might cause skin diseases, abstains from contact with lower-class women deemed "unclean," and feels a revulsion toward blood. Nothing more—at least not much more.

The nature of a priestly aristocracy itself explains why such societies are prone to dangerously intensifying opposing values at an early stage. These oppositions carve deep divisions into the social fabric, creating chasms that even the boldest free thinkers might hesitate to cross. From the beginning, there is something inherently diseased about priestly aristocracies, and this affliction permeates their way of life. Their aversion to direct action fosters a peculiar blend of introspection and intense emotional volatility. This results in a kind of introspective morbidity and nervous exhaustion—neurasthenia—that seems to cling inevitably to priests across all times and places.

As for the remedies these priestly societies devised for their own maladies, the philosopher can only observe that these so-called cures have often proven far more harmful than the original disease they sought to treat. Humanity still bears the scars of the naïve "cures" of priestly societies. Consider their dietary restrictions (such as abstaining from meat), their fasting, their insistence on sexual continence, and their withdrawal into wilderness isolation—a form of treatment reminiscent of the Weir - Mitchell rest cure, though without the system of excessive feeding and strengthening that effectively counters the hysteria of the ascetic ideal.

Reflect also on the metaphysical systems created by priests, with their war on the senses, their weakening effects, and their obsessive attention to minute details. Consider their practices of self-hypnosis, modeled on the principles of the fakir and Brahman (using metaphysical concepts like Brahman as a kind of fixation device). And finally, note the culmination of this path in an overwhelming desire for annihilation—disguised as a union with God. The longing for unio mystica with God mirrors the Buddhist's yearning for nothingness: Nirvana—and nothing else.

In priestly societies, everything operates on a more dangerous scale—not only their remedies but also their pride, vengeance, cunning, ecstasy, love, ambition, virtue, and even their morbidity. It is fair to say that on the soil of this inherently perilous form of human society, the priestly society, humanity first became an interesting animal. It was within this framework that the human soul reached new depths and developed its capacity for evil. These two traits—depth and evil—remain the fundamental markers of humanity's superiority over every other animal.

The reader will likely have already guessed how easily the priestly mode of valuation could diverge from the knightly-aristocratic mode and develop into its direct opposite. This opposition is further fueled in situations where the priestly and warrior castes confront each other with mutual jealousy, unable to agree on who should hold the highest status.

The knightly-aristocratic values are rooted in a careful cultivation of physical strength and vitality—a flourishing, rich, and exuberant health that exceeds mere survival. These values celebrate war, adventure, hunting, dancing, tournaments, and all forms of bold, free, and joyous action. In contrast, the priestly- aristocratic mode of valuation, as we have seen, rests on entirely different assumptions. For this caste, war itself is an undesirable affair! And yet, as is well known, priests are the most dangerous of enemies—why? Because they are the weakest.

Their weakness fuels a hatred that grows into something vast and sinister— subtle, cunning, and venomous. Throughout history, the greatest haters have always been priests, who are also the most intelligent haters. Compared to the ingenuity of priestly revenge, all other forms of cleverness pale into insignificance. Without the cleverness of the weak, human history would be unbearably dull. Consider the most striking example of this: all the efforts directed against the aristocrats, the powerful, the masters, and the rulers of society are insignificant compared to what the Jews—a priestly nation— achieved in their struggle.

The Jews, that priestly people, discovered that their ultimate weapon against their enemies and oppressors was a radical transvaluation of values, which was simultaneously the most ingenious act of revenge. This strategy was uniquely suited to a nation of priests, deeply steeped in the jealousy and resourcefulness of priestly vengeance. Opposing the aristocratic equation of "good = noble = beautiful = happy = loved by the gods," the Jews had the audacity to propose and fiercely uphold the opposite equation. With a terrifying logic and the deepest hatred—the hatred born of weakness—they asserted:

"The wretched are the only ones who are good. The poor, the weak, the lowly—they alone are good. The suffering, the needy, the sick, and the loathsome—they are the pious, the blessed, and only they shall be saved. But you, aristocrats, you men of power, you are evil for all eternity! You are the horrible, the greedy, the insatiable, the godless! Eternally cursed and damned shall you be!"

We know who inherited this Jewish transvaluation. In the context of the monumental and far-reaching consequences of the Jews' initiative—arguably the most fundamental declaration of war in history—I am reminded of something I wrote elsewhere (Beyond Good and Evil, Aphorism 195): that it was with the Jews that the slave revolt in morality began. This revolt, with its roots two millennia deep, has endured through history and, in our present age, has simply disappeared from view—because it has triumphed.

But you do not understand this? You cannot see the power that took two thousand years to achieve its victory? There is no surprise in that: all long processes are difficult to perceive and even harder to grasp. Yet this is what happened: from the trunk of that tree of revenge and hatred—Jewish hatred, the most profound and sublime hatred, capable of creating ideals and transforming old values into something entirely new and unparalleled on earth— there emerged a phenomenon just as incomparable: a new kind of love, the deepest and most sublime form of love ever known. And from what other trunk could such a love have grown?

But do not mistake this love as a negation of the thirst for revenge, as an opposition to Jewish hatred. Quite the opposite! This love grew out of that hatred, becoming its ultimate crown, its victorious crown. It expanded ever outward, basking in the light and fullness of the sun, while still pursuing the goals of hatred— its victory, its spoils, its cunning strategies—with the same fervor as the roots of that tree of hatred drove deeper and deeper into the dark and evil depths of existence, growing ever more stable, ever more insatiable.

Consider Jesus of Nazareth, the living embodiment of the gospel of love, this "Redeemer" who brought salvation and victory to the poor, the sick, and the sinful. Was he not, in truth, the most sinister and irresistible form of temptation? A temptation to adopt the tortuous path toward precisely those Jewish values and ideals? Did Israel not, through this "Redeemer," achieve the ultimate goal of its sublime revenge, despite his appearance as Israel's opponent and destroyer?

Could it be that this extraordinary outcome—Israel's triumph— was the result of the dark genius of a truly great policy of revenge? A revenge that was slow, far-seeing, and methodical, digging deeply into the fabric of time and history? Is it not possible that Israel had to renounce and condemn, before the eyes of the world, the very instrument of its revenge—nailing it to the cross—so that the world, all of Israel's enemies, might unsuspectingly take the bait?

Could any human mind, with all its ingenuity, have devised a bait more dangerous, more insidious? Could anything else rival the seductive, intoxicating, corrupting power of the symbol of the holy cross? This terrifying paradox of "a god on the cross," this unfathomable mystery of a god's self-crucifixion for the salvation of humanity—does it not represent the ultimate, supreme horror, a horror so profound that it defies comprehension?

It is certain, at least, that sub hoc signo—under this sign—Israel, through its revenge and its transvaluation of all values, has consistently triumphed over all other ideals, including the more aristocratic ones.

"But why speak of nobler ideals? Let us face the facts: the people have triumphed—whether you call them the slaves, the masses, the herd, or whatever other name suits you. If this triumph came through

Translated by Tim Zengerink

the Jews, so be it! In that case, no nation has ever had a greater mission in the history of the world. The 'masters' have been overthrown, and the morality of the common man has prevailed. This victory may be likened to a kind of blood-poisoning, as it has blended the races together—I do not deny this—but it cannot be disputed that this intoxication has succeeded. The 'redemption' of humanity (that is, its liberation from the masters) is proceeding smoothly. Everything is clearly becoming Judaised, Christianised, or vulgarised—what difference does the label make? The poisoning seems unstoppable as it spreads through the entire body politic of humanity.

However, perhaps from this point forward, its tempo can be slowed, its progress made more refined, more subtle, quieter, and more restrained—there is no rush. In this context, one might ask: does the Church still serve a necessary purpose? Does it even have a right to exist? Could humanity now do without it? Quaeritur. It seems that the Church hinders and slows this process instead of accelerating it. Perhaps that is precisely its utility.

Certainly, the Church remains a crude and clumsy institution, offensive to any mind with even a hint of delicacy or to anyone with genuinely modern tastes. Should it not, at the very least, learn to refine itself a little? Today, it repels more people than it attracts. Which of us would even bother to be a freethinker if not for the Church? It is the Church that drives us away, not its poison— because, apart from the Church, we actually like the poison."

These are the parting words of a freethinker responding to my argument— a respectable man by his own standards (as he has often demonstrated) and a democrat as well. He had listened to me patiently but could not endure my silence on this matter. As for me, there is indeed much on this subject about which I prefer to remain silent.

The revolt of the slaves in morality begins with the principle of resentment becoming creative and giving rise to values. This resentment is experienced by those who, unable to act directly, are forced to channel their frustrations into an imagined revenge. While aristocratic morality originates in a triumphant affirmation of its own existence and values, slave morality begins by saying "no"—a rejection of everything "outside itself," "different from itself," and "not itself." This "no" is its creative act.

This reversal of the valuing process—a shift from affirming the self to focusing on the external—is characteristic of resentment. Slave morality depends on an external, objective world as a condition for its very existence. To use a physiological metaphor, it requires external stimuli to activate itself; its essence is reaction, not action. It lacks the spontaneous, self-generating energy of aristocratic morality.

In the case of aristocratic values, action and growth occur naturally and independently. The aristocratic morality does not need an adversary to define itself but instead seeks an antithesis only to enhance its joyful and emphatic "yes" to itself. Its negative concepts—"low," "vulgar," "bad"—are mere afterthoughts, secondary contrasts to its primary, life-affirming essence. This essence is rich with vitality and passion, grounded in the aristocrat's self-perception: "We aristocrats, we good ones, we beautiful ones, we happy ones."

When the aristocratic morality goes astray and violates reality, this misstep is confined to the particular sphere with which it is not sufficiently familiar—a sphere that it deliberately avoids understanding and disdains to engage with. It often misjudges, in certain instances, the sphere it holds in contempt: that of the common, vulgar man and the lower classes. However, it is important to note that even if its disdain falsely represents the object of its contempt, this misrepresentation will always be far less egregious than the fabrications and grotesque distortions born of the vindictive hatred and vengefulness of the weak when they attack their enemies. Contempt inherently carries too much nonchalance, casualness, boredom, impatience, and even personal exhilaration to ever transform its object into a complete caricature or monstrosity.

Attention should be drawn to the almost benevolent nuances infused by the Greek nobility into the terms they used to distinguish the common people from themselves. Observe how, in such words, there often lingers a kind of pity, care, and consideration that softens their tone. Eventually, many of these terms evolved into expressions meaning "unhappy" or "worthy of pity." For example, words like δειλός, δείλαιος, πονηρός, and μοχθηρός, initially used to describe the vulgar man as a laborer or beast of burden, ultimately acquired connotations of misfortune. Similarly, terms for "bad," "low," and "unhappy" in Greek carried a resonance in which "unhappy" was the dominant note. This linguistic inheritance from noble morality reflects how, even in scorn, it remained consistent with its values.

The "well-born" naturally felt themselves to be the happy ones. They did not need to manufacture their happiness artificially by focusing on their enemies or delude themselves into happiness through false narratives, as is common among resentful men. Their happiness arose organically, as an outpouring of their strength and energy. To them, happiness and action were inseparable concepts; to act was to be happy. This is reflected in the etymology of the Greek phrase εὖ πράττειν ("to fare well"), which originally meant "to act well." In contrast, the happiness of the weak and oppressed is fundamentally passive—it is a sedative, a tranquilizing state of rest, peace, and quiet, akin to a Sabbath for the soul, a relaxation of the body and mind.

The aristocratic man, confident and at ease with himself, exemplified sincerity and straightforwardness. The Greek term γεννα ῖος ("noble-born") emphasizes this quality of being candid and perhaps even naïve. By contrast, the resentful man is neither sincere nor honest with himself. His soul is crooked; his mind thrives in hidden corners, on secret paths, and in backdoor dealings. For him, the concealed and indirect are his refuge, his safety, and his comfort. He is a master of silence, grudge-holding, waiting, and self-deprecation.

Over time, a race of resentful individuals necessarily becomes more prudent than any aristocratic race. For them, prudence is not a luxury or refinement, as it is for the aristocrats, but a critical necessity for survival. Among aristocratic men, prudence carries an air of indulgence and refinement. It plays a secondary role compared to the reliable functioning of their instincts and unconscious drives, or even a certain recklessness in their actions. They might charge boldly into danger or battle or exhibit bursts of passionate emotion—whether in love, reverence, or gratitude. Such displays of vitality and spirit have always been the hallmarks of noble souls.

When the aristocratic man experiences resentment, it expresses itself immediately and exhausts itself in the reaction, leaving no lingering venom. In many situations, aristocratic resentment does not even arise, where in weaker individuals it would be unavoidable. Their inability to dwell on their enemies, injuries, or misfortunes signals the fullness of their nature. Their excess of energy heals wounds and fosters forgetfulness. Mirabeau provides a modern example of this disposition; he bore no memory of the insults and petty wrongs committed against him. His inability to forgive was simply a byproduct of his tendency to forget. Such men shrug off insults like worms that would otherwise burrow into others.

In these individuals, we see the possibility—if it exists at all—of a true "love of one's enemies." An aristocratic man respects his enemies, and this respect can act as a bridge to love. He demands that his enemies be worthy adversaries—men he can admire, whose character holds much to honor and nothing to despise. He tolerates no enemy who is beneath his contempt.

In contrast, consider how the resentful man conceives of his enemy. It is here that his creativity emerges. He imagines the "evil enemy," the "wicked one," and from this fabricated figure, he derives a contrasting and corresponding idea: the "good one." This "good one" is none other than himself. Through this inversion, the resentful man defines his identity by vilifying those he opposes.

The method of the resentful man is entirely opposite to that of the aristocratic man. The aristocratic man forms the concept of "good" spontaneously and directly—arising naturally from his own being. From this starting point, he then creates the idea of "bad," which serves as a secondary concept, an afterthought. In contrast, the resentful man's concept of "evil" emerges from the cauldron of unfulfilled hatred. The aristocratic "bad" is merely a nuance, an imitation, an addition; the resentful "evil," however, is original, foundational, the central act in the creation of slave morality.

These two words—"bad" and "evil"—mark an immense difference, even though they share a common opposition in the idea of "good." But the idea of "good" itself is not the same in the two systems. Let us ask instead: W ho is truly evil according to the morality of resentment? The answer, given with full seriousness, is this: precisely the good man of the aristocratic morality—the noble, the powerful, the ruler—transfigured and distorted through the venomous lens of resentment into something entirely different, into a figure of malevolence.

This much must be admitted: the man who came to know these "good" ones only as enemies also came to know them only as evil enemies. Those same aristocratic men, who among their equals were bound by strict conventions, respect, customs, and gratitude—and even more by mutual vigilance and jealousy—these same men, who within their circle displayed countless forms of courtesy, self-restraint, refinement, loyalty, pride, and friendship, behaved in entirely different ways outside their group. Toward those beyond their circle, where the foreign begins, they were little better than beasts of prey set loose.

In the wilderness, freed from the constraints of societal control, they released the pent-up tension created by their confinement in the order and peace of their own society. There, they returned to the innocence of the predator's conscience, reveling like jubilant monsters in their wild freedom. Emerging from acts of murder, arson, rape, and torture, they carried themselves with a moral ease, even a sense of playfulness, as if these horrors were nothing more than a rowdy prank from students on a spree—utterly convinced that poets would celebrate their deeds in song and story.

It is impossible to overlook the beast of prey that lies at the core of all aristocratic races. This magnificent, blonde brute, driven by a relentless hunger for plunder and victory, is a defining feature of these noble classes. This primal force demands an outlet; the beast must occasionally break free, returning to the wilderness. We see this need in the Romans, Arabs, Germans, and Japanese nobility, in the Homeric heroes, and in the Scandinavian Vikings. All these groups share this essential trait: the need to unleash their inner beast and revel in the unrestrained innocence of their savage nature.

It is the aristocratic races that have left the imprint of the word "barbarian" along every path they have traveled. Indeed, an awareness of this very barbarism, and even a pride in it, is evident even in their most advanced civilizations. For example,

Pericles, in his famous funeral oration, declares to the Athenians, "Our audacity has forced a way over every land and sea, rearing everywhere imperishable memorials of itself for good and for evil."

This audacity of aristocratic races, however reckless, absurd, and spasmodic its manifestations may seem, reflects the unpredictable and extravagant nature of their endeavors. Pericles especially highlights the ϱα θυμία of the Athenians—their nonchalance, their disregard for safety, bodily well-being, life, and comfort. He celebrates their terrifying joy and intense delight in destruction, in the ecstasies of victory, and even in cruelty. These traits— when viewed by those who have suffered at their hands—become crystallized into the image of the "barbarian," the "evil enemy," or figures like the "Goth" and the "Vandal."

The profound, icy mistrust that the German provokes as soon as he attains power—even today—is a lingering echo of the inextinguishable horror with which Europe regarded the wrath of the blonde Teutonic beast for centuries. This mistrust persists despite the fact that there is now barely any psychological, let alone physical, continuity between the ancient Germans and modern ones. I have previously pointed out Hesiod's difficulty when he attempted to describe the series of social ages in terms of gold, silver, and bronze. Hesiod faced a contradiction when trying to reconcile the Homeric world, which aristocratic families remembered as a glorious age filled with their heroic ancestors, with its simultaneously dreadful and violent reality. He resolved this by splitting one age into two: the heroic age of demigods, as it was remembered by the aristocracy, and the bronze age, as it appeared to the descendants of the oppressed, the enslaved, and the exiled. To them, it was a brutal and merciless era—a true age of bronze—hard, cold, and unfeeling, crushing everything and staining all it touched with blood.

If we accept the modern theory, now widely believed, that the very essence of civilization lies in taming humanity's beastly instincts and transforming humans into domesticated and civil animals, then it follows that the real tools of civilization must include the instincts of reaction and resentment. These are the very instincts by which aristocratic races, along with their ideals, were eventually degraded and defeated. However, this does not imply that the bearers of these tools of civilization were themselves representatives of civilization. On the contrary—this is not merely probable but evident even today.

These bearers of vindictive instincts, compelled to repress their vengeance and resentment, are the descendants of all European and non-European slaves, particularly the pre-Aryan populations. These people, I assert, represent not the advancement of humanity but its decline.

These "tools of civilization" are a disgrace to humanity and, in truth, provide more reason to question and distrust civilization than to defend it. While it is perfectly reasonable to be wary of the blonde beast that lies at the heart of all aristocratic races and to remain vigilant against it, who would not prefer to live with fear—and at the same time, admiration—than to endure the constant, revolting sight of the deformed, the dwarfed, the stunted, and the poisoned? Is that not our current condition? What drives our disgust with "man" today? For it is clear that we suffer from man—there is no denying it.

It is not fear that troubles us. Rather, it is that there is nothing left to fear from men. The worm that is "man" now crawls to the forefront, multiplying endlessly. The "tame man," the pitiful, mediocre, uninspiring creature, has come to see himself as the goal, the pinnacle, the meaning, the historic principle—the "higher man." Worse still, he may even be right to see himself this way. Compared to the overwhelming deformity, sickness, exhaustion, and decay that now pollutes Europe, he may indeed represent a kind of relative success. At least he still says yes to life.

At this point, I cannot help but express a sigh and one last hope. What is it that I find so intolerable? What chokes me, suffocates me, and makes me faint? Bad air! Bad air! The stench of something misshapen, the foul odor of the insides of a malformed soul near me—that is what I cannot endure. Beyond that, what hardship could not be borne? What privation, bad weather, illness, toil, or solitude would be insurmountable? In truth, one can endure anything, being born to dig, to battle, to survive. One always finds the light again, always experiences life's golden moment of triumph, and stands again as one was born: unbroken, tense, and ready for something more challenging, something more distant. Like a bow, stretched tauter by every strain, one prepares for the next shot.

But I beg—if there are goddesses beyond good and evil who can grant such things—grant me, from time to time, just one glimpse. Just one glimpse of something perfect, fully realized, mighty, triumphant. Grant me the sight of something that still inspires fear! Let me see a man who justifies humanity's existence. A man whose happiness, realized and embodied, redeems the idea of mankind. A man for whom one might cling to belief in humanity!

The reality, however, is bleak. The dwarfing and flattening of European man is our greatest danger. It is this trend that wears us down, for we see nothing today that strives to grow greater. The trajectory appears to move ever backward—toward something smaller, more insipid, more calculating, more comfortable, more mediocre, more indifferent, more Chinese, more Christian. There is no doubt: man is becoming "better." And it is precisely this process—this loss of fear of man—that has also robbed us of hope in man, even of the will to be man.

The sight of man now wearies us. What is modern nihilism, if not this? We are tired of man.

But let us return to the subject. The problem of a differ ent origin of "good"—as it has been imagined by the resentful man—requires an answer. It's no surprise that lambs might hold a grudge against the great birds of prey. But this doesn't mean we should blame the birds of prey for hunting the lambs. When the lambs say among themselves, "These birds of prey are evil, and anyone who is the opposite of them, who is not a bird of prey but a lamb—such a person is good," there's nothing particularly objectionable about this view. It is natural for the lambs to create such an ideal. At the same time, however, the birds of prey might mockingly say to themselves, "We don't bear any grudge against these good lambs. In fact, we like them—there's nothing tastier than a tender lamb."

To demand that strength should not show itself as strength—that it should not seek to dominate, to overcome, to rule, to thirst for challenges, opponents, and victories—is just as absurd as expecting weakness to behave like strength. A force is simply what it is: movement, will, and action—it cannot be separated from these expressions. Force is not something separate from what it does. Yet language (and the flawed reasoning built into it) misleads us. It tempts us to see every action as requiring a subject behind it, a "doer" behind the deed.

For example, people separate lightning from its flash. They think of the flash as something done by the lightning, as if lightning itself were a kind of being or subject that causes the flash to happen. In the same way, popular morality separates strength from its actions, imagining that there is some neutral, independent force behind a strong person, one that can choose whether or not to act with strength. But this is a false idea. There is no "being" behind the doing, no "doer" behind the act. The action itself is everything. The so-called "doer" is just a shadow of the action, a label we attach to it.

This is like saying the lightning "flashes," as though the flash were something separate from the lightning itself. It's a kind of doubling of the same event— making the lightning both the cause and the effect of its own flash. Scientists, too, fall into this trap when they say things like, "Force moves," or "Force causes." Even modern science, despite its cold objectivity, remains ensnared by the tricks of language. It cannot let go of the old superstition of the "subject." The atom, for instance, is one such imaginary subject, just like Kant's "Thing-in-itself."

Is it any wonder, then, that suppressed feelings of revenge and hatred seize upon this belief for their own purposes? Nothing fuels these emotions more than the idea that "the strong have the choice to be weak, and the bird of prey has the option to be a lamb." This belief gives the oppressed and downtrodden a way to hold the birds of prey accountable for being what they are. The weak and powerless, driven by their resentment, convince themselves that the strong are to blame for their strength, and that the predators are at fault for being predators.

"Let us be different from evil, let us be good! And good is anyone who does not oppress, who does not harm others, who does not attack, who does not seek revenge, who leaves vengeance to God, who keeps himself hidden as we do, who avoids evil, and who asks little from life; in short, someone like us—patient, meek, and just." Yet, when this sentiment is stripped of its pretenses and interpreted coldly and without bias, it means little more than, "The weak are weak, and it is good to avoid doing anything beyond our strength."

This grim prudence, this lowest form of survival instinct, is no different from what insects demonstrate when they feign death in the face of great danger, avoiding any action that could cost them too much. Yet this basic instinct, through the self-deception and trickery of weakness, has been dressed up in the grandeur of an ascetic, silent, and expectant virtue. It pretends, as if by choice, that the weakness of the weak—their very nature, their being, their actions, their inescapable reality—is a deliberate decision, a conscious act of will, a merit, a virtue.

Such individuals rely on the belief in a neutral, free-choosing "subject"—or, in simpler terms, the soul. This belief is essential for their self-preservation and self-assertion, where every lie about themselves can be sanctified. The notion of the subject, or soul, has perhaps been the most effective dogma ever devised because it enables the weak, the oppressed, and the frail masses to engage in the ultimate self-deception: interpreting their weakness as a form of freedom, seeing their condition—whether being one thing or another—not as necessity but as merit.

Who dares to peer into the secret of how ideals are created in this world?

Who has the courage to confront it? Come forward!

Here, a glimpse is granted into these dark and grimy workshops. But wait! Just a moment, curious and reckless soul—your eyes must first adjust to this strange, shifting light. Now, look carefully! Enough! Speak! What is happening down there, in the depths? Tell us what you see, you with the most dangerous curiosity—for now I will listen.

"I see nothing, but I hear much more. It is a careful, spiteful, soft whispering and murmuring from every corner and crevice. It seems to me they are lying; every sound is coated with a sugary sweetness. Weakness is being turned into merit—there's no question about it. It is exactly as you say."

Go on!

"And the inability to retaliate is being called 'goodness.' Cowardly baseness is being rebranded as meekness. Submission to those they hate is renamed obedience—obedience, they say, to someone who supposedly commanded this submission, whom they call God. The harmlessness of the weak, their abundance of cowardice, their standing at the door and waiting because they have no other choice—these things are given noble labels like 'patience,' which they even call a virtue. Their inability to take revenge is transformed into not wanting revenge, perhaps even forgiveness (as if they know not what they do— though we know well enough what they do). They speak of 'love for their enemies' and sweat as they say it."

Go on!

"They are wretched, without a doubt—all these whisperers and forgers in the corners, though they huddle together for warmth. And yet they tell me their misery is a special favor and distinction granted to them by God, much like one beats the dogs one loves most. They even say this misery is a preparation, a test, a form of training. Perhaps, they say, it is more than that—it might one day be repaid with immense interest, in gold or in happiness. This they call 'blessedness.'"

Go on!

"Now they are trying to convince me that not only are they better people than the mighty, than the lords of the earth—whose spittle they are forced to lick (not out of fear, of course, oh no, not out of fear! But because God commands that all authority must be honored)—but also that they have a 'better time.' If not now, then one day they will surely have a 'better time.' But enough! Enough! I can bear no more. Bad air! Bad air! These workshops where ideals are created—they reek of the rankest lies!"

Wait, hold on! You're not mentioning the masterpieces crafted by these virtuosos of black magic, these masters who can transform blackness into whiteness, guilt into innocence, and darkness into light. Have you not noticed the level of refinement they achieve in their ultimate work, their most daring, subtle, ingenious, and deceitful trick?

Be careful! These creatures of the cellar, filled with revenge and hatred—what do they make out of that revenge and hatred? Do you hear their words? Would you ever guess, if you trusted only their words, that you are among people seething with resentment and nothing else?

"I understand now—I prick up my ears (ah! ah! ah!—and hold my nose). Now, for the first time, I truly hear what they have always said: 'We are the good, we are the righteous.' What they demand is not called revenge; they call it 'the triumph of righteousness.' What they hate is not their enemies; no, they claim to hate 'unrighteousness' and 'godlessness.' What they believe in and hope for is not the joy of revenge, not the intoxicating sweetness of revenge (did not Homer call it 'sweeter than honey'?), but rather the victory of God—the righteous God— over the 'godless.' What is left for them to love in this world? Not their brothers in hate, but their 'brothers in love,' as they say: all the good and righteous people of the earth."

And what do they call that vision that comforts them through the hardships of life—their grand illusion of future blessedness?

"What? Am I hearing this correctly? They call it 'the Last Judgment,' the coming of their kingdom, 'the Kingdom of God.' But for now, they say they live 'in faith,' 'in love,' and 'in hope.'"

Enough! Enough!

Faith in what? Love for what? Hope for what? These weaklings! It is clear they also wish to be strong one day. There is no doubt about it—their kingdom must come someday. They call it "the Kingdom of God," as already mentioned. They are so meek in everything, so patient! Yet to experience that kingdom, they must live long—beyond death itself. Yes, eternal life is required to finally compensate for this earthly life of "faith," "love," and "hope."

Compensate for what? Compensate with what?

Dante, I believe, made a glaring error when, with terrifying brilliance, he inscribed over the gates of his Hell, "Me too made eternal love." Surely, the following inscription would be far more fitting over the gates of the Christian Paradise and its so-called "eternal blessedness." "Me too made eternal hate." That is, of course, assuming one is willing to put a truth above the entrance to a lie.

What is this "blessedness" of Paradise, exactly? Perhaps we could guess, but it's better to let an authority explicitly state it— someone whose expertise in such matters is beyond question: Thomas Aquinas, the great teacher and saint.

"Beati in regno celesti," says Thomas Aquinas, as softly as a lamb, "videbunt paenas damnatorum, ut beatitudo illis magis complaceat." ("The blessed in the heavenly kingdom will witness the punishment of the damned, so that their bliss will be all the greater.")

Or, if you wish to hear a stronger tone, let us take the words of a triumphant early Church Father, warning his followers against the cruel pleasures of public spectacles. Why? Because, he explains, faith offers something far greater. De Spectaculis (Chapter 29 and following) lays it out plainly: thanks to redemption, we have access to joys of an entirely different kind. Instead of athletes, we have martyrs. Do we crave blood? Then we have the blood of Christ. But what will await us on the day of His return, on the day of His triumph?

Then this enraptured visionary continues:

"But indeed, other spectacles await us—that final and eternal day of judgment, that day unexpected by the nations, that day scorned by them, when the vast age of the world and all its generations will be consumed in one fir e. What a spectacle will that be! What shall I marvel at? What shall I laugh at? Where shall I rejoice? Where shall I exult, as I watch so many mighty kings, who were once proclaimed to be taken into heaven, groaning in the deepest darkness along with Jupiter himself and their own witnesses! Then, too, the governors, those persecutors of the name of the Lord, being consumed in fir es more savage than the flames with which they tormented Christians! And what about those wise philosopher s, ashamed as they burn alongside their disciples, those same philosophers who taught that nothing pertained to God, who declared that souls either did not exist or would not return to their bodies! What of the poets, trembling not before Rhadamanthus or Minos but before the unexpected tribunal of Christ! Then, truly, the tragedies will be heard again, with voices much louder and screams far more violent in their own calamities. Then, the actors will be seen, more unrestrained in their movements through the flames. Then, the charioteer s will be on fiery wheels, their whole bodies blazing red. Then, the athletes will be thrown not in the gymnasiums, but into fire.

Unless, of course, I prefer not to see them alive even then, for I would rather direct my insatiable gaze to those who were most cruel against the Lord. 'Her e he is,' I will say, 'the carpenter 's son or the child of a prostitute' (as the following passages and especially the description of Mary in the Talmud make clear , Tertullian is here refer ring to the Jews). 'Her e he is, the break er of the Sabbath, the Samaritan possessed by a demon. Her e he is, the one whom you purchased from Judas, the one who was beaten with a reed and struck with fists, who was defiled with spit, given gall and vinegar to dr ink. Her e he is, the one whose body his disciples supposedly stole to claim he had risen—or per haps the gardener took it, to prevent visitors from trampling his lettuce!' To witness such things, to revel in such spectacles—what praetor, what consul, what priest could offer you such gifts from their generosity? And yet we already have a foretaste of these things, in a way, through faith, as the Spirit brings them to us in vivid imagination. But how much more magnificent are those things that eye has not seen, nor ear heard, nor the heart of man imagined (1 Corinthians 2 :9). I believe they will be far more pleasing than any arena or stage, whether comedic or tragic."

And so it is written: Perfidem—by faith.

Let us come to a conclusion. The two opposing value systems—"good and bad" versus "good and evil"—have waged a terrible battle across the centuries. This thousand-year struggle has shaped the world, and though the "good and evil" morality has long held the upper hand, there are still places where the outcome remains undecided. It could even be said that this conflict continues to escalate, reaching ever higher levels of complexity and intensity. It has become increasingly psychological, so much so that one might argue there is no greater mark of a higher or more psychological nature than to embody this very contradiction—to still serve as a battlefield for these opposing values.

The symbol of this struggle, etched into history in a script still worth reading, is encapsulated in the phrase: Rome against Judea, Judea against Rome. This conflict, this confrontation, this antagonism remains unparalleled in significance. There has been no greater event in history than this fight, no more profound question than the one it poses.

To Rome, the Jew represented the embodiment of the unnatural, a being utterly monstrous in its opposition to the Roman way of life. The Romans saw in the Jews a race consumed by hatred for all of humanity—and they were right, insofar as the well-being and future of humanity were tied to the unconditional dominance of aristocratic values, the values of Rome. Conversely, what did the Jews feel toward Rome? This can be gleaned from countless hints, but it is enough to turn to the Book of Revelation (the Johannine Apocalypse), which stands as perhaps the most obscene of written outbursts, a text steeped in the spirit of vengeance.

And yet, consider the profound irony—and the cunning logic—of the Christian instinct, which labeled this very book of hate with the name of the "Disciple of Love." This is the same disciple to whom the ecstatic and passionate Gospel was attributed. There is a fragment of truth in this association, even if it required considerable literary forgery to make it plausible.

The Romans were a strong and aristocratic people—perhaps the strongest and most aristocratic the world has ever known, or even imagined. Every relic of their civilization, every inscription, inspires awe, provided one can perceive the spirit behind the words. In contrast, the Jews were the quintessential priestly nation of resentment, endowed with a singular genius for shaping popular morality. To fully appreciate their exceptionalism, compare the Jews to other nations with similar tendencies, such as the Chinese or the Germans. It is only after such a comparison that one can grasp what is truly first-rate and what is merely fifth-rate.

Which of the two has been provisionally victorious, Rome or Judea? There can be no doubt. Just look at whom, even today, people bow to in Rome itself, as though before the embodiment of the highest values. And not only in Rome, but across nearly half the world—everywhere humanity has been tamed or is in the process of being tamed—people bow before three Jews and one Jewess: Jesus of Nazareth, Peter the fisherman, Paul the tent- maker, and Mary, the mother of Jesus. This fact is extraordinary. Rome has undoubtedly been defeated.

At least, that is the case for now. During the Renaissance, there was a brilliantly sinister resurgence of the classical ideal, the aristocratic valuation of all things. Rome, like a man shaking off a deep sleep, seemed to stir under the weight of the Judaised Rome that had been built over it—a Rome that had become an ecumenical synagogue and called itself the "Church." But just as quickly, Judea triumphed again, this time through that fundamentally popular (German and English) movement of revenge called the Reformation. Along with it came the inevitable restoration of the Church and, with it, the return of the graveyard peace of classical Rome.

Judea triumphed once more, and even more decisively, during the French Revolution. Here, the victory was deeper and more profound than ever. The last political aristocracy in Europe—the French aristocracy of the seventeenth and eighteenth centuries— was shattered by the instincts of a resentful populace. Never before had the world heard such jubilant celebration, such uproarious enthusiasm. And in the midst of it all, something monstrous and unexpected occurred: the ancient ideal itself was revived, parading before the conscience of humanity with unprecedented brilliance and vitality.

Against the cry of resentment—the call for equality, abasement, and the levelling of humanity, for regression into mediocrity— there resounded a counter-cry, terrible and seductive: the prer ogative of the few.

As though marking a final crossroads, there appeared Napoleon, the most singular and violent anachronism to have ever lived. In Napoleon was embodied the very problem of the aristocratic ideal itself—an ideal both magnificent and monstrous. Napoleon was a synthesis of the Monster and the Superman. Consider carefully what a profound problem he represents.

Was that the end? Was the greatest of all conflicts between ideals thereby laid to rest forever? Or was it merely postponed— postponed for a long time? Might there not come a day when the old fire reignites, more terrifying and more deliberately prepared than ever before? And further—should one not wish for such a culmination with all their strength? Should one not will it, demand it, strive for it with every fiber of their being?

For those who, like my readers, begin to reflect and think more deeply on these questions, it will not be easy to arrive quickly at a conclusion. This is reason enough for me to bring my own reflections to a close here, trusting that my meaning has by now become sufficiently clear. Surely it is evident what I mean by the dangerous motto inscribed on the body of my last book: Beyond Good and Evil. At the very least, it should be understood that this is not synonymous with "Beyond Good and Bad."

Note. I take this opportunity afforded by this treatise to express openly and formally a wish that I have, until now, shared only in casual conversations with scholars. I hope that some Faculty of Philosophy might earn the honor of advancing the study of the history of morals by initiating a series of prize essays on the subject. Perhaps this book may serve as a compelling impetus for such an endeavor.

In connection with this possibility, the following question deserves thoughtful consideration. It merits the attention not only of philologists and historians but also of professional philosophers:

"What can philology, and particularly the study of etymology, tell us about the historical evolution of moral ideas?"

At the same time, it is equally crucial to encourage physiologists and doctors to take an interest in these problems—specifically, the value of the valuations that have prevailed throughout history. In this effort, professional philosophers should act as spokesmen and intermediaries. But this requires first transforming the traditionally cold and suspicious relationship between philosophy, physiology, and medicine into one of mutual respect and productive collaboration.

Indeed, every historical and cultural "table of values"—every "thou shalt" known to history and ethnology—needs to be examined and interpreted primarily from a physiological perspective, rather than exclusively a psychological one. Additionally, all these values demand critique from the standpoint of medical science. The question, "What is the value of this or that table of values or morality?" must be examined from a variety of perspectives. For instance, the question "valuable for what?" cannot be analyzed too carefully or in too much detail.

What might have value for one purpose—such as promoting a race's capacity for endurance, its adaptability to a particular climate, or even the survival of the greatest number—might have far less value if the goal is the evolution of a stronger species. In evaluating values, the interests of the majority and those of the minority represent fundamentally opposing perspectives. It is left to the naïveté of English biologists to assume that the former perspective— the good of the majority—is inherently superior.

All the sciences must now work to prepare the ground for the philosopher's future task: to solve the problem of value. This task requires the philosopher to establish and define a hierarchy of values.

Chapter 2
Guilt, Bad Conscience, and The Like

The cultivation of an animal capable of making promises—is this not the paradoxical task that nature has set for itself in regard to humanity? Is this not the very essence of the problem of man? The fact that this problem has been largely solved is extraordinary, especially to those who recognize the immense power of forgetfulness that works against it. Forgetfulness is not simply a passive inertia, as many superficial thinkers assume. Rather, it is an active force—a positive and deliberate function. It prevents what we have lived through, experienced, and absorbed from constantly intruding upon our consciousness, just as the processes of physical digestion and assimilation operate without entering our awareness.

Forgetfulness provides a temporary closing of the doors and windows of consciousness, offering relief from the ceaseless activity of the subconscious organs working together in harmony or conflict. It allows a moment of quiet, a clean slate, so to speak—a tabula rasa— to make space for new experiences and, more importantly, for higher functions like governance, planning, and decision-making. The human organism, like an oligarchy, requires this order to function properly. Active forgetfulness, therefore, is the guardian and nurturer of mental order, peace, and proper conduct. Without it, there can be no happiness, joy, hope, pride, or even a sense of the present.

A person in whom this preventive apparatus of forgetfulness is damaged is like a dyspeptic who cannot "digest" anything, and this comparison is not merely figurative. Such a person cannot "let go" of anything. Yet this same human animal, who depends so much on forgetfulness for health and vitality, has developed within himself an opposing power: memory. Memory functions to curb forgetfulness when necessary—in situations where promises must be kept.

This memory is not a mere passive inability to forget impressions once made or words once spoken. It is an active refusal to let go. It is the persistence of the will, a deliberate desire to continue what has once been decided. It creates a bridge between the original "I will" and the ultimate execution of that will. This memory ensures that even amidst a world of new and unforeseen circumstances, distractions, and desires, the chain of intent does not break.

But what is the foundation for this remarkable ability? To regulate the future in this way, man had to learn to distinguish between what is necessary and what is accidental. He had to think causally, to envision the distant future as though it were present, to anticipate, and to determine with precision the relationship between ends and means. Above all, he had to learn to calculate and to reckon. He had to become disciplined, predictable, and reliable—even to himself. Only then could man begin to promise, to guarantee himself as a being with a future.

This is, in essence, the long history of how responsibility came into being. The task of creating an animal capable of making promises includes, as we now understand, the preliminary task of shaping man to be, in some sense, necessary, predictable, consistent with his kind, orderly, and therefore calculable. The immense undertaking I refer to as the "morality of custom" (see Dawn of Day, Aphorisms 9, 14, and 16)—the actual, painstaking work that humanity has done on itself throughout its longest and most prehistoric periods—derives its meaning and justification from this goal. Despite all its inherent harshness, despotism, rigidity, and occasional foolishness, the morality of custom made man truly calculable.

If we now consider this colossal process from its endpoint, where the tree of humanity finally bears its mature fruit—when society and its morality of custom have achieved their purpose—we find the sovereign individual. This individual is unlike anyone else, having freed himself from the constraints of the morality of custom. He is autonomous, a being who stands "beyond morality" (for autonomy and morality are mutually exclusive). He is, in short, a man of personal, enduring, and independent will—a man capable of making promises.

This individual possesses a proud awareness, felt in every fiber of his being, of what he has achieved and brought to life within himself: a genuine sense of power, freedom, and human perfection. This person, who has grown into true freedom and who is capable of binding himself with promises, is a master of his own will, a sovereign. How could he not be aware of his immense superiority over all beings incapable of committing themselves to promises or acting as their own guarantee? How could he not recognize the trust, reverence, and awe he inspires? He has earned all these. With mastery over himself, he is also granted mastery over circumstances, over nature, and over all creatures with weaker wills and less reliability.

For the free man, the man of the enduring and unbreakable will, this strength becomes his measure of value. From this vantage point, he looks outward, evaluating others. He honors and respects his equals—the strong and the reliable, those who, like him, can bind themselves with promises. Such individuals promise sparingly, carefully, and deliberately. They give their trust rarely, and when they do, it is an act of conferring honor. Their word is reliable because they know they possess the strength to uphold it, even in the face of calamity or fate.

Conversely, the sovereign man has no patience for the empty and thoughtless, for those who promise without reason or capability. He stands ready to crush the hollow fools who make promises they have no business making and to chastise the liar who breaks his word even as it leaves his lips.

The proud knowledge of this extraordinary privilege—the privilege of responsibility—and the deep awareness of this rare freedom, this power over oneself and over fate, become ingrained in him as an instinct, a ruling instinct. What does he call this instinct, this governing force within him, if he feels the need to name it? There can be no doubt: the sovereign man calls it his conscience.

His conscience? One quickly realizes that the idea of "conscience," seen here in its highest and most striking form, must have undergone a long history of development. The ability to guarantee oneself with pride, to say yes to oneself—that is a mature fruit, but also a late one. How long this fruit must have hung sour and bitter on the tree! And for an even longer period, there was no sign of it at all. No one had yet dared to promise such a thing, even though everything on the tree had been preparing and ripening for that very purpose.

"How does one create a memory in the human animal? How can an impression be so deeply fixed in this fleeting, half-thoughtless, and half- oblivious creature—this embodiment of forgetfulness— that it remains present permanently?" It is easy to imagine that this ancient problem was not solved with gentle answers or kind methods. Perhaps nothing in early human history is as dreadful and sinister as humanity's first system of mnemonics.

"Something must be burned into memory to ensure it stays there: only what continues to cause pain is remembered." This axiom comes from the oldest—and, unfortunately, the longest- lasting— psychology known to the world. One could even say that wherever we now find solemnity, seriousness, mystery, and grim colors in the lives of people and nations, we see remnants of the terror that once accompanied all promises, pledges, and obligations. The past, with all its vastness, depth, and cruelty, breathes its influence into us when we grow "serious."

When humanity deemed it necessary to forge a memory for itself, it did so through blood, torture, and sacrifice. The most horrifying sacrifices (including the sacrifice of first-born children), the most repulsive mutilations (such as castration), and the cruelest rituals of religious cults (for all religions, at their core, are systems of cruelty) all originate from this instinct that found its strongest mnemonic tool in pain.

In this sense, asceticism itself can be understood as part of this process. Certain ideas had to be rendered indelible, ever-present, and fixed in such a way that they could dominate the nervous and intellectual system. Ascetic practices and lifestyles served to eliminate competing ideas, ensuring these chosen ones became "unforgettable."

The less capable humanity was of remembering, the more horrific the signs and customs it employed. The harshness of ancient penal laws, for example, reveals how difficult it was for humans to overcome forgetfulness and hold a few basic social principles firmly in mind. These laws were directed at people ruled by every fleeting emotion and passing desire, those incapable of maintaining even the simplest agreements.

We Germans may not see ourselves as particularly cruel or hard-hearted, and certainly not as frivolous or careless. But a glance at our old penal codes reveals the tremendous effort required to evolve into a "nation of thinkers." By this, I mean the European nation that still today represents the pinnacle of reliability, seriousness, bad taste, and pragmatism—a nation that, thanks to these traits, claims the right to train Europe's intellectual elite, its mandar ins.

The Germans employed horrific means to create for themselves a memory strong enough to overcome their deeply ingrained plebeian instincts and the raw brutality of those instincts. Consider the old German punishments: stoning (as described in legend, where a millstone crushes the guilty man's head), breaking on the wheel (an original and uniquely German invention in the realm of punishment), dart-throwing, tearing or trampling by horses (the infamous "quartering"), boiling criminals in oil or wine (practiced even into the 14th and 15th centuries), the gruesomely popular flaying ("slicing into strips"), cutting flesh from the chest, and besmearing the offender with honey before exposing him to flies under the blazing sun.

It was through such vivid and horrifying images that humanity learned to retain in its memory a mere five or six "thou shalt nots," essential for societal coexistence. These were promises that man had to remember in order to enjoy the benefits of living in society. And it was, indeed, through such methods that man eventually attained r eason! But alas, reason, seriousness, control over emotions—all those somber and weighty achievements we now call reflection, all the supposed privileges and crowning glories of humanity—what a steep price they have demanded! How much blood and cruelty have laid the foundation for all the so-called "good things" in life!

But how did that other bleak phenomenon—the consciousness of sin, the pervasive sense of a "bad conscience"—enter the world? This question brings us back to our genealogists of morality. For the second time, I must say—or perhaps for the first time—that they are utterly inadequate. They possess nothing more than a few narrow spans of modern experience, lacking any deep knowledge of the past, and showing no real desire to gain such knowledge. Even less do they possess the historical instinct, that essential "second sight" needed for this kind of inquiry. Yet, despite this, they attempt to write the history of morals, and their conclusions are inevitably far removed from the truth—so far that their efforts deserve no more than a condescending glance.

Have these so-called genealogists ever entertained even a vague understanding, for example, that the fundamental moral concept of "ought" originated in the very material idea of "owe"? Or that punishment initially developed as retaliation, entirely independent of any consideration of free will or determinism? It was only when civilization reached a high level of development that humans began making more subtle distinctions such as "intentional," "negligent," "accidental," "responsible," and their opposites— distinctions which are now used in evaluating punishment.

The idea that "the wrongdoer deserves punishment because he could have acted differently," though today it seems self-evident and foundational to the notion of justice, is in fact a very late and highly refined form of human judgment. To retroactively project this idea back to the origins of human society is to commit a crude violation of the principles of early psychology.

For the vast majority of human history, punishment was never based on the offender's responsibility for their actions. It was never about punishing only the guilty. Instead, punishment functioned much like the way parents still punish their children: out of anger for a wrong suffered. This anger, often raw and instinctive, would mechanically vent itself on the source of the injury—the wrongdoer. Over time, this anger became moderated and shaped by the notion that every injury has an equivalent pr ice that could be repaid, even if the repayment took the form of pain inflicted on the perpetrator.

But from where does this deeply entrenched and seemingly indestructible idea of equivalence between harm and pain draw its strength?

I have already traced the origin of this idea to the contractual relationship between creditor and debtor, a relationship as old as the concept of legal rights itself. This points further back to the most basic forms of purchase, sale, barter, and trade.

The recognition and enforcement of these contractual relationships naturally provoke suspicion and resistance toward the primitive societies that created and upheld them. In such societies, promises were made, and mechanisms were devised to ensure the promiser would remember and honor them. These societies, as we might expect, often resorted to harshness, cruelty, and pain to achieve their goals. To instill confidence in their promise to repay, to affirm the seriousness and sanctity of that promise, and to etch the duty of repayment into their own conscience, debtors would pledge something they still owned or controlled. This might include their life, their spouse, their freedom, their body—or under certain religious frameworks, even their salvation, their soul, or their peace in the afterlife. In ancient Egypt, for example, even the corpse of a debtor could be denied rest in the grave if the debt remained unpaid—a particularly grave matter from the Egyptian perspective.

Moreover, creditors were often granted the legal right to inflict pain or torture on the debtor's body as a form of repayment. They might cut off an amount of flesh proportionate to the debt owed. This practice gave rise to elaborate, often grotesque systems of valuation for different body parts, which were meticulously detailed and legally sanctioned. Such schemes reflect the harsh precision with which early societies attempted to ensure the fulfillment of obligations.

A step forward in legal thinking—and an indicator of a freer, less pedantic, and more Roman perspective on law—can be seen in the Roman Code of the Twelve Tables. It stated that the amount creditors could cut off in such cases did not matter: "si plus minusve secuerunt, ne fraude esto" ("if more or less is cut, it shall not be considered fraud").

Let us unpack the logic behind this entire system of equivalence. It is, indeed, a strange and revealing logic. The equivalence here does not consist of direct compensation for the injury— no payment in money, land, or goods. Instead, the creditor is compensated with a kind of emotional satisfaction. This is the satisfaction of exercising power over someone powerless, the perverse pleasure of inflicting harm simply for the sake of doing so—" de faire le mal pour le plaisir de le faire" ("to do harm for the pleasure of doing it"). This joy in cruelty is often most intense for creditors of lower social standing, as it allows them a fleeting sense of power and superiority. For them, it might even feel like a foretaste of a higher social position.

By punishing the debtor, the creditor momentarily participates in the privileges of the ruling class. For once, the creditor experiences the gratifying sense of being able to despise and mistreat another being as an "inferior." Even when the power to punish has already been transferred to authorities, the creditor still enjoys witnessing the debtor being despised and punished. Thus, compensation for the creditor is effectively a claim to cruelty—a right to exercise or benefit from the infliction of suffering.

It is within the realm of contractual law that we find the origins of the entire moral framework surrounding ideas such as "guilt," "conscience," "duty," and the "sacredness of duty." As with all great beginnings in human history, this moral world is steeped in blood. Should we not also acknowledge that this world has never entirely lost its connection to blood and torture—not even in the philosophy of old Kant, whose categorical imperative carries the faint yet unmistakable scent of cruelty?

In this same domain of contracts arose the dark and perhaps inseparable link between the ideas of "guilt" and "suffering." But why, again, can suffering serve as compensation for "owing"? Because the infliction of suffering brings an intense kind of satisfaction. The injured party receives, in exchange for their loss (and the frustration accompanying it), an extraordinary compensation: the pleasure of inflicting pain. This act becomes a feast for the senses—a reward that grows all the more delectable the greater the disparity in rank and social standing between creditor and debtor.

These are speculative thoughts, of course, for it is difficult, both intellectually and emotionally, to delve into such depths. The crude notion of "revenge" often introduced as a connecting concept only obscures the issue rather than clarifying it. Revenge merely redirects us to the same question: Why does inflicting suffering bring satisfaction?

It is unsettling—perhaps repellent—to the sensibilities of modern, "tame" humans (ourselves included) to fully confront how deeply cruelty once permeated human joy and pleasure. Ancient man, with a simplicity and innocence we might now find shocking, openly embraced cruelty as a natural and delightful part of life. He even institutionalized "disinterested malice" (what Spinoza calls sympathia malevolens) as a fundamental trait of human nature, something the conscience could unreservedly approve.

The more insightful observer will already have recognized this primal and enduring joy in cruelty. In Beyond Good and Evil (Aphorism 188) and earlier in The Dawn of Day (Aphorisms 18, 77, 113), I have cautiously hinted at the ongoing "spiritualization" and "deification" of cruelty that runs through the entire history of higher civilizations—indeed, that largely defines it. The time is not so distant when royal weddings or grand national celebrations were unthinkable without accompanying executions, tortures, or perhaps an auto- da-fé. Similarly, aristocratic households often required the presence of a victim—someone to be baited and tormented for the amusement of the household.

Consider Don Quixote at the court of the Duchess. Today, we read Don Quixote with a bitter taste in our mouths, almost as if we are enduring a form of torture. This reaction would have been utterly foreign to Cervantes and his contemporaries, who saw the book as one of the most joyful of all comedies, a work to laugh at until they could laugh no more.

The sight of suffering soothes; the act of inflicting suffering soothes even more. This harsh principle is ancient, powerful, and fundamentally human. Perhaps even apes would agree, as they seem to demonstrate in their own inventions of bizarre cruelties— acts that prefigure and foreshadow their future humanity. Without cruelty, there can be no feast. This lesson comes from the oldest and most enduring history of mankind. Even in punishment, there has always been something of the festive.

Considering these ideas, I must clarify—let me say this in passing—that I am fundamentally opposed to providing pessimists with more fuel for their mills of dissatisfaction and despair. On the contrary, it should be emphasized that when humanity was unashamed of its cruelty, life was brighter and more vibrant than it is now, in this age of pessimism. The darkening of human existence has always paralleled the growth of man's shame in himself. The weary, pessimistic outlook, the suspicion that life itself is a problem, the icy denial born of boredom and disgust—these are not the signs of humanity's most depraved era. Rather, they bloom, like swamp flowers, only when the swamp itself comes into being— when diseased refinement and over- moralization take root, teaching "animal man" to feel ashamed of his instincts.

On the path to becoming "angelic" (to avoid using a harsher term), humanity has developed a kind of moral dyspepsia, complete with a sickly stomach and coated tongue. These have rendered not only the joy and innocence of animal existence repugnant to him but also life itself. At times, humanity stands before itself in revulsion, pinching its nose as though life stinks. Pope Innocent III's infamous list of human horrors—"unclean generation, loathsome nutrition in the womb, the vile material from which man develops, the stench of excretion, saliva, urine, and feces"— captures this attitude perfectly.

Today, suffering is trotted out as the ultimate argument against existence, the most damning indictment of life. How different this is from earlier times when people thought quite the opposite. They valued the infliction of suffering, seeing it as something magical and even a seductive lure to life itself.

Perhaps, for the more sensitive souls among us, it will be comforting to hear that pain may not have hurt as much in those days as it does now. Any physician who has treated individuals of less "refined" cultures (for instance, some African groups taken to represent prehistoric man) might confirm this. These patients, even when suffering from severe internal inflammations that would drive a modern European to the brink of despair, often endure their pain with surprising resilience. Pain simply does not have the same impact on them.

Indeed, the curve of human sensitivity to pain seems to drop dramatically, almost suddenly, once one steps beyond the narrow band of over-civilized humanity. I am personally convinced that a single painful night endured by a highly-strung, cultured woman might well outweigh the collective suffering of all the animals subjected to scientific experiments with knives.

Even now, the human craving for cruelty has likely not disappeared—it has merely been transformed. With pain now more keenly felt, this impulse has undergone a kind of sublimation and refinement. It has been redirected to the realm of imagination and the psyche, camouflaged by euphemisms so artfully contrived that even the most delicate and hypocritical consciences remain oblivious to their true nature. Terms like "tragic pity" and "the nostalgia of the cross" are among these deceptive labels, concealing the enduring appetite for cruelty beneath a veil of moral respectability.

What truly stirs indignation against suffering is not the suffering itself but its apparent senselessness. This sense of meaninglessness, however, was absent in Christianity, which framed suffering as part of a grand, mysterious system of salvation. Nor did it exist for the naive ancient peoples, who found meaning in suffering from the perspective of the spectator or the one inflicting the pain. To remove the notion of hidden, unseen suffering from the world, it became almost essential to invent gods and a hierarchy of beings—figures who could wander through secret places, peer into darkness, and never miss an intriguing or painful spectacle. Through these inventions, life managed a remarkable feat: the justification of itself, including its evils.

In our time, such justifications might require different devices (such as framing life as a riddle or a problem to be solved). But for primitive people, the logic was simple: "Every evil is justified if a god can find it edifying." And was this sentiment truly limited to primitive people? Hardly. The idea of gods as connoisseurs of cruelty extends deeply into our European civilization, even today. One might recall the perspectives of Luther or Calvin in this context. It is certain, at any rate, that even the Greeks found no greater spice for the happiness of their gods than the delights of cruelty.

What mood, one wonders, does Homer ascribe to his gods as they gaze upon the fates of mortals? What ultimate meaning lies behind the Trojan War and other such tragic horrors? There can be no doubt: these events were conceived as festival games for the gods. Moreover, since poets are of a more "godlike" breed than ordinary men, such events were also games for the poets themselves. Later, in the same spirit, Greek moral philosophers envisioned the gods' eyes fixed upon the moral struggles, heroism, and self-torture of virtuous humans. Heracles, embodying the duty-bound hero, performed on a stage and was fully conscious of his audience. For this society of actors, virtue without witnesses was utterly unthinkable.

Indeed, how could one not conclude that the bold and fateful invention of "free will"—a concept then entirely new to Europe—was created specifically to justify the notion that the gods' interest in human virtue and vice was boundless? This invention ensured that the stage of the free-will world would never lack truly fresh, novel, and exciting situations, dramatic conflicts, and catastrophic endings. In contrast, a world governed entirely by deterministic principles would be too predictable for the gods and would quickly bore them. This was reason enough for the philosophers of the time—those loyal allies of the gods—to reject the idea of a deterministic universe.

All of ancient humanity was steeped in consideration for the spectator, embodying a world where public display and theatricality were central. For them, happiness was inseparable from spectacles and festivals. And, as mentioned before, even in acts of great punishment, there was something inherently celebratory, a ritual festivity woven into the spectacle of human suffering.

The sense of "ought," of personal obligation (to return to our inquiry), originated in the oldest and most fundamental personal relationship: the relationship between buyer and seller, creditor and debtor. In this context, one individual confronted another, measuring themselves against each other. No stage of human civilization, however primitive, has been found to lack some trace of this relationship. Setting prices, assessing values, calculating equivalents, and exchanging goods—these activities dominated the earliest human thoughts so thoroughly that they essentially constituted the very act of thinking itself.

It was in this sphere that the first form of human intelligence developed, along with humanity's earliest sense of pride and superiority over other animals. Perhaps even our word "Mensch" (manas) retains a hint of this self-pride: it identified man as the creature who measures and values, the assessing animal par excellence.

Commerce—sale and purchase—along with the psychological processes they entail, predates any organized form of society or community. Instead, the awareness of exchange, trade, debt, obligation, and compensation first emerged from the most basic forms of individual interaction. This consciousness was then applied to the earliest social groups, particularly in their relations with one another. It extended the practice of comparing force against force, measuring, and calculating.

Man's focus was shaped by this perspective, and with the unyielding consistency typical of ancient thought—slow to start but relentless in its course—humanity soon arrived at a sweeping generalization: everything has a price, everything can be paid for. This concept formed the oldest and most straightforward moral code of justice and laid the foundation for ideas of fairness, goodwill, and objectivity in the world.

In this early stage, justice was essentially an agreement between individuals or groups of roughly equal power to settle disputes and restore balance through mutual understanding. As for the weaker parties, justice often involved compelling them to accept terms of settlement imposed by the stronger. This basic willingness—or enforced necessity—to come to terms marked the beginnings of what we now call fairness and equity.

When viewed through the lens of antiquity (and this kind of antiquity can arise or reemerge in any era), the relationship between the community and its members resembles that of a creditor to its debtors. Man lives within a community, enjoying its benefits—what tremendous benefits these are, though we sometimes underestimate them today. He lives protected, spared, in peace and trust, shielded from the dangers and hostilities that constantly threaten those outside the community, the "peaceless" ones. (A German might recognize this from the original meaning of the word Elend, signifying "exile" or being without a homeland.) This security is granted because the individual has pledged himself to the community, entering into obligations in exchange for this protection from harm and enmity.

But what happens when this agreement is broken? When the individual fails to uphold his obligations, the community—now the wronged creditor—will demand repayment, one way or another. In such cases, the specific harm caused by the offender becomes almost secondary. The true transgression lies in his breach of trust, his breaking of the pact with the entire community, which had granted him its protection and benefits. The criminal is not just someone who fails to repay his debt; he actively attacks his creditor. Consequently, he forfeits not only the advantages and security of communal life but also receives a forceful reminder of just how valuable those benefits were.

The wrath of the injured community strips him of his rights and casts him back into the "wild" status he had previously been protected from. The community rejects him, and in doing so, opens the door for all manner of hostility and vengeance to be unleashed upon him. At this stage of civilization, punishment serves as a grim mimicry of how one treats a despised, defeated enemy. Such an enemy is not only stripped of all rights and protection but also shown no mercy. Here we see the full enactment of vae victis— "woe to the vanquished"— in its most brutal and unrelenting form.

This perspective also explains why war itself, along with its associated sacrificial rituals, has shaped all the forms of punishment that have emerged throughout human history. The treatment of the criminal mirrors the treatment of a conquered foe, embodying the mercilessness and cruelty of a victorious celebration over the defeated.

As a community grows stronger, it begins to view individual offenses as less threatening to its overall stability. The misdeeds of individuals no longer seem as revolutionary or dangerous to the existence of the group as a whole. As a result, the wrongdoer is no longer cast out or subjected to the unrestrained wrath of the community. Instead, the community actively shields and protects the wrongdoer, particularly from the anger of those directly harmed by the offense.

With the evolution of penal law, certain patterns become increasingly evident: efforts are made to moderate the wrath of the injured party, to contain the conflict, and to prevent it from escalating or spreading. The focus shifts toward finding equivalents, settling disputes (compositio), and ultimately attempting to separate the offender from the offense itself. The more powerful and self-assured a community becomes, the more its system of justice softens. Conversely, when a community's stability is threatened or its power diminishes, the harshest and most severe forms of justice tend to resurface.

This dynamic parallels the relationship between creditors and debtors: as the creditor becomes wealthier, they grow more lenient and humane in their dealings. The true measure of their wealth becomes the degree of harm they can endure without genuinely suffering. One can even imagine a society with such immense confidence in its power that it embraces the luxury of allowing wrongdoers to go unpunished. Such a society might say, "What harm do these parasites do to me? Let them live and thrive—I am strong enough to handle it."

Justice, which began with the principle "everything can be paid off, everything must be paid off," eventually transforms into something that allows even those who cannot pay to escape punishment. Like all good things on Earth, justice ultimately undoes itself. This self-destruction of justice bears a charming name: Gr ace. And as is evident, grace remains the privilege of the strongest— their super- law.

A word of caution is necessary here regarding recent attempts to trace the origins of justice back to resentment. Allow me to offer a suggestion to psychologists who wish to study revenge up close: this particular emotion thrives most vibrantly today among anarchists and anti-Semites. Like the hidden violet, it blooms discreetly—though it carries a vastly different scent. Given that similar forces tend to create similar outcomes, it's hardly surprising that such circles often attempt to glorify revenge by rebranding it as justice. The claim seems to be that justice is nothing more than an advanced form of the consciousness of injury, which serves to validate revenge and elevate reactive emotions as a whole.

I have no fundamental objection to reevaluating these reactive emotions— indeed, from a biological perspective, their value has likely been underestimated. However, I wish to highlight that the very spirit of revenge underpins this so- called new scientific "equity." This perspective, while appearing fair at first, quickly dissolves into outright hostility and bias the moment other emotions, particularly those of higher biological value, come into play. These active emotions—like personal ambition and the drive for tangible achievement— deserve far greater scientific recognition than reactive feelings such as hate, envy, and resentment. (E. Dühring's writings, such as Value of Life and Course of Philosophy, are key examples of this bias.)

To address Dühring's claim that justice originates in the realm of reactive feelings: the truth requires us to assert the exact opposite. The final domain that justice conquers is the sphere of reactive emotions. When a truly just individual remains impartial even toward their injurer—when they go beyond being merely calm, restrained, or indifferent—this represents a rare and extraordinary achievement. True justice is an active state. To maintain an objective, clear, and balanced perspective even in the face of insult, contempt, or slander is an extraordinary form of mastery. Such an individual exhibits a profound, gentle clarity—a perfection that is almost beyond human capacity.

That said, even the most just among us is vulnerable to small provocations. A mere hint of malice, hostility, or innuendo is often enough to cloud their objectivity and inflame their emotions. Justice, for all its loftiness, is a delicate and challenging ideal to sustain.

The active man, the attacking, aggressive man, is always a hundred degrees nearer to justice than the man who merely reacts; he certainly has no need to adopt the tactics, necessary in the case of the reacting man, of making false and biased valuations of his object. It is, in point of fact, for this reason that the aggressive man has at all times enjoyed the stronger, bolder, more aristocratic, and also freer outlook, the better conscience. On the other hand, we already surmise who it really is that has on his conscience the invention of the "bad conscience,"— the resentful man! Finally, let man look at himself in history. In what sphere up to the present has the whole administration of law, the actual need of law, found its earthly home? Perchance in the sphere of the reacting man? Not for a minute: rather in that of the active, strong, spontaneous, aggressive man? I deliberately defy the abovementioned agitator (who himself makes this self-confession, "the creed of revenge has run through all my works and endeavours like the red thread of Justice"), and say, that judged historically law in the world represents the very war against the reactive feelings, the very war waged on those feelings by the powers of activity and aggression, which devote some of their strength to damming and keeping within bounds this effervescence of hysterical reactivity, and to forcing it to some compromise. Everywhere where justice is practised and justice is maintained, it is to be observed that the stronger power, when confronted with the weaker powers which are inferior to it (whether they be groups, or individuals), searches for weapons to put an end to the senseless fury of resentment, while it carries on its object, partly by taking the victim of resentment out of the clutches of revenge, partly by substituting for revenge a campaign of its own against the enemies of peace and order, partly by finding, suggesting, and occasionally enforcing settlements, partly by standardising certain equivalents for injuries, to which equivalents the element of resentment is henceforth finally referred. The most drastic measure, however, taken and effectuated by the supreme power, to combat the preponderance of the feelings of spite and vindictiveness—it takes this measure as soon as it is at all strong enough to do so—is the foundation of law, the imperative declaration of what in its eyes is to be regarded as just and lawful, and what unjust and unlawful: and while, after the foundation of law, the supreme power treats the aggressive and arbitrary acts of individuals, or of whole groups, as a violation of law, and a revolt against itself, it distracts the feelings of its subjects from the immediate injury inflicted by such a violation, and thus eventually attains the very opposite result to that always desired by revenge, which sees and recognises nothing but the standpoint of the injured party. From henceforth the eye becomes trained to a more and more impersonal valuation of the deed, even the eye of the injured party himself (though this is in the final stage of all, as has been previously remarked)—on this principle "right" and "wrong" first manifest themselves after the foundation of law (and not, as Duhring maintains, only after the act of violation). To talk of intrinsic right and intrinsic wrong is absolutely nonsensical; intrinsically, an injury, an oppression, an exploitation, an annihilation can be nothing wrong, inasmuch as life is essentially (that is, in its cardinal functions) something which functions by injuring, oppressing, exploiting, and annihilating, and is absolutely inconceivable without such a character. It is necessary to make an even more serious confession:—viewed from the most advanced biological standpoint, conditions of legality can be only exceptional conditions, in that they are partial restrictions of the real life-will, which makes for power, and in that they are subordinated to the life-will's general end as particular means, that is, as means to create larger units of strength. A legal organisation, conceived of as sovereign and universal, not as a weapon in a fight of complexes of power, but as a weapon against fighting, generally something after the style of Duhring's communistic model of treating every will as equal with every other will, would be a principle hostile to life, a destroyer and dissolver of man, an outrage on the future of man, a symptom of fatigue, a secret cut to Nothingness.

A word more on the origin and end of punishment—two problems which are or ought to be kept distinct, but which unfortunately are usually lumped into one. And what tactics have our moral genealogists employed up to the present in these cases? Their inveterate naivety. They find out some "end" in the punishment, for instance, revenge and deterrence, and then in all their innocence set this end at the beginning, as the causa fiendi of the punishment, and— they have done the trick. But the patching up of a history of the origin of law is the last use to which the "End in Law" ought to be put. Perhaps there is no more important principle for any kind of history than the following, which, difficult though it is to master, should nonetheless be mastered in every detail.

The origin of the existence of a thing and its final utility, its practical application and incorporation in a system of ends, are completely opposed to each other— everything, anything, which exists and which prevails anywhere, will always be put to new purposes by a force superior to itself, will be commandeered afresh, will be turned and transformed to new uses; all "happening" in the organic world consists of overpowering and dominating, and again all overpowering and domination is a new interpretation and adjustment, which must necessarily obscure or absolutely extinguish the existing "meaning" and "end." The most perfect comprehension of the utility of any physiological organ (or also of a legal institution, social custom, political habit, form in art or in religious worship) does not for a minute imply any simultaneous comprehension of its origin: this may seem uncomfortable and unpalatable to the older men, for it has been the immemorial belief that understanding the final cause or the utility of a thing, a form, an institution, means also understanding the reason for its origin: to give an example of this logic, the eye was made to see, the hand was made to grasp. So even punishment was conceived as invented with a view to punishing. But all ends and all utilities are only signs that a Will to Power has mastered a less powerful force, has impressed thereon out of its own self the meaning of a function; and the whole history of a "Thing," an organ, a custom, can on the same principle be regarded as a continuous "sign- chain" of perpetually new interpretations and adjustments, whose causes, so far from needing to have even a mutual connection, sometimes follow and alternate with each other absolutely haphazard. Similarly, the evolution of a "Thing," of a custom, is anything but its progress to an end, still less a logical and direct progress attained with the minimum expenditure of energy and cost: it is rather the succession of processes of subjugation, more or less profound, more or less mutually independent, which operate on the thing itself; it is, further, the resistance which in each case invariably displays this subjugation, the Protean wriggles by way of defense and reaction, and, further, the results of successful counter-efforts. The form is fluid, but the meaning is even more so—even inside every individual organism, the case is the same: with every genuine growth of the whole, the "function" of the individual organs becomes shifted—in certain cases a partial perishing of these organs, a diminution of their numbers (for instance, through annihilation of the connecting members), can be a symptom of growing strength and perfection.

What I mean is this: even partial loss of utility, decay, and degeneration, loss of function and purpose, in a word, death, are part of the conditions of genuine progress; which always appears in the form of a will and way to greater power, and is always realized at the expense of innumerable smaller powers. The magnitude of a "progress" is gauged by the greatness of the sacrifice it requires: humanity as a mass sacrificed to the prosperity of the one stronger species of Man—that would be a progress. I emphasize all the more this cardinal characteristic of the historic method, for the reason that in its essence it runs counter to predominant instincts and prevailing taste, which must prefer to put up with absolute casualness, even with the mechanical senselessness of all phenomena, than with the theory of a power-will, in exhaustive play throughout all phenomena. The democratic idiosyncrasy against everything which rules and wishes to rule, the modern misarchism (to coin a bad word for a bad thing), has gradually but so thoroughly transformed itself into the guise of intellectualism, the most abstract intellectualism, that even nowadays it penetrates and has the right to penetrate step by step into the most exact and apparently the most objective sciences: this tendency has, in fact, in my view already dominated the whole of physiology and biology, and to their detriment, as is obvious, in so far as it has spirited away a radical idea, the idea of true activity. The tyranny of this idiosyncrasy, however, results in the theory of "adaptation" being pushed forward into the van of the argument, exploited; adaptation— that means to say, a second- class activity, a mere capacity for "reacting"; in fact, life itself has been defined (by Herbert Spencer) as an increasingly effective internal adaptation to external circumstances. This definition, however, fails to realize the real essence of life, its will to power. It fails to appreciate the paramount superiority enjoyed by those plastic forces of spontaneity, aggression, and encroachment with their new interpretations and tendencies, to the operation of which adaptation is only a natural corollary: consequently, the sovereign office of the highest functionaries in the organism itself (among which the life-will appears as an active and formative principle) is repudiated. One remembers Huxley's reproach to Spencer of his "administrative Nihilism": but it is a case of something much more than "administration."

To return to our subject, which is punishment, we need to make two important distinctions: first, the relatively permanent element, the custom, the act, the "drama," a fixed sequence of steps in the process; and second, the more fluid element, the meaning, the purpose, and the expectations that come with the way the procedure works. At this point, we should assume, by analogy (following the historical method we've talked about earlier), that the procedure itself is older than its use in punishment. This use was added and interpreted into the procedure (which had been around for a long time, but with a different meaning). In short, the situation is not what our naïve moral and legal historians have thought—that the procedure was created specifically for punishment, just as the hand was once thought to have been made for grasping. Now, when we look at the second element of punishment, the more fluid one—the meaning of punishment— it's clear that in very advanced societies (for example, in contemporary Europe), punishment doesn't just have one meaning, but rather a complex mix of meanings. The general history of punishment, and how it has been used for many different purposes, eventually comes together in a kind of unity that's difficult to break down into separate parts, and this unity, it should be emphasized, can't be easily defined. (Today, it's impossible to say for sure the exact reason for punishment: all ideas that lump together a whole process in one definition tend to escape definition; only things that have no history can be clearly defined.) In earlier times, however, that collection of meanings was much less fixed and much more flexible; we can see how, in each case, the elements of the meaning shift in importance and position. Sometimes, one meaning will stand out and dominate, and in certain cases, one element (like the goal of deterring crime) might even seem to take over and eliminate all the others. To give a clearer picture of how uncertain, extra, and accidental the meaning of punishment can be, and how one procedure can be used and adapted for very different purposes, I will now provide a list based on relatively small and random examples.

- Punishment as making the criminal harmless and unable to harm others.
- Punishment as a form of compensation for the injury suffered by the victim, in any form, including sentimental compensation.
- Punishment as isolating what disrupts the balance, to stop the disturbance from spreading.
- Punishment as a way to inspire fear in those who decide and carry out the punishment.
- Punishment as a kind of compensation for the benefits the wrongdoer had enjoyed up until that point (for example, when the wrongdoer is forced into slavery in the mines).
- Punishment as removing an element of decay (sometimes even a whole part, as in Chinese laws, for the purpose of purifying the race or preserving a social type).
- Punishment as a festival, where an enemy who has been defeated is violently oppressed and humiliated.

- Punishment as a reminder, either for the person being punished (the so-called "correction") or for the witnesses of the punishment being carried out.
- Punishment as the payment of a fee, required by the power that protects the wrongdoer from the excesses of revenge.
- Punishment as a compromise with the natural act of revenge, in so far as revenge is still seen as a privilege of the stronger groups.
- Punishment as a declaration of war against those who oppose peace, law, order, and authority—those who are fought by society with the weapons of war because they are seen as a danger to the community, as someone who breaks the social contract, as a rebel, a traitor, or someone who disturbs the peace.

This list is clearly not complete; it is obvious that punishment is packed with a variety of purposes. This makes it even more reasonable to dismiss one supposed purpose, which is often considered, at least by most people, to be its most essential purpose. This idea is also the one that still provides the strongest support for the belief in punishment, a belief that is already unsteady for many reasons. Punishment is believed to have the value of awakening in the guilty person a sense of guilt; punishment is seen as the proper tool to create that psychological reaction known as a "bad conscience" or "remorse." However, this theory, even from the perspective of the present day, does not reflect reality or psychology. It is even more inaccurate when we consider the long stretch of human history, particularly the early, primitive periods.

Genuine remorse is undeniably rare among wrongdoers and those who are punished. Prisons and correctional facilities are not the environments where this "worm of remorse" tends to flourish. This is the unanimous conclusion of all honest observers, many of whom arrive at this judgment reluctantly and against their personal expectations. In general, punishment tends to harden and desensitize people. It causes individuals to become more focused and sharpens their awareness of their alienation. It strengthens their ability to resist. When punishment does succeed in breaking a person's spirit and reducing them to a pitiful state of submission and misery, the result is even less healthy than the more typical effects of punishment, which are marked by harshness and grim stubbornness.

When we consider those prehistoric times, we are led to the clear conclusion that punishment actually delayed the development of the sense of guilt—at least among those subjected to the power of punishment. Moreover, we should not underestimate the extent to which the spectacle of legal and enforcement actions prevents the wrongdoer from recognizing that their deed and its nature are inherently wrong. This is because they can plainly see similar actions being carried out in the name of justice, labeled as good, and performed with a clear conscience. These actions include espionage, deceit, bribery, entrapment, and all the cunning and covert strategies employed by law enforcement officers and informants. The system of punishment itself—a system driven not by passion but by principles—relies on acts such as stealing, oppressing, insulting, imprisoning, torturing, and even killing.

The wrongdoer sees all of this and notices that these actions are not treated as inherently blameworthy or condemnable but only as problematic in specific contexts or uses. It was not on this foundation that the "bad conscience," one of the most troubling and fascinating aspects of human nature, came into being. In fact, for a long stretch of history, the idea of dealing with a "guilty person" did not even exist in the minds of those who judged and punished. They saw themselves as dealing with someone who caused harm, an unaccountable force of fate. For the individual on whom punishment fell, it did not bring about any deeper internal suffering. Instead, it was experienced as no different from an unforeseen and unavoidable event, such as a devastating natural disaster, an avalanche that struck without warning, against which no resistance was possible.

This truth crept subtly into the mind of Spinoza, much to the frustration of his commentators (such as Kuno Fischer, for instance, who made great efforts to misunderstand him on this point). One afternoon, as Spinoza sat reflecting on who knows what memories, he began to ponder what remained for him personally of the famous morsus conscientiae—the "sting of conscience." Spinoza, who had dismissed the notions of "good and evil" as products of human imagination, passionately defended the honor of his "free" God against those who blasphemed by claiming that God acted sub r atione boni—in accordance with the concept of good. To Spinoza, such an idea subordinated God to fate, which he considered the greatest absurdity.

For Spinoza, the world had returned to the state of innocence it had known before the discovery of the bad conscience. What, then, became of the morsus conscientiae? He finally defined it for himself as "the opposite of joy—a sadness accompanied by the memory of a past event that turned out contrary to all expectation" (Ethics, Part III, Proposition 18, Scholium I and II). For thousands of years, wrongdoers faced with punishment felt much like Spinoza described regarding their "offense." They thought, "Here is something that went wrong, contrary to what I expected," rather than, "I should not have done this." They accepted punishment in the same way one endures illness, misfortune, or death—with a fatalistic and resigned stubbornness. This kind of acceptance, even today, gives people like the Russians an advantage over Westerners in dealing with the challenges of life.

In those times, if actions were judged critically, the standard was prudence. Punishment's actual effect was primarily to sharpen the sense of prudence, strengthen memory, and encourage a more cautious, secretive, and suspicious approach to life. It taught people to recognize their limitations and inspired a form of self-criticism. Punishment's broader effects on both humans and animals included increasing fear, sharpening cunning, and controlling desires. In this way, punishment tamed people but did not make them "better." In fact, one could argue the opposite: "Injury makes a man cunning," as the saying goes, and as it sharpens cunning, it often makes people worse. Thankfully, it also often makes them less intelligent.

At this point, I must offer a tentative and provisional explanation of my own hypothesis about the origin of the bad conscience. This idea is difficult to fully grasp and requires careful thought, sustained attention, and reflection. I consider the bad conscience to be the serious illness that humanity inevitably developed during its most radical transformation: when people found themselves confined within the structures of society and forced to live in peace.

Just as water-dwelling creatures faced a crisis when they had to either adapt to life on land or face extinction, so too did early humans, who were like half- animals. These creatures had thrived in a world of war, roaming, and adventure, perfectly suited to that wild life. Suddenly, their instincts became useless and "switched off." From that point on, they had to support themselves, to "carry themselves," just as water creatures had to walk on land after being carried by the water. This shift brought a crushing weight upon them. They struggled to obey even the simplest commands. Faced with a new and unfamiliar world, they could no longer rely on the instincts that had unconsciously guided them to safety in the past. Instead, they were forced to think, to reason, to calculate, and to connect causes and effects—relying on their weakest and most unreliable tool, their "consciousness."

I doubt there has ever been such a profound sense of misery in the world, such a feeling of leaden discomfort. Meanwhile, those old instincts did not disappear overnight. They continued to demand satisfaction, but it was now difficult, and often impossible, to fulfill them. Broadly speaking, these instincts were forced to find expression in new, covert ways, like a shadow of their former selves. When instincts cannot find an outlet in the external world, they turn inward. This is what I call the process of man's growing "internalization." It was through this process that what we later called the soul first began to develop.

The inner world of humanity, originally as thin and fragile as if stretched between two layers of skin, now burst open and expanded. It gained depth, breadth, and height as the external outlets for human instincts were blocked. The powerful defenses created by social organization to suppress the old instincts of freedom—especially punishment—forced these instincts to turn back against the human being himself. Feelings like hostility, cruelty, the joy of hunting, the thrill of surprise, destruction, and change—all these were now directed inward, against their possessor. This, I believe, is the origin of the "bad conscience."

Human beings, no longer facing external enemies and obstacles, found themselves trapped in the suffocating monotony and narrowness of social customs. In their frustration, they lashed out at themselves, tormenting, punishing, gnawing at, and terrifying themselves. It was like a wild animal in captivity, smashing itself against the bars of its cage. It was this being, longing desperately for the wild freedom of the past, who turned their inner life into a place of adventure, a chamber of torture, a dangerous and unpredictable desert. This homesick and despairing prisoner created the concept of the "bad conscience."

With this invention, humanity introduced a profound and sinister illness— one from which we have not yet recovered. This is the suffering of humankind caused by its own nature, a sickness born from the violent severing of humanity from its animal past. It was like a sudden, wrenching leap into a new way of life, a rejection of the instincts that had once been the source of human strength, joy, and fearsome power.

Yet, this turning of the human mind against itself produced something so new, so deep, so unprecedented, so complex, and so full of potential that it transformed the very face of the world. This was a phenomenon so dramatic, so paradoxical, so filled with possibilities that only divine observers could truly grasp its significance. The drama that began then is still unfolding, with no clear end in sight. It is too intricate, too extraordinary, too paradoxical to have happened meaninglessly or unnoticed on some random, grotesque planet.

From this moment onward, humanity must be seen as one of the most unexpected and astonishing outcomes of the game played by Heraclitus' "great child," whether you call it Zeus or Chance. Humanity now inspires interest, excitement, and hope. It even gives the impression that it is not the final goal, but a stepping stone, a bridge, an interlude—a great promise of something yet to come.

The hypothesis about the origin of the bad conscience begins with the idea that this transformation was neither gradual nor voluntary. It was not an organic adaptation to new circumstances but rather a rupture, a sudden break, a necessity imposed by fate. This change came without resistance or even a spark of resentment. Furthermore, this transformation—the shaping of a previously unrestrained and chaotic population into a rigid form—was initiated through violence and could only be maintained through violence. The earliest "state" thus emerged as a horrifying tyranny, a relentless and grinding machine that molded the raw, semi-animal masses into something pliable, structured, and disciplined.

By "state," I mean what is self-evident: a herd of blonde beasts of prey—a race of conquerors and rulers. This race, armed with all the tools of war and organization, descended with ferocious claws upon a population that, though numerically much larger, was unformed and nomadic. This is the true origin of the "state." The fanciful theory that the state began with a social contract is easily dismissed. Those who can command, who are natural masters, those whose very being is forceful and decisive—what would they have to do with contracts? These individuals are beyond calculation. They arrive like fate, without cause, without justification or warning. They are like lightning:

too powerful, too sudden, too undeniable, and too alien to even inspire personal hatred.

Such beings instinctively create and impose forms. They are the most involuntary, unconscious artists to exist. Their arrival immediately establishes a living order of sovereignty, one in which roles and functions are defined and assigned. In this order, no part exists unless it serves a meaningful role in relation to the whole. These born organizers are utterly unfamiliar with concepts like guilt, responsibility, or consideration. They embody a terrifying, artistic egoism that shines like polished metal, fully convinced of its eternal justification in its creations, just as a mother sees her child as her unquestionable right.

It was not in these individuals that the bad conscience first grew—this is a fundamental point. Yet, the bad conscience could not have developed without them. For all its repulsiveness, the bad conscience arose because their hammer blows, their violent artistry, expelled a tremendous amount of freedom from the world. This freedom was not destroyed but rendered invisible and latent.

This instinct for freedom, repressed and confined, is the key. The instinct for freedom, forced back, trampled down, imprisoned within itself, and eventually finding expression only within its own confines—this is where the bad conscience begins. It is this imprisonment, this inward turning of freedom, that marks the origin of the bad conscience.

Do not dismiss this phenomenon lightly just because of its initially painful and ugly appearance. At its core, it is the same active force at work on a grander scale in powerful artists and organizers who build states. Here, however, this force operates internally, on a smaller, more personal scale, with a tendency to turn backward on itself. It becomes a bad conscience in what Goethe calls the "labyrinth of the breast." It constructs negative ideals. This is, as I've said, the very same instinct of fr eedom (or, in my own terms, the will to power). The only difference is the material on which this force is unleashed.

In the grander, external phenomenon, the material is other people— other men. But here, it is man himself, his entire old animal self, that becomes the target.

This secret self-tyranny, this artistic cruelty, this pleasure in shaping oneself as though one were a difficult, resistant, and suffering material—this burning desire to impose a will, a critique, a contradiction, a disdain, or a rejection upon oneself— this dark and dreadful labor of love performed by a soul divided against itself, inflicting suffering upon itself for the delight of suffering, is what we call the active bad conscience. It is this same bad conscience, brimming with creative energy as the source of idealism and imagination, that has ultimately produced an extraordinary wealth of new and astounding beauty and affirmation. Indeed, it might even be said to have given birth to beauty for the first time.

What would beauty be, after all, if its opposite had not first been made conscious? If ugliness had not first declared, "I am ugly"? With this realization, the problem of tracing idealism and beauty in ideas such as selflessness, self- denial, and self-sacrifice becomes much less perplexing. It becomes clear that the original character of the pleasure felt by the selfless, the self-denying, and the self- sacrificing is rooted in cruelty.

This, then, is a preliminary explanation of the origin of "altruism" as a moral value and an outline of the soil from which this value has grown. It is the bad conscience—the will to self-punishment— that creates the conditions necessary for altruism to emerge as a value.

Undoubtedly, the bad conscience is an illness, but it is an illness in the same way that pregnancy is an illness. If we examine the conditions under which this illness reaches its most extreme and profound heights, we can begin to uncover what first brought it into the world. To do this, however, we must take a deep breath and return once more to an earlier perspective.

The relationship in civil law between debtor and creditor (which we have already discussed in detail) has been interpreted in a way that is both historically fascinating and deeply suspicious. It has been reimagined as a relationship between the current generation and its ancestors—a concept that is perhaps more incomprehensible to us today than to any other era. In the original tribal associations of primitive times, each living generation recognized a legal obligation to the generations that came before, especially to the earliest ancestors who founded the family. This obligation was far more than a sentimental one. During the longest period of human history, the mere idea of sentimental obligation was far from certain.

Instead, these early generations believed that their very existence depended on the sacrifices and efforts of their ancestors and that this debt had to be repaid through sacrifices and services. The debt was considered ongoing, growing ever larger, as the ancestors, now regarded as powerful spirits, continued to grant new privileges and advantages to the tribe. Did these benefits come for free? Certainly not, according to the harsh and "mean-souled" mindset of that era. What could be given in return? Sacrifices—at first, nourishment in its most basic form—then festivals, temples, tributes of reverence, and above all, obedience. For all customs, as works of the ancestors, were also seen as their commands and precepts. But was it ever enough to repay the ancestors? The suspicion lingered and grew over time. This suspicion occasionally demanded great acts of atonement, extravagant repayments to the creditors—such as the notorious sacrifices of the firstborn, or the spilling of blood, including human blood.

The fear of the ancestors and the sense of indebtedness to them grew stronger in direct proportion to the success of the tribe. As the tribe became more victorious, independent, respected, and feared, so too did the fear of the ancestors' power increase.

This, not the reverse, is the truth. Every step toward decay, every disaster, and every sign of degeneration or collapse diminished the fear of the ancestors' spirits and eroded the belief in their wisdom, foresight, and presence.

Imagine this crude kind of logic carried to its extreme: the ancestors of the most powerful tribes must, in proportion to the increasing fear they inspire, grow into immense, almost unimaginable figures. They become shrouded in the darkness of divine mystery and are ultimately transformed into gods. Perhaps this is the very origin of the gods: born out of fear! And for those who wish to add, "but also out of piety," it would be difficult to support that claim in relation to the earliest and longest period of human history. It is even harder to maintain with respect to the middle period—the formative era of aristocratic races. These aristocratic races repaid their founders, their ancestors (now seen as heroes or gods), with interest, attributing to them all the qualities they themselves developed over time—the qualities of the aristocrat.

Later, we will briefly examine the process of ennobling and elevating the gods (which is quite different from their sanctification). For now, however, let us follow to its conclusion this development of the consciousness of "owing."

According to historical accounts, the sense of owing a debt to the deity did not vanish with the disintegration of clan-based social structures. Just as humanity inherited the concepts of "good" and "bad" from the aristocratic nobility—along with their tendency to create social distinctions—it also inherited from the racial and tribal gods the oppressive burden of unpaid debts and the enduring desire to repay them. This inheritance was transmitted through vast populations of slaves and bondsmen, who, whether by force or through submission and imitation, adopted the religions of their masters. Through this channel, these inherited obligations spread across the world.

For centuries, the feeling of debt owed to the deity grew steadily, keeping pace with the growing prominence and exaltation of the idea of God among humanity. (The entire history of ethnic conflicts, triumphs, reconciliations, and amalgamations— everything leading to the eventual merging of social elements into grand racial syntheses—

is reflected in the chaotic genealogies of their gods, in myths of battles, victories, and reconciliations. Progress toward universal empires consistently corresponds to progress toward universal deities; despotism, by crushing the independence of the nobility, always clears the path for some form of monotheism.)

The advent of the Christian God, the most exalted deity to date, simultaneously brought with it the greatest degree of guilt consciousness. Now, if humanity has begun a reversal of this trajectory, there is reason to believe that the gradual decline in belief in the Christian God has corresponded to a significant decline in humanity's sense of moral obligation. Indeed, we can foresee the complete triumph of atheism as potentially liberating humanity from this feeling of obligation to its origin—its causa prima. Atheism might usher in a kind of second innocence, a fresh beginning free of this burden.

This, then, is a rough outline of the connection between the concepts of "ought" (owing) and "duty" with the foundations of religion. Up until now, I have deliberately avoided addressing the moralization of these concepts—their integration into the bad conscience, or more specifically, the fusion of the bad conscience with the idea of God. In the last paragraph, I even implied that such moralization did not occur and that these ideas would naturally dissipate as faith in the "creditor," in God, eroded. However, the reality is far grimmer.

The moralization of "ought" and "duty," their absorption into the bad conscience, marked the first attempt to reverse the development we have described—or at least to halt its progress. At this point, even the hope of eventual redemption is locked away in the prison of pessimism. Here, humanity's gaze recoils hopelessly from an unyielding impossibility. The concepts of "guilt" and "duty" turn backward—but against whom? There can be no doubt: they turn primarily against the debtor, the "ower," in whom the bad conscience takes root, expands, and consumes everything like a parasitic growth.

As the impossibility of repaying the debt becomes undeniable, so too arises the idea of the impossibility of atonement. This leads to the concept of inexpiable guilt—the notion of "eternal punishment."

Eventually, the bad conscience turns against the creditor as well. Whether this creditor is seen as the causa prima of humanity— the origin of the human race, its father, now cursed ("Adam," "original sin," "the bondage of the will")— or as Nature itself, the womb from which humanity emerged, and which is now held responsible for the principle of evil (the "demonization of Nature")—or as existence in general, viewed as an absurd and unbearable burden. This logic leads to nihilistic despair: the rejection of life, the desire for nothingness, or for some other form of existence, as seen in Buddhism and similar philosophies.

It is here that humanity arrives at a paradoxical and terrifying solution: the ingenious creation of Christianity. In this system, God sacrifices himself for humanity's debt. God pays himself by offering his own flesh. God, the ultimate creditor, becomes the scapegoat for his debtor—all out of love. Can you believe it? Out of love for his debtor!

The reader may already have guessed what unfolded both on the stage and behind the scenes of this drama. The will for self- torture— the turned-inward cruelty of human beings, who, once introspective and frightened by their confinement (caged within the framework of "the State" as part of their taming)—gave rise to the bad conscience as a way to hurt themselves when their natural outlet for cruelty was blocked. This man of the bad conscience seized upon the religious hypothesis to drive his self-inflicted torment to unimaginable extremes.

The idea of owing a debt to God became his tool for self- torture. In God, he imagined the ultimate antithesis to his own ineradicable animal instincts. He reinterpreted these instincts as offenses against what he "owes" to God—as hostility, rebellion, and defiance toward the "Lord," the "Father," the "Creator," the very "Beginning of the world." He trapped himself in the agonizing contradiction between "God" and "Devil." Every denial he wished to make against himself, against his nature, his naturalness, and his very reality, he twisted into an affirmation of God's existence. He transformed these negations into declarations of God's holiness, judgment, punishment, and transcendence— into eternal torment, infinite guilt, and unending hell.

This represents a madness of the will in the realm of psychological cruelty unlike anything else. Humanity's will to find itself guilty and beyond forgiveness, its will to think of itself as punished without any possibility of atonement, and its will to poison the foundations of the universe with the problem of guilt and punishment—all serve to trap humanity within this labyrinth of fixed ideas. It is a will to construct an ideal—that of the "holy God"—before which humanity can eternally prove its unworthiness.

Alas, for this despairing and deranged creature called man! What wild fantasies it conjures, what fits of perversity, hysterical irrationality, and mental savagery erupt whenever it is restrained from being the beast of action! All of this is deeply fascinating, yet it is also dark, oppressive, and draining, compelling us to resist gazing too long into these depths. Here is a sickness, undoubtedly the most horrifying disease that has ever afflicted humanity.

And if someone still has the capacity to hear—though modern man now often turns a deaf ear to such things—they may recognize that, within this night of torment and absurdity, the cry of love once echoed. It was the cry of the most intense ecstasy, the yearning for redemption through love. But anyone who truly listens to this cry recoils in unspeakable horror. For within humanity, there is so much that is monstrous. For far too long, the world has been a madhouse.

Let this be sufficient, once and for all, regarding the origin of the "holy God." The idea of gods does not inherently lead to the degradation of human imagination that we have just described. The fact that there are nobler ways to use the concept of gods—ways that do not involve the self-crucifixion and self- debasement of humanity, which has characterized the last two thousand years of Europe—remains clear. We only need to look at the Greek gods to see this. These gods were reflections of noble and grand men, mirrors in which the animal within humanity felt deified rather than destroyed by inward madness.

The Greeks used their gods in a completely different way. For them, the gods served as buffers against the "bad conscience," allowing them to preserve their inner freedom. This stands in stark contrast to Christianity's approach to its god. The Greeks, those magnificent and courageous people, embraced this principle wholeheartedly. Even the Homeric Zeus himself occasionally reminded them not to take life too lightly. Take, for instance, his commentary on the case of Aegisthus, a truly egregious example:

"Wonderful how they grumble, the mortals against the immortals.

They claim all evil comes from us, yet in their folly, They fashion their own doom, against all fate."

Yet note how this Olympian observer and judge is neither angry with mortals nor condemns them. Instead, he views their misdeeds with a certain amused detachment. "How foolish they are," he seems to think. For the Greeks, even in their strongest and most valiant era, the causes of evil and disaster were not rooted in sin but in folly, in imprudence, in a kind of temporary disturbance of the mind. Folly, not sin—do you see the distinction?

Even this "brain disturbance," however, presented a puzzle to the Greeks. "How could this happen?" they wondered. "How could such foolishness find its way into the minds of men like us— men of noble ancestry, men of wealth, men with fine natural gifts, men of the best upbringing, men of virtue?" For centuries, the Greek aristocracy asked this question whenever one of their peers committed some incomprehensible outrage or act of sacrilege. Eventually, they settled on an answer: "It must be that a god has deceived him," they concluded, nodding their heads.

This solution is quintessentially Greek. In their worldview, the gods did not punish humanity for its failings; instead, they took upon themselves the responsibility for human guilt. This approach justified human actions to a certain extent, even when those actions were evil. In those days, the gods were not seen as dispensers of punishment but as bearers of guilt—a role far nobler than that of executioner.

I conclude with three questions, as you will notice. "Is an ideal being established here, or is one being torn down?" you may ask. But have you truly considered the cost of creating every ideal in the history of the world? How much truth has had to be distorted and misunderstood, how many lies have been sanctified, how much conscience disturbed, and how many sacrifices of "God" have been made each time? To build a sanctuary, another must be destroyed— this is an unyielding law. Show me a single instance where it has not held true!

We modern men have inherited an ancient tradition of vivisecting our consciences and inflicting cruelty on our natural, animal selves. This is where we have undergone our most rigorous training, where we have perhaps honed our artistic talents—or, at the very least, indulged our dilettantism and perverted tastes. For far too long, humanity has regarded its natural instincts with suspicion, branding them as evil. Over time, these instincts have become intertwined with the bad conscience.

Wouldn't it be possible to attempt the opposite? Couldn't we attach this bad conscience to all our unnatural inclinations—our transcendental aspirations that oppose sense, instinct, nature, and our very humanity? Couldn't we apply it to all the ideals, past and present, that reject life and defame the world? But who today would be strong enough to undertake such a reversal? To whom could one turn with such aspirations?

It is precisely the "good" people who would rise against us if we tried. Alongside them would be the indolent, the conformists, the vain, the hysterical, and the weary. Nothing is more alienating or offensive than hinting at the stern rigor with which we treat ourselves. And yet, how readily the world embraces us when we simply "let ourselves go" and do as it does. For such a transformation, we would need spirits of an entirely different caliber than those of this feeble and introspective age—spirits strengthened by wars and victories, who crave conquest, adventure, danger, and even suffering.

Such spirits would need to be accustomed to rarefied air, to the sharpness of winter wanderings, to both literal and metaphorical ice and mountains. They would need a sublime malice, a supreme and conscious audacity born of great health. In summary, they would require nothing less than this great health.

Is this even conceivable today? Perhaps not. But someday, in an age stronger than this decaying and inward-looking present, such a redeemer must come. This redeemer, a spirit of great love and great scorn, will create anew. Driven by his own power, he will rebound from every transcendental ideal, not to escape reality but to penetrate it. Diving deep into existence, he will return to the surface with the means to redeem it—redeeming reality from the curse imposed upon it by the old ideal.

This man of the future will free us from the old ideal and its inevitable companions: great nausea, the will to nothingness, and nihilism. He will be the herald of a new dawn, restoring freedom to the will, purpose to the world, and hope to humanity. He will be the Antichrist and the Antinihilist, the conqueror of God and Nothingness. He must come.

But what am I saying? Enough. Enough! At this moment, the only course left to me is silence—otherwise, I overstep into a realm that belongs to someone younger, stronger, more "future" than I. This realm belongs to Zarathustra, Zarathustra the godless.

Chapter 3
What Is the Meaning of Ascetic Ideals?

What is the meaning of ascetic ideals? For artists, they mean either nothing or far too much. For philosophers and scholars, they reflect a kind of instinct or "flair" for the conditions that best support advanced thinking and intellectual pursuits. For women, at best, they add an extra layer of charm, a faint touch of delicacy on a beautiful body, the angelic quality of a plump, attractive creature. For those who are physically weak or chronic complainers (the majority of humanity), they serve as a way to appear "too good" for the world, a holy excuse for indulgence. Ascetic ideals become their main weapon in dealing with lingering pain and boredom. For priests, they represent true priestly belief, their greatest tool of power, and the ultimate justification for that power. For saints, ascetic ideals offer a reason for retreat, a longing for the ultimate glory of nothingness—"God"—and serve as a form of madness.

Yet, the fact that ascetic ideals have meant so much to humanity reveals something fundamental about the human will: its horror of emptiness. Humans need a goal, and they would rather will nothingness than have no will at all. Do you understand me? Have I made myself clear? No? "Certainly not, sir?" Well, let's start over from the beginning.

What is the meaning of ascetic ideals? Or, to take a specific example I've often been asked about: why would an artist like Richard Wagner embrace chastity in his later years? True, he had always done so in a certain way, but only near the end of his life did he do so in a fully ascetic sense. What explains this change, this complete reversal in his attitude? Wagner turned into the opposite of what he had been. What does it mean when an artist transforms into their own opposite? Let's pause to consider this question.

Think back to the boldest, happiest, and most creative period of Wagner's life. This was when he was deeply involved with the idea of

Luther's Wedding. Who knows what twist of fate led us to have The Master singer s instead of this wedding music? And how much of the latter might still echo the former? There is no doubt, however, that Luther 's Wedding would have celebrated chastity. Yet, it would also have celebrated sensuality, and it would have been entirely fitting— entirely Wagnerian. There is no inherent contradiction between chastity and sensuality. Every true marriage, every genuine and heartfelt love, transcends this division.

I believe Wagner could have shown his fellow Germans this beautiful reality through a daring and elegant "Luther Comedy." It would have reminded them that chastity and sensuality can coexist, even complement each other. Among the Germans, there have always been many critics of sensuality, but perhaps Luther's greatest achievement was his courage to embrace it. He called it, quite charmingly, "evangelical freedom." Even in situations where the conflict between chastity and sensuality does arise, there is no reason for it to be tragic. At least, this should be true for those who are healthy in both mind and body, who do not see the balance between "animal" and "angel" as a fundamental challenge to life itself. The most brilliant spirits, such as Goethe and Hafiz, even found this balance to be one of life's greatest charms. These so-called "conflicts" can actually make life more alluring.

On the other hand, it is painfully clear that when broken, miserable people worship chastity, they do so because it represents the opposite of what they are. They see chastity as the antithesis of their own ruined nature. And when such people worship chastity, the result is tragic. You can imagine the desperate grunting and pathetic eagerness with which they embrace it. They celebrate this painful, unnecessary conflict, the very conflict Wagner seemed to want to set to music and display on stage in his later years. But why? What purpose could it possibly serve? What did these broken souls mean to him? What do they mean to us?

At this point, it's impossible to avoid asking what Wagner really intended with that rustic, unmanly character, that naïve and unfortunate soul, Parsifal, whom he ultimately turned into a Catholic through such dubious means. Was Parsifal meant to be taken seriously? One might hope not—one might even suspect the opposite. Perhaps Wagner intended Parsifal to be a lighthearted farewell, akin to the final act of a trilogy or asatyric drama. Perhaps he, the great tragedian, wanted to bid farewell to us, to himself, and above all to tragedy itself, in a manner fitting his stature: by parodying the very idea of the tragic, mocking the grim seriousness and earthly sorrows of the past. This parody would also mock the most grotesque and unnatural aspects of the ascetic ideal, a phase that he had finally overcome.

Such an interpretation would indeed be worthy of a great tragedian. Every true artist reaches the height of their greatness only when they can look down on themselves and their work, when they can laugh at their own creations. Could Parsifal be Wagner's secret laugh at himself? The triumph of ultimate artistic freedom and transcendence? We might wish it so. For what else could Parsifal amount to if taken seriously? Are we to see in it, as some have suggested, a work driven by an insane hatred of knowledge, reason, and the body? A curse against flesh and spirit uttered in one breath of bitter contempt?

Could Parsifal be Wagner's retreat into the sickly ideals of Christianity, his return to a decayed and obscurantist morality? Was it a self-negation, a complete reversal by an artist who had previously poured all his will into the highest artistic expressions of both soul and body? And not just in his art, but in his life as well? Recall the enthusiasm with which Wagner once followed Feuerbach's teachings. Feuerbach's motto of "healthy sensuality" was, during the 1830s and 1840s, like a word of salvation to Wagner and many other Germans, especially the so-called "Young Germans."

Did Wagner later change his mind about this? It certainly seems that he wanted to change his message on the subject. This shift isn't only apparent in the Parsifal trumpets resounding onstage; it echoes in the somber, constrained, and troubled writings of his later years. In countless passages, Wagner reveals a hidden desire, a hesitant and unspoken will to preach retreat, to advocate for conversion, Christianity, medievalism. It's as if he wanted to say to his followers, "All is vanity! Seek salvation elsewhere!" At one point, he even invokes the "blood of the Redeemer."

What, then, are we to make of all this? Could Wagner's Parsifal truly represent the turning point where he gave up his earlier ideals and turned toward something entirely opposed to what he once stood for? Or is it something else altogether?

This list is certainly not complete; it is obvious that punishment is overloaded with utilities of all kinds. This makes it all the more permissible to eliminate one supposed utility, which passes, at any rate in the popular mind, for its most essential utility, and which is just what even now provides the strongest support for that faith in punishment which is nowadays for many reasons tottering. Punishment is supposed to have the value of exciting in the guilty the consciousness of guilt; in punishment is sought the proper instrumentum of that psychic reaction which becomes known as a "bad conscience," "remorse." But this theory is even, from the point of view of the present, a violation of reality and psychology: and how much more so is the case when we have to deal with the longest period of man's history, his primitive history! Genuine remorse is certainly extremely rare among wrongdoers and the victims of punishment; prisons and houses of correction are not the soil on which this worm of remorse pullulates for choice— this is the unanimous opinion of all conscientious observers, who in many cases arrive at such a judgment with enough reluctance and against their own personal wishes. Speaking generally, punishment hardens and numbs, it produces concentration, it sharpens the consciousness of alienation, it strengthens the power of resistance. When it happens that it breaks the man's energy and brings about a piteous prostration and abjectness, such a result is certainly even less salutary than the average effect of punishment, which is characterised by a harsh and sinister doggedness. The thought of those prehistoric millennia brings us to the unhesitating conclusion, that it was simply through punishment that the evolution of the consciousness of guilt was most forcibly retarded—at any rate in the victims of the punishing power. In particular, let us not underestimate the extent to which, by the very sight of the judicial and executive procedure, the wrong-doer is himself prevented from feeling that his deed, the character of his act, is intrinsically reprehensible: for he sees clearly the same kind of acts practised in the service of justice, and then called good, and practised with a good conscience; acts such as espionage, trickery, bribery, trapping, the whole intriguing and insidious art of the policeman and the informer—the whole system, in fact, manifested in the different kinds of punishment (a system not excused by passion, but based on principle), of robbing, oppressing, insulting, imprisoning, racking, murdering.—All this he sees treated by his judges, not as acts meriting censure and condemnation in themselves, but only in a particular context and application. It was not on this soil that grew the "bad conscience," that most sinister and interesting plant of our earthly vegetation—in point of fact, throughout a most lengthy period, no suggestion of having to do with a "guilty man" manifested itself in the consciousness of the man who judged and punished. One had merely to deal with an author of an injury, an irresponsible piece of fate. And the man himself, on whom the punishment subsequently fell like a piece of fate, was occasioned no more of an "inner pain" than would be occasioned by the sudden approach of some uncalculated event, some terrible natural catastrophe, a rushing, crushing avalanche against which there is no resistance.

What, then, is the meaning of ascetic ideals? In the case of an artist, we are starting to understand their meaning: Nothing at all… or so much that it is almost nothing. So, what is the point of them? For a long time now, artists have not taken an independent enough stance, either in the world or against it, to make their views and the changes in these views worth paying attention to. They have always been the servants of some morality, philosophy, or religion. And, unfortunately, they have often been excessively obedient courtiers to their clients and patrons, and overly curious sycophants to the existing powers, or even to new powers that are rising. To put it simply, they always need a shield, a support, some established authority: artists never stand on their own. Standing alone goes against their deepest instincts. So, for example, when the time came, Richard Wagner took the philosopher Schopenhauer as his shield, his support. Who would even think it possible that he would have had the courage for an ascetic ideal without the backing of Schopenhauer's philosophy, without the authority of Schopenhauer, which ruled Europe in the 1870s? (This is without considering whether an artist could have even existed without the support of an orthodoxy.) This leads us to a deeper question: What does it mean for a real philosopher to embrace the ascetic ideal, a truly independent intellect like Schopenhauer's, a man with the courage to be himself, who knows how to stand alone without waiting for others to protect him, and without needing approval from his superiors? Now, let us think about Schopenhauer's remarkable attitude toward art, an attitude that even fascinates certain types of people. This is clearly the reason why Richard

Wagner suddenly turned to Schopenhauer (as we know, influenced by the poet Herwegh), turning so completely that it caused a major shift in his views, creating a sharp contradiction between his earlier and later aesthetic beliefs. His earlier ideas are expressed in his work *Opera and Drama*, while his later writings, starting in 1870, show his change of heart. In particular, from that time on (and this is the change that most alienates us), Wagner had no hesitation in changing his opinion on the value and role of music itself. What did he care if, until that point, he had seen music as a tool, a medium, a "woman" that needed an end, a "man"—that is, drama—in order to thrive? He suddenly realized that much more could be achieved by applying Schopenhauer's theory to music, in *majorem musicae gloriam*—meaning, through the idea of music's sovereignty, as Schopenhauer understood it. Music was now seen as separate from and opposed to all other arts, as the independent art in itself—not like other arts, which reflect the world of appearances, but as the voice of the will itself, speaking directly from the "abyss" as the most personal, original, and direct expression. This huge increase in the value of music (which seemed to grow from Schopenhauer's philosophy) was accompanied by an unprecedented rise in the status of the musician. He became an oracle, a priest—no, more than a priest, a kind of spokesperson for the "intrinsic essence of things," a messenger from another world. From then on, he spoke not just of music, this ventriloquist of God, but also of metaphysics. So, is it any surprise that, eventually, he spoke of ascetic ideals?

Schopenhauer made use of the Kantian approach to the aesthetic problem—but he certainly did not see it in the same way as Kant. Kant thought that he honored art by emphasizing those qualities of beauty that also contribute to the dignity of knowledge: impersonality and universality. This is not the place to discuss whether this was a complete mistake; all I want to highlight is that Kant, like many other philosophers, did not approach the aesthetic problem from the perspective of the artist (the creator). Instead, he only considered art and beauty from the perspective of the spectator, and in doing so, he unknowingly brought the spectator into the very idea of the "beautiful"! But if only the philosophers of beauty had a better understanding of this "spectator"!—an understanding of him as a great personality, as a rich experience, as a wealth of powerful and most individual events, desires, surprises, and raptures within the realm of beauty! But, as I feared, the opposite was always the case. And so, from the very beginning, we get definitions from philosophers that are burdened with a coarse mistake, like Kant's famous definition of beauty. "That is beautiful," says Kant, "which pleases without interest." Without interest! Now, compare this definition with another, made by a true "spectator" and "artist"—by Stendhal, who once called beauty *une promesse de bonheur*

(a promise of happiness). Here, at the very least, the one point Kant makes in his aesthetic theory—disinterest—is rejected and eliminated. Who is right, Kant or Stendhal? When, after all, our aesthetes never tire of pointing to the fact that under the magic of beauty, men can look at even naked statues of women "without interest," we can certainly laugh a little at their expense. In this respect, the experiences of artists are much more "interesting," and, at any rate, Pygmalion was not necessarily an "unaesthetic man." Let us think all the better of the innocence of our aesthetes, reflected in such arguments. Let us, for example, count as a point in Kant's favor the country-parson naivety of his doctrine on the peculiar character of the sense of touch! And here we return to

Schopenhauer, who was much closer to the arts than Kant was, yet still never fully escaped the Kantian definition. How can this be? The situation is remarkable: he interprets Kant's phrase "without interest" in the most personal way, drawing on an experience that must have been a part of his regular routine. Few topics are discussed with such certainty by Schopenhauer as the workings of aesthetic contemplation: he claims that it simply counteracts sexual interest, like hops and camphor. He never tires of glorifying this escape from the "will to live" as the great advantage and utility of the aesthetic state. In fact, one might be tempted to ask whether his fundamental idea of Will and Idea—the thought that freedom from the "will" can only be achieved through the "idea"—didn't stem from a generalization of this sexual experience. (And, by the way, in all discussions of Schopenhauer's philosophy, one should never forget that it reflects the thinking of a young man of twenty- six, so it carries not only the peculiarities of Schopenhauer's life but also the characteristics of that particular stage in his life.) Let us now listen to one of the most striking passages he wrote in praise of the aesthetic state (from *World as Will and Idea*), and pay attention to the tone, the suffering, the happiness, and the gratitude with which these words are spoken: "This is the painless state that Epicurus praised as the highest good and the state of the gods; during this moment, we are freed from the vile pressure of the will. We celebrate the Sabbath of the will's hard labor, and the wheel of Ixion stands still." What power in the language! What images of agony and long-lasting revulsion!

How extreme is the contrast between "that moment" and everything else— the "wheel of Ixion," "the hard labor of the will," and "the vile pressure of the will." But even if Schopenhauer was absolutely right for himself, how does that help us understand what the beautiful really is? Schopenhauer describes one effect of beauty— the calming of the will—but is this effect something that usually happens? As mentioned before, Stendhal, who had a more balanced and happier nature than Schopenhauer, highlights a different effect of beauty. "The beautiful promises happiness." To him, the excitement that beauty creates in us, the "interest," is what matters most. And doesn't Schopenhauer leave himself open to criticism here, by claiming he understands Kant's view on beauty when he really doesn't? Kant defined beauty as something that pleases without making us feel any personal interest in it. But Schopenhauer actually found beauty interesting—perhaps even through the most personal kind of interest of all, the feeling of relief from suffering, like a tortured person escaping their pain. So, if we return to our original question—"What does it mean for a philosopher to admire ascetic ideals?"—we get our first clue: he wants to escape from suffering.

Let's be careful not to overly focus on the word "torture"—there is definitely room for some criticism and even some humor here. We shouldn't ignore the fact that Schopenhauer, who treated sexuality as an enemy (and even woman, whom he saw as "the instrument of the devil"), needed enemies to keep himself in a good mood. He loved using dark, bitter, and harsh words. He often raged just for the sake of raging, out of sheer passion. Without his enemies—without Hegel, without women, without sensual pleasures, and without the "will to live"—Schopenhauer would have become ill. He would have become a pessimist (although he wasn't really one, despite wanting to be). Without his enemies, he wouldn't have been able to continue at all. He would have given up. But his enemies kept him going. They always dragged him back into life, and his anger, just like that of the ancient

Cynics, was his source of strength, his way of coping, his way of finding relief and happiness.

So much for what is most personal in Schopenhauer's case; on the other hand, there is still a lot that is typical of him— and now we return to our main question. It is an accepted and undeniable fact, as long as there are philosophers in the world, and wherever philosophers have existed (from India to England, for example, at opposite ends of the spectrum of philosophical ability), that philosophers often feel irritated or even angry at sensuality. Schopenhauer is just the most passionate, and if you can listen closely, the most captivating and enchanting example of this. There is also a real philosophical bias and love for the entire ascetic ideal; there should be no illusions about this. Both of these feelings, as I have mentioned, are common in the type of philosopher we are talking about. If a philosopher lacks both of them, you can be sure that he is, at best, only a "pseudo- philosopher."

What does this mean? This situation must first be understood: in itself, it stands there, pointless and unchanging, like any "Thing- in-itself." Every living creature, including the "philosophical beast," naturally strives for the best conditions where it can fully express its power, and experiences the most satisfaction in doing so. Similarly, and with a keen sense that is even sharper than reason, every animal, including humans, instinctively fears any kind of disturbance or obstacle that could block or prevent its ability to reach these optimal conditions (I am not talking about happiness here, but about the way to power, action, and the most powerful actions, which often lead to unhappiness). Likewise, the philosopher deeply fears marriage, along with anything that could lead to it—marriage is seen as a deadly obstacle to reaching the ideal conditions for intellectual freedom.

So far, how many great philosophers have been married? Heraclitus, Plato, Descartes, Spinoza, Leibniz, Kant, Schopenhauer— they were not married, and one can't even imagine them being married. A married philosopher is something of a joke—that is my rule. As for the exception of Socrates—he married out of a kind of ironic humor, seemingly just to prove this very rule. Every philosopher would say, just as Buddha said when he heard that he had a son: "Rahoula has been born to me, a fetter has been forged for me" (Rahoula here means "little demon"); every "free spirit" must have his moment of reflection, just like Buddha did at one point: "Life is too narrow in a house; it is a place of impurity; true freedom is found by leaving the house." Because Buddha thought this way, he left his house.

There are so many ways to seek independence shown in the ascetic ideal, that philosophers can't help but feel joy and excitement when they hear the stories of those who, with great resolve, said no to all forms of servitude and chose to live in the desert— though they may have been, in reality, just strong donkeys, far from strong minds. So, what does the ascetic ideal mean for a philosopher? This is my answer—it probably won't surprise you: when a philosopher sees this ideal, he smiles because he sees it as a perfect condition for the highest and boldest intellectual freedom. By embracing this ideal, he doesn't reject "existence" as a whole; on the contrary, he affirms only his own existence, and perhaps even to the point where he is not far from wishing in a blasphemous way, "let the world perish, but let philosophy, let the philosopher, let me, exist!"

These philosophers, you see, are by no means untainted witnesses or judges of the value of the ascetic ideal. What do they think of themselves—what does the "saint" mean to them? They think of what is most essential to them personally; of freedom from force, disturbance, and noise; freedom from work, responsibilities, and worries; of a clear head; of the flow and freedom of thoughts, like a dance or spring or flight; of good air—fresh, clear, free, dry air, like the air at high altitudes, where every living creature becomes more intellectual and gains wings; they think of peace in every room; of all the hounds neatly chained, with no barking of anger or rough hatred; no regrets from wounded pride; quiet and obedient internal organs, busy like mills, but unnoticed; a heart that is distant, transcendent, future, even posthumous— to sum it up, they mean by the ascetic ideal the joyful asceticism of a deified and newly born animal, one that sweeps through life instead of resting. We know the three main ideas of the ascetic ideal: poverty, humility, chastity; and if you closely examine the lives of all the great, creative, and inventive minds, you will repeatedly find these three qualities, to a certain extent. Not for a moment, of course, as if these were their virtues—what does this type of person have to do with virtues?—but as the most essential and natural conditions of their best existence, their greatest productivity.

In this regard, it is possible that their strong intellectualism had to first control a proud or easily irritated nature, or an excessive sensualism, or that it had to work hard to keep its desire for the "desert" against a temptation for luxury, indulgence, or even a generous and excessive nature. But their intellect did all this because it was the dominant instinct that carried out orders over all the other instincts. It still does: if it stopped, it would simply no longer be dominant. But there is not the slightest trace of "virtue" in all of this. Moreover, the "desert" I just mentioned, where strong, independent, and well-prepared minds retreat to their hermitages—oh, how different it is from the dream of a desert that the cultured classes have! In some cases, the cultured classes themselves are the desert. It is certain that none of the intellectual giants could tolerate this desert for even a minute. It is not romantic enough, not enough like the mystical, Syrian deserts they dream of! Yes, there are still many donkeys here, but the resemblance stops there. But what a desert means today is something more like this—it might be a deliberate obscurity; a way of getting away from one's own self; a fear of noise, fame, papers, influence; a small office, a daily task, something that hides rather than reveals; sometimes associating with harmless, cheerful animals or birds, the sight of which refreshes; a mountain for company, but not a dead one, one that has life (that is, with lakes); and sometimes, even a room in a busy hotel where one can count on not being recognized, and be able to speak freely to everyone—this is the desert—oh, it is lonely enough, believe me! I admit that when

Heraclitus retreated to the courts and halls of the massive temple of Artemis, that "wilderness" was worthier; why do we lack such temples? (Perhaps we do not lack them: I just think of my wonderful study in Piazza di San Marco, in spring, of course, and in the morning, between ten and twelve.)

But what Heraclitus avoided is still what we try to avoid today: the noise and endless chatter of the Ephesians, their politics, their news from the "empire" (which I mean, of course, Persia), their market-trade in "the things of today"— for there is one thing from which we philosophers especially need rest—from the things of "today." We honor the quiet, the cold, the noble, the distant, the past—everything that, in fact, does not force the soul to tense up and defend itself— something we can connect with without needing to speak out loud. Just listen to the way a spirit speaks; each spirit has its own tone and loves its own tone. That one over there, for example, must be an agitator, a hollow mind, an empty vessel: whatever goes into him, everything comes back from him dull and thick, heavy with the echo of an empty space. That spirit over there almost always speaks hoarsely: has he, perhaps, thought himself hoarse? Maybe so—ask the physiologists—but he who thinks in words, thinks as a speaker, not as a thinker (this shows that he does not think about objects or think objectively, but only about his relationship with objects—that, in fact, he only thinks of himself and his audience). This third one speaks aggressively, coming too close to us, his breath touching us—we involuntarily shut our mouths, even though he is speaking to us through a book: his tone of style explains why—he has no time, he has little faith in himself, and he thinks this is his one chance to express himself. But a spirit who is sure of himself speaks softly; he seeks privacy, he lets himself be awaited. A philosopher is recognized by the fact that he avoids three bright and noisy things—fame, princes, and women—which is not to say that they do not come to him. He avoids any glaring light: that is why he avoids his time and its "daylight." In this way, he is like a shadow; the lower the sun sinks, the longer and darker the shadow becomes. As for his humility, he accepts, just as he accepts darkness, a certain dependence and obscurity: also, he fears the shock of lightning, he shudders at the danger of a tree that is too isolated and too exposed, where every storm blows with full force. His "maternal" instinct, his secret love for that which grows within him, leads him into states where he is relieved from the need to take care of himself, much like the "mother" instinct in women has always kept women in a dependent position. After all, philosophers demand very little; their favorite motto is, "He who possesses is possessed." All of this is not, as I must say again and again, due to a virtue, or a worthy desire for moderation and simplicity: but because their highest master demands it of them, demands it wisely and relentlessly; their master who cares for only one thing, and for which he gathers and hoards everything—time, strength, love, attention. This type of man does not like to be disturbed by enemies, nor by friends; he is a person who forgets or despises easily. He finds it bad form to play the martyr, "to suffer for the truth"—he leaves all of that to the ambitious, to the stage-heroes of the intellect, and to everyone, in fact, who has enough time for such luxuries (the philosophers themselves have real work to do for truth). They use big words sparingly; they are said to dislike the word "truth" itself: it sounds too pompous. Finally, when it comes to the chastity of philosophers, the creativity of this type of mind clearly lies in a different area than that of having children; perhaps in some other area as well, they achieve a kind of immortality, a small, lasting legacy (philosophers in ancient India would be even bolder in expressing this: "What use is posterity to someone whose soul is the world?"). In this mindset, there is no trace of chastity because of any ascetic belief or hatred of the body, just as an athlete or jockey's abstaining from women is not really chastity. It is simply the will of the dominant instinct, at least during their period of deep philosophical reflection. Every artist understands how sexual activity can harm the mind during times of intense focus and preparation; for the greatest artists and those with the most refined instincts, this is not necessarily learned through hard experience—it is just their "maternal" instinct, which, in order to nurture the growing work, carelessly uses up (beyond all its usual resources) the strength of their physical life; the stronger power then takes over the weaker. Let's now apply this idea to Schopenhauer, a case we have already discussed: for him, the sight of beauty acted like a kind of irritant that triggered the main power of his nature (the power of deep thought and intense focus); so this strength erupted and suddenly took control of his consciousness. But this doesn't rule out the possibility that the special sweetness and fullness of the aesthetic state, which is linked to sensuality (just like the "idealism" seen in young girls at puberty), could also come from this same source. Therefore, it may be that sensuality isn't removed when the aesthetic state arises, as Schopenhauer thought, but instead, it transforms and no longer enters the mind as sexual desire. (I will come back to this point later, when discussing the more detailed aspects of the physiology of the aesthetic experience, a topic that has been largely unexplored and not well explained up until now.)

A certain asceticism, a serious yet joyful renunciation, is, as we have seen, one of the most favorable conditions for the highest intellectualism. And, as a result, it will not surprise us that philosophers, in particular, always have a certain affection for the ascetic ideal. A serious historical investigation shows that the bond between the ascetic ideal and philosophy is even tighter and stronger than we might expect. It could be said that it was only in the leading strings of this ideal that philosophy really learned to take its first steps and baby paces—oh, how clumsily, oh, how crossly, oh, how ready to tumble down and lie flat was this shy little creature with its bandy legs! The early history of philosophy is like that of all good things; for a long time, they lacked the courage to be themselves. They kept always looking around to see if anyone would come to their help; moreover, they were afraid of everyone who looked at them. Just enumerate in order the particular tendencies and virtues of the philosopher— his tendency to doubt, his tendency to deny, his tendency to wait (to be "ephectic"), his tendency to analyze, search, explore, dare, his tendency to compare and to equalize, his will to be neutral and objective, his will for everything to be "without anger and prejudice."

Has it yet been realized that for quite a long time, these tendencies were opposed to the first demands of morality and conscience? (Let us not even speak of reason, which even Luther called "Frau Klüglin," the sly whore.) Has it yet been recognized that a philosopher, upon arriving at self-consciousness, must indeed feel himself an incarnate "we strive for the forbidden," and thus guard himself against "his own sensations," against self-consciousness? It is, I repeat, the same with all good things, on which we now pride ourselves; even judged by the standard of the ancient Greeks, our whole modern life, as far as it is not weakness but strength and the awareness of strength, appears as pure "Hybris" and godlessness. The things that are the complete opposite of those we honor today have long had conscience on their side and God as their guardian. "Hybris" is our entire attitude toward nature nowadays, our violation of nature with the help of machinery, and all the unscrupulous inventiveness of our scientists and engineers. "Hybris" is our attitude toward God, that is, toward some alleged teleological and moral spider behind the webs of the great trap of cause and effect. Like Charles the Bold in his war with Louis the Eleventh, we could say, "I fight the universal spider"; "Hybris" is our attitude toward ourselves—for we experiment on ourselves in a way we would not allow with any animal, and with curiosity, we open our souls in our living bodies: what does the "salvation" of the soul matter to us now? We heal ourselves later: being ill is instructive, we do not doubt it, even more instructive than being well—inoculators of disease seem to us today even more necessary than any medicine-men or "saviors." There is no doubt that we do violence to ourselves today, we crackers of the soul's kernel, we incarnate riddles, who are forever asking riddles, as though life were nothing more than cracking a nut; and even through this, we must inevitably become more and more worthy of being asked questions and worthy of asking them, and in this way, we perhaps also become more worthy to—live?

All good things were once bad things; from every original sin, an original virtue has grown. For example, marriage was once seen as a violation of the rights of the community. A man used to pay a fine for the audacity of claiming one woman for himself (this idea connects to things like the jus primae noctis, the right of the priest to be the first to sleep with a bride, which is still a custom in Cambodia today, as a part of the "old traditions").

The soft, kind, yielding, and sympathetic feelings we now value so highly were once looked down upon by those who had them. Gentleness was once a source of shame, just as hardness is seen as a fault now (see Beyond Good and Evil, Aph. 260). The submission to law: how difficult it was for the noble people around the world to give up their personal vendettas and accept the law's power over them! Law was once considered forbidden, a blasphemy, an unwelcome change; it was forced upon people like a power they reluctantly accepted with personal shame.

Every small step forward in the world used to come at the cost of great mental and physical suffering. Today, the idea that not just progress, but any step forward, any movement or change, required countless martyrs sounds strange to us. I mentioned this in Dawn of Day, Aphorism 18. "Nothing is bought more dearly," says the same book a little later, "than the small amount of human reason and freedom that we now take pride in. But that pride is why it's almost impossible for us to sympathize with those vast periods in history, the 'Morality of Custom,' that shaped the early stages of the 'world's history,' and set the course for human nature. I repeat, during those times, suffering was seen as a virtue, cruelty as a virtue, deceit as a virtue, revenge as a virtue, and rejecting reason as a virtue. Meanwhile, well-being was seen as a danger, the desire for knowledge as a danger, pity as a danger, peace as a danger, being pitied as a shame, work as a shame, madness as divinity, and change as immorality and corruption!"

In the same book, Aphorism 12, there is an explanation of the burden of unpopularity under which the earliest group of contemplative men had to live— despised almost as widely as they were first feared! Contemplation first appeared on earth in a disguised shape, in an ambiguous form, with an evil heart and often with an uneasy head: there is no doubt about it. The inactive, brooding, unwarlike element in the instincts of contemplative men long invested them with a cloud of suspicion: the only way to combat this was to excite a definite fear. And the old Brahmans, for example, knew to a nicety how to do this! The oldest philosophers were well versed in giving their very existence and appearance meaning, firmness, background, by reason whereof men learned to fear them; considered more precisely, they did this from an even more fundamental need, the need of inspiring in themselves fear and self-reverence. For they found even in their own souls all the valuations turned against themselves; they had to fight down every kind of suspicion and antagonism against "the philosophic element in themselves." Being men of a terrible age, they did this with terrible means: cruelty to themselves, ingenious self- mortification—this was the chief method of these ambitious hermits and intellectual revolutionaries, who were obliged to force down the gods and the traditions of their own soul, so as to enable themselves to believe in their own revolution. I remember the famous story of the King Vicvamitra, who, as the result of a thousand years of self-martyrdom, reached such a consciousness of power and such a confidence in himself that he undertook to build a new heaven: the sinister symbol of the oldest and newest history of philosophy in the whole world. Every one who has ever built anywhere a "new heaven" first found the power thereto in his own hell... Let us compress the facts into a short formula. The philosophic spirit had, in order to be possible to any extent at all, to masquerade and disguise itself as one of the previously fixed types of the contemplative man, to disguise itself as priest, wizard, soothsayer, as a religious man generally: the ascetic ideal has for a long time served the philosopher as a superficial form, as a condition which enabled him to exist... To be able to be a philosopher he had to exemplify the ideal; to exemplify it, he was bound to believe in it. The peculiarly etherealized abstraction of philosophers, with their negation of the world, their enmity to life, their disbelief in the senses, which has been maintained up to the most recent time, and has almost thereby come to be accepted as the ideal philosophic attitude—this abstraction is the result of those enforced conditions under which philosophy came into existence, and continued to exist; inasmuch as for quite a very long time philosophy would have been absolutely impossible in the world without an ascetic cloak and dress, without an ascetic self-misunderstanding. Expressed plainly and palpably, the ascetic priest has taken the repulsive and sinister form of the caterpillar, beneath which and behind which alone philosophy could live and slink about... Has all that really changed? Has that flamboyant and dangerous winged creature, that "spirit" which that caterpillar concealed within itself, has it, I say, thanks to a sunnier, warmer, lighter world, really and finally flung off its hood and escaped into the light? Can we today point to enough pride, enough daring, enough courage, enough self-confidence, enough mental will, enough will for responsibility, enough freedom of the will, to enable the philosopher to be now in the world really— possible?

And now, after we've seen the ascetic priest, let's address our main question. What does the ascetic ideal really mean? This is when it becomes very serious— critically serious. We are now facing the real representatives of seriousness. "What is the meaning of all seriousness?" This even deeper question might already be on our minds: it's a question more for scientists, but we will skip it for now. In this ideal, the ascetic priest finds not only his beliefs, but also his will, his strength, and his interest. His right to exist depends on this ideal. No wonder we run into a fierce opponent (assuming, of course, that we are the ones opposing this ideal), someone fighting for his very survival against those who reject this ideal! On the other hand, it's already unlikely that such a biased attitude towards our problem will help him much; the ascetic priest will hardly be the best champion of his own ideal (just like a woman often fails when she tries to defend "woman")—let alone being the most objective critic or judge of this debate. So, it's clear that we will more likely have to help him defend himself properly against us, rather than worry about him defeating us too easily. The idea we're debating is the value of life from the perspective of the ascetic priests: this life (and everything it's part of—"Nature," "the world," everything that is always changing) is seen by them in relation to a different kind of existence, which it pushes away unless life denies itself: in the case of the ascetic life, life is seen as a way to get to another existence. The ascetic views life as a puzzle, where one must move backwards to find where it began; or he sees it as a mistake that must be corrected by action: he demands that others follow him; he enforces his view of existence wherever he can. What does this mean? Such a strange view is not a rare case, or a curiosity in history: it's one of the most common and enduring facts we have. If we looked at the big picture of human life from the perspective of a distant star, we might think that Earth is especially ascetic, a place full of unhappy, proud, and ugly creatures, who never stop hating themselves, the world, and all of life, and who hurt themselves out of the pleasure of causing pain—probably their only pleasure. Let's think about how regularly, how universally, the ascetic priest appears: he doesn't belong to any one group; he thrives everywhere; he comes from all walks of life. It's not that he inherited this view and passed it down—quite the opposite. There must be a deep, powerful need that makes this kind of person, so hostile to life, appear again and again.— Life itself must have a reason for letting this type of self- contradiction continue. For the ascetic life is a self-contradiction: it is based on deep resentment, the resentment of a never-satisfied desire and ambition, wanting to control not just one part of life, but life itself, with all its deepest, strongest, and most basic forces. The ascetic tries to use power to block the sources of power. The green-eyed jealousy even targets physical well-being, especially things like beauty, happiness, or pleasure, while the ascetic finds satisfaction in suffering, decay, pain, misfortune, ugliness, and even in punishing and sacrificing themselves. This is all deeply paradoxical: we're faced with a split that chooses to be a split, that enjoys the suffering, and only becomes more confident and victorious as its own basis—its physical life—diminishes. "Triumph in the greatest agony": this is the symbol under which the ascetic ideal has fought throughout history; in this mix of temptation, pleasure, and torture, it found its brightest light, its salvation, and its final victory. Crux, nux, lux—all three in one.

If a will so driven by contradiction and unnaturalness is compelled to philosophize, where will it direct its peculiar obsession? It will aim its skepticism at those things most firmly believed to be true and real. It will seek out error precisely where the instinct for life has most confidently established truth. Following the example of the ascetics of Vedanta philosophy, it might declare matter to be an illusion, dismiss pain and multiplicity as errors, and even reject the logical distinction between "subject" and "object" as falsehoods. To abandon belief in one's own self, to deny one's own "reality"—what a victory!

This is a higher kind of triumph, not just over the senses or the physical, but an act of violence and cruelty against reason itself. This ecstasy reaches its peak in ascetic self-contempt, where reason, despised and scorned, is forced to decree: there exists a realm of truth and life, but reason is excluded from it. Even Kant's idea of the "intelligible character of things" retains traces of this schism so beloved by ascetics—the tendency to turn reason against itself. In Kant's view, the "intelligible character" of things refers to a quality that reason can only understand as being beyond comprehension.

Despite this, as seekers of knowledge, we should not be entirely ungrateful for such radical reversals of perspectives and values. The mind's relentless rebellion against itself, even when it seems futile, has value. The very act of seeing the world from a different angle, the very desire to do so, serves as a form of training for the intellect, preparing it for true objectivity. Here, objectivity is not understood as "disinterested contemplation"—a concept that is impossible and absurd—but as the ability to command both sides of an argument and to shift perspectives at will, using the contrast between viewpoints and emotional interpretations to advance understanding.

However, let us, as philosophers, be cautious of the dangerous mythology surrounding ancient ideas that have enthroned concepts like a "pure, will-less, painless, timeless subject of knowledge." Let us be wary of such contradictory notions as "pure reason," "absolute spirituality," or "knowledge-in-itself." These ideas demand something absurd: they require an eye that does not see, an eye without direction, stripped of the active and interpretive functions that make perception possible. In these theories, seeing is divorced from context, and vision itself is reduced to nonsense.

There is no seeing without perspective, no knowing without a viewpoint. The more emotions we engage with, the more perspectives we apply, the more different "eyes" we turn toward an object, the fuller and more complete our understanding of it becomes—this is true objectivity. But to eliminate all will, to silence every emotion—if such a thing were even possible—what would we call that? Surely it would amount to nothing less than intellectual castration.

But let us return to the topic. The apparent contradiction seen in ascetics— "life turned against life"—is, from a physiological standpoint (and not merely a psychological one), complete nonsense. It can only seem to be a contradiction. It must be a temporary explanation, a formula, a misunderstanding—a psychological attempt to explain something deeper, something that could not be fully understood or articulated for a long time. It is merely a term placed over an old gap in human knowledge.

Let me state the facts more plainly: the ascetic ideal arises from the instincts of self-preservation and self-defense found in a decaying form of life. It is a strategy employed by a life form struggling to hold its ground and fight for its survival. This ideal signals a state of partial physiological exhaustion and decline, against which the strongest and most intact life instincts continually battle, creating new tools and strategies. The ascetic ideal is one such tool. Its purpose is precisely the opposite of what its worshippers imagine—life fights within and through this ideal against death. The ascetic ideal is a strategy for sustaining life.

History provides an important clue to this. The dominance of the ascetic ideal, particularly in times and places where human civilization and taming were most developed, reveals something significant: the diseased condition of humanity up to now. Specifically, the condition of tamed humanity shows a physiological struggle against death—or more accurately, against the weariness of life, exhaustion, and the longing for an end. The ascetic priest embodies the desire for another kind of existence, one on a different plane. He represents the highest point of this yearning, its official ecstasy and passion. Yet it is this very strength of the desire that binds him to earthly life. It makes him a tool for creating better conditions for human existence on this plane. Paradoxically, this power is what allows the ascetic priest to keep the entire herd of failures, distortions, outcasts, and self- tormentors tethered to life, even as he himself leads them forward, instinctively acting as their shepherd.

Do you see it now? This ascetic priest, this supposed enemy of life, this denier of life—he is, in fact, one of life's greatest conservative and affirmative forces.

What, then, is the cause of this diseased condition? For it is certain that man is sicker, more uncertain, more changeable, and more unstable than any other animal. He is the sick animal—there is no question about it. But why? Certainly, man has also dared, innovated, and risked more than all other creatures combined. He is the great experimenter with himself, the restless and insatiable being who challenges beasts, nature, and even gods. He is ever striving for mastery, driven relentlessly forward by the future pressing upon the present. How could such a bold and resourceful creature not also be the most endangered, the one with the longest and deepest sickness of all the sick animals?

Man grows weary of himself. Entire epidemics of this weariness have swept through humanity, as during the Dance of Death in 1348. But even this exhaustion, this disgust with himself, is transformed into something powerful. Man discharges his nausea and fatigue with such force that it becomes a new chain that binds him to life. His "no" to life somehow conjures countless graceful "yeses." Even in wounding himself, this master of destruction and self- destruction is forced by the wound itself to continue living.

The more common this sickness in humanity becomes—and we cannot deny its prevalence—the more we should honor those rare individuals who possess both mental and physical strength, the true gifts of humanity. These exceptional individuals should be protected even more carefully from the worst kind of environment—the atmosphere of the sickroom. But is that being done? The sick pose the greatest threat to the healthy. It is not the strong who harm the strong, but the weak. Do we recognize this?

On a larger scale, it is not fear of humanity that we should wish to diminish. Fear forces the strong to remain strong, even to be fearsome at times, preserving the vitality of humanity's healthiest type. What is truly dangerous is not the fear of humanity but the nausea with humanity—and just as much, the excessive pity for humanity. If these two emotions were ever to merge, they would unleash the greatest monstrosity imaginable: the ultimate will of humanity, the will to nothingness—Nihilism. The path toward this is already well-paved. Anyone who uses their senses—who not only smells but also sees and hears—can detect the faint yet pervasive odor of madness and sickness wherever they go. I am speaking, of course, of the so-called cultured regions of humanity, of every "Europe" that exists in the world today.

It is the sick who are the greatest danger to humanity, not the evil or even the "beasts of prey." Those who are flawed from the start, crushed, broken— these are the weakest among us, and they undermine the ground beneath humanity's feet. They inject the most dangerous poison into our trust in life, in humanity, and in ourselves. How can we escape it? How can we avoid the covert glance of the malformed and miserable, a glance that leaves us deeply saddened? That glance, turned away from life, reveals their inner monologue: "I wish I were something else, but there is no hope. I am what I am. How could I escape myself? And truthfully—I am sick of myself!"

From such soil—this swampy ground of self-contempt—springs a weed, a poisonous growth. It is small, hidden, ignoble, and sickeningly sweet. Here, the worms of revenge and resentment crawl. The air reeks of secrecy and unmentionable things. In this foul environment, a malicious web is spun—a conspiracy of the suffering against the healthy and the victorious. Here, the sight of success and strength is met with hatred. And yet, what efforts they make to conceal this hatred! What grand words and virtuous postures they adopt! What skillful lies they tell to disguise their bitterness!

These wretched beings—what a noble tone their complaints take on! How their eyes ooze sugary humility and submission! But what do they really want? Above all, they want to appear righteous, loving, wise, and superior. This is the ambition of the "lowest" and the sick. How clever this ambition makes them! You cannot help but marvel at the skill with which they counterfeit virtue, even forging the golden seal of righteousness. They have taken virtue for themselves, beyond all doubt. "We alone are the good and the righteous," they declare. "We alone are the homines bonae voluntatis—the people of good will." They move among us as living accusations, as warnings, as if health, strength, pride, and the joy of power were sins for which we must one day atone. How they long, in their hearts, to make us atone! How they thirst to become our executioners!

Among them are countless vengeful individuals masquerading as judges, constantly invoking the word "righteousness" as if it were a venom they are ready to spit. Their mouths are always pursed, prepared to attack anything that does not wear a mask of discontent, anything that dares to move through life with cheerfulness and ease. Among them, too, is the most repulsive type of the vain and deceitful—those twisted creations who present themselves as "pure souls," peddling their warped sensuality disguised as "purity of heart," wrapped in poetic verses and other such coverings. They are the self-comforters, the ones who indulge in their own illusions, masturbators of their own souls.

The sick have a relentless will to project some form of superiority, to seek out devious paths that lead to power over the healthy. Where can this will to dominate—the will to power of the weakest— not be found? Especially in the sick woman: no one surpasses her in inventiveness when it comes to ruling, oppressing, and tyrannizing. The sick woman spares nothing—neither the living nor the dead. She digs up even the most buried and forgotten things. (As the Bogos say, "Woman is a hyena.") Look into the private lives of families, communities, and institutions: everywhere you will see this ongoing, silent battle of the sick against the healthy. It is often fought with subtle poisons, pinpricks, and spiteful grimaces disguised as patience. Yet sometimes, it escalates into a diseased kind of self-righteousness, a pure pantomime of "moral indignation."

This battle even reaches into the sacred spaces of knowledge, where the yelping of these sick hounds can be heard. Their lying and frenzied moralism infect even the noblest pursuits. Think, for instance, of that Berlin preacher of revenge, Eugen Dühring, who shamelessly exploits the most vile moral refuse in modern Germany. He stands out even among the Anti-Semites as the loudest and most repugnant moral hypocrite of the age.

These individuals are consumed by resentment. They are physiological distortions, worm-eaten remnants of humanity, a kingdom of festering revenge. They are tireless, insatiable in their attacks on the happy and equally ingenious in finding ways to disguise and justify their revenge. When will they reach their ultimate triumph? Likely when they succeed in planting their misery—and all misery— into the minds of the happy. At that point, the happy might begin to feel ashamed of their happiness and say to one another, "It is wrong to be happy when there is so much suffering."

But there could be no greater or more disastrous misunderstanding than for the healthy, the strong, and the joyful to doubt their right to happiness. Away with this "perverse world"! Away with this sickly sentimentality! Preventing the sick from infecting the healthy—this must be our highest goal. To achieve this, it is essential that the healthy remain separate from the sick, guarding themselves even from their gaze, avoiding any association with them. Is it their mission to play nurse or doctor to the sick? Certainly not. To do so would be the grossest denial of their true purpose. The higher must never degrade itself into becoming a tool for the lower. The pathos of distance must always maintain this separation.

The right of the happy to exist, the right of full-toned bells to ring above the discordant cracked bells, is infinitely greater. The happy, the healthy, and the strong are the true guarantees of humanity's future. They alone are bound to its destiny. What they can and must do, the sick cannot and should not attempt. But for the healthy to fulfill their unique role, they cannot waste themselves as the doctors, comforters, or "saviors" of the sick.

…And so, good air! Good air! Let us move away, at all costs, from the madhouses and hospitals of civilization. Let us seek good company—our own company—or, if need be, solitude. But at any rate, let us escape the foul stench of inner decay and the rotting corruption of the sick. This, my friends, is how we must defend ourselves, if only for a little longer, against the two worst afflictions that could ever befall us: the great nausea with man and the great pity for man.

If you have truly grasped—deeply and profoundly—the reasons why it is impossible for the healthy to act as nurses for the sick, to take on the task of healing them, then you must also understand another necessity: the need for doctors and nurses who are themselves sick. And now, with both hands, we hold the essence of the ascetic priest. The ascetic priest must be understood as the predestined savior, shepherd, and defender of the sick herd. It is only through this lens that we can comprehend his terrifying historical role. His domain is the rule over sufferers; this is his kingdom, his instinct, his unique art, his craft, and even his form of happiness.

To fulfill this role, he must be sick himself, a kin to the sick and the deformed, so that he can understand them and communicate with them. Yet, at the same time, he must also be strong—stronger than both himself and others. He must possess an unshakable will to power to win the trust and reverence of the weak. He becomes their anchor, their bulwark, their guide, their overseer, their tyrant, even their god. His duty is to protect the herd—but against whom? Against the healthy, of course, and against the envy the herd feels toward the healthy.

The priest naturally opposes every form of untamed, wild, predatory strength and power. He is the first embodiment of a more refined creature, one that scorns more easily than it hates. He will inevitably find himself in conflict with the beasts of prey, but his weapons are not brute force; they are cunning and spirit. He may even need to summon from within himself, or at least project, a new form of predator—a hybrid monstrosity, part polar bear, part stealthy panther, and part fox. This combination is as mesmerizing as it is terrifying.

When necessary, the priest appears with the gravity of a bear—serious, wise, cold, and full of deceitful superiority. He presents himself as the voice of mysterious powers, even venturing into the realm of other predators. His goal is to sow suffering, discord, and self-doubt among them, and he is certain of his skill to remain the master of sufferers at all times.

The priest arrives with salves and balms, but before healing, he first wounds. And as he soothes the pain of the wound, he poisons it further. He excels at this, this wizard and beast-tamer, who turns everything healthy sick and makes the sick docile. He guards his herd well—this strange shepherd—protecting them even from themselves. He shields them from the sparks of malice, deceit, and wickedness that smolder within the herd, for these are the ailments of the sick.

He fights tirelessly, using cunning, harshness, and secrecy, to stave off anarchy and the ever-present danger of the herd's collapse. For within the herd, resentment—the most dangerous and volatile of all explosives—constantly accumulates. It is the priest's task to manage this brewing storm, to keep the herd together and obedient, even as he strengthens his own rule.

Diverting this volatile resentment in a way that prevents it from destroying both the herd and the herdsman—this is the true achievement of the ascetic priest. It is his most significant function. If one were to summarize the value of the priestly life in the briefest formula, it would be this: the priest is the diverter of resentment. Every sufferer instinctively seeks a cause for their suffering. More specifically, they seek a doer—an agent they can hold responsible. Even more precisely, they long for a sentient, accountable being upon whom they can place the blame. In short, they need something alive, something tangible, upon which to direct their emotions. Whether this target is real or symbolic, it serves the same purpose: it provides an outlet for the sufferer's pent-up emotions.

For the sufferer, venting emotions becomes their most desperate attempt at relief—a kind of self-induced numbness, a narcotic they turn to in their struggle to deaden any kind of pain. This phenomenon, in my judgment, reveals the true physiological root of resentment, revenge, and related emotions. These are not merely defensive reflexes, as they are often misunderstood. They are not the protective reactions that help one avoid further harm, like the way a decapitated frog might reflexively react to corrosive acid. No, the purpose here is different. It is not about avoiding harm but about numbing a deep, persistent, almost unbearable pain by replacing it with a more violent emotion—any violent emotion will do.

For this purpose, an excuse is needed to provoke such emotion. The more intense the emotion, the more effective it is in temporarily driving the pain out of consciousness. This is why sufferers instinctively conclude, "It must be someone's fault that I feel this way." This reasoning is universal among those in pain, but it becomes more pronounced the less they understand the true physiological cause of their suffering. The source of their pain could be anything—an imbalance in the nervous system, an excess of bile, a deficiency in vital minerals like potassium, intestinal pressure disrupting blood flow, ovarian degeneration, and so forth. Yet, instead of addressing these actual causes, sufferers turn to imaginative and emotional explanations.

Sufferers possess an almost inexhaustible creativity in finding excuses to amplify their painful emotions. They revel in jealousy, wallow in dark suspicions, and relive supposed injustices. They dig through the depths of their past and present, searching for hidden grievances that allow them to indulge in torturous doubt and drink deeply from the poison of their own malice. They reopen old wounds, make scars bleed once more, and transform loved ones— friends, spouses, children—into perceived enemies. Their inner voice constantly repeats, "I suffer; it must be someone's fault."

This is where the ascetic priest steps in. He speaks to the suffering sheep and says, "Yes, my sheep, it is someone's fault—but that someone is you. You are the one to blame. It is your fault, and it is your fault alone." Bold, even false, as this declaration may be, it achieves one critical outcome: it redirects the resentment inward.

Now you see the purpose of the ascetic priest's role, the remedy that life's instinct has attempted through him. To achieve this, the priest employed a temporary tyranny of paradoxical and extreme ideas such as "guilt," "sin," "sinfulness," "corruption," and "damnation." The goal was not to heal the sick in any real physiological sense. Instead, it was to make them harmless, to a certain extent, by turning their destructive tendencies inward. The incurable were, in effect, destroyed by their own self-accusations. The milder cases were redirected toward self-discipline, self- surveillance, and self-mastery. Their resentment became a tool for controlling and policing themselves.

It is evident that this emotional "medication" never aimed to truly heal the sick. Healing, in the physiological sense, was never the goal of this instinct of life. Instead, two outcomes were achieved. First, there was a kind of consolidation and organization of the sick—a systematized management of suffering, which we often call the "Church." Second, a provisional safeguarding of the comparatively healthy was achieved. A deliberate separation was created between the healthy and the sick—a rift that kept the two groups distinct.

For a long time, this was all that could be achieved, and yet it was significant. It was a great deal—more than could have been imagined in such a state of widespread suffering and decline. It was an accomplishment of enormous importance.

As you can see, I am proceeding in this essay from a hypothesis that, for the kind of readers I address, does not need proof: the idea that "sinfulness" in humanity is not an actual fact but rather an interpretation of a fact—a physiological discomfort viewed through a moral and religious lens that no longer holds authority over us. Therefore, the feeling of being "guilty" or "sinful" is not evidence that one is justified in feeling so, any more than feeling healthy is proof of actual health. Consider, for example, the infamous witch trials. Even the most intelligent and humane judges of the time firmly believed they were dealing with guilt. The so-called witches themselves believed it. And yet, guilt was absent.

Let me expand on this hypothesis. I do not accept the concept of "pain in the soul" as a fact. Rather, I see it as an explanation—a temporary one—for phenomena that could not previously be clearly defined. In this sense, it is still unsubstantiated and scientifically unsupported, a convenient term that takes the place of a question mark. When someone cannot escape their "pain in the soul," the cause lies not in the "soul" itself but far more likely in the body—in the stomach, for instance. (I speak crudely, though I do not mean to encourage a crude interpretation of my words.)

A strong and well-balanced individual processes their experiences—both their deeds and misdeeds—just as they digest their food, even when some morsels are tough to swallow. If they fail to "digest" an experience, this indigestion is physiological as much as it is psychological. In fact, the two forms of indigestion are often interlinked, with one contributing to the other. You could embrace this perspective and still remain, in principle, an opponent of materialism.

But is the ascetic priest truly a physician? We already have reasons to hesitate before calling him one, no matter how much he enjoys portraying himself as a "savior" and being worshipped as such. His efforts are focused entirely on addressing the sufferer's discomfort, not the root cause of the suffering or the underlying illness itself. This is the most fundamental objection to priestly "medicine."

However, if you adopt the priest's perspective, it is difficult not to marvel at what he has seen, sought, and achieved from this vantage point. His genius lies in mitigating suffering, in providing consolation. Consider the inventiveness with which he has interpreted his role as a consoler and the boldness with which he has selected the tools for his task. Christianity, for instance, could be considered a vast treasure trove of ingenious consolations. It has amassed a remarkable storehouse of remedies—refreshing, soothing, even numbing drugs. Christianity has ventured some of the most daring and dangerous psychological strategies. With unparalleled refinement, often with a distinctly Oriental subtlety, it has identified emotional stimulants capable of countering the profound depression, crushing fatigue, and black melancholy of those who are physiologically unwell.

Indeed, all religions share this common goal: combating a kind of weariness that weighs down life. It is likely, even inevitable, that in certain times and places large portions of the population would experience waves of physiological depression. Without the scientific understanding of bodily health that we possess today, such depression would not have been recognized as physiological. Instead, its causes and cures were sought within the realm of moral and psychological explanations. This, I propose, is the most general framework for what is often called "religion."

Religions, then, can be seen as grand systems of consolation, designed to manage the fatigue of life that spreads among societies. By addressing this fatigue, they provide temporary relief and create narratives that help individuals endure the burdens they cannot fully understand or escape. This is the ascetic priest's domain: offering solace for suffering while leaving its true sources untouched.

Such feelings of depression can arise from a wide variety of causes, each shaped by unique circumstances and influences. For example, depression may result from the intermingling of races or classes that are too different from each other. Genealogical and racial distinctions often manifest in class structures, and the European "Weltschmerz" or the pessimism of the nineteenth century can be traced back to absurd and abrupt class mixing. Similarly, depression may be triggered by ill-fated migrations, such as when a race moves into a climate it cannot adequately adapt to, as in the case of the Indians in India.

Other causes might include the natural decline brought on by old age and fatigue, such as the Parisian pessimism that emerged after 1850, or poor dietary habits like the rampant alcoholism of the Middle Ages or the peculiar nonsense of vegetarianism, even though vegetarianism has been endorsed humorously by figures such as Sir Christopher in Shakespeare. Further contributors include deteriorating blood health or diseases like malaria and syphilis, which devastated Germany after the Thirty Years' War and left behind a population marked by submissiveness and timidity.

When such widespread depression arises, humanity instinctively wages war against it on a grand scale. This battle unfolds in various practices and stages. For brevity, I leave aside the philosophical struggles against depression, which often accompany these efforts. These philosophical battles, though intellectually engaging, are largely ineffective and impractical. They are riddled with abstract theorizing, such as the notion that pain is merely a mistake to be corrected—an assumption that, when tested, invariably fails to make the pain disappear.

The dominant approach to combating depression is through methods that reduce life's intensity to its absolute minimum. The strategy seeks to suppress the consciousness of life itself, lowering it as much as possible. This often involves eliminating desires and avoiding anything that provokes emotion or "stirs the blood." Practitioners of such methods might abstain from salt (as in the hygiene of fakirs), avoid love and hate, embrace equanimity, renounce revenge, wealth, and labor, and sometimes even resort to begging. They shun the company of women or limit their interactions with women to the barest minimum. Intellectually, this strategy aligns with Pascal's principle, "il faut s'abêtir"—the need to dull one's mind.

In ethical and psychological terms, these practices are labeled as "self- annihilation" or "sanctification." Physiologically, they resemble a form of "hypnotism," an effort to simulate the human equivalent of hibernation in animals or aestivation in tropical plants. The goal is to achieve a minimal level of metabolism and assimilation, allowing life to persist without fully entering consciousness. An extraordinary amount of human energy has been invested in achieving this state—possibly to no avail.

Still, it is undeniable that such "saintly athletes," who have appeared throughout history in nearly every culture, often find genuine relief from the physiological depression they battle. Through rigorous training and their system of hypnotism, they have managed to escape the deepest forms of depression in countless cases. This success places their methods among the most universal practices documented in ethnology.

It is incorrect to dismiss such strategies, aimed at starving the physical desires and instincts, as mere madness. While some blunt, roast-beef-eating "freethinkers" and Sir Christophers may be eager to label these practices as insanity, their view is overly simplistic. That said, there is no doubt that such methods frequently lead to mental disturbances. These may include experiences of "inner light," auditory or visual hallucinations, ecstatic raptures, or heightened sensualism, as exemplified in the cases of the Hesychasts of Mount Athos or St. Theresa.

The victims of these phenomena often provide explanations filled with fanatical falsehoods. Yet, even in their explanations, one detects a profound tone of gratitude—a sense that their suffering has granted them a higher understanding. They interpret their final state of salvation, the ultimate goal of their hypnotic practices, as a profound mystery beyond words. To them, it is a return to the essence of existence, a liberation from illusions, desires, and all forms of action. It is seen as a state beyond Good and Evil, transcending every boundary and dichotomy.

As the Buddhists say, "Good and Evil are both chains. The perfect man is the master of both."

"The done and the undone," says the disciple of the Vedanta, "do him no harm; the good and the evil he shakes off, for he is wise. His kingdom remains unaffected by actions; he transcends both good and evil." This is a thoroughly Indian conception, shared by both Brahmanism and Buddhism. In neither Indian nor Christian doctrines is "redemption" achieved through virtue or moral improvement, no matter how much they might value the hypnotic power of virtue. This is a key point to understand—and it aligns entirely with reality. The fact that these traditions stayed true to this principle may be one of the best examples of realism within the otherwise morality-saturated framework of the three great religions.

"For those who know, there is no duty." Redemption, according to these teachings, is not something attained by accumulating virtues. Redemption means unity with Brahman, who cannot gain perfection because he is already perfect. Similarly, it is not about shedding faults, for Brahman, with whom unity constitutes redemption, is eternally pure. These ideas are well-articulated in the commentaries of Cankara, as cited by Paul Deussen, one of the first true European experts on Indian philosophy and a personal friend.

We must, therefore, give due respect to the concept of "redemption" in these great religions, but it is hard to remain entirely serious when faced with how these exhausted pessimists—too weary even to dream—praise deep sleep. To them, deep sleep is seen as a merging into Brahman, the ultimate unification with God, the unio mystica.

The oldest and most revered scriptures express it this way: "When he has completely gone to sleep and reached perfect rest, so that he sees no more visions, then, oh dear one, he is united with Being. He has entered his true self—enclosed by the Self with its absolute knowledge. He has no more consciousness of anything within or without. Day and night do not cross these bridges, nor do age, death, suffering, good deeds, or evil deeds." Similarly, the adherents of this deepest of the three great religions claim, "In deep sleep, the soul rises out of this body, enters the supreme light, and takes its true form: it becomes the supreme spirit itself. There, it moves about freely, rests, plays, and enjoys itself—whether with women, chariots, or friends. Its thoughts no longer return to the burdens of the body, to which the vital breath ('prana') is yoked like an animal to a cart."

Yet, as with the concept of "redemption," we must note that this elaborate and extravagant Oriental imagery ultimately conveys the same critique of life as did the Greek philosopher Epicurus. His approach, while clear and cold in its simplicity, expressed the same underlying sentiment. The hypnotic sensation of nothingness, the peace of deep sleep, and the numbness of complete anesthesia— this is what the suffering and utterly dejected regard as their highest good, their ultimate value.

For them, this state of absolute negation becomes something positive, the essence of what they consider the highest achievement. By this same emotional logic, all pessimistic religions declare that nothingness is God. In their eyes, to embrace the void is to find peace, and the absence of everything is exalted as the ultimate liberation.

This hypnotic dulling of sensitivity and resistance to pain—requiring rare qualities like courage, disregard for public opinion, and intellectual stoicism—is far less common than another, simpler method often employed to combat depression: mechanical activity. Undeniably, the burden of a painful existence can be significantly lightened through such activity. Today, this phenomenon is often referred to, somewhat crassly, as the "blessing of work."

The relief it provides comes from its ability to divert the sufferer's attention entirely away from their pain. By monopolizing the consciousness with constant action, little room is left for suffering to take hold. After all, human consciousness is a narrow space, easily filled. Mechanical activity, combined with its byproducts—absolute regularity, rigid and unthinking obedience, the monotony of routine, the total occupation of time, and even a certain freedom found in impersonality—becomes a powerful tool. This "training in impersonality" or incuria sui (carelessness about the self), has been utilized with great skill by the ascetic priest in his ongoing war against pain.

When addressing the lower classes—slaves, prisoners, or women (who, in many cases, exist as a blend of laborer and captive)— the priest requires little effort beyond linguistic manipulation. By renaming and reinterpreting their circumstances, he can make them view their hated conditions as blessings. It is important to note that dissatisfaction with one's lot as a slave was not a creation of the priests, but the priests were adept at redirecting that discontent.

A complementary and equally popular method for combating depression is the prescription of small joys, particularly joys that are easy to attain and can be integrated into daily routines. This remedy often works alongside the discipline of mechanical activity. Among the most common forms of this "medication" is fostering joy through producing joy—acts such as doing good, giving gifts, helping others, offering comfort, praising someone, or extending kindness. These acts of generosity are often linked with the moral commandment to "love your neighbor."

The ascetic priest, however cautiously, also prescribes a controlled stimulation of one of the strongest and most vital instincts: the Will to Power. Even the smallest feeling of superiority, which naturally accompanies acts of helping, comforting, or praising others, becomes a profound source of consolation for the afflicted. Physiological distortions and those suffering from depression wisely use this instinct to their advantage, finding happiness in the smallest affirmations of power. Where this instinct is not harnessed constructively, the same drive often leads to harmful actions, as people injure one another in their pursuit of even the most minor dominations.

An exploration of Christianity's origins in the Roman world reveals that cooperative organizations for addressing poverty, illness, and burial emerged among the lowest social strata. These groups deliberately fostered the antidote of shared, mutual benefits as a way to combat depression. At the time, this approach may have been a novel discovery—a true innovation. By promoting cooperation, family structures, community life, and gatherings in shared spaces (Caenacula), these groups stimulated the Will to Power on a communal level, albeit in modest doses. This collective drive for mutual aid blossomed into a more potent and expansive manifestation of that instinct.

The development of these herd organizations marked a genuine advancement in the battle against depression. As communities grew, individuals often found a new focus of interest that drew them away from their personal despair or self-loathing—what Geulincx termed despectus sui (contempt for oneself). Through communal bonds and shared purposes, individuals could escape the narrower confines of their own dissatisfaction, finding solace and meaning in collective life. This was, in many ways, a triumph—not only for the community but for the individuals within it, who discovered a form of redemption through their integration into something greater than themselves.

All sick and suffering individuals instinctively strive for herd organization, driven by a deep desire to alleviate their overwhelming discomfort and sense of weakness. The ascetic priest recognizes and nurtures this instinct, fostering the formation of herds. Wherever herds arise, they are the product of the instinct of the weak, who crave union, and the cunning of priests, who structure and lead them. This dynamic reflects a natural divide: the strong, by necessity, strive for isolation as much as the weak seek union.

When the strong join together, it is not out of love for community but rather a reluctant alliance aimed at achieving aggressive collective action and fulfilling their shared Will to Power. Such cooperation is often against their individual inclinations, each strong individual wrestling internally against this compromise. Conversely, the weak unite with genuine delight in the organization, feeling their instincts gratified. For them, the herd is a source of solace and strength, whereas for the "born master"— the solitary predator type of man— any form of organization is a wound to their very nature, an affront to their instincts.

History teaches us an inescapable lesson: lurking within every oligarchy is the seed of tyranny. Oligarchies are perpetually tense, as each individual member must constantly suppress their own tyrannical desires. (The Greeks exemplify this dynamic; Plato, with his deep understanding of his contemporaries—and himself—revealed it time and again in his writings.)

The ascetic priest's methods, which we have already examined— suppressing vitality, enforcing mechanical labor, offering small joys, and promoting "love your neighbor"—are all tools for herd organization. By awakening a shared sense of communal power, the priest enables individuals to find joy in the success of the group, thus overshadowing their disgust with themselves. These strategies, according to contemporary standards, are considered "innocent" methods in combating depression.

Let us now turn to the "guilty" methods, which are far more intriguing. These methods center on the deliberate creation of emotional excess, a strategy used to provide temporary relief from the chronic pain of depression. Emotional excess acts as a powerful anesthetic, dulling the sufferer's awareness of their agony. This need for intense emotion has driven priestly ingenuity to extraordinary lengths, leading to the invention of countless techniques to provoke overwhelming feelings.

This may sound harsh. One might prefer a gentler phrasing: "The ascetic priest has always harnessed the enthusiasm inherent in strong emotions." But why should we sugarcoat this for the delicate sensibilities of modern listeners? To do so would only cater to the verbal Pecksniffianism of our age. For a psychologist, to indulge in such euphemisms would not only be hypocritical but nauseating. Good taste—or perhaps what some might call integrity—demands that we challenge the sickly moralized language that infects modern discourse about humanity and the world.

Do not be deceived: the defining trait of modern souls and modern literature is not outright dishonesty but the innocence that accompanies their intellectual dishonesty. This innocence is what makes modern psychology such a distasteful and dangerous enterprise. It is a path that leads directly to the "great nausea"—a revolt against the sugary moralism and falsity saturating contemporary culture.

I am well aware of the role modern works, and modernity as a whole, will serve for future generations (should they endure and should a healthier, stricter generation eventually arise): modernity will function as an emetic. It will purge the moral and intellectual systems of those future people, ridding them of the cloying sweetness, the ingrained softness and false idealism that masquerades as high-mindedness today.

Our contemporary "cultured" men and "good" men do not lie—this much is true. Yet this is hardly to their credit. Their unwillingness to lie is not a sign of virtue but a reflection of the same ingrained dishonesty that defines them. It is not a conscious choice but a symptom of their weakness, their inability to confront or express uncomfortable truths. Such is the state of modern idealism, cloaked in moral sugar and falsehood, steeped in the sentimental idealism they mistake for greatness. And such is the legacy that modernity will leave behind: a purgative for a future stronger, healthier humanity.

The real lie—the deliberate, intentional, and "honest" lie, the kind Plato speaks of so highly—is far too bold and difficult for most people to handle. Asking them to embrace it would require them to do something they are fundamentally unwilling to do: look inward, confront their own truths, and learn to differentiate between what is true and what is false within themselves. Instead, the dishonest lie is what suits them best—a lie that fools even the "good" man. Such people are entirely incapable of being anything other than dishonorable liars, absolute liars, yet they remain innocent liars, virtuous liars, and naïve, well-meaning liars.

These "good men" are completely steeped in morality, so much so that their sense of honor has been irreparably corrupted. They are morally tainted, disgraced for all eternity. Which of them could withstand hearing more truths about humanity—or, more specifically, about themselves? Who among them could bear the weight of an honest biography? A few examples will suffice. Lord Byron once wrote a deeply personal autobiography, but Thomas Moore, being "too good" for such raw honesty, burned his friend's papers. Similarly, Schopenhauer's executor, Dr. Gwinner, is said to have destroyed many of Schopenhauer's self-reflective writings, including some that may have even been critical of himself (εἰς ἑαυόν). And consider the virtuous American Thayer, who, while writing Beethoven's biography, abandoned the project partway through. At a certain point, even he could no longer continue exposing the truths of Beethoven's otherwise noble and simple life.

The moral here is clear: who among us, in this age, would dare to write an honest word about themselves? To do so would require one to belong to an order of holy fools, a rare breed indeed. An autobiography from Richard Wagner is promised, but does anyone doubt that it will be anything less than a carefully constructed narrative? Consider the outrage caused by the Catholic priest Janssen in Germany with his overly simplistic and harmless depictions of the Reformation. Now imagine the chaos that would erupt if a true psychologist were to present us with an authentic account of Luther—not with the timid modesty of a Protestant historian or the moralizing simplicity of a parish priest, but with the fearless precision of someone like Taine, whose boldness comes not from deference to power but from genuine inner strength. (The Germans, by the way, already have a classic example of such deference in Leopold Ranke, the quintessential advocate of every causa fortior, a master of opportunism disguised as objectivity.)

But you can see my point. To put it simply, there are plenty of reasons why we psychologists must approach even ourselves with a degree of mistrust. It is quite likely that we too are still "too good" for the work we attempt to do. Despite whatever contempt we may feel for the modern obsession with morality, we are not immune to its influence. We are, perhaps, still its slaves and victims. This moral infection seeps into even our own judgments. What else could that diplomat have meant when he warned his colleagues, "Distrust your first impulses, gentlemen! They are almost always good"? This should be the mantra of every psychologist when speaking to their peers.

And so, we return to our problem, which demands a certain level of rigor and mistrust, especially of first impulses. The ascetic ideal as a tool for inducing emotional excess—those who recall my earlier thoughts will already understand part of what I mean. This ideal seeks to unsettle the human soul completely, throwing it into states of terror, ecstasy, rapture, and despair, as though through a sudden lightning strike. This method aims to jolt the individual out of their unhappiness, depression, and discomfort. But which paths lead to such a result? And which of them are the safest?

In truth, all strong emotions hold the potential to achieve this, provided they find a sudden and dramatic outlet. Rage, fear, lust, revenge, hope, triumph, despair, and cruelty—any of these can provide a release. The ascetic priest has never hesitated to employ the entire arsenal of human emotions, unleashing them selectively to awaken people from prolonged melancholy. He chases away their dull pain and misery, if only temporarily, always under the guise of religious meaning and justification.

Of course, this emotional excess comes at a cost. It must be repaid—it inevitably worsens the condition of the sick. For this reason, such remedies are deemed "guilty" by modern standards. Still, the priest's methods are undeniably effective, even if the price is steep and the long-term consequences dire.

Fairness requires us to acknowledge that this remedy was applied by the ascetic priest with a good conscience. He prescribed it with a profound belief in its necessity and effectiveness, even though he often struggled with the very pain he created in others. The priest, as a healer of sorts, genuinely believed this was the best path forward. Even the severe physiological consequences of these methods— sometimes leading to mental disturbances— were not entirely inconsistent with the purpose of the remedy. After all, the priest was not attempting to cure diseases in a conventional sense but to combat the misery of depression and its accompanying unhappiness. The goal was to alleviate and numb the pain of existence, and in that sense, the remedy succeeded.

The central tool that the ascetic priest used to pluck every agonizing and ecstatic chord in the human soul was the feeling of guilt. As I have previously explained, the origins of guilt lie in animal psychology—it began as a primal feeling tied to the instincts of creatures struggling with survival. In its raw, unshaped form, guilt was a simple mechanism of conscience. Yet, in the hands of the priest, this crude feeling was transformed into something far more elaborate and dangerous—a masterwork of emotional manipulation.

The priest gave this new version of guilt a name: "sin." Sin became the religious reinterpretation of the animal's bad conscience, a reversal of cruelty turned inward. Up to now, "sin" has been the most monumental event in the history of the human soul afflicted by disease. It is, without question, the most perilous and fatal creation of religious interpretation.

Imagine a man already suffering, burdened by his existence, trapped in a cage of his own making, and without understanding why. He searches desperately for reasons—anything to explain his suffering—and for remedies, perhaps even narcotics, to dull the pain. When he turns to the ascetic priest, the priest provides him with his first "answer": the cause of his suffering lies within himself, in his guilt, in a piece of his past. His suffering, the priest explains, is a punishment—a direct consequence of his own actions.

The man hears and understands. But now he is trapped, like a hen that has had a line drawn around it, unable to step outside the circle. The sick man becomes the sinner. And for thousands of years, humanity has been haunted by the image of this new invalid, the sinner. Can we ever escape it?

Everywhere we look, we see the hypnotic gaze of the sinner, always fixated on guilt as the sole cause of suffering. Everywhere is the evil conscience—what Luther called the "ghastly beast"—obsessed with the past, distorting actions through the lens of guilt and fear of punishment. The sinner's suffering is endlessly misunderstood, transformed into feelings of blame and a terror of divine retribution. The consequences are everywhere: the scourge, the hair shirt, the starving body, acts of contrition. We see the sinner breaking themselves on the wheel of a restless, insatiable conscience. We see silent pain, overwhelming fear, hearts tormented by their own guilt, and cries for redemption.

And yet, this system achieved its intended purpose. The old depression, dullness, and lethargy were completely vanquished. Life, once heavy and meaningless, became deeply interesting again—so much so that it burned with an almost unbearable intensity. The sinner became a figure of endless energy, awake and sleepless, consumed by his inner fire. Exhausted but never allowed to rest, humanity, as the sinner, was thrust into a state of perpetual tension and spiritual urgency.

The ascetic priest, the master manipulator, had triumphed. His kingdom had arrived. No longer did people complain about pain; instead, they began to crave it. "More pain! More pain!" became the cry of his followers, his initiates, echoing through the centuries. What had begun as a fight against depression and despair was transformed into an insatiable hunger for suffering—a perverse new vitality born from the ashes of misery.

Every form of emotional excess that inflicted pain—everything that shattered, overwhelmed, crushed, exalted, or transported the soul—became a tool for the ascetic priest. The horrors of torture chambers, the twisted ingenuity of hell itself, and every imaginable torment were uncovered, imagined, and exploited to serve the triumph of his ideal: the ascetic ideal. "My kingdom is not of this world," he proclaimed, both at the beginning and the end of his work. But did he truly still have the right to say so? Goethe once claimed there are only thirty-six tragic situations. If we didn't know better, we might assume Goethe was no ascetic priest—because the priest surely knows more.

Regarding this "guilty" form of priestly medicine—the emotional excess prescribed by the ascetic priest to his ailing followers— criticism is almost unnecessary. The idea that such methods have genuinely helped any sick person seems laughable. Who could seriously argue that emotional extremes, wrapped in sacred language and applied under the guise of divine purpose, have ever truly cured anyone? If by "be of use" one means that these methods have reformed individuals, I won't dispute it. But let's clarify: "reformed," to my understanding, means something closer to "tamed," "weakened," "discouraged," "refined," "delicate," or "emasculated"—all of which amount to a form of harm.

When dealing primarily with the sick, depressed, and downtrodden, such treatments might indeed make them seem "better," but they also make them far worse. Ask any physician who treats mental illness: what is the outcome of systematically applying penance- tortures, acts of contrition, and ecstatic salvation experiences? The result is clear—a nervous system further shattered, piled atop whatever existing malady the sufferer endured. History corroborates this. Everywhere the ascetic priest implemented this "cure," disease spread rapidly, infecting not only individuals but entire populations.

What were the results of these methods? Time and again, they left communities and nations riddled with broken nerves and deep psychological scars. Consider the epidemic of epileptic fits in the Middle Ages, such as the St. Vitus and St. John dances—mass outbreaks of uncontrollable convulsions, born out of penance and redemption training. Another result was the emergence of chronic depression and twisted emotional states that reshaped entire cities or nations, like Geneva or Basel, transforming their temperaments into something permanently somber and repressed.

This training was also directly responsible for the witch-hysteria—epidemics of mass delusion akin to somnambulism. Between 1564 and 1605 alone, there were eight significant outbreaks of this phenomenon. Similarly, we find entire populations gripped by suicidal fervor, like the mass death-cravings of certain periods in Europe, where crowds would shout the horrifying cry, "Evviva la morte!" (Long live death!). These episodes often swung unpredictably between orgiastic ecstasy and a destructive frenzy, a pattern seen wherever the doctrine of sin and asceticism found success. Religious neuroses are unmistakably tied to these symptoms—what else could they be? (Quaeritur— we must ask).

The ascetic ideal, along with its lofty moral cult, stands as one of humanity's most ingenious, reckless, and dangerous systems of emotional excess. It has left a terrifying and indelible mark on the history of mankind, a scar that is both unforgettable and undeniable. Worse still, this history is not confined to the past. Its influence continues to manifest in the present, haunting us with its legacy of suffering and manipulation.

I can scarcely think of any force that has harmed the health and vitality of European people more than the ascetic ideal. It can rightly be called the true catastrophe in the history of European health. At most, it can be compared to the uniquely German influence: the widespread poisoning of Europe with alcohol. This plague, running parallel with the rise of German political and racial dominance, left its mark wherever their influence extended—not only their blood but also their vice was spread. Third in this grim sequence is syphilis, though the gap between these calamities is significant (magno sed proximo intervallo).

Wherever the ascetic priest has gained control, he has corrupted the health of the soul. And, inevitably, where he has corrupted the soul, he has also corrupted taste in the arts and literature—he continues to do so even now. "Inevitably," I say. I trust I will be granted this conclusion without the need to prove it exhaustively here. Allow me to offer one striking example: consider the chief book of Christian literature, their ultimate standard, their "book above all books." This book was born in the midst of the Graeco- Roman splendor—a golden age for books, when the ancient world still brimmed with literary treasures that had not yet been lost to decay and ruin.

Imagine a time when people could still read works that we, today, would trade half our modern literature to possess. Yet, in this era of greatness, Christian agitators—those we now call the "Fathers of the

Church"—had the audacity to declare: "We too have our classical literature; we have no need of the Greeks." They held up their books of legends, their apostles' letters, and their apologetic pamphlets with pride. The comparison is almost absurd, akin to how the English Salvation Army today pits its tracts against Shakespeare and other "heathens" with similar misplaced self- importance.

Let me say it plainly: I do not like the New Testament. In fact, it nearly unsettles me to admit how isolated I feel in my disdain for this highly esteemed and excessively praised scripture. Two thousand years of admiration and reverence weigh against me— but so be it! "Here I stand; I cannot do otherwise." I have the courage of what some might call my bad taste.

The Old Testament, on the other hand—that is something entirely different. It commands respect! Within its pages, I find great men, a landscape full of heroic grandeur, and one of the rarest phenomena in history: the raw, unpretentious naivety of a strong heart. In the Old Testament, I see a people, a true collective identity. But in the New Testament? It is nothing more than a crowded hostel for petty sects, a spiritual rococo with its ornate twists, exaggerated flourishes, and overly sentimental embellishments. The air of small religious gatherings permeates it, a stifling atmosphere with hints of provincial sweetness that belong more to the Hellenistic world of the Roman provinces than to anything truly Jewish.

Here, meekness and bravado stand awkwardly side by side. The New Testament is filled with noisy, emotional chatter that nearly drowns out all else. There is hysteria in abundance, but no true passion; theatrical gestures, but no substance. These "pious little people" lack all dignity. How can they make such a spectacle of their minor failings, parading them with such earnestness? Who cares about their petty sins—let alone God?

And then, they have the audacity to demand the crown of eternal life. For what? On what grounds? The arrogance of it all is almost unbearable. An immortal Peter? Who could endure such a figure?

These small, self-important provincials seem convinced that their trivial troubles and mundane lives are matters of cosmic significance, as though the universe itself were obligated to revolve around their personal struggles. They never tire of dragging God Himself into the midst of their insignificant grievances, entangling the divine in their narrow, self-absorbed misery.

This is the New Testament: a book born of small minds and small ambitions, written by and for people who elevate their everyday struggles into the grand stage of universal importance. It is impossible not to see the absurdity—and, in some cases, the insufferable insolence—of it all.

And what about the dreadful form of this constant, intrusive familiarity with God? This Jewish—and not solely Jewish— endless pleading and clawing at the divine, this desperate, shameless insistence? There are small, so-called "heathen" tribes in East Africa from whom the first Christians could have learned much, especially a bit of tact in worship. These tribes do not even speak their god's name aloud—a delicacy so refined it far surpasses anything the early Christians could have mustered. It is certainly too refined, not just for primitive Christians, but also for the loud and irreverent worshippers that came later. For contrast, just think of Martin Luther—the most "eloquent" and audacious peasant Germany has ever known. Recall the tone of Luther in his personal exchanges with God, where he felt most at home: blunt, brash, and utterly without restraint.

Luther's rebellion against the medieval saints and the Church— especially his animosity toward "that devil's hog, the Pope"— was, at its core, the revolt of a crude man offended by the etiquette of worship. That code of priestly conduct maintained the sacred distance between the divine and the profane, admitting only the initiated and reverent to the holy of holies while shutting out the unrefined masses. Luther, the peasant, could not abide this. It was not "German" enough for him. He wanted to speak directly, personally, and without ceremony to his God—straightforward and plain. And he succeeded.

Yet, as you might guess, the ascetic ideal has never been a school for good taste, much less for refined manners. At its best, it has taught a particular form of priestly decorum—a manner fundamentally opposed to all genuine civility. Its essence is one of excess, a relentless defiance of balance and moderation, a refusal to adhere to any proper limits. It is the ultimate "non plus ultra" of poor taste and unchecked fanaticism.

But the damage caused by the ascetic ideal extends far beyond health and taste. It corrupts in countless ways—third, fourth, fifth, and sixth dimensions of ruin. Listing all its effects would be endless, and exhausting the catalogue would serve little purpose. Instead, my aim is not to enumerate its outcomes but to uncover what it means, to reveal the foundation it rests on, the forces lurking beneath it, and the hidden motives it expresses—often in vague, distorted, and misleading ways.

This is why I have not spared my readers a look at its disastrous consequences: to prepare them for the ultimate and most terrifying question—what is the true meaning of the ascetic ideal? What is the source of its immense, monstrous power? Why does it wield such dominance? Why is it given so much space to flourish, and why is there no stronger resistance to it? The ascetic ideal embodies a single will. But where is the opposing will—the counter-ideal that resists and stands against it?

The ascetic ideal has one clear aim: to make every other interest in human life seem small and unimportant by comparison. It interprets entire eras, nations, and people solely in relation to this goal. It rejects and accepts, denies and affirms, only within the confines of its own interpretation. Is there any other system of meaning that has been so thoroughly worked out? The ascetic ideal refuses to submit to any other power. Instead, it claims precedence over all forces, asserting that nothing powerful in the world can exist without first being assigned meaning, value, and legitimacy by the ideal itself.

Everything is treated as a tool for its purpose, a means to its singular end.

So, where is the counterpart to this vast, all-encompassing system of will and interpretation? Why is such a counterpart absent? Where is the alternative "one aim"?

I am told that this counterpart is not absent—that it has long fought against the ascetic ideal, successfully challenging it, and has even gained dominance over it in some respects. Look, they say, to modern science—the purest form of real- world philosophy. Science, they argue, has achieved what the ascetic ideal never could: the courage to believe in itself, the will to exist on its own terms, unburdened by God, another world, or the ascetic virtues of denial and negation. Science, they say, is the true conqueror of the ascetic ideal.

All their loud, clumsy agitation leaves me unmoved; these self-proclaimed heralds of reality are poor performers, incapable of producing a sound deep enough to resonate with true understanding. They are not the voice of science's vast and profound abyss—for modern science is an abyss. In their mouths, the word "science" is reduced to a vulgarity, an abuse, an insult to its true meaning. The reality is quite the opposite of what the ascetic ideal's defenders claim. Science today has no faith in itself, much less in any ideal greater than itself. And wherever science still possesses passion, love, dedication, or even suffering, it is not an adversary of the ascetic ideal—it is its finest and most advanced form.

Does this sound strange? Perhaps, but consider this: even now, there are plenty of diligent and honorable workers among the learned, people who are genuinely pleased with their small spheres of activity. Because they enjoy their work, they sometimes become embarrassingly loud in demanding that everyone else should be content as well, especially with science. After all, they say, "There is so much useful work to do in science!"

I do not deny this; indeed, I would be the last to interfere with the joy these honest laborers find in their tasks. Their enthusiasm for their craft brings me some delight as well. But the fact that science requires hard work, or that it has contented workers, is no evidence that science as a whole possesses a unified purpose, a shared will, a single ideal, or a deep passion rooted in faith. On the contrary, the truth is precisely the opposite.

When science is not functioning as the newest incarnation of the ascetic ideal—a rare occurrence, reserved only for the most exceptional and refined cases—it often serves instead as a refuge for all kinds of cowardice, doubt, guilt, and self-loathing. It becomes a sanctuary for those plagued by a lack of ideals, those suffering from the absence of a great passion, and those tormented by their enforced restraint and moderation. Oh, how much does science obscure today? How much, at the very least, does it try to obscure?

The tireless diligence of our most accomplished scholars, their obsessive industriousness, their endless sacrifices at the altar of intellectual labor—how often is the true purpose of all this effort simply to avoid seeing a particular truth? Science, in such cases, acts as a form of self-anesthesia. Have you noticed this?

Anyone who spends time with scholars knows the experience: a single harmless word, unintentionally spoken, can wound them deeply. What you might think is a compliment can provoke an extreme bitterness, not because you intended offense, but because you failed to recognize the nature of the people you were dealing with. These scholars are sufferers—though they might not admit it even to themselves. They are dazed, unaware of their own condition, gripped by one overriding fear: the fear of becoming fully conscious.

Now, turn your attention to the other side—to those rare figures I previously mentioned, the supreme idealists among philosophers and scholars today. Could it be that we have found in them the true opponents of the ascetic ideal—its genuine anti-idealists? These "unbelievers" (for they all claim that title) believe so; they cling to this belief as their last vestige of faith. They are so earnest, so fiery in their declarations and gestures, so insistent that they stand in opposition to the ascetic ideal. But does their belief make it true?

We, who claim to "know," have become deeply suspicious of all believers, no matter their creed. Over time, this suspicion has led us to draw the opposite conclusions from those drawn by others. Where belief is strongest, we suspect the greatest difficulty in proving it; the strength of a belief often signals its actual improbability. We do not deny that faith brings comfort or even salvation; in fact, it is precisely because of this that we doubt faith proves anything at all. Strong faith, capable of creating happiness, raises suspicions about its object rather than validating its truth. Instead, it points to the likelihood of illusion.

What, then, is the situation with these figures—these solitary spirits, these self-proclaimed deniers, these champions of intellectual purity, these heroic seekers of truth? They are the pride of our age: pale atheists, anti-Christians, immoralists, Nihilists, sceptics, and "ephectics" (those who suspend judgment) as well as "hectics" (those burning with intellectual fever). These are the highest idealists of knowledge, the sole bearers of the intellectual conscience in our time. They believe themselves to be as distant as possible from the ascetic ideal, thinking of themselves as "free spirits."

And yet, if I may speak the truth they cannot see—for they are too close to themselves—this ideal is their ideal. They are, in fact, its most spiritualized embodiment. They are its most refined scouts, its sharpest weapon, and its most subtle and persuasive expression. If I am at all adept at unraveling riddles, then let me propose this: for some time, there have been no truly free spirits. Why? Because they still believe in truth.

Consider the Christian Crusaders in the East who encountered the infamous Order of Assassins—a group that epitomized free spirits, disciplined far beyond anything the strictest monastic orders could achieve. Among their highest initiates was shared a secret motto: "Nothing is true; everything is permitted." This was the ultimate expression of freedom in thought—freedom that rejected even the belief in truth. Have any Europeans, any self-proclaimed freethinkers, ever truly confronted this idea? Have they grappled with its consequences or ventured into the labyrinth it creates? I doubt it. No, I know otherwise.

The so-called "free spirits" of today are, in fact, bound tighter than ever. Their belief in truth has an absolutism that is unmatched, even fanatical. I speak from experience, having encountered it firsthand. This belief binds them to a form of dignified intellectual asceticism— a stoicism of the mind that prohibits negation as firmly as it does affirmation. They remain paralyzed before the brute fact, the factum brutum, as though standing still is their ultimate virtue.

This small-minded fatalism, this "petit faitalism" (as I term it), is especially evident in the French scientific mindset, which tries to claim moral superiority over the German approach. But this renunciation of interpretation—this refusal to modify, challenge, or creatively engage with facts—this so-called objectivity is nothing more than a modern variation of ascetic virtue. It is, in essence, another form of the same repudiation of the senses, merely disguised under a new guise. At its core, it is still the ascetic ideal in operation, perpetuating itself through intellectual austerity.

The force that drives science into its relentless pursuit of truth is none other than faith in the ascetic ideal itself, even when this faith operates as an unconscious imperative. Do not be mistaken—this is still faith, faith in the metaphysical value and intrinsic worth of truth, a belief that is legitimized and sustained only within the framework of the ascetic ideal. This ideal upholds and guarantees the worth of truth; if the ideal falls, so does the belief in the inherent value of truth.

Strictly speaking, there is no science without its guiding "hypotheses." The very concept of a science that stands independent of assumptions is illogical, even inconceivable. Before science can take form, there must first be a philosophy, a faith, something that provides it with direction, meaning, boundaries, methods, and ultimately, the right to exist. Anyone who imagines otherwise—who claims, for instance, to establish philosophy on a "purely scientific basis"—must first overturn not only philosophy itself but also truth as we understand it. This would be the gravest affront to both, an unforgivable insult to the foundations of thought.

Make no mistake: the unwavering pursuit of truth, conducted with such daring and extremity as demanded by the faith in science, inherently asserts the existence of a world distinct from life, nature, and history. By affirming such a world, does it not simultaneously reject its counterpart—this world, our world? This paradox was already noted in my earlier work, The Joyful Wisdom (Book V, Aphorism 344): "The one who pursues truth in this radical, uncompromising way presupposes the existence of another world. And in so doing, must they not reject this one— the very world in which we live?"

Even now, we so-called knowers, we godless opponents of metaphysics, remain bound to a legacy born of ancient belief. Our zeal for truth, the very fire that drives us, is drawn from a thousand-year-old blaze ignited by faith—a Christian faith, a Platonic faith. This faith declared that God is truth and that truth is divine. But what happens when this belief crumbles? What if nothing proves to be divine except error, blindness, and lies? What if God Himself turns out to be the oldest and most tenacious lie?

At this point, we must pause to consider the consequences carefully. Science, which has long appeared as self-justifying, now finds itself in need of justification. This is not to say such justification necessarily exists; rather, it highlights a fundamental problem that has been ignored by nearly all philosophers, ancient and modern alike. Why this blind spot? Because all philosophy to date has been shaped by the ascetic ideal, where truth was enshrined as absolute—whether as Being, God, or the ultimate arbiter of reality.

Truth was sanctified, removed from scrutiny, and treated as unquestionable. Do you grasp the significance of this "unquestionable"?

Once belief in the God of the ascetic ideal is rejected, a new and pressing question arises: what is the value of truth itself? This becomes a problem for the first time—a question that the ascetic ideal never allowed to surface. The Will to Truth, which has driven humanity for centuries, now demands a critique. This is the task we must take upon ourselves: to examine, even challenge, the value of truth itself.

If this seems overly concise, I encourage readers to revisit The Joyful Wisdom, particularly the aphorism titled "How Far We Too Are Still Pious" (Aphorism 344) and the entirety of its fifth book. For further reflection, the preface to The Dawn of Day also offers valuable insights into this ongoing inquiry. Through these works, one might better understand the profound questions we must now face in our reevaluation of truth, its worth, and the faith that has sustained it for so long.

No, you cannot deceive me with science when I seek the natural opposition to the ascetic ideal or when I ask: "Where is the counter-will, the opposing ideal that expresses itself against it?" Science is far too dependent to fulfill this role. In every field, science relies on an ideal, a value-creating force that gives it direction, a purpose in which it can believe. Science does not create values on its own. Its relationship to the ascetic ideal is not inherently antagonistic. On the contrary, it often acts as a driving force in the inner evolution of that ideal.

If we examine more closely, science does not attack the core of the ascetic ideal but merely its outward manifestations—its rigid forms, surface expressions, and dogmas. Science liberates the inner life of the ideal by stripping away its superficialities, but it does not overthrow the ideal itself. In fact, both science and the ascetic ideal rest on the same foundation: an overvaluation of truth, or more precisely, a shared belief in the impossibility of questioning or valuing truth itself. This shared foundation makes them allies. If one is to critique the ascetic ideal, one must also critique science. Recognize this connection; it is crucial.

Art, in contrast, holds a far more genuine opposition to the ascetic ideal. Art, where deception is sanctified, and the will to create illusions is celebrated, stands fundamentally opposed to the ascetic ideal. Plato understood this deeply; he was the greatest adversary of art that Europe has ever known. His opposition to Homer reflects the full antagonism: on one side, Plato represents the life- denying transcendentalist, the great critic of existence. On the other side, Homer stands as life's unconscious celebrant, its golden admirer. For art to serve the ascetic ideal is the deepest corruption of its essence— a sad but frequent reality, as artists are often susceptible to such compromise.

Physiologically speaking, both science and the ascetic ideal stem from similar conditions: a certain decline in vitality, a frugality of life. Both reflect a cooling of emotions, a slowing of life's tempo, and the replacement of instinct with analysis and reason. Seriousness becomes their shared hallmark—a clear sign of life's struggle, a strenuous effort to maintain balance. Consider the eras in which scholars and intellectuals gain prominence; they often coincide with periods of cultural fatigue, societal decline, and the fading of confidence in life and the future.

The ascendancy of intellectuals, like the rise of democracy, arbitration instead of war, equal rights for women, or religions based on pity, are all symptoms of life's weakening vitality. They signify moments when a society has shifted from the vitality of creation to the slower rhythms of maintenance and decline. Science, when considered as a problem, raises questions about its very meaning and purpose. For a deeper exploration of this, one might refer to the preface of The Birth of Tragedy.

Modern science, despite its celebrated independence, often acts as the unwitting ally of the ascetic ideal. This partnership is subtle and unconscious, but it is undeniable. Science and the ascetic ideal have long reinforced one another. Their apparent opposition is misleading; they serve the same underlying purpose. Even the so-called victories of science often strengthen the ideal, not weaken it. When science dismantles a theological framework, it does not destroy the ideal itself. Instead, it refines it, making it more elusive, abstract, and insidious.

For instance, did the collapse of theological astronomy herald the end of the ascetic ideal? Hardly. If anything, the need for transcendental solutions to life's mysteries has only grown stronger. Since Copernicus, humanity has seen a continuous process of self-diminishment. The idea that we are mere accidents in a random and indifferent universe has not freed us from the ascetic ideal but has intensified our longing for meaning. This relentless will to belittle ourselves, to make existence seem smaller and more inconsequential, reveals the enduring grip of the ascetic ideal.

Science, with all its achievements, has yet to confront this core issue. It has not provided an alternative to the ascetic ideal but has instead evolved alongside it, refining and reinforcing its foundations. The need for critique remains. Only by addressing the shared underpinnings of science and the ascetic ideal can we begin to question the deeper values that continue to shape humanity.

Alas, humanity's belief in its own dignity, uniqueness, and indispensable role in the grand scheme of existence has eroded. Once, man regarded himself as almost divine—"a child of God," or even a "demi-God." But now, that sense of sacredness is gone, and he sees himself as nothing more than an animal—plain, literal, unremarkable, and unqualified. Since Copernicus, it feels as though mankind has been slipping down a steep incline, rolling faster and faster away from the perceived center of existence. But to where? Into the void? Into the "thrilling sensation of his own nothingness"?

Perhaps this descent is merely a direct path back to the old ideal. Consider how all branches of science—whether astronomy or even philosophy, including the harsh self-examination of reason itself—have labored to dismantle man's lofty opinion of himself. Kant, for instance, confessed to feeling diminished by the discoveries of astronomy, admitting it "annihilates my own importance." Science seems to take a strange pride in this project, finding its satisfaction in maintaining the very state of self-contempt it worked so hard to cultivate in humanity. For science, this disdain for man becomes his final and most profound claim to self-worth—a bitter, stoic form of pride. After all, only one who understands value can truly despise something, even himself.

But does this mean science has effectively countered the ascetic ideal? Hardly. If anything, it reinforces it. Take Kant's so-called "victory" over theological dogmas concerning God, the soul, freedom, and immortality. Many theologians believed this victory marked a blow to the ascetic ideal, but has it really? In truth, transcendentalists have thrived since Kant. Freed from direct ties to theologians, they've found a new respectability under the guise of science. Kant taught them the tools and methods to pursue their deepest aspirations without theological oversight, cloaked in scientific respectability.

Consider the agnostics, who revere the unknown and the absolute mystery. These modern worshippers elevate their very questioning into a form of divinity. They have turned their reverence for what they cannot comprehend into a new kind of faith. Xaver Doudan remarked on this phenomenon, noting how the habit of admiring the unintelligible has led to confusion, displacing a simpler stance of merely accepting the unknown. Ancient peoples, he speculated, may have been spared such ravages.

Suppose that everything humanity has ever come to know contradicts or horrifies its desires. In such a situation, how convenient it is to shift the blame— not onto the desires themselves but onto the act of knowing! "There is no knowledge; therefore, there is a God."

What an elegant syllogism! What a masterstroke for the ascetic ideal! It manages to transform humanity's dissatisfaction with the world into a divine affirmation of its own worldview. In doing so, the ideal emerges not weakened but stronger, perpetuating its hold over humanity.

Or, does modern history seem to reflect a greater confidence in life or its ideals? Quite the opposite—it prides itself on being merely a mirror, rejecting any teleological purpose or claims of proving anything. It disdains judgment, deeming such roles beneath it, which it might call an act of "good taste." Instead, it avoids both assertions and denials, merely fixing its gaze and "describing." This approach, while seemingly detached, is highly ascetic and, even more so, deeply nihilistic. Make no mistake about that.

Consider the historian's gaze: it is stern, somber, and determined, much like that of a solitary explorer in the Arctic, peering outward as if to avoid looking within or back. What does he see? A barren wasteland. Life lies silent beneath the snow, and the only echoes are bleak murmurs: "Whither?" "Vanity," "Nothingness." This desolate landscape yields nothing—no growth, no vitality— except perhaps the hollow intellectualism of "meta-politics" in St. Petersburg or Tolstoy's overwrought pity.

And then there is that other, perhaps even more modern, school of historians—a group enamored with life and the ascetic ideal alike. They romanticize and fetishize the contemplative life, praising it as though it were an art form, and establishing for themselves a smug little corner of pseudo- intellectual worship. These "sweet intellectuals," with their pretentious adoration of winter landscapes and ascetic ideals, inspire in me a deep and furious longing—for action, for vitality, even for the icy mists of historical nihilism. Yes, I'd prefer the company of those historical nihilists trudging through grey, cold fog over these effete, self- satisfied contemplators.

But worse still are the "objective" historians—those detached scholars perched on their worm-eaten chairs, feigning neutrality while oozing hypocrisy.

They are neither fully priests nor wholly men of passion; instead, they are grotesque hybrids, half-priest and half-satyr, their entire existence marked by a false refinement. Renan, for instance, reeks of perfume but lacks substance, a perfect example of this type. Such figures make me bristle with irritation. They sap my patience, and their very presence enrages me more than the supposed "play" of history itself. How could one not feel disdain? These eunuchs of thought, these weak-kneed admirers of ascetic ideals, deserve nothing but contempt.

Nature, in its wisdom, granted horns to the bull and teeth to the lion. For what purpose did it give me feet, if not to kick? Yes, kick—to trample down these cowardly intellectuals, these groveling contemplators who flinch at vitality and flirt shamelessly with ascetic ideals. They are hypocrites, eunuchs, and frauds, wrapping themselves in the guise of wisdom or objectivity, but inside, they are hollow. They are tragic clowns posing as priests, agitators masquerading as heroes, and opportunists exploiting idealism for personal gain.

Take, for example, the modern Anti-Semites, who cloak themselves in the supposed virtue of "Christian-Aryan honour." They roll their eyes and posture with cheap moralistic tricks, aiming to manipulate the most gullible elements of society. Their success reveals the sad state of modern intellectual life, particularly in Germany, where the mind has been dulled by an unhealthy diet of newspapers, politics, beer, and Wagnerian bombast. Combine this with the isolationist arrogance of "Germany above all," and you have the perfect storm of intellectual stagnation, a kind of mental paralysis that grips the nation and prevents any genuine progress or vitality.

All reverence to the ascetic ideal, but only insofar as it is honest and believes in itself. When it plays no games or flirts with pretensions, it retains a certain dignity. But the insipid bugs who cling to it, feeding on its infinite aspirations, until even the infinite stinks of their corruption—I cannot abide them. Nor can I stomach the empty facades of life these hypocrites parade, the exhausted souls wrapped in hollow wisdom, or the theatrical agitators hiding their triviality behind grand ideals. They represent everything that stifles life, everything that dulls the spark of vitality and replaces it with the rotting specter of pretense and decay.

Europe today seems consumed by its craving for stimulation. It overflows with ingenious means of excitement, as if it knows no greater need than for stimulants, whether intellectual or alcoholic. This has led to a widespread counterfeit of ideals—a flood of artificial inspirations and theatrical displays of passion. The atmosphere is thick with a pseudo-alcoholic stench of pretense, suffocating and false.

I can only imagine how many shipments of fake idealism, heroic posturing, and melodramatic moralism would need to be exported from Europe to cleanse its air. How many barrels of saccharine pity labeled as "the religion of suffering"? How many props for limp-minded intellects—crutches of righteous indignation? How many actors parading as champions of the Christian moral ideal? There's clearly a new business opportunity here: a trade in small, mass-produced idols of idealism and compliant "idealists." The market is wide open! With boldness—or perhaps just a free, uninhibited hand—one might imagine rebranding the entire world under these ready-made ideals.

But enough! Let's set aside these absurdities and grotesque spectacles of the modern spirit. They elicit as much ridicule as revulsion, and our present problem—the meaning of the ascetic ideal—does not depend on them. I will address these matters in more depth elsewhere, under the title "A Contribution to the History of European Nihilism." This will appear in a larger work I am preparing, The Will to Power: An Attempt at a Transvaluation of All Values. My only reason for mentioning them here is to note a peculiar irony: the ascetic ideal's most dangerous adversaries are not its critics, but its comedians. These performers of the ideal inspire distrust, undermining its seriousness.

In all other domains where intellectual work is done earnestly and authentically, without counterfeit, the ideal is often dispensed with entirely. This abstention is popularly labeled "Atheism," but even this so-called rejection is deceptive. The will to truth, which persists even in atheism, is in fact the most distilled and severe formulation of the ascetic ideal. Stripped of its adornments and external structures, this will to truth represents the ideal's core, not its remnant.

Consider this carefully: unadulterated, honest atheism—breathed in by the most intellectually rigorous minds of our time—does not oppose the ascetic ideal as it might seem. Rather, it is one of its final, logical expressions. It is a culmination, an awe-inspiring catastrophe born from two millennia of training in the pursuit of truth. This discipline has finally forbidden itself from indulging in the "lie" of belief in God.

This trajectory is not unique to Europe. A strikingly similar development occurred in India, providing independent and therefore illustrative evidence of the pattern. The same ideal drove to the same conclusion centuries earlier, culminating with Buddha around 500 years before the European era. This evolution began in the Sāmkhya philosophy and was later popularized by Buddha, transforming it into a religion.

The parallel is fascinating: two cultures, separated by vast distances, reaching the same endpoint through the relentless logic of their ideals. Europe, following its path of rigorous devotion to truth, finds itself arriving at a stark, godless reality—not an opposition to the ascetic ideal, but its ultimate refinement. The story of this ideal is not yet finished, and its ramifications continue to unfold in ways both profound and disquieting.

What, I ask in all seriousness, has truly triumphed over the Christian God? The answer is stated in my Joyful Wisdom, Aphorism 357: "Christian morality itself has triumphed—the idea of truth, taken with increasing seriousness, the intricate subtlety of the Christian conscience transformed and elevated into the scientific conscience, into an intellectual rigor at any cost." Viewing nature as proof of God's benevolence, interpreting history as evidence of divine reason and a moral order, seeing personal experiences as though every event were orchestrated for the salvation of the soul—such ideas are now entirely overturned. The sharper conscience rejects these interpretations, deeming them dishonorable, cowardly, and false. This severity, this demand for intellectual integrity, makes us, indeed, good Europeans, inheritors of the most rigorous self- discipline Europe has ever known.

All great things, however, crumble by their own weight, by acts of self- destruction; this is the law of life, the rule of inevitable "self- mastery" intrinsic to existence itself. Even the lawgiver must eventually face the verdict of his own law: pater e legem quam ipse tulisti—"submit to the law you have made." Christianity as a dogma fell through the consequences of its own morality, and now Christianity as a morality is unraveling in the same way. We are on the verge of this event. Christian truthfulness has led, step by step, to conclusions that ultimately turn against itself. It culminates in the question: "What is the meaning of all will for truth?"

Here lies our challenge, my unknown friends (for I know of no friends yet): what is the sense of our existence if not that the will for truth has become self- aware in us as a problem? With this self- awareness, morality as we know it collapses. This is the grand drama of the next two centuries in Europe—the most terrifying, enigmatic, yet potentially hopeful of all dramas.

Without the ascetic ideal, man—the human animal—lacked meaning. His existence had no purpose, no justification. The question "What is man for?" was met with silence. There was no will for man or the world; a vast emptiness surrounded human existence. Behind every great life echoed an even greater refrain of "Vanity!" The ascetic ideal answered this vacuum. It signified that something was missing—

that man needed justification, explanation, affirmation. He suffered not just physically but from the problem of his own meaning.

Man's issue was not suffering itself, but rather the lack of an answer to the searing question: "Why do we suffer?" The bravest and most resilient of creatures, man does not inherently reject suffering; he embraces it when it has meaning. He seeks suffering if it serves a purpose. What humanity could not bear was the meaninglessness of suffering, and the ascetic ideal gave it meaning. For the first time, suffering was explained. The immense void was filled. The door to suicidal nihilism was shut.

Granted, the explanation brought new and more agonizing suffering— more corrosive, more brutal—but it gave suffering purpose. It recast suffering through the lens of guilt. Despite this, humanity was saved. Man now had meaning and could "will" something—anything. The content of the will mattered less than the act of willing itself. The will was preserved, and with it, humanity was saved from nihilism.

This ascetic ideal, however, expressed profound contempt for life. It represented a hatred of the human, a disdain for the animal, and an aversion to the material. It loathed the senses, feared reason, rejected happiness, and recoiled from beauty. It yearned to escape illusion, change, growth, decay, desire—even life itself. At its core, the ascetic ideal revealed a will for Nothingness—a will fundamentally opposed to life. Yet it remains a will.

And as I said at the start: humanity would rather will Nothingness than not will at all.

Peoples and Countries

The Europeans today see themselves as the highest examples of humanity on Earth.

A common trait of Europeans is the inconsistency between their words and actions, unlike the people of the East, who stay true to themselves in daily life. The way Europeans established colonies can be explained by their nature, which resembles that of a predator.

This inconsistency stems from Christianity having abandoned the class it originally came from.

This marks a significant difference between us and the Greeks: their morals were shaped by the ruling classes. The morality we see in Thucydides is the same as the one that erupted in Plato's time. Honesty, for example, saw an effort during the Renaissance, often to benefit the arts. Michelangelo's view of God as the "Tyrant of the World" reflected an honest perspective.

I hold Michelangelo in higher regard than Raphael because Michelangelo, through all the Christian limitations of his era, glimpsed a nobler cultural ideal than the one embodied by Christian-Raphaelite art. Raphael merely and respectfully celebrated the values handed down to him without striving for something beyond. Michelangelo, in contrast, grappled with the immense challenge of creating new values. He sought to embody the conqueror perfected, the one who must first overcome his inner hero, a figure standing at the highest pedestal, mastering even his pity, and ruthlessly destroying anything that does not reflect his vision. Michelangelo at times surpassed his age and Christian Europe. However, he often yielded to the softer, eternal feminine elements of Christianity. In the end, it seems he abandoned the bold ideal of his greatest moments—a vision too immense for anyone but a man in his prime to carry. As he aged, he could no longer bear it. To fulfill his ideal, he would have had to destroy Christianity itself, but he lacked the philosophical depth to do so.

Perhaps only Leonardo da Vinci among the artists achieved a truly post- Christian perspective. Leonardo seemed to carry within him an understanding of the East—the "land of dawn"— both internally and externally. There is something transcendent and silent about him, a trait shared by all who have seen too much of both the good and the bad in the world.

How much we have learned in just fifty years! The Romantic School and its belief in "the people" have been entirely discredited. Homeric poetry is not "popular" poetry. The powers of nature are no longer deified. Relationships between languages no longer imply relationships between races. There is no mystical contemplation of the supernatural, no hidden truth in religion.

The question of truthfulness has become a completely new challenge. I am amazed. From this perspective, figures like Bismarck seem guilty due to carelessness, and Richard Wagner seems culpable for his lack of humility. Even Plato's noble falsehoods (pia fraus) and Kant's derivation of the Categorical Imperative now appear flawed, as these ideas were not truly their own beliefs.

In the end, even doubt turns upon itself, leading to doubt about doubt. The question of the value of truthfulness and how far it should go lies before us.

What I appreciate in the German character is its Mephistophelian quality. However, to truly understand this, one must have a greater concept of Mephistopheles than Goethe had. Goethe reduced Mephistopheles to make his "inner Faust" appear larger. The true German Mephistopheles is far more dangerous, daring, wicked, and cunning—yet also more open and honest. Consider the character of Frederick the Great or, even more so, Frederick II of Hohenstaufen.

The true German Mephistopheles crosses the Alps and claims everything he sees as his own. Then, like Winckelmann or Mozart, he collects himself. He views Faust and Hamlet as exaggerated figures made for ridicule, and he even looks at Luther the same way. Goethe, during his better German moments, likely laughed quietly at such things. But even Goethe could not avoid slipping back into his more somber moods.

Perhaps the Germans simply grew up in the wrong environment! There is something within them that could have been Hellenic—something that stirs when they come into contact with the South, as seen in Winckelmann, Goethe, and Mozart. However, we must remember that as a culture, the Germans are still young. Luther remains their last significant historical figure, and their most recent defining book is still the Bible. The Germans have never truly "moralized" in a philosophical sense. Even their diet has been a curse, contributing to a certain Philistinism.

The Germans are a dangerous people, experts at inventing intoxicants of all kinds. Gothic art, rococo (as Semper described), their sense of history and exoticism, Hegel, Richard Wagner— even Leibniz, who still exerts influence today—all are evidence of this. They even turned the servile spirit into an ideal, celebrating it as the virtue of scholars, soldiers, and the humble-minded. Germans may well be the most complex and mixed people on Earth.

They are "the people of the middle," inventors of porcelain and a peculiar type of bureaucratic Privy Councillor, resembling something out of Chinese tradition.

The smallness and pettiness of the German soul were not caused by their history of small states. History shows that people from even smaller states could still be proud and independent. Nor does a large state automatically foster freer, stronger souls. A man whose spirit bows to the command, "Thou shalt and must kneel!"—a man whose very body instinctively submits to titles, medals, and favors from above—will bow even lower under a greater ruler than under a lesser one. There is no doubt about this.

In contrast, in the lower classes of Italy, there is still a sense of aristocratic self-assurance. The discipline and self-respect that come from a long history of greatness are still visible. A poor Venetian gondolier cuts a more impressive figure than a Privy Councillor from Berlin and is, in many ways, the better man. Ask the women—they know this.

Most artists, even the greatest among them, have historically come from the serving classes. Whether they served nobility, princes, women, or the masses, they remained tied to their patrons, not to mention their dependence on the Church and moral conventions.

Rubens, for example, painted the nobility of his time, but he adhered to their vague notions of taste rather than his own sense of beauty. He worked against his personal standards.

Van Dyck, however, was nobler in this regard. He elevated those he painted, infusing them with qualities he admired most. He did not lower himself to match them; instead, he brought them up to his level through his art.

The artist's submissive humility to his audience, which Sebastian Bach revealed in bold and shocking terms in the dedication of his High Mass, may be harder to detect in music, but it is deeply ingrained. If I were to explain my views on this subject, I might not even find a willing audience.

Chopin, like Van Dyck, carried himself with distinction. Beethoven had the proud spirit of a peasant, while Haydn carried the pride of a servant. Mendelssohn, too, had a natural elegance, much like Goethe.

German scholars with wit have always been few—countable on one hand— while the rest possess understanding, and some, fortunately, that famous "childlike quality" that enables them to intuitively sense things. This ability has led German science to uncover phenomena that we can scarcely imagine—and which, perhaps, do not exist. Yet, this quality of "divination" is not shared by the Jews among the Germans.

Just as French scholars reflect the wit and courtesy of French society, Germans mirror the deep, contemplative seriousness of their mystics and musicians, along with a certain naive childishness. Italians, on the other hand, exude a sense of republican refinement and artistry; they can appear noble and proud without slipping into vanity.

It is my hope that more of Germany's talented individuals will eventually gain enough self-control to abandon their poor taste for affectation and sentimental gloom. Such men will, I trust, turn against the influences of Richard Wagner and Schopenhauer. These two figures, dangerous as they are, flatter Germany's most perilous traits and lead the nation toward decline. Instead, a stronger and more promising future lies with the legacy of Goethe, Beethoven, and Bismarck, not with such deviations from the path. After all, Germany has yet to produce true philosophers.

The peasant represents the most common form of nobility because he relies primarily on himself. Peasant blood remains the strongest in Germany, as seen in figures like Luther, Niebuhr, and Bismarck. Regarding Bismarck, one cannot ignore his Slavic ancestry. German faces often reveal this mixture—those with vigorous, masculine blood left Germany for foreign lands, while the remaining population, largely docile and subservient, saw improvement through an infusion of Slavonic elements. Today, the Brandenburg and broader Prussian nobility, as well as the peasants from specific northern regions, embody the most masculine natures in Germany. It is natural for such men to rule; indeed, the future of German culture rests with the sons of Prussian officers.

Germany has always suffered from a lack of wit. Even average minds achieve high honors there simply because they are uncommon. Qualities like diligence, persistence, and a dispassionate, critical perspective are what Germany values most. These traits have allowed German scholarship and the German military system to dominate Europe.

Parliaments can be of use to a strong and capable statesman; they provide something stable to rely on, something that can bear responsibility. However, Germany should not adopt the counting obsession and faith in majorities seen in Latin nations. There is still an opportunity to innovate in politics, and universal suffrage, which is relatively new and could easily be uprooted, should not be allowed to take deeper root. It was introduced only as a temporary solution to pressing problems.

Can anyone genuinely care about the German Empire as it stands? Where is its new and innovative thinking? If it is merely a new combination of power, that's even worse—especially if it lacks a clear vision. Peace and laisser - aller are not the kind of politics I respect. What interests me in Germany is the potential to rule effectively and to champion the most elevated ideas.

The greatest threat in the world today is England's narrow-mindedness. Remarkably, I observe more ambition for greatness among Russian Nihilists than among English Utilitarians. To achieve true mastery, Germany must forge a union with the Slavic races and incorporate the skills of the Jews, who are the most capable financiers.

To achieve this, several elements are necessary: (a) A firm grasp of reality. (b) Abandoning the English principle of popular representation and replacing it with representation of major interests. (c) An unconditional alliance with Russia and a joint strategy to ensure that English schemes have no influence in Russia. The future must not be Americanized. (d) Nationalistic politics are unsustainable, and the entanglement of Christian ideals is a major hindrance. In Europe, all rational minds are skeptics, even if they do not openly admit it.

I see beyond these national conflicts, new empires, and whatever else appears on the surface. My true concern is with what I perceive slowly taking shape—the vision of a United Europe. This has been the only meaningful labor, the singular impulse in the souls of all the broad-minded and forward-thinking individuals of this century. Their aim has been to prepare a new synthesis, an effort to anticipate and shape the future of "the European." Only in moments of weakness or as they grew older did they revert to the narrow nationalism of "Fatherland" sentiments—then they once again became "patriots." Figures such as Napoleon, Heinrich Heine, Goethe, Beethoven, Stendhal, and Schopenhauer come to mind. Perhaps even Richard Wagner, with his peculiar brand of German obscurity, belongs among them, though his inclusion warrants some hesitation.

Supporting the minds that seek this unity is a significant and clarifying economic reality: the small states of Europe—our current kingdoms and empires—will soon become economically unsustainable. The frenzied, unregulated competition for control of local and international trade is pushing Europe toward amalgamation into a single power. Money is driving this necessity. For Europe to effectively engage in the looming struggle for global dominance (and it is easy to imagine against whom this struggle will be fought), an agreement with England will likely become unavoidable. England's colonies will be essential in this endeavor, just as modern Germany, in its emerging role as broker and middleman, will find itself reliant on the colonial assets of Holland.

It is clear that no one believes England can maintain its current global role alone for another fifty years. The impossibility of preventing homines novi from entering government will undermine her stability, while the constant rotation of political parties will obstruct any efforts requiring long-term planning. Today, a man must first be a soldier to secure his reputation as a merchant later. Suffice it to say, the next century will likely follow the path laid by Napoleon—the foremost figure of his era and the most innovative and visionary of modern times. For the challenges of the coming century, the methods of popular representation and parliamentary governance seem woefully inadequate.

Europe's condition in the next century will once again demand the cultivation of manly virtues, as life will be defined by constant danger. Universal military service already serves as a curious counterbalance to the softness introduced by democratic ideals, born as it was out of the nations' struggles. And what is a nation?

A group of people who speak the same language and consume the same news. These groups call themselves "nations" and are all too eager to trace their ancestry and history to a single, unbroken source. Yet, even with the help of the most outrageous falsehoods about the past, they have never fully succeeded in doing so.

What confusion and falsehood must exist for questions of "race" to even be raised in the chaotic mixture that is modern Europe! (Assuming, of course, that the origins of these writers are not in some far-off place like Horneo or Borneo.) A simple principle: avoid associating with anyone who participates in the deceitful "race" charade.

With the freedom of travel available today, people of like minds and shared heritage can gather and create communities with shared customs and practices. This is how nations can be overcome. To make Europe a true center of culture, we must rise above the foolishness of national divisions. At higher levels, there is already an interconnectedness that we cannot ignore. Think of France and German philosophy, Richard Wagner and Paris during the 1830s to 1850s, or Goethe and Greece. There is a natural momentum toward unifying Europe's past in the minds of its greatest thinkers.

Humanity still has much ahead of it—how could anyone believe the ideal lies in the past? Perhaps the past can only offer meaning when seen in contrast to our present, which might well be a lower phase of development.

This persistent uncertainty haunts us, keeping us awake, raising questions that no one wants to acknowledge. It's our riddle, our Sphinx, standing near more than one precipice. We suspect that today's Europeans are deeply mistaken about what they value most, and some indifferent, childlike force—a pitiless demon— seems to toy with our passions and ideals, just as it has perhaps toyed with all that has lived and loved before us.

I suspect that much of what we Europeans admire today—values like "humanity," "sympathy," and "pity"—might have some worth only because they weaken and tame certain powerful, primal drives. Over time, however, these virtues seem to shrink the potential of the human type, reducing us to mediocrity. If I may use a desperate phrase for a desperate situation: all of this leads to the belittling of man. For an epicurean god watching this human comedy unfold, it must be amusing to see Europeans believe, with all their moral earnestness and self-satisfaction, that they are advancing. The truth, however, is that they are sinking—lower and lower. By cultivating herd-friendly virtues and suppressing the contrary qualities that could create a new, stronger, and more masterful race, we are merely refining the herd-animal within man. And yet, man remains the animal that has not yet stabilized itself.

Genius and the times in which it arises are intricately connected. Heroism, for example, is not a form of selfishness—it often leads to ruin. The strength of an individual often finds its direction shaped by the era into which they are born, giving rise to the misconception that such a person is a product of their time. In reality, this strength could manifest in many different ways. There is always a disconnect between the individual and their time. Public opinion tends to celebrate the herd instinct—the instinct of the weak—while the strong individual fights for ideals that defy this collective mindset.

The looming fate of Europe is clear: her strongest individuals emerge rarely, and even then, often too late in life. In their youth, they are already burdened by sorrow, disillusionment, and a darkness of mind. This happens because, with the intensity of their strength, they confront the full weight of their era's despair— the despair of knowledge and disillusionment—and drain it completely. Yet, this is the ultimate test of their power: they must rise above the sickness of their age to find their own health. Their distinction is marked by their late blooming—late joy, late folly, and a late but exuberant springtime of spirit.

But here lies the danger of our time: everything we cherished in our youth has betrayed us. Even our last love—the one we placed in Truth herself— threatens to betray us if we are not careful. Let us guard this final love with vigilance, for it represents our deepest acknowledgment and our most profound hope.

The End

Twilight of the Idols

Friedrich Nietzsche

Prologue

To stay cheerful while dealing with a grim and extremely serious task is no small artistic skill. Yet, what could be more essential than cheerfulness? Nothing is ever truly successful unless vibrant energy has helped create it. Only extra strength proves real power. A rethinking of all values—a question so dark and massive that it even casts a shadow over the one who raises it—is a task so heavy with consequence that anyone who takes it on must occasionally step into the sunlight to shake off a seriousness that becomes overwhelming, unbearably so. This goal justifies any method, and every event along the way becomes an unexpected benefit. Above all, war. War has always been the ultimate strategy for those who have delved too deeply into their own thoughts or grown too profound; a wound provokes the strength to heal.

For many years, I've lived by a saying, though I'll keep its origin a secret from curious scholars: "The spirit grows, virtue flourishes through a wound."

At other times, another way to recover, one I prefer even more, is to question idols. There are more idols than truths in the world, and this is why I have such a "sharp eye" for this world. It is also why I have such a "sharp ear." To ask questions of these idols with a hammer, and maybe hear that familiar hollow sound that comes from something empty—what joy this brings to someone who listens carefully, even with a mind attuned to what isn't spoken. For an old psychologist and Pied Piper like me, even the things that wish to remain silent cannot help but reveal themselves.

This book, as its title suggests, is mainly a kind of relaxation, a flash of light, a playful escape for a psychologist in his free time. But could it also be a new kind of battle? Are we once again questioning new idols? This small work is a bold declaration of war. As for questioning idols, this time, it isn't just the idols of the present day but the eternal ones that are struck with a hammer, as though they were tuning forks. These idols are certainly the oldest, the most self-assured, and the most puffed-up. None are more hollow. Yet this doesn't change the fact that they are believed in more than any others. They are never even called idols—at least, not the most revered ones among them.

Chapter 1
Maxims – And Missiles

Idleness is the root of all psychology. What? Does that mean psychology is a kind of vice? Even the bravest among us rarely has the courage to face what they truly know. Aristotle said that to live alone, a person must be either an animal or a god. But there's a third option missing: one must be both—a philosopher.

"All truth is simple."—Isn't that a double lie? Sometimes, I choose to remain blind to certain things. Wisdom places limits even on knowledge. A person recovers best from their extraordinary nature—from their intellect—by letting their instincts take over for a while.

So which is it? Is humanity just a mistake made by God? Or is God simply a mistake made by humanity?

From life's school of war: That which doesn't kill me makes me stronger.

Help yourself, and others will help you too. This is the true meaning of loving your neighbor.

A person should never be ashamed of their actions. Once a deed is done, they shouldn't disown it. Feelings of guilt are indecent.

Can a donkey be tragic? To be crushed under a burden it can neither carry nor throw off—isn't this the fate of a philosopher?

If someone knows why they exist, they can figure out how to live. Happiness isn't the goal of life; only the English make that their aim.

Man created woman—out of what? Out of a rib taken from his god, from his "ideal."

What are you searching for? Do you wish to multiply yourself tenfold, a hundredfold? Are you seeking followers? Look for zeros, not people!

Those of us who belong to the future, like myself, are harder to understand than those who mirror their time, but we're treated with more respect. Simply put: we are never fully understood— that's why we have authority.

On women: "Truth? Oh, you don't understand truth! Isn't it an insult to all our sense of modesty?"

There is an artist after my own heart, humble in his needs. He only desires two things: his bread and his art—panem et Circem.

Those who cannot impose their will onto the world at least give it some meaning. They believe there's already a will within it. (This is the essence of faith.)

What? You chose virtue and a heart full of passion, yet you still glance enviously at the rewards of the shameless? But by choosing virtue, you've renounced all "advantages"... (this belongs nailed to the door of an anti-Semite).

The perfect woman writes literature as if it were a minor vice, a passing experiment, all the while looking around to see if anyone is noticing—and hoping that someone does.

One should only choose situations where fake virtues are unnecessary, where, like a tightrope walker on their rope, one must either fall, stand firm, or find a way out.

"Evil men have no songs."—How, then, do the Russians have songs?

"German intellect"—for eighteen years this phrase has been a contradiction in terms.

When a man tries to find the origins of everything, he becomes like a crab. The historian always looks backward; eventually, he even starts believing backward.

Feeling content keeps a person from catching a cold. Has a woman who knew she was well-dressed ever gotten sick?—No, not even if she was barely covered by rags.

I distrust anyone who builds elaborate systems and avoid them. The desire to create a system shows a lack of honesty.

Man thinks women are profound—why? Because he can never fully understand them. Women are not even shallow.

When a woman has masculine virtues, she can make you want to run away.

When she doesn't have any masculine virtues, she runs away herself.

"How often conscience used to sting in the past! It must have had strong teeth back then! But today, what's gone wrong?"—A question for the dentist.

Mistakes made in haste rarely come alone. The first time, a person always overdoes things. Because of that, they make a second mistake, where they end up doing too little.

When a worm is stepped on, it curls up. This shows its caution— it lowers the chances of being stepped on again. In moral terms, this is called humility.

There is a kind of hatred for lies and deceit that comes from a sharp sense of humor. There is also the same hatred, but born from cowardice—the fear of lying because it's forbidden by divine law. Too cowardly to lie...

What tiny things bring happiness! The sound of bagpipes. Life without music would be a mistake. The German even imagines God as a singer.

"One can only think and write while sitting" (G. Flaubert). Now I've got you, you nihilist! Living a sedentary life is the true sin against the Holy Spirit. Only the thoughts that come to you while walking have any real worth.

Sometimes, we psychologists are like restless horses, growing uneasy as we see our own shadow rise and fall before us. A psychologist must look away from himself if he wants to see anything clearly.

Do we immoralists harm virtue in any way? No more than anarchists harm royalty. In fact, only after being shot at have princes returned to their thrones with greater strength. The moral of the story: morality must be tested by attack.

Are you rushing ahead?—Are you doing so as a leader or as an exception? Or perhaps you're just running away?... This is the first question of conscience.

Are you authentic, or are you just acting? Are you the real thing or merely a representative of it? Or, worse, are you just a copy of an actor?... This is the second question of conscience.

The disappointed man says: "I searched for great men, but all I found were imitators of their ideals."

Are you someone who observes from the sidelines, or someone who lends a hand? Or are you someone who looks away or even turns their back? This is the third question of conscience.

Do you want to follow, lead, or walk your own path alone? A person must know what they desire—and that they truly desire something. This is the fourth question of conscience.

They were merely rungs on my ladder, steps I used to climb higher. For that purpose, I had to move past them. But they thought I wanted to stop and rest on them.

Does it matter whether others agree that I'm right? I am far too right. And the one who laughs best today will also laugh last.

The formula for my happiness: a Yes, a No, a straight path, and a goal.

Chapter 2
The Problem of Socrates

Throughout history, the wisest minds have always agreed on one thing: life is not good. No matter the time or place, their words have been the same— filled with doubt, sadness, weariness, and even hostility toward life. Even Socrates, in his final moments, said: "To live is to be sick for a long time. I owe a cock to the god Æsculapius." Even Socrates had had enough of life. But what does that mean? What does it suggest? In the past, people would have said—and it was said loudly, especially by the Pessimists—"Surely there must be some truth in this! The agreement of the wisest proves it." Should we say the same thing today? Can we?

Instead, we now respond: "Surely there must be some sickness here." These so-called great thinkers of every age need to be examined more closely! Could it be that they all shared something physically or mentally fragile, something decadent? Is it possible that wisdom comes to earth like a crow drawn to the faint smell of decay?

This bold and disrespectful thought—that these great thinkers were actually signs of decline—first came to me in connection with a case where both scholarly and common opinions stood firmly against my own view. I came to see Socrates and Plato as symptoms of a culture in collapse, as tools of the disintegration of Greece, as fake Greeks, even anti-Greek (this was my argument in The Birth of Tragedy, 1872). The agreement of these sages— the consensus sapientium, as I increasingly realized—was not evidence that they were right about life. Instead, it suggested that they all shared some underlying physical or mental weakness that made them take the same negative stance toward life. Their judgments about life, whether positive or negative, are not true in themselves. Their value lies only in what they reveal about their creators. Such judgments are symptoms, and nothing more. In themselves, these opinions about life are meaningless.

You must grasp this critical idea: the value of life cannot be measured. A living person cannot judge it because they are too involved—they are part of the conflict, not a neutral observer. A dead person cannot judge it either, for obvious reasons. For a philosopher to see life's value as a problem suggests something is flawed in their perspective. It raises a question about their wisdom—or even their lack of wisdom.

Could it be that all these so-called great thinkers were not only signs of decline but also not wise at all? Let us now return to the case of Socrates.

Judging by his origins, Socrates came from the lowest social class—Socrates was part of the common mob. You know, and can still observe in the descriptions of him, how remarkably ugly he was. In Greek society, where beauty was highly valued, ugliness was not only an objection but often taken as evidence of deeper flaws. Was Socrates truly Greek? Ugliness often reflects a thwarted or disrupted development, or perhaps one stunted by mixed influences. In other cases, it signals a degenerative decline. Anthropologists who study criminals say that the typical criminal is often ugly: monstrum in fronte, monstrum in animo—a monster in appearance, a monster in spirit. Does that mean the criminal is a degenerate? Was Socrates, then, a typical criminal?

This idea wouldn't conflict with the infamous judgment made about Socrates by a physiognomist, which deeply upset his friends. While passing through Athens, a foreigner skilled in reading faces told Socrates directly that he was a monster and that his body harbored every kind of vice and passion. Socrates simply replied: "You know me, sir!"

Not only do Socrates' wild and chaotic instincts point to degeneracy, but so do his extreme reliance on logic and the peculiar malice that seemed tied to his disfigured features. We must also not forget his auditory hallucinations, which he religiously interpreted as "the demon of Socrates." Everything about him was excessive, exaggerated, almost comical—a caricature. His nature was also secretive, filled with hidden motives and underlying currents. I attempt to understand the strange personality behind the Socratic equation: Reason = Virtue = Happiness. This is perhaps the strangest formula ever devised, and it fundamentally contradicted the instincts of the earlier Greeks.

With Socrates, Greek taste shifted toward dialectics. What happened as a result? First, the refined and noble taste of earlier Greek culture was overthrown. Dialectics allowed the common crowd to rise to prominence. Before Socrates, the art of argument was avoided in polite society; it was considered improper and even disgraceful. Young men were warned against indulging in it. Arguing and constantly explaining oneself were seen as suspicious behaviors. Honest people, like honest things, don't need to constantly justify themselves. It was considered poor form to put everything on display. Anything that required proof was seen as having little inherent value.

In societies where authority was respected, where people gave commands rather than explanations, the dialectician was viewed as a kind of jester. People laughed at him and didn't take him seriously. Yet Socrates, a master of dialectics, managed to make people take him seriously. How did this happen? What was going on?

A person resorts to dialectics only when they have no other options available. People know that using it creates suspicion and that it's not particularly persuasive. Nothing is more easily overturned than the effect of a dialectical argument—this is clear from the experience of any debate or discussion. Dialectics can only be a last resort, the weapon of someone who has no other tools left. One must be desperate to demand their rights this way; otherwise, they wouldn't need to rely on it. This is why the Jews became skilled in dialectics.

Reynard the Fox was a dialectician. But what about Socrates—was he one too?

Is Socratic irony a form of rebellion, a weapon of resentment from the common people? Did Socrates, oppressed and suffering, enjoy his inherent cruelty by inflicting sharp attacks through his arguments? Was he taking revenge on the noblemen he managed to charm? As a dialectician, a person wields a ruthless weapon; they can dominate and even humiliate their opponents. By defeating someone in debate, the dialectician undermines them; their victory is always a compromise. The dialectician forces their opponent to prove they're not a fool, which often provokes anger and renders them defenseless. A dialectician paralyzes their opponent's thinking. Could dialectics, for Socrates, have been a form of revenge?

I have explained why Socrates could repel people; now it's just as important to understand why he was so captivating. One reason is that he invented a new kind of Agon, a competitive struggle, becoming the first master of verbal combat in Athens' elite circles. He charmed others by appealing to the Greek love of competition—he transformed intellectual debate into a new kind of contest between men and youths. Socrates also had an intense and magnetic personality, one deeply rooted in eroticism.

But Socrates saw even further. He understood his noble Athenian peers better than they understood themselves. He recognized that his situation—his unusual inner conflict—was not unique. The same kind of decline was quietly spreading everywhere: ancient Athens was dying. Socrates realized that the entire world needed him—his method, his remedy, and his unique technique for self-discipline and survival. Everywhere, instincts were in chaos; everywhere, people were teetering on the edge of excess. The monstrum in animo—the monster within—had become a widespread threat. "Instincts must be tamed," he thought. "We need to find a counterforce, a ruler stronger than they are."

When the physiognomist unmasked Socrates, calling him a volcano of evil desires, Socrates, the great Master of Irony, uttered a few revealing words that explain his nature. "That is true," he admitted, "but I overcame them all."

How did Socrates manage to master himself? His case was, at its core, simply the most extreme and visible example of a widespread crisis. It was a time when no one could control themselves, and instincts constantly clashed with one another. As the clearest example of this disorder, Socrates fascinated people. His shocking ugliness made him impossible to ignore, and his ability to present himself as a solution—a cure for this state— made him even more compelling.

When a man feels compelled, as Socrates did, to turn reason into a tyrant, it is a clear sign that something else is attempting to seize control. In Socrates' case, reason was seen as a savior. Neither Socrates nor his followers had the freedom to choose whether to be rational—they had no choice. At that time, being rational was mandatory, a last resort. The intensity with which all of Greek thought embraced reason reveals the severity of their situation: humanity was at a critical crossroads. The options were stark— either perish or cling desperately to excessive rationality.

The moral focus of Greek philosophy from Plato onward, and its reverence for dialectics, stemmed from a pathological state. The equation Reason =

Virtue = Happiness essentially meant: we must follow Socrates' example and constantly confront our dark passions with the light of reason. We must prioritize cleverness, precision, and clarity above all else. To yield to instinct or the unconscious was seen as a descent into chaos.

I have now explained why Socrates was so captivating: he appeared as a healer, a savior. But should we examine the flaws in his faith in "reason at any cost"? It was an illusion, a self- deception among philosophers and moralists, to believe they could free themselves from decline simply by fighting against it. This approach cannot lead to liberation. The tools they used, the path they chose as a solution, were themselves symptoms of the very degeneration they sought to overcome. They only altered the form of the problem—they did not eliminate it. Socrates was a misunderstanding. The entire morality of "improvement," including that of Christianity, was also a misunderstanding.

The brightest light of reason—this insistence on clarity, coldness, caution, and conscious control—opposed to instinct and detached from it, was itself a disease, simply a different kind of sickness. It was not a path back to "virtue," "health," or "happiness." To be forced to fight against one's instincts is the very definition of degeneration. As long as life is ascending, happiness is synonymous with instinct.

Did Socrates, the most intelligent of self-deceivers, understand this? Did he admit it to himself at the end, in his brave acceptance of death? Socrates wanted to die. It wasn't Athens that gave him the hemlock—it was his own hand. He pushed Athens to hand him the poisoned cup. "Socrates is not a doctor," he may have whispered to himself. "Only death can heal this. Socrates himself has simply been sick for a very long time."

Chapter 3

"Reason" In Philosophy

You ask me what defines the peculiarities of philosophers? For example, their lack of a sense of history, their disdain for the idea of change, and their obsession with preserving things like the ancient Egyptians did. They believe they honor something by removing it from its history, placing it "under the aspect of eternity"—essentially turning it into a mummy. For thousands of years, philosophers have dealt with mummified ideas; nothing alive has ever emerged from their work. These worshippers of concepts kill and preserve things when they idolize them—they endanger the life of everything they claim to revere. To them, death, change, aging, and even growth and creation are flaws, even arguments against life itself. What is, they claim, cannot change; and what changes, they insist, is not real.

All philosophers believe—desperately—in the idea of Being. But because they cannot grasp it, they search for reasons why this understanding is denied to them. "There must be some illusion, some trick, preventing us from knowing the true nature of Being," they say. "Where is this deceiver?" Then, triumphantly, they declare: "We've found it—it's sensuality!" The senses, they argue, are immoral in other ways and deceive us about the true world. The moral they draw is this: we must rid ourselves of the illusion brought by the senses, of change, of history, of lies. For them, history is nothing but belief in the senses, belief in falsehood. Their conclusion: we must reject everything the senses tell us. We must reject humanity and everything connected to it. Let us become philosophers—mummies, believers in monotony, grave-diggers! Above all, they cry, let us cast aside the body, this miserable obsession of the senses. The body, they claim, is infected with every flaw of logic and is neither real nor possible, even though it has the audacity to pretend otherwise.

With great respect, I make an exception for Heraclitus. While other philosophers dismissed the senses because they revealed variety and change, Heraclitus dismissed them because they seemed to show permanence and unity. Yet even Heraclitus was unfair to the senses. The senses do not lie, as the Eleatics thought, nor as Heraclitus believed. They don't lie at all. It is our interpretation of what the senses reveal that introduces falsehood—the lies of unity, matter, substance, and permanence. Reason is the source of these distortions. As long as the senses show us a world of change and impermanence, they are truthful. Heraclitus was entirely correct, however, in saying that the idea of Being is an empty illusion. The "apparent" world is the only world that exists; the so-called "true world" is nothing but a false add-on to it.

What delicate instruments our senses are! Take the human nose, for example—no philosopher has ever spoken of it with the reverence and gratitude it deserves. Yet, for now, it is the most finely tuned instrument we have. It can detect even the tiniest changes in motion, subtleties that even a spectroscope cannot measure. Our scientific achievements today reach as far as we have trusted our senses, sharpened them, enhanced them, and followed their evidence to its limits. What lies beyond that is incomplete and not yet science—it is metaphysics, theology, psychology, epistemology, or abstract systems like logic and mathematics. In all of these fields, reality is not even considered, not even as a problem, just as the broader value of these symbolic conventions like logic is not questioned.

Another strange trait of philosophers is just as dangerous. They confuse the last things with the first. They take what appears last—unfortunately, as it often shouldn't appear at all—"the highest concept," the most general, emptiest, and vaguest shadow of reality, and place it at the beginning, treating it as the origin. This, too, reflects their habit of reverence: the highest thing must not have arisen from anything lower, it must not have grown or developed at all. Their moral: anything of the highest rank must be causa sui—its own cause. If something derives from something else, it loses value and becomes suspect.

All the so-called higher values—like Being, the Absolute, Goodness, Truth, and Perfection—are assumed to be of the highest rank. They cannot have evolved; they must be self-caused. Moreover, these concepts must be alike, never in conflict with one another. And so they arrive at their grand concept of "God," the final, most diluted, and emptiest thing, which they declare to be the first cause, the ens r ealissimum, the ultimate reality. Imagine humanity taking the mental cobwebs spun by these diseased minds seriously! And yet, humanity has paid a high price for doing so.

Let us contrast this with how we approach the problem of error and deception in things (and notice, I politely say "we"). In the past, people saw change and evolution as proof that the world was deceptive, that something was leading us astray. Today, however, we understand that the real source of error lies in our rational thinking. Whenever we insist on unity, identity, permanence, substance, cause, materiality, or Being, we are driven into error— despite knowing from careful study that the error lies here.

This is similar to how people once believed their eyes deceived them about the sun's motion. In this case, it isn't our eyes but our language that keeps reinforcing these mistaken concepts. Language was developed in a time when human psychology was still very primitive. If we look at the origins of language metaphysics—that is, reasoning itself—we find it rooted in a kind of fetishism. Language imposes the idea of a doer behind every deed; it assumes that willpower is a cause and that the self, the "ego," is a kind of Being or substance. This faith in the ego as a substance is then projected onto the world, creating the concept of "things." From the ego alone comes the idea of Being.

At the root of all this is a grave mistake: the belief that the will is something active, a force. Now we know it's just a word. Much later, in a far more enlightened world, philosophers marveled at how certain and reliable these categories of reason seemed. They concluded that these concepts could not have come from experience since experience actually contradicts them. Where, then, do they come from? In both India and Greece, people made the same mistake: "We must have lived in a higher world once," they thought, "because we possess reason!" But the truth is, we came from a much simpler and less developed state.

Nothing has been more convincing than the error of Being, as first proposed by the Eleatics. Their concept of Being is supported by every word and sentence we speak! Even those who opposed the Eleatics fell into the trap of their idea, such as Democritus with his theory of the atom. "Reason" in language—what an old and cunning deceiver it is! I suspect we will never rid ourselves of the idea of God as long as we believe in grammar.

To make this important and novel perspective clear, I will summarize it in four points to simplify understanding and encourage discussion.

Proposition One. The arguments claiming this world is only "apparent" actually support its reality. No other kind of reality can be proven.

Proposition Two. The qualities people attribute to the "true Being" of things are actually qualities of nonexistence. The "true world" was constructed by denying the real world, and it is indeed an illusion—a moral and optical trick.

Proposition Three. Imagining another world makes no sense unless there is a deep, instinctual urge to slander, diminish, and distrust this life. In that case, this imaginary "better" world is just an act of revenge against the life we live.

Proposition Four. Dividing the world into a "true" and "apparent" world, whether in Christianity or Kant's philosophy (which is essentially Christianity in disguise), is a sign of decline and a symptom of decaying life. The fact that an artist values appearances more than reality does not contradict this. For the artist, "appearance" is reality, but in a refined, intensified, and improved form. The tragic artist is not a pessimist—they affirm even the most troubling and terrifying aspects of life. They are Dionysian.

Chapter 4
How The "True World"
Ultimately Became a Fable the History of An Error

The true world is reachable by the wise, the virtuous, and the devout. They live in it—they are it.

(This earliest version of the idea was relatively simple, clever, and convincing. It was essentially a rewording of "I, Plato, am the truth.")

The true world, though unattainable for now, is promised to the wise, the virtuous, and the devout—especially to the sinner who repents.

(The idea evolves: it becomes subtler, more deceptive, more elusive. It takes on a new form—it becomes feminine, it becomes Christian.)

The true world is beyond reach. It cannot be proven or promised, but merely thinking about it provides comfort, obligation, and direction.

(This is essentially the same old sun, but seen through a haze of doubt and skepticism. The idea becomes lofty, pale, northern—Königsbergian.)

The true world—is it unattainable? In any case, it is unattained. And because it is unattained, it is also unknown. As something unknown, it can no longer comfort, save, or command. How could the unknown demand anything of us?

(The first light of dawn. Reason begins to stir and stretch. The cockcrow of positivism.)

The "true world"—an idea that no longer has any use, that no longer demands anything—a pointless, unnecessary idea, now discarded: let us get rid of it!

(The brightness of morning; breakfast; the return of common sense and joy.

Plato blushes in shame, and all free spirits celebrate wildly.)

We have abolished the true world. What remains? The apparent world, perhaps? Certainly not! By getting rid of the true world, we have also done away with the world of appearances!

(Noon; the time of the shortest shadows; the end of the longest mistake; the height of humanity. Thus Spoke Zarathustra begins.)

Chapter 5
Morality as The Enemy of Nature

There is a time when all passions are destructive, dragging people down with their reckless force. But there comes a much later time when passions merge with the spirit and refine themselves—they become "spiritualized." In the past, because of the inherent foolishness of passion, people waged war against it. They committed themselves to eradicating it. All ancient moralists agreed on this point: "Il faut tuer les passions"—passions must be killed. The most famous version of this idea is found in the New Testament, in the Sermon on the Mount, where, let's be clear, things are hardly viewed from an elevated perspective. It says there, for example, about sexuality: "If your eye offends you, pluck it out." Thankfully, no Christian truly follows this advice.

Destroying passions and desires simply because of their foolishness or to avoid the unpleasant outcomes of their excess now seems to us like an even greater form of foolishness. We no longer admire dentists who pull teeth just so they won't ache again. On the other hand, it's fair to say that the soil from which Christianity grew could never have allowed for the idea of "spiritualizing passion" to take root. Everyone knows the early Church waged war on intelligence in favor of the "poor in spirit." Under those conditions, how could passions have been fought intelligently? The Church combats passion through methods of removal and suppression. Its solution, its "remedy," is castration. It never asks, "How can desire be refined, elevated, or even sanctified?"

Throughout history, the Church's discipline has always focused on eradicating passions entirely—on destroying sensuality, pride, the thirst for power, the desire for wealth, and even the urge for revenge.

But attacking passions at their roots is the same as attacking life at its source. The Church's approach is fundamentally hostile to life itself.

The same methods—castration and eradication—are instinctively chosen to battle passions by those who are too weak-willed or degenerate to impose some form of moderation. These are the kinds of people who, metaphorically (or even literally), need La Trappe or some extreme declaration of war against their desires, a vast gulf separating them from temptation. Only degenerates need such drastic methods. A weak will—or, more precisely, an inability to resist reacting to stimuli—is itself a form of degeneration.

A radical and absolute hatred of sensuality is always a suspicious sign. It gives good reason to doubt the overall health of the person who takes such an extreme stance. Moreover, this hatred reaches its peak only when such people no longer have the strength of character to commit to the ultimate remedy—to renounce their inner "Satan."

Consider the history of priests, philosophers, and even artists. The most venomous attacks on the senses have not come from those who are impotent or naturally ascetic, but from those who found it necessary to become ascetics. These were people whose inner struggles forced them into extreme positions, and their attacks on sensuality reflect their personal battles more than any genuine wisdom.

The spiritualization of sensuality is called love: this represents a great victory over Christianity. Another triumph is the spiritualization of hostility. This means we are beginning to deeply understand the value of having enemies. In short, we now act and think in the exact opposite way from how we once did. Throughout history, the Church sought to destroy its enemies. But we, the immoralists and Antichrists, see an advantage in the Church's survival. Even in politics, hostility has become more refined—more cautious, thoughtful, and restrained. Nearly every political party now sees its self-interest in ensuring its opposition doesn't collapse. The same is true in global politics.

A new creation—such as the new Empire—needs enemies more than friends. It only becomes necessary as a contrast to what opposes it; it defines itself through opposition. We approach our inner conflicts in much the same way. Here too, we have spiritualized enmity and come to understand its value. A person is productive only when they are rich in opposing instincts; they stay youthful only so long as their soul resists comfort and rejects the yearning for peace.

The "peace of the soul," which Christianity holds as its highest goal, has become entirely foreign to us. Nothing could make us less envious than the moral complacency and contentment of a clean conscience—the happiness of a "moral cow." A man who renounces conflict also renounces a life of grandeur.

Of course, in many cases, what people call "peace of the soul" is really something else, disguised and unable to name itself honestly. Let me, without hesitation or bias, suggest a few examples.

"Peace of the soul" could be the radiant glow of abundant animal energy within the realm of morality or religion. Or it might be the first sign of fatigue, the shadow cast by the evening, as all evenings cast shadows. Or it could be a signal of humid air and southern winds on the horizon. Perhaps it is an unconscious gratitude for good digestion, sometimes mistaken for "brotherly love." It could also be the calmness of someone recovering from illness, savoring every flavor of life anew and waiting patiently. Or it might follow the satisfaction of a powerful passion, the comfort of an unfamiliar fullness.

"Peace of the soul" might be the weariness of our will, desires, and vices as they grow old. Or it could be laziness, dressed up by vanity in the clothes of morality. Sometimes, it's the relief that follows the end of long periods of uncertainty, even if that end is marked by terrible certainty. It might also be the expression of mastery during a creative effort, the deep, steady breathing of someone who has achieved true freedom of will.

Who knows? Perhaps even The Twilight of the Idols is nothing more than a form of "peace of the soul."

Let me lay down a principle: all natural morality—that is, every healthy morality—is guided by the instinct for life. It fulfills one of life's fundamental laws by creating definite rules like "you shall" or "you shall not," and in doing so, it clears obstacles from the path of life. In contrast, morality that opposes nature—which describes almost every morality that has been taught, praised, and preached so far—is aimed directly against life's instincts. It secretly or openly condemns these very instincts. When it says, "God sees into the heart of man," it denies the deepest and most vital desires of life, turning God into life's enemy. The saint, whom God supposedly favors, is nothing more than an ideal eunuch. Life ends where the "Kingdom of God" begins.

If you understand the wickedness of this rebellion against life, which Christian morality has made almost sacred, you also see its emptiness, its falseness, and its absurdity. For any condemnation of life by a living being is merely a symptom of a specific kind of life. The question of whether such a condemnation is right or wrong doesn't even arise. To even approach the question of life's value, one would need to be outside life itself and yet know it as completely as everyone who has ever lived. This makes the question entirely inaccessible to us.

When we speak of values, we do so under the influence and perspective of life itself. Life urges us to create values; life evaluates through us. This means that even morality that opposes life—one that sees God as the rejection and condemnation of life—is still an evaluation of life. But what kind of life does it reflect? I have already answered: it is the perspective of declining, weakened, exhausted, and doomed life. Morality, as it has been understood up to now—as Schopenhauer put it in his idea of

"The Denial of the Will to Life"—is the instinct of degeneration turned into a command. It says, "Perish!" It is the death sentence pronounced by those already marked for death.

Now, consider how absurdly simple it is for someone to say, "Man should be like this or that!" Reality shows us a wondrous abundance of types, an endless variety of forms and transformations. Yet the first petty moralist who comes along declares, "No! Man should be different!" This self-righteous fool even imagines he knows what man should be like. He draws his own face on the wall and proclaims: "Behold the man!"

Even when the moralist addresses an individual and says, "You should be this way or that way!" he still makes a fool of himself. The individual, with their past and future, is part of fate—a law, a necessity added to the universe. To say to someone, "Change yourself," is the same as demanding that the entire world change, even retroactively. These moralists have been consistent in their madness—they wanted man to be different, to be virtuous, to reflect their own image. In doing so, they denied the world itself. This is no small form of insanity! Nor is it a humble kind of arrogance!

Morality, when it condemns for the sake of condemnation itself—without any regard for life's goals, needs, or motives—is a specific kind of error. It is a degenerative quirk that has caused immeasurable harm, and no one should feel pity for it. We, the immoralists, on the other hand, have opened our hearts to understanding, acceptance, and affirmation. We do not reject life lightly; instead, we take pride in saying "yes" to things.

Our vision has widened to include the economy of life—a system that knows how to use even what priests and moralists reject. It finds value even in what the sanctimonious or the sickly-minded condemn. It turns the so-called repulsive elements—priests, bigots, and the "virtuous"—to its own advantage. What is that advantage? We, the immoralists, are the living answer to that question.

Chapter 6
The Four Great Errors

The error of confusing cause and effect—there is no more dangerous mistake than mistaking the effect for the cause.

I call this mistake the fundamental perversion of reason. Yet, this error has been one of humanity's oldest habits, and one that persists even today. In some parts of the world, it has even been elevated to sacred status, taking the form of "religion" and "morality." Every principle put forth by religion and morality is built upon this very error. Priests and moral lawgivers have been the most enthusiastic promoters of this distortion of reason.

Take, for example, the famous book by Cornaro, in which he promotes a strict, modest diet as the key to a long, happy, and virtuous life. This book, widely read and still reprinted in large numbers, has likely caused more harm and shortened more lives than almost any other well-intentioned work—except, of course, the Bible. Why? Because it confuses cause and effect. Cornaro believed his longevity was caused by his restricted diet. However, the truth is that his unique physiology, marked by an unusually slow rate of molecular change and low energy expenditure, was the actual cause of his meager diet. His constitution didn't allow him to eat much—if he had eaten more, he would have fallen ill.

For most people, especially those with a different metabolism, such a diet would be disastrous. A modern scholar, for example, whose nervous energy is rapidly consumed, would waste away on Cornaro's diet. Crede exper to— trust someone who knows from experience.

The same confusion of cause and effect lies at the heart of every religion and morality. Their central message is always: "Do this and avoid that, and you will be happy. Otherwise—" This "otherwise" is an unspoken threat. Every moral or religious imperative repeats this same formula. I call this the original sin of reason—immortal unreason.

But in my hands, this principle is turned on its head. This is the first example of my "transvaluation of all values." A well-constituted person, one who is a masterpiece of nature, instinctively performs certain actions and avoids others. Such a person embodies the natural order and harmony their body expresses. Their virtue is not a cause but an effect of their excellent constitution. Their longevity and ability to have many children are not rewards for their virtue; rather, these qualities result from their robust and healthy nature. This is the true basis of what I call Cornarism.

In contrast, the Church and traditional morality assert, "A race or a people perishes because of vice and luxury." My reinstated reason says the opposite: when a people are already in decline, when they are physically degenerating, vice and luxury naturally emerge. These are not the causes of their downfall but symptoms of their exhaustion. Their declining energy leads them to crave stronger and more frequent stimuli, which is typical of all weakened natures.

Consider a young man who becomes pale and sickly. His friends may blame an illness, but I say the illness itself is merely a symptom of his already weakened state, the result of hereditary exhaustion. Similarly, when a political party makes a fatal mistake, the common view is that the mistake leads to its demise. But my superior understanding of politics says: a party capable of making such errors is already in its death throes. It has lost its instinctual certainty.

Every error, in any context, is the consequence of a degeneration of instincts and a disintegration of the will. This is the essence of what we call "evil." Everything truly valuable arises from instinct and is therefore effortless, necessary, and free. Strain and effort are objections to value. The divine is characterized not by struggle but by lightness—the god has light feet, unlike the hero who battles against obstacles.

The error of false causality also runs deep. Throughout history, humans have believed they understood causality. But where did this belief come from? What gave us such confidence in causality? It came from what we call the "inner facts of consciousness." Yet not one of these so-called facts has ever been proven.

We assumed we were the causes of our own actions, that our will was an undeniable proof of causality. We believed that all the motives for our actions could be found in our consciousness, as if they were sitting there waiting to be uncovered. Without these motives, we thought, we wouldn't be free or responsible. Finally, we believed that thoughts themselves were caused by the ego, the "self."

But now, we have come to our senses. Today, we know none of this is true. The "inner world" is a collection of illusions. The will doesn't cause anything; it doesn't explain anything. It merely accompanies processes and sometimes isn't even present. What we call "motive" is another falsehood, a surface ripple that often conceals the deeper causes of action rather than revealing them. As for the ego, it is now nothing more than a myth, a fiction, an empty word.

What's the result of all this? There are no such things as spiritual causes. The entire foundation of popular experience—our belief that the world is built on causes and effects, wills and spirits—has collapsed. Humanity blissfully projected its own inner illusions onto the world, turning it into a vast system of agents and actions. Man imagined his ego as the root of all things and built the concept of "Being" upon this illusion.

Even the concept of the atom, cherished by physicists, still carries remnants of this old psychological error. And the metaphysicians' notion of the "thing-in- itself" is the ultimate example of this confusion—a disgraceful relic of primitive thinking.

The greatest error of all has been to regard the spirit as a cause, to mistake it for reality, and to use it as a measure of the real. This error was even elevated to the status of a deity—it was called God.

The Error of Imaginary Causes

Starting in the realm of dreams, we often ascribe causes to sensations after the fact. Take, for instance, the sound of a distant cannon shot in a dream. We frequently weave a story around such sensations, turning them into little dramas where we ourselves are the central figures. The sensation lingers, echoing and intensifying, until our instinct for causality demands an explanation. But instead of recognizing the sensation as random, we interpret it as something meaningful—a direct result of a fabricated cause. In dreams, this often leads to a reversal of the natural order of events: the sensation, which should be the starting point, is made the result of the imagined cause. The cannon shot is explained as though it were caused by events that supposedly happened earlier in the dream.

What occurs here? Ideas associated with a particular sensory state are misinterpreted as the cause of that state. This same process happens when we are awake. Many of our general sensations— like tension, pressure, obstacles, or explosions in the interplay of our bodily systems, particularly in the sympathetic nervous system— trigger the instinct to search for a cause. We need an explanation for why we feel good or bad, ill or well. It is not enough for us to simply recognize that we feel a certain way. We only become fully conscious of the feeling when we have assigned it a cause.

Memory plays a key role in this process, unconsciously recalling past states that were similar, along with the causal interpretations we previously attached to them. However, memory rarely retrieves the actual causes. Instead, it presents familiar interpretations. The belief that our thoughts or conscious processes are the causes of these sensations stems from the way memory works. This mechanism leads us to accept a fixed interpretation of causes, one that often hinders or entirely blocks us from investigating the real causes of our sensations.

The Psychological Explanation

Why do we trace the unfamiliar back to the familiar? Because doing so brings relief, comfort, and a sense of control. The unfamiliar provokes fear, anxiety, and unease. Our most basic instinct is to eliminate these uncomfortable feelings. Thus, our first principle becomes: any explanation is better than none at all. Since our goal is simply to free ourselves from troubling ideas, we are not overly picky about the explanations we adopt. The first explanation that makes the unfamiliar seem familiar gives us such comfort that we readily accept it as true.

This process relies on the "proof" of happiness or relief to determine truth. In this way, the instinct for causality is closely tied to feelings of fear and the need to alleviate it. Whenever possible, the question "why?" doesn't just seek any cause but rather a particular kind of cause—one that comforts, liberates, and reassures us.

The easiest way to achieve this is by attributing causes to something we already know, something familiar and stored in memory. The new, unfamiliar factor is excluded from consideration as a possible cause. We prefer explanations that remove the sensation of strangeness, novelty, or unpredictability. Over time, a particular way of explaining causes becomes dominant, solidifies into a system, and eventually crowds out alternative explanations.

For example, a banker instinctively attributes everything to business, a Christian sees sin behind every event, and a young woman interprets everything through the lens of her love life.

The Domain of Morality and Religion as Imaginary Causes

The entire realm of morality and religion can be categorized under the heading of "imaginary causes." Consider how unpleasant sensations are explained in these frameworks. Such sensations are often attributed to malevolent external forces, like evil spirits. For example, the hysteria of women in the past was frequently interpreted as possession by witches. Similarly, feelings of guilt or sinfulness are seen as evidence of moral failings, yet they are often just symptoms of physiological imbalances. People have always found reasons to be dissatisfied with themselves, projecting these feelings onto moral or religious explanations.

Religions often go further, interpreting unpleasant sensations as punishment for wrongdoing, as if suffering proves guilt or sinfulness. Schopenhauer took this idea to its extreme, claiming that all great suffering reveals what we deserve, as it could not happen without a reason rooted in guilt. In this way, morality and religion turn life's natural challenges into accusations and condemnations.

Even physiological conditions like exhaustion or illness are interpreted through this lens. The passions and bodily senses are blamed as causes, and their effects are deemed deserved punishments for indulging in sinful behavior. This moralization of suffering twists natural occurrences into a system of guilt and penalty.

Similarly, pleasant sensations are explained through imaginary causes. They are attributed to faith, good deeds, or divine favor. A "good conscience," for instance, may simply be the result of good digestion, yet it is often interpreted as a reward for moral virtue. Even successful outcomes of endeavors are misattributed; a hypochondriac or someone like Pascal, for example, would not feel general happiness simply because of a fortunate result.

Religious virtues like faith, love, and hope are also misinterpretations. The feelings of strength and abundance that underpin these states are mistaken for their causes. A person trusts in God because they feel strong and peaceful, not the other way around.

Morality and Religion as Psychology of Error

At their core, morality and religion belong to the psychology of error. They consistently confuse cause and effect. They mistake feelings of pleasure or pain for their supposed causes and interpret them through a lens of moral or religious belief. They turn subjective states of consciousness into explanations, obscuring the true causes behind these sensations.

In every case, morality and religion invert the relationship between cause and effect, making them systems of misinterpretation. Truth is conflated with the effects of what is believed to be true, and the underlying processes that produce sensations are hidden behind a false dialect of moral and religious explanations. These systems are not rooted in reality but are deeply embedded in the errors of human psychology.

The Error of Free Will

Today, we have no patience for the concept of "free will." We know too well what it really is: the most audacious theological trick ever devised to make humanity "responsible" in a theological sense— that is, to make humanity dependent on theologians. Let me explain the psychology behind how this sense of responsibility is instilled.

Whenever people assign responsibility to someone, it is driven by the instinct for punishment and judgment. The innocence of Becoming—the natural unfolding of events—is destroyed the moment any state of affairs is attributed to a will, intentions, or deliberate actions. The doctrine of the will was invented primarily as a tool for punishment, specifically to assign guilt.

The entire foundation of ancient psychology, or the psychology of the will, arose because its creators—the priests who ruled early societies—sought to justify their power to punish. They wanted to grant themselves, or their gods, the right to judge and condemn. To make this possible, humanity had to be considered "free," so that individuals could be judged and held guilty. Consequently, every action was framed as voluntary, and the origin of every action was imagined to lie in conscious choice. This fraud became the foundation of psychology: the deliberate falsification of human nature to serve the interests of power and control.

Now, we are moving in the opposite direction. We immoralists are working tirelessly to eliminate the concepts of guilt and punishment from the world. We aim to cleanse psychology, history, nature, and all social customs and institutions of these poisonous ideas. Our most determined adversaries in this effort are the theologians, who still cling to the notion of a "moral order of things." They continue to pollute the innocence of Becoming with the concepts of punishment and guilt. Christianity, in this regard, is nothing more than the metaphysics of the executioner.

What, then, can our teaching be? It is this: No one gives a person their qualities—not God, not society, not parents, not ancestors, and certainly not the person themselves. This nonsensical notion, which has been perpetuated for centuries, was called "intelligible freedom" by Kant and perhaps even earlier by Plato. But it is utterly refuted here.

No one is responsible for their existence, for being the way they are, or for the circumstances in which they find themselves. A person's existence is inextricably linked to the entire chain of events that has been and will be. It is not the product of an intention, a will, or an aim. There is no striving for some "ideal man," "ideal happiness," or "ideal morality." To think otherwise is absurd.

The concept of "purpose" is something we invented—it does not exist in reality. There is no purpose driving existence. Each individual is a necessary part of the whole, a fragment of fate, inseparably bound to the totality of existence. No one can judge, measure, or condemn an individual's existence because to do so would mean judging, measuring, and condemning the entirety of existence. But there is nothing outside the whole to serve as a basis for such judgment.

The liberation we offer is this: no one can be made responsible. Existence cannot be traced to a causa prima—a first cause. The world is not an entity driven by a central consciousness, a divine spirit, or a purpose. This realization restores the innocence of Becoming. It frees the world from the burden of guilt and condemnation.

The concept of "God" has been the greatest obstacle to accepting existence as it is. For centuries, God has been used to justify the idea of ultimate responsibility, judgment, and guilt. But we deny God. We deny responsibility in God. Only by doing so can we truly save the world. This denial restores the innocence of existence and frees us from the chains of metaphysical guilt. This is the great liberation.

Chapter 7
The "Improvers" Of Mankind

You are familiar with my demand upon philosophers: that they rise above the notions of Good and Evil, leaving behind the illusion of moral judgment. This demand arises from a perspective I was the first to articulate—that there are no moral facts. Moral judgment, like religious judgment, believes in unrealities, in things that do not exist. Morality is merely an interpretation of certain phenomena—or, more accurately, a misinterpretation.

Moral judgment belongs to a stage of ignorance, a time when the very idea of reality, the distinction between what is real and imagined, had not yet emerged. At this stage, "truth" was applied to a multitude of things we now consider imaginary. For this reason, moral judgment should never be taken literally. On its own, it is nonsense. However, as a system of signs, it is invaluable to those who understand it. It offers insight into the cultural and psychological conditions of societies that lacked the knowledge to understand themselves. Morality, in essence, is a kind of language, a symptomatology. To make use of it, one must already grasp what it signifies.

Let me offer a preliminary example. Throughout history, certain individuals have sought to "improve" humanity—a goal that has always been closely tied to morality. But beneath this single word, vastly different tendencies are concealed. The "improvement" of humanity has sometimes meant the taming of the wild animal in man, while at other times it has meant the cultivation of a specific type of human being. These two approaches are fundamentally distinct, though both are described as moral.

Take the taming of an animal as an example. To call this process an "improvement" seems almost laughable to modern ears. Anyone who has observed a menagerie knows that animals are not improved there—they are weakened. Their natural power and danger are subdued through fear, pain, and deprivation, transforming them into sick, broken creatures. The same holds true for humanity under the influence of the priestly "improvers."

Consider the Middle Ages, when the Church acted as a menagerie for humanity. The Church hunted down the most vital and noble individuals—the "blond beasts," such as the Germans—and set about "improving" them. But what did this "improved" person look like after the process? He became a shadow of himself, a distorted caricature of humanity. Lured into monasteries, stripped of his instincts, and imprisoned behind oppressive concepts of sin and guilt, he was rendered sick and wretched, filled with self- hatred and suspicion of all that is strong and joyful in life. In short, he became a Christian.

From a physiological standpoint, this "improvement" was no different than what one does to an animal: weakening it by making it sick. The Church understood this strategy well. It ruined man, drained his strength, and then claimed to have made him better.

Now, let us consider a very different example of morality: the deliberate cultivation of a particular type of humanity. The most striking example of this is found in Indian morality as laid out in the Law of Manu. This text describes the structured breeding of four distinct castes: priests, warriors, merchants and farmers, and finally servants (the Sudras). Here, we are no longer dealing with the taming of wild animals. To conceive of such a system presupposes a level of mildness and rationality far beyond that of the lion-tamer.

Emerging from the Christian atmosphere of prisons and hospitals, one can breathe more freely in the world of Manu. Here, the goal is not to break humanity but to cultivate it. The vision is vast, orderly, and noble. By comparison, the New Testament reeks of pettiness and decay. Yet even this grand system had to confront challenges, particularly from those who did not fit into its carefully crafted structure—the "non-caste" people, the Chandala.

For the Chandala, the morality of Manu was as harsh as the Church's morality was to the strong. Unable to assimilate these "mixed" people into the system, Indian morality sought to render them weak and harmless by making them sick. This was a struggle against the sheer numbers of the Chandala, whose very existence threatened the structure of the caste system.

Some of the measures taken against the Chandala are repugnant to modern sensibilities. For instance, the Avadana- Sastra decrees that their diet should consist solely of garlic and onions; they were forbidden access to grains, clean water, or fire. Their drinking water had to be drawn from ditches and animal tracks, and they were prohibited from washing themselves or their clothing. Chandala women were barred from assisting one another during childbirth, and Sudra women were forbidden from helping them as well.

Such sanitary regulations had predictable results: deadly epidemics and venereal diseases ravaged the Chandala population. In response, the Law of the K nife—circumcision for males and genital mutilation for females—was introduced. Manu himself described the Chandala as the offspring of adultery, incest, and crime. Their clothing was to be made from rags taken from corpses, their utensils from broken pottery, and their jewelry from old iron. They were to worship malevolent spirits, wander endlessly, and were even forbidden to write using their right hand or in the direction reserved for virtuous people.

This is the logical outcome of a morality focused on breeding: the deliberate dehumanization of those who threaten the system. The Chandala were treated as the living embodiment of chaos, their suffering justified as the necessary cost of order.

The stark contrast between these two examples—the Christian taming of man and the Indian cultivation of castes—reveals the true diversity hidden within the concept of morality. While both systems aimed to "improve" humanity, their methods and goals were fundamentally different. The Christian moralist sought to weaken and break the strong, while the Indian lawgiver aimed to build a structured and lasting society. Yet both relied on the same principle: to make the undesirable elements weak and subservient, even at the cost of their health and humanity.

These regulations are profoundly revealing: they offer a glimpse into the primal and unfiltered humanity of the Aryans. From them, we see that the concept of "pure blood" is far from innocent—it carries with it a profound and often ruthless seriousness. At the same time, these regulations help us identify the people in whom a deep-seated hatred of this Aryan humanity—the Chandala hatred—has been immortalized. Among these people, this hatred was transformed into both religion and genius.

From this perspective, the gospels are invaluable historical documents, and the Book of Enoch is even more significant. Christianity, having sprung from Jewish roots and comprehensible only in the context of this heritage, represents the exact opposite of the morality of breeding, race, and privilege. Christianity is, at its core, an anti-Aryan religion. It is the transvaluation of all Aryan values— a complete reversal. It is the triumph of Chandala values, the gospel of the poor, the lowly, and the oppressed.

Christianity embodies the general uprising of the downtrodden— the miserable, the failed, and the broken—against the concept of "race." It is the eternal revenge of the Chandala, disguised as the "religion of love."

When comparing the morality of breeding to the morality of taming, we see that the methods employed by each are equally ruthless. Both rely on a deep commitment to immorality in order to enforce their respective visions of morality. One could even propose a principle: to create morality, one must possess an absolute will to immorality.

This paradoxical principle forms the basis of a profound and perplexing problem that I have studied for years: the psychology of those who claim to "improve" humanity. This problem first presented itself to me in the form of a seemingly trivial yet deeply significant phenomenon known as the pia fraus— the "pious fraud." This concept, the shared legacy of all philosophers and priests who have sought to improve mankind, opened the door to my exploration of this issue.

Figures like Manu, Plato, Confucius, and the teachers of Judaism and Christianity have all relied on the pia fraus. None of them ever doubted their right to deceive. Moreover, they never questioned their right to many other tools of manipulation and control.

To summarize this idea in a formula: every method ever used to make humanity "moral" has been, at its core, thoroughly immoral.

Chapter 8

Things the Germans Lack

Among Germans today, it is not enough to simply possess intellect; one must actively claim it, assert it, even lay hold of it.

Perhaps I know the Germans well enough to tell them a few uncomfortable truths. Modern Germany possesses a vast reserve of inherited and cultivated abilities, so vast that it could afford to spend this accumulated wealth liberally for some time. However, what has emerged in modern Germany is not a superior culture, nor refined taste, nor noble instincts for beauty. Instead, it is a set of virtues— admirable, yes, but also heavily pragmatic—more robust and "manly" than those of other European nations.

Germany still demonstrates a remarkable level of good spirits and self- respect, along with strength in human relationships and a reliable sense of mutual obligations. There is an abundance of industriousness and perseverance, paired with an inherited sobriety that seems to require stimulation rather than restraint. It is worth noting that Germans still know how to obey without feeling that obedience diminishes them, and they maintain respect for their opponents rather than despising them.

You can see that I wish to be fair to the Germans; it is my intention not to betray my commitment to balance, even when critiquing them. But fairness requires me to voice my objections as well. Achieving a position of power comes at a cost, for power inevitably stultifies.

Once upon a time, the Germans were known as a nation of thinkers. But do they truly think anymore? Today, Germans seem bored by intellect, mistrustful of it. Politics has consumed the seriousness once reserved for intellectual pursuits. The rallying cry, "Ger many, Ger many above all," seems to have delivered a fatal blow to German philosophy. Abroad, people ask me, "Are there still German philosophers? Are there still German poets? Are there any good German books?" I feel ashamed, though I muster the courage to answer, even in my moments of despair, "Yes, Bismarck!"

But could I dare to reveal what books are actually being read in Germany today? The curse of mediocrity dominates.

What could German intellect have become? Who has not lamented this question! For nearly a thousand years, this nation has deliberately dulled its own edge. Nowhere else have Europe's two great narcotics—alcohol and Christianity—been so excessively and destructively consumed as in Germany. To these, a third opiate has been added, one that could alone have sufficed to extinguish the spark of intellectual daring: music. German music—ponderous, bloated, and stifling—has completed the paralysis of German thought. How much sluggishness, heaviness, dampness, lethargy, and beer-fueled languor are entangled in German intellect!

How can it be that young men who dedicate their lives to intellectual pursuits lack the most basic instinct for intellectual self-preservation and drink beer? The alcoholism of academic youth doesn't prevent them from becoming scholars—after all, one can be a great scholar without being truly intelligent. But in every other respect, this is a disaster. What kind of intellectual softness, what kind of dull degeneration, comes from beer?

I once pointed out an infamous example of this kind of intellectual degeneration: the decline of David Strauss, once a leading German free spirit, who devolved into the author of a pedestrian gospel and a "New Faith." His intellect succumbed not just to mediocrity but to the very spirit he himself had celebrated—"the dear old brown liquor," to which he remained faithful to the end.

This kind of degeneration—soft, indulgent, and self-defeating—offers a troubling reflection of the broader intellectual culture in Germany, one that undermines the potential for brilliance with a relentless embrace of comfort, conformity, and the narcotics of religion, alcohol, and art.

I have spoken about the state of German intellect, noting that it has become coarser and shallower. But is that enough? In truth, what concerns me far more is the steady and alarming decline of German seriousness, depth, and passion in intellectual matters. It is not just intellect that has diminished; even the emotional force— what we might call the pathos—behind intellectual pursuits has been transformed.

When I occasionally encounter German universities, I am struck by the atmosphere that prevails there. What barrenness! What smug, tepid intellectuality! These institutions have grown content with mediocrity, and the once-earnest German intellectual spirit now feels lukewarm, drained of vitality.

Some might point to German science as a counterargument to my observations. Such a claim would only prove they have misunderstood me and failed to grasp even a single page of my writings. For seventeen years, I have devoted myself to exposing the dehumanizing and de-intellectualizing effects of modern scientific pursuits. The rigid, mechanical labor demanded by the vast scope of modern sciences has left individuals shackled, unable to cultivate the fuller, richer, and deeper natures that once thrived in intellectual endeavors.

Our age suffers from an overabundance of shallow dilettantes and fragmented personalities—half-formed individuals who flit aimlessly through life. The universities, though unintentionally, have become factories for producing this kind of intellectual decay, training people whose instincts for genuine intellectuality have withered. And this problem is not confined to Germany. All of Europe is beginning to recognize this trend. Large-scale politics, the realm in which Germany has invested so much, fools no one. Germany is becoming, ever more clearly, the flatland of Europe, a place devoid of the peaks of culture and thought.

I am still searching for a German with whom I could engage in the kind of seriousness that defines my way of thinking. And even more elusive is a German with whom I could share genuine cheerfulness. The Twilight of the Idols— what man today could grasp the kind of seriousness from which a philosopher recovers in such a work? Of all things, our cheerfulness is the most misunderstood.

Now let us shift our focus slightly. It is not just that German culture is visibly in decline; there are also clear reasons behind this fall. No one, whether an individual or a nation, can expend more energy than they possess. If your resources of reason, seriousness, will, and self-discipline are poured entirely into pursuits such as political power, economics, large-scale commerce, parliamentary systems, or military ambitions, then you cannot also spend them on culture.

Culture and the state are fundamentally opposed to one another. Let no one be misled: the idea of a "culture-state" is a modern illusion. One thrives at the expense of the other. Throughout history, every great period of culture coincided with political decline. That which is culturally great is always unpolitical, even anti-political.

Consider Goethe. His heart swelled with hope at the rise of Napoleon, a figure of cultural vitality, but it closed at the thought of the "Wars of Liberation," which signaled Germany's move toward becoming a political power. Similarly, when Germany emerged as a dominant force in global politics, France rose anew as a cultural powerhouse. Even now, much of Europe's intellectual seriousness and passion have migrated to Paris. Questions of pessimism, the works of Wagner, and other psychological and artistic debates are approached in France with a level of subtlety and depth that Germany seems incapable of matching.

In matters that truly define culture—those that demand intellectual and artistic earnestness—the Germans are no longer relevant. This shift marks a profound displacement of Europe's intellectual center of gravity. In the history of European culture, the rise of the German Empire signifies not progress but a retreat from cultural significance.

I challenge you to name a single German thinker today who can stand alongside the great figures of Europe's intellectual past. Where is the modern equivalent of Goethe, Hegel, Heinrich Heine, or Schopenhauer? The absence of any contemporary German philosopher worthy of comparison with such minds is an ever-growing marvel—and a deeply troubling one.

The entire higher educational system in Germany has lost sight of everything that truly matters—both the ultimate goals and the means to achieve them. People seem to have forgotten that education itself is the goal, the process of cultivation an end in itself—not "the Empire" or any other external objective. They forget that education demands true educators, not merely public- school teachers or university scholars. What is needed are educators who are themselves cultivated, superior, and noble minds—individuals who can demonstrate their worth at every moment of their lives through their words and their actions. These are individuals who are ripe and refined products of culture.

Instead, Germany is plagued by an abundance of learned louts— "superior wet-nurses"—foisted upon its youth by public schools and universities. These are not educators in the true sense, but mere functionaries. What Germany lacks, with few exceptions, is the very foundation of education: genuine educators. And without educators, there can be no culture. This deficit has led to the decline of German culture.

One of those rare exceptions, and a man I deeply respect, is my friend Jacob Burckhardt of Bâle. It is to him, above all, that Bâle owes its position as a center of true human culture. He stands as a shining example of what an educator should be.

What, then, do Germany's higher schools actually achieve? They ruthlessly and rapidly train vast numbers of young men to become useful and exploitable servants of the state. This process prioritizes utility over cultivation, treating education as a means to an end rather than an end in itself. The very concept of "higher education" contradicts the idea of catering to the masses. True higher education can only concern the exceptional few; it is a privilege reserved for those capable of appreciating and embodying it.

Great and beautiful things cannot belong to the masses. As the Latin phrase goes, pulchrum est paucorum hominum—the beautiful is for the few. This democratization of education— this attempt to make cultivation "general" and common—is one of the root causes of Germany's cultural decline. When higher education is treated as a universal right rather than a privilege, it inevitably deteriorates in quality.

Another factor undermining German education is the influence of the military profession. The privileges associated with military careers drive far too many people into the higher schools, flooding the system and degrading its standards. In modern Germany, no parent has the freedom to provide their children with a noble education. The teachers, curricula, and goals of the higher schools are all built on a fundamentally mediocre foundation.

Everywhere one looks, haste reigns supreme. It is as if something vital would be lost if a young man were not "finished" by the age of twenty-three, or if he were unable to answer the all-important question: "What career should I choose?" But the superior individual, the one truly capable of higher culture, does not think in terms of "careers." Such a person feels called to something higher and cannot simply conform to the idea of a "calling" imposed by society.

The superior individual takes their time—they must take their time. For such a person, the idea of being "finished" is absurd. In the realm of higher culture, a man of thirty is still a beginner, still a child.

Meanwhile, our overcrowded public schools and the mass production of mediocre teachers are nothing short of a scandal. While some may present serious motives for defending this state of affairs—like the professors at Heidelberg recently did—there can be no legitimate reasons to support it. The rush to "complete" education and the focus on quantity over quality are destroying the very foundation of culture.

Germany's educational system is not cultivating exceptional individuals; it is churning out uniform, functional tools for the state. This is a betrayal of what education should be and a clear indication of the decline of German intellectual and cultural life.

To remain true to my affirmative nature—a nature that deals with contradictions and criticism only reluctantly and as a secondary matter—I will begin by stating the three essential goals for which we require educators. People must learn to see, they must learn to think, and they must learn to speak and write. These three abilities are the foundation of a noble culture.

To learn to see means to train the eye in calmness, patience, and the ability to let things present themselves. It involves postponing judgment and approaching every individual case from all possible angles. This is the first and most essential preparation for intellectual development. One must not react immediately to stimuli; one must cultivate the instincts of restraint and isolation. To learn to see, as I understand it, is closely related to what is popularly referred to as "strength of will." Its core is the ability not to want to see immediately, to defer decisions, and to resist impulses.

All lack of intellectuality and all vulgarity stem from the inability to resist stimuli. Such people feel compelled to respond to every impulse and indulge every reaction. In many cases, this immediate response is a sign of decline, a symptom of exhaustion or morbidity. Most of what common language calls "vices" is simply the physiological inability to refrain from reacting.

To illustrate what it means to have learned to see, consider a person who has undergone this training. As a learner, this individual will likely become cautious, slow, and resistant. With a calm and almost hostile skepticism, they will allow strange and unfamiliar things to approach them but will refrain from immediately engaging or forming judgments. They will withdraw their hand, metaphorically speaking, as the new comes near, watching and observing instead.

In contrast, to be perpetually open, to have the "doors of one's soul" flung wide for every trivial fact, to constantly lie in submission before the flood of external impressions—this is what modern people call "objectivity." But such objectivity is in poor taste; it is vulgar and cheap. It is the intellectual equivalent of being at the mercy of every passing whim, ready to leap into others' souls and experiences without discernment or control.

As for learning to think—our schools have long since abandoned any understanding of this process. Even at the universities, among scholars of philosophy, the discipline of logic is withering away, both as a theory and as a practical skill. Look into any German book, and you will find no trace of the understanding that thinking has a technique, a structure, and a discipline. There is no recognition that thinking must be learned, much like dancing must be learned. Thinking, like dancing, demands practice and a will to mastery.

Who among the Germans today knows, from experience, the subtle joy— the delicate shudder—that comes when intellectual movements are as graceful as light footfalls? Instead, intellectual clumsiness abounds. Awkward postures of the mind and a heavy-handed approach to grasping ideas are so distinctly German that outside of Germany, they are mistakenly equated with the German spirit itself. The German mind has no "fingers" for fine nuances.

The Germans' tolerance for their philosophers, particularly for Kant—the most malformed and crippled figure in the realm of ideas—speaks volumes about their lack of elegance. Kant is a testament to their coarse intellectual habits and their inability to recognize intellectual grace.

In truth, no noble education can exclude dancing in all its forms. This includes dancing with one's feet, but also with ideas, with words, and, above all, with the pen. Writing is, in its highest form, a kind of intellectual dance, requiring rhythm, precision, and lightness. Yet at this point, I must acknowledge that these thoughts will likely remain utterly incomprehensible to most German readers.

Chapter 9
Skirmishes in A War with The Age

My Impossible People.—Seneca, the showman of virtue, performing like a bullfighter in the ring of morals. Rousseau, the preacher of returning to nature, lost in his own unpolished, raw state. Schiller, the trumpet of morality, blasting his tunes from Säckingen with little depth behind the noise. Dante, the scavenger who writes poetry over the graves he haunts. Kant, whose moral preaching is nothing more than a cleverly disguised form of empty rhetoric. Victor Hugo, a beacon on the vast sea of nonsense, shining brightly but without direction. Liszt, master of chasing not only after musical greatness but also after women. George Sand, overflowing with creativity, like a cow with an endless supply of beautiful milk. Michelet, all fire and passion, but dressed casually in the everyday garb of enthusiasm. Carlyle, the voice of pessimism, but one born of a poorly digested meal rather than deep reflection. John Stuart Mill, whose clarity is so sharp it feels almost offensive. The brothers Goncourt, two literary warriors battling Homer with their pens, their drama set to Offenbach's music.

Zola, who finds inspiration in the repulsive and thrives in the stench of decay.

Renan. Theology personified, corrupted by the original sin of Christianity. His thoughts are tainted with the contradictions of faith. Even when Renan dares to take a stance, to say "yes" or "no" on a major issue, he almost always misses the point entirely. He tries to combine science with nobility, seemingly unaware that science is inherently democratic and cannot be aligned with his aristocratic ideals. He dreams of an intellectual aristocracy, yet at the same time, he bows down to the gospel of humility and grovels before it. What good is his modern free-spiritedness, his wit, his irony, and his intellectual acrobatics, if deep inside he remains tied to the faith of a Christian, a Catholic, and even a priest?

Renan's strength, much like that of a Jesuit or a confessor, lies in his ability to seduce. His intellect has the same unctuous, self-satisfied tone as a parson. Like all priests, he becomes dangerous when he loves, because his love distorts the truth. He has a rare talent for worshipping dangerous ideas in such a way that they appear benign. But his intellect, rather than invigorating, weakens and softens. For France, already suffering from a broken will and diminishing strength, Renan is one more calamity—a soothing voice at a time when sharp clarity and decisiveness are needed.

Sainte-Beuve. There is nothing manly about him. He is filled with petty malice toward all strong and noble spirits. He drifts aimlessly, subtle yet spiteful, always restless and curious. He listens at keyholes, gathering whispers, but never facing things head-on. At heart, he is more like a woman, full of revenge and sensuality. As a psychologist, he is a genius of slander, endlessly creative in his ability to add a touch of poison even to his praise. His instincts are plebeian, closely aligned with the resentful spirit of Rousseau. This makes him a Romanticist, for beneath all Romanticism lies Rousseau's vengeful nature, grumbling and restless.

Sainte-Beuve is a restrained revolutionary, his actions kept in check by fear. He flinches before strength, whether it comes in the form of public opinion, the Academy, the court, or even the cloistered thinkers of Port Royal. He is filled with bitterness toward all that is great, toward everything that has confidence in itself. He is enough of a poet, enough of a sensualist, to recognize power when he sees it, but he writhes under its weight like a worm being trodden upon.

As a critic, Sainte-Beuve lacks a foundation—no standard of judgment, no clear principles, no backbone. While he speaks with the versatility of a worldly libertine, chattering endlessly about countless subjects, he lacks the courage to own his own libertinism. As a historian, he has no philosophical depth, no ability to see history as a coherent whole. This lack of vision leads him to avoid making judgments, opting instead for a mask of "objectivity" in matters of importance.

Yet when it comes to things that demand subtlety and refined taste, Sainte- Beuve finds his footing. Here, he dares to embrace his true nature, enjoying his own personality and even achieving mastery. In this sense, he is a precursor to Baudelaire, though without Baudelaire's courage to push boundaries.

"The Imitation of Christ." This is a book I cannot even touch without feeling physically repulsed. It reeks of the "eternally feminine," a cloying sweetness that can only appeal to French sensibilities or to Wagnerites. Its saintly musings on love are delivered in a tone so saccharine that even the most worldly Parisian women might find themselves intrigued.

I have been told that Auguste Comte, the clever Jesuit disguised as a man of science, took inspiration from this book in his attempt to lead his countrymen back to Rome by way of science. I can believe it. This is the essence of the "religion of the heart"—a sentimental, deceptive path back to the old faith, cloaked in modern rhetoric. It is as much a symbol of decline as it is of misplaced devotion.

G. Eliot.—They have let go of the Christian God, yet they cling even harder to Christian morality. This is a very English way of thinking, and while it might seem strange, one can hardly blame moral women like George Eliot for following it. In England, even the smallest step away from theology must be balanced by an extreme embrace of morality. It's their way of making amends, their form of penance. Anyone who begins to stray from religious belief feels compelled to prove their virtue by becoming a moral fanatic.

We, however, are different. When we abandon Christian faith, we also give up any claim to Christian morality. This connection might not be obvious to everyone, but it must be emphasized repeatedly, especially to counter the shallow thinkers so common in England. Christianity is not a loose collection of values; it is a complete system, a worldview where every part supports the whole. If you remove its central pillar—the belief in God—the entire structure collapses. What remains is empty, lifeless, and without meaning.

Christianity assumes that humans cannot know what is good or bad for themselves. It teaches that only God knows these things. Christian morality, therefore, is not a product of human reasoning but a divine command. It is immune to criticism because it rests entirely on the belief that God is the ultimate truth. Without God, Christian morality loses its foundation and cannot stand on its own.

The English, however, seem to believe otherwise. They think they can intuitively know what is good or evil without needing Christianity to guide them. But this belief only shows how deeply Christian values still shape their thinking. Their moral standards remain rooted in Christian teachings, even when they deny the religion itself. This is not evidence of independence; it is proof of how strong Christianity's influence remains. The English no longer recognize the origins of their morality, nor do they realize how fragile it is without its theological base. For them, morality is not a question to be examined—it is simply assumed, a problem they have yet to confront.

George Sand.—I recently read the first Lettres d'un Voyageur, and like everything influenced by Rousseau, it felt artificial, exaggerated, and insincere. The style reminded me of cheap wallpaper—bright, decorative, but ultimately shallow. The writing seems overly concerned with appearing noble and generous, yet lacks any genuine depth. What struck me most was Sand's affected masculinity, which came across as forced and unconvincing, like the awkward swagger of a poorly mannered schoolboy.

And how cold she must have been beneath this performance! She seemed like a machine, wound up and ready to produce her work, writing not out of passion but out of routine. This coldness is not unique to her; it is the hallmark of Romanticists like Hugo and Balzac, whose writing often feels detached from true feeling. Sand's self-satisfaction is evident in her prolific output, as if she took pride in her ability to churn out words endlessly. There was something undeniably German in her style—not in the good sense, but in the clumsy, heavy-handed way that marks the decline of true French taste. And yet Renan adores her!

A Moral for Psychologists.—Never engage in psychology just for the sake of observing. Observing for its own sake leads to a distorted view of things, to exaggeration, and to a forced perspective. Experiencing something intentionally, with the purpose of analyzing it, is not helpful. When in the middle of an experience, a person should not turn their attention inward to observe themselves. In such moments, even the clearest vision becomes clouded—it turns into the "evil eye." A true psychologist avoids observing for the sake of observation. The same is true for a true artist. A born painter, for instance, does not work directly "from nature." Instead, they rely on their instinct, their internal lens, to filter and shape their perception of reality. For them, only the general idea, the final impression, reaches conscious thought. They do not bother with the painstaking process of building conclusions from small, particular details.

But what happens when someone approaches this differently? Take, for example, the Parisian novelists who practice "note-book psychology," recording every detail, large or small, that catches their attention. Such people are constantly spying on life, collecting observations like trinkets to carry home at the end of each day. The result? A chaotic mess, at best resembling a mosaic of unrelated fragments. Their work is restless and garish, more like a patchwork quilt than a coherent picture. The Goncourts are the worst offenders in this regard. They cannot write three sentences without causing pain to anyone with an eye for psychology or aesthetics.

From an artistic perspective, nature is no model to imitate. Nature exaggerates, distorts, and leaves gaps—it is full of accidents. To study "from nature" is, in my view, a bad sign. It shows submission, weakness, and a kind of fatalism. This slavish worship of trivial facts is beneath a true artist. The ability to see "what is" belongs to a different kind of intellect altogether—one that is practical and matter-of-fact, not artistic. An artist must know who they are and what their purpose is, rather than bowing before the randomness of nature.

To make art possible—that is, to create an aesthetic way of acting and seeing—a certain physiological state must come first: ecstasy. Without this heightened state of being, art simply cannot exist. Ecstasy heightens the sensitivity of the whole body and mind, making them more receptive and powerful. Many kinds of ecstasy can lead to art, no matter how they arise. Sexual excitement, for example, is the oldest and most fundamental form of ecstasy. Similarly, ecstasy can come from powerful desires, intense passions, the energy of celebration, the thrill of a battle, the bravery of a daring act, the joy of victory, or the rush of destruction. Even seasonal changes, such as the vibrancy of spring, or the use of drugs can trigger this state. Another form of ecstasy arises from a strong surge of willpower, when one feels driven and overflowing with determination.

At its core, ecstasy creates a feeling of increased strength and abundance. In this state, a person projects their inner wealth onto the world around them. They impose their energy onto things, forcing them to reflect their own richness and power. This act of projecting oneself onto the world is called idealizing. Contrary to popular belief, idealizing does not mean removing details or simplifying things. Instead, it emphasizes the main characteristics so powerfully that lesser details fade away.

In this state of abundance, a person enriches everything they encounter. Whatever they see or desire appears to them as larger, stronger, and more alive. They transform objects and ideas until these reflect their own strength and perfection. This drive to transform things into something beautiful is what we call art. Through art, a person celebrates themselves as a reflection of perfection, even in things they are not.

It is also possible to imagine the opposite of this artistic state—an anti- artistic condition. In such a state, a person drains energy from everything around them. Instead of enriching and enhancing, they weaken and impoverish. These individuals lack vitality and draw from others to sustain themselves. History is full of such anti-artists—individuals like Pascal, whose Christian faith exemplifies this draining tendency. A true Christian, by nature, cannot also be an artist. Even suggesting otherwise by pointing to figures like Raphael misses the point entirely. Raphael affirmed life, celebrated beauty, and said "yes" to the world, which means he was not a Christian in the true sense.

The terms Apollonian and Dionysian, which I introduced to aesthetics, represent two opposing forms of ecstasy. Apollonian ecstasy sharpens vision, giving the eye a heightened ability to see and understand. This type of ecstasy inspires painters, sculptors, and epic poets, who are fundamentally visionaries. On the other hand, Dionysian ecstasy awakens the entire system of passions, intensifying them and causing them to pour out in a flood of expression. This state drives transformation and imitation, releasing all forms of mimicry and artistic display at once. The Dionysian artist is incredibly sensitive to every emotion and suggestion. They instinctively grasp and communicate emotions, transforming themselves into whatever role or passion they encounter. Music, as we understand it today, is a surviving fragment of this broader Dionysian expression—a remnant of a once richer form of emotional discharge. For music to become its own art form, many other senses, such as the sense of touch and movement, had to be partially suppressed. Rhythm, however, still appeals to our physical senses to some extent, linking music to its Dionysian roots.

Actors, mimes, dancers, musicians, and lyricists all share a common foundation in their instincts. Over time, however, they have specialized, developing their own distinct fields of art, even to the point of becoming opposites. Among these, lyricists remained closely connected to musicians for the longest period, while actors were similarly linked to dancers. Architects, however, represent something different. Their art is born not from

Dionysian or Apollonian ecstasy but from the overwhelming will to create. Architecture expresses human pride, triumph over nature, and the will to power in physical form. Great men have always inspired architects, who in turn translate this power into structures that symbolize strength and security. Architecture becomes a language of power, speaking through form. It can persuade, command, or simply exist with quiet confidence. True grandeur in architecture reflects power that is self-assured, needing no validation, unconcerned with opposition, and relying only on itself.

Recently, I read about Thomas Carlyle's life, a mix of unintended comedy and moral posturing. Carlyle was a man of dramatic words and gestures, forever in search of a strong faith that he could not find. This unfulfilled longing makes him a quintessential Romantic. The desire for strong faith, however, is not a sign of having it but rather the opposite. A person with true faith can afford the luxury of doubt and skepticism because their foundation is firm. Carlyle's loud proclamations of reverence for those with strong faith, combined with his anger at those who lacked it, reveal his inner turmoil. He needed noise—both literal and figurative—to distract himself from his doubts.

Carlyle's defining trait was his persistent dishonesty with himself. This quality makes him fascinating, though it also explains why he was so admired in England. Honesty, as the English understand it, often overlaps with hypocrisy, and Carlyle fits this mold perfectly. At heart, he was an atheist who stubbornly refused to admit it, making his struggle with faith all the more dramatic and emblematic of the English spirit.

Emerson is far more enlightened, versatile, and refined than Carlyle, and most importantly, he is happier. He lives instinctively, enjoying the best parts of life while discarding what he finds unpleasant. Compared to Carlyle, Emerson has better taste and a lighter, more joyous intellectuality. Carlyle, who admired him greatly, complained that Emerson "does not give us enough to chew." While this criticism may be true, it hardly counts as a flaw—it is simply a reflection of Emerson's different approach. Emerson's cheerfulness shields him from the heaviness of life. He does not burden himself with excessive seriousness, and he approaches existence with a kind of perpetual youthfulness, blissfully unaware of his age or the weight of time. He might have described himself, in Lope de Vega's words, as someone who constantly succeeds himself, always renewing and reimagining his life. His mind naturally seeks reasons to be content, even grateful, and he often approaches a carefree joyfulness akin to the bourgeois simplicity of a man returning from a romantic escapade, satisfied with life's fleeting pleasures.

The "struggle for existence," a centerpiece of Darwinian thought, strikes me as more of an assumption than an established fact. It does happen, but it is the exception, not the rule. Life's general state is not one of scarcity and competition but one of abundance, extravagance, and even absurd excess. Where struggle does occur, it is more often a struggle for power than for mere survival. The idea of nature as fundamentally Malthusian is misleading. Even if the struggle for existence does take place, its outcomes are often the opposite of what Darwin and his followers might hope. Instead of favoring the strong, the exceptional, and the privileged, it often benefits the weak, simply because they are the majority and frequently more cunning. Darwin overlooked the role of intellect—an oversight that seems distinctly English. The weak are often more intelligent, driven by necessity to develop cleverness and adaptability. By contrast, the strong, having less need for such traits, may grow complacent and neglect their intellect, letting it atrophy. Intellect, after all, demands caution, patience, and subtlety—qualities the powerful may disdain in favor of brute strength.

Those who study humanity deeply often have ulterior motives. A politician, for instance, uses his understanding of people to gain power or advantage. But what of the so-called disinterested observer, the one who claims to seek no personal benefit? A closer look often reveals a darker purpose: the desire to feel superior, to distance oneself from humanity, to no longer belong. This kind of person despises mankind, even if they claim objectivity and fairness. By contrast, the more "self-serving" politician may actually be more humane, for at least he sees himself as part of the same world as those he studies.

The German approach to intellect and psychology leaves much to be desired, as evidenced by certain cultural missteps. Consider, for example, the pairing of names like Goethe and Schiller, or worse, Schiller and Goethe, as if they were equals. Has no one yet recognized the vast gulf between them? And then there are other egregious pairings, such as Schopenhauer and Hartmann. Such thoughtless associations reflect a lack of discernment and an inability to appreciate true intellectual refinement.

The most intelligent and courageous individuals often endure the greatest tragedies because they confront life's most daunting challenges. Yet, paradoxically, these struggles lead them to honor life all the more, for it forces them to grapple with its fiercest adversaries. In this way, their suffering becomes a testament to their strength and their profound engagement with existence.

In today's world, genuine hypocrisy has become increasingly rare. Hypocrisy requires a strong belief, a faith so deeply held that one is willing to outwardly adopt another, contradictory stance while maintaining one's inner conviction. Such duality thrives only in an era of fervent faith, where abandoning one's belief is unthinkable. Modern culture, however, allows for a multiplicity of beliefs, making hypocrisy almost obsolete. People no longer feel the need to maintain a façade; instead, they adopt multiple convictions and live comfortably with them, ensuring these beliefs never truly conflict or demand consistency.

This tolerance for contradictions is both a sign of our age and a symptom of its weaknesses. Modern individuals avoid compromising themselves by avoiding consistency. They cultivate convenience rather than conviction, preferring a life free of challenges or demands on their integrity. Even vices, once expressions of strong will, have degenerated into virtues in this climate of comfort and ease. The few hypocrites I've encountered are mere imitations of the real thing, like actors playing a role. They lack the depth and complexity of true hypocrisy, reduced instead to shallow performances in a world that no longer requires or even understands the profound struggles of belief and deceit.

Beautiful and Ugly:—Our sense of the beautiful is deeply relative, tightly bound to the limitations of human perception and context. To try and separate beauty from the joy humans derive from their surroundings, especially other humans, would be to sever it from its grounding altogether. "Beauty in itself" is nothing more than an abstract phrase, a hollow idea without true substance or universal agreement. In perceiving beauty, humans essentially declare themselves as the measure of perfection. At times, in exceptional circumstances, they even idolize themselves as that ultimate standard. This impulse stems from the most basic instinct of survival and self-preservation. Even the loftiest ideas of beauty are, at their core, expressions of humanity's need to affirm and expand itself.

Man views the world as brimming with beauty, failing to recognize that he is the source of this projection. The beauty he perceives is merely a reflection of himself, a human imprint upon the world. Alas, it is not a universal beauty, but rather one that is all-too-human. In truth, man mirrors himself in everything he beholds, deeming things beautiful because they resonate with his own image.

The judgment of beauty is thus the vanity of the human species, an echo of its own self-love. A skeptic might wonder, "Is the world genuinely beautiful because man finds it so?" Perhaps not. Perhaps all man has done is to humanize the world, to imprint it with his desires and perceptions. Yet, there is no definitive proof that man is the ultimate standard of beauty. What if, in the eyes of a more refined judge of taste, mankind appeared peculiar, comical, or arbitrary? Imagine Dionysus teasing Ariadne about her ears during a philosophical conversation, playfully suggesting, "Why are they not a little longer?" The joke may contain a deeper truth.

From this perspective, nothing in itself is beautiful; it is man alone who declares beauty. Aesthetic sensibility begins with this innocent assumption, the first axiom of aesthetics. Alongside it stands a second principle: nothing is truly ugly except the degenerate man. Together, these principles define the bounds of aesthetic judgment. From a physiological standpoint, ugliness weakens and demoralizes. It reminds humanity of fragility, decay, and the loss of vitality. In the presence of ugliness, man's strength diminishes, as if the sight itself drains him of energy. This reaction, measurable even by a dynamometer, reveals a deep instinctual response: ugliness signals something threatening, something that disrupts the will to power.

When a man feels a sudden drop in confidence or courage, it often stems from encountering something that he perceives as ugly. This reaction emerges from deep within his instincts, stored with countless associations between appearances and their inferred meanings. Ugliness is perceived as a symptom of decline and degeneration. Anything that even faintly suggests a deterioration of the human type—be it physical exhaustion, aging, stiffness, or the crudeness of decomposition—is judged as ugly. Colors, smells, and forms associated with decay, even when abstracted into mere symbols, provoke the same visceral rejection.

This response is not simply distaste; it is hatred, a primal and profound aversion. What is it that man hates in ugliness? He hates the signs of decline in his own kind. This hatred is rooted in the deepest instincts of survival, resonating with the need to preserve the strength and vitality of his type. It is a hatred tinged with horror and caution, expressing a far-sighted instinct for the preservation of life. This reaction is not shallow; it is the most profound hatred man possesses, one that is etched into the very fabric of his being.

It is this hatred of decline, this refusal to accept degeneration, that gives art its depth. Art draws from the profound tension between man's yearning for beauty and his rejection of what threatens his sense of vitality and perfection. In this way, art is more than an expression of the beautiful; it is an affirmation of life, shaped by man's most primal fears and desires.

Schopenhauer, the last German thinker of significance, stands alongside figures like Goethe, Hegel, and Heinrich Heine as a European, not merely a national, event. For a psychologist, he is a fascinating case of the highest order. His work represents a cunning and skillful effort to turn the most life-affirming aspects of human existence—such as art, heroism, genius, beauty, deep compassion, the pursuit of truth, and even the grandeur of tragedy—into arguments for a nihilistic rejection of life. In this, Schopenhauer engages in what could be called one of history's greatest intellectual forgeries, rivaled only by Christianity. He reinterpreted all the noble affirmations of life as if they were but expressions of the denial of the "will to live" or as steps leading inevitably toward that denial.

When scrutinized more closely, Schopenhauer appears as an inheritor of the Christian worldview, repackaged for a secular age. Unlike Christianity, which outright rejects many aspects of human culture, Schopenhauer found a way to nihilistically "approve" of them. To him, these elements of culture—art, beauty, and even human striving—were not ends in themselves but tools to draw the soul toward "salvation," mere appetizers to stimulate a hunger for deliverance from life itself.

Take, for example, his view of beauty. Schopenhauer speaks of beauty with a sorrowful intensity, valuing it as a bridge to something beyond, a fleeting liberation from the burdens of the "will to live." He sees beauty as a temporary escape, particularly from the "burning core" of the will—sexuality. To him, beauty negates the reproductive instinct, offering a glimpse of salvation. Singular saint, indeed! But someone challenges this notion— Nature herself. Why does Nature create beauty in sound, color, fragrance, and rhythm if not to affirm life and reproduction? Why does beauty compel and captivate? Schopenhauer's own idol, Plato, offers a striking contradiction to his thesis.

Plato, whom Schopenhauer venerates as a divine authority, takes an entirely different view. For Plato, beauty is not a denial of life; it is an irresistible lure toward creation and procreation. Beauty inspires both the lowest sensual desires and the highest intellectual pursuits. With a Greek innocence utterly foreign to the Christian mindset, Plato claims that without the beauty of young men in Athens, there would have been no Platonic philosophy. It was their radiance that stirred the philosopher's soul, igniting a passion that refused to rest until it had planted the seeds of great ideas in such captivating soil. Plato himself, then, was a singular saint of a different kind—one for whom the aesthetic and the erotic were deeply intertwined.

This reveals a starkly different approach to philosophy in Athens, where it was pursued openly, even playfully. Unlike the cloistered, abstract cogitations of later thinkers such as Spinoza with his intellectual love of God, Platonic philosophy was an extension of the Greek tradition of competitive games, agon, infused with an erotic dimension. Plato's philosophy was, in many ways, an elevated and spiritualized form of the Greek gymnastic competitions, with dialectics becoming a new art form born of this philosophic eroticism.

In defense of Plato and against Schopenhauer's austere view, it is worth noting that much of the higher culture and literature of classical France also flourished on the fertile ground of sexual interests. Whether in gallantry, the passions, sexual rivalry, or the role of women, these themes pervade French culture and cannot be overlooked. The sensual and the intellectual intertwined seamlessly, revealing that higher culture, far from denying life, often springs from its most vibrant and primal energies.

The idea of l'ar t pour l'ar t—art for art's sake—has often been interpreted as a rebellion against the notion that art must serve a moral purpose or improve humanity. This phrase essentially declares, "Let morality go to hell!" Yet, even in this rejection, we see how deeply entrenched the moral bias remains. The act of opposing morality in art still acknowledges its overwhelming influence. If art is stripped of its role as a preacher of morals or a tool for human betterment, this does not mean it is left entirely without purpose or meaning. To say that art has no purpose, no point, no sense—this is what l'art pour l'art suggests. It is like a snake biting its own tail: a pure passion insisting, "No purpose at all is better than a moral purpose."

But a psychologist must question this: What does art actually do? Does it not praise? Does it not elevate certain ideas while diminishing others? Does it not highlight and amplify? In doing so, art reinforces or diminishes certain values. Can this be dismissed as an incidental outcome or a mere accident, independent of the artist's intentions? Or is it, rather, a fundamental instinct of the artist to shape and serve life through art? Is the artist's true drive concerned with art itself, or does it instead lie in the aim of art—to enrich and enhance life, to advocate for a specific way of living? Art is a tremendous stimulus to life; how, then, can it be seen as pointless or purposeless? It is not simply l'art pour l'art.

And what of the dark and unsettling aspects that art sometimes reveals? When art exposes what is ugly, harsh, or deeply troubling, does it not risk making life unbearable? Some philosophers have thought so. For example, Schopenhauer argued that the purpose of art, especially tragedy, was to free us from the relentless desires of the will and to lead us toward resignation. Tragedy, for him, was valuable because it made us more willing to renounce life. But this view reflects a pessimistic perspective—a deeply negative outlook. To understand art, we must consult the artist, not the pessimist. What does the tragic artist convey to us? Surely it is not resignation but rather a fearless embrace of life's terrors and uncertainties. The artist shows us how to face profound suffering with courage and strength. This attitude is a triumph in itself, and those who have experienced it know it is something to be revered. The artist must share this perspective. A true artist and a genius in communication cannot help but share it.

The tragic artist exalts a heroic spirit, one that confronts overwhelming challenges, sublime catastrophes, and terrifying mysteries with dignity and resolve. This spirit celebrates itself in tragedy, finding joy even in suffering. The tragic artist extends this "cup of sweetest cruelty" to those who are attuned to hardship, who seek it out and embrace it as a defining aspect of life. Tragedy is not about giving up; it is about finding meaning and affirmation in struggle.

A related notion is the idea of hospitality in one's soul. To welcome anyone and everyone into one's inner world may seem generous, but it lacks discernment. A truly noble heart holds its finest chambers in reserve, waiting for worthy guests—guests who are not merely anybody but rather individuals of real substance. Such hearts are rich in depth, with shutters closed and windows veiled, not out of fear or selfishness, but in anticipation of those who merit their best.

Too often, we undervalue ourselves when we attempt to articulate the deepest contents of our souls. Our most profound experiences are not verbose; they are beyond words and would resist even the most earnest attempts at expression. The very act of finding words for something suggests that it has already been overcome or rendered less significant. Speech itself diminishes, for in speaking, we simplify and vulgarize. Words are the currency of the average, the mundane, the communicable. To speak is to betray the depth of what one truly feels, revealing instead only a shadow of the truth. This recognition might well serve as a moral guide for philosophers and others who value the unspoken.

And what of those who strive for objectivity, who pride themselves on their detached and impartial perspectives? Their wisdom, patience, and tolerance may seem impressive, even virtuous, but it often comes at the cost of passion and genuine self-control. Such individuals, drenched in their indulgence and sympathy, should occasionally permit themselves a dose of raw emotion, even a small emotional vice. It may feel uncomfortable, even ridiculous, to them, but it serves as a form of self-discipline—a kind of asceticism for those who have mastered detachment but risk losing touch with their own humanity.

In becoming personal, the so-called "objective" individuals reveal their own virtues, for objectivity often masks a deeper desire: the need to feel above the fray, detached from the common lot. Yet true nobility lies not in keeping oneself apart but in knowing when and how to connect with others authentically. The virtues of objectivity are limited without the courage to embrace and engage with life's messy, subjective truths.

Excerpt from a doctor's exam paper: "What is the ultimate goal of all advanced education?" To transform a human being into a machine. "What methods are employed to achieve this?" Teaching the individual how to endure boredom. "And how is this boredom instilled?" Through the concept of duty. "What model of duty is presented to the student?" The philologist, who embodies the art of relentless, uninspired diligence. "Who, then, is the ideal human being?" The government official. "And which philosophy provides the definitive framework for this ideal?" Kant's philosophy: envisioning the government official as the ultimate abstraction—the thing- in-itself— presiding over his worldly role as mere appearance.

The Right to Stupidity: Picture the exhausted worker, his breath measured, his demeanor mild, his actions guided by inertia rather than intent. This archetype, a product of our era of relentless labor (and "Empire"), now inhabits every class. This weary figure seeks escape and leisure, claiming even Art for himself—books,

newspapers, and, most notably, beautiful landscapes like Italy. This man of the evening, with his "wild instincts lulled," as Faust might say, requires his summer holidays, his coastal retreats, his alpine glaciers, and his pilgrimage to Bayreuth. In times like these, Art gains the right to be utterly frivolous—a playful retreat for wit, spirit, and emotion. Wagner, of course, understood this well. Pure silliness becomes a form of refreshment, a tonic for the fatigued.

A Further Question of Discipline: Consider the methods Julius Caesar used to safeguard himself against illness and headaches: grueling marches, a life stripped to its simplest essentials, constant exposure to the elements, and enduring hardships without respite. These strategies represent the necessary defenses and survival tactics for those intricate, high-performing organisms called geniuses. Such lives, always teetering at the edge of their capacity, demand such rigorous measures to maintain their vitality.

The Immoralist Speaks: Nothing is more repugnant to true philosophers than observing man in the act of wishing. When they see man purely in his actions—this most fearless, cunning, and resilient of animals, navigating life's calamities with remarkable ingenuity—he earns their admiration. They may even encourage him.

Yet the moment man begins to wish or pursue "ideals," he becomes contemptible in their eyes. They reject not only the man of desires but also the very concept of "desirability" and all the ideals and aspirations that humans project upon the world.

Were a true philosopher inclined to nihilism, it would not be because of the absence of meaning but because every human ideal reveals not grandeur but something base: futility, absurdity, frailty, cowardice, fatigue, and the residue left over from life's excesses. Why is it that man, so admirable in his tangible existence, becomes unworthy of respect the moment he begins to desire? Is it some kind of cosmic balancing act? Must the heights of his reality be counterbalanced by the lowliness of his imagination and aspirations? Humanity's history of desires has always been its most shameful chapter; one would be wise not to delve too deeply into it.

What redeems mankind is not its dreams or ideals but its tangible reality. This reality justifies humanity—now and forever. A real man, living and acting in the world, is infinitely more valuable than the mere shadow of a man shaped by desires, fantasies, and delusions. Any ideal man, no matter how elevated he may seem, pales in comparison to the flesh-and-blood individual who embodies the truth of existence. And it is precisely the "ideal man"—the product of abstractions, longings, and lies—that a philosopher finds most insufferable.

The Natural Value of Egoism: The worth of selfishness depends entirely on the inherent value of the individual who practices it. This value may be immense, or it may be insignificant and even contemptible. Every person can be evaluated based on whether they represent the ascending or descending trajectory of life. Once this determination is made, it becomes possible to measure the value of their egoism. If a person embodies the upward movement of life—its growth, strength, and vitality—then their worth is extraordinary. For the collective progress of humanity, which advances through such individuals, it is essential to focus on ensuring their well-being and creating the optimal conditions for them to thrive. These individuals are not isolated entities, mere atoms, or passive inheritors of history; instead, they represent the entire trajectory of humanity culminating in their existence.

Conversely, if an individual represents decline, degeneration, or chronic decay, their value diminishes significantly. Sickness, for instance, is often the result, rather than the cause, of such decline. In such cases, it would be most equitable if these individuals took as little as possible from those who are nature's fortunate creations. These declining individuals become parasitic, drawing from the vitality of others without contributing to life's upward momentum.

The Christian and the Anarchist: When the anarchist, as the voice of the decaying elements in society, cries out for "rights," "justice," or "equality," it is not an enlightened demand but a symptom of their deeper ignorance. They do not understand the true source of their suffering: a poverty not of material possessions but of life itself. An instinct for finding blame is at work here; someone must bear responsibility for their discomfort and unease. Their anger, their dramatic indignation, serves as a fleeting relief—a kind of temporary intoxication that offers them a sense of power, however small. To complain, to bewail one's condition, even to hurl accusations, is a twisted consolation. It allows them to endure their existence by adding a layer of satisfaction to their misery.

There is always an element of revenge in lamentation. In every complaint lies the unspoken accusation: "Because I suffer, you ought to suffer too." This logic, though bitter, is the foundation of revolutions. To grumble about one's plight, however, is always degrading. It stems from weakness, whether one blames others or oneself for one's suffering. The socialist blames society; the Christian, by contrast, blames themselves. But both share a common flaw—the need to identify a scapegoat for their pain. This shared instinct, ignoble in both cases, is driven by the desire to alleviate suffering with the sweet, temporary balm of revenge.

The targets of this vengeful instinct are often incidental, chosen simply because they offer a convenient outlet. The Christian turns their blame inward, condemning their own sinfulness, while the anarchist directs their anger outward, railing against society and its perceived injustices. Yet, both are products of decline, symptoms of decadence. Even the Christian, in their acts of condemnation, slander, and defamation, mirrors the same instinct that drives the socialist worker to vilify society. The ultimate Christian fantasy— the Last Judgment—is nothing more than a dramatic extension of this need for vengeance, a cosmic reckoning that satisfies their desire to see wrongs avenged on the grandest scale.

In this way, the Christian's idea of the "Beyond" serves as nothing more than a tool to defame the "Here." It is not born out of a genuine belief in transcendence but from the need to disparage and denigrate this world. Similarly, the anarchist's dream of revolution is merely a more immediate expression of the same instinct—a wish for upheaval to punish those they blame for their suffering. Whether through the promise of an apocalyptic reckoning or the hope for societal collapse, both use these fantasies to lash out at life, unable to embrace its reality or its challenges.

An "altruistic" morality, one that causes selfishness to weaken and fade away, is always a troubling sign. This holds true not only for individuals but especially for nations. When selfishness starts to diminish, it signals the absence of the best and strongest qualities. To instinctively choose what harms oneself or to be drawn to so-called "selfless" motives is nearly a definition of decadence. The idea of "not prioritizing one's own interests" is nothing more than a moral disguise for a deeper problem, a physiological one: the person no longer knows what truly benefits them. This is the collapse of instincts, the breakdown of life's natural guidance system. A person who becomes overly altruistic is on a dangerous path. Instead of admitting honestly, "I am no longer any good," the lie that decadents tell themselves through morality is, "Nothing is any good— life itself is worthless."

This kind of judgment is deeply harmful, as it can spread like a poison, infecting others. On the polluted soil of society, such ideas grow wildly and take root, appearing now as religion, like Christianity, or as philosophy, like Schopenhauer's worldview. In some cases, even the faintest trace of such toxic ideas, sprouting as they do from the decay of life itself, can harm humanity for thousands of years.

The sick man, in this context, becomes a parasite to society. There are times when continuing to live becomes indecent. When life's meaning and one's right to live have been lost, clinging to existence through doctors and treatments should be viewed with disdain. Doctors themselves should be the ones to instill this sense of contempt; instead of prolonging such lives with prescriptions, they should daily serve their patients a dose of disgust. A new duty should fall upon the doctor—to mercilessly prevent and eliminate degenerate life in cases where the higher interests of life demand it. This would include defending the right to be born, the right to live, and even the right to procreate. One should embrace death proudly when living proudly is no longer possible. Death should be a conscious choice, welcomed at the right time, with clarity and joy, and shared with loved ones in a way that allows a proper farewell. A person should remain fully themselves, able to reflect on their achievements and measure the value of life itself before departing.

This vision is the complete opposite of the grotesque drama that Christianity has turned the moment of death into. Christianity has abused the vulnerability of dying people, violating their conscience and exploiting their final moments as a way of judging them and their lives. For this, Christianity deserves no forgiveness. It is our duty to restore the dignity of death, reclaiming it as a natural, physiological process, even though "natural death" is often nothing more than a euphemism for suicide. No one perishes because of someone else; one dies only because of their own nature. Yet the kind of death that happens by chance, at the wrong time, or under cowardly circumstances, is the most disgraceful. Out of love for life itself, one should strive for a death that is deliberate and free, neither accidental nor unexpected.

Let me offer some advice to the pessimists and other decadents among us. We cannot undo the fact of our birth—that mistake, if it was one—but we can choose to correct it if we wish. The act of taking one's own life can be the most honorable deed. In fact, the person who ends their life almost earns the right to live for having had the strength to do so. Such an act benefits society—and life itself—far more than a life wasted in weakness, self-denial, or other so-called virtues. At the very least, the one who takes their own life spares others the burden of their existence and removes one more objection to the value of life.

Pure pessimism can only truly be proven by the actions of pessimists themselves. They must go further in their logic. To merely deny life in theory, as Schopenhauer did in The World as Will and Idea, is not enough; the next step is to deny Schopenhauer himself. Incidentally, pessimism, no matter how contagious it might appear, does not actually increase the decay of an era or a species. It merely reflects the decay that already exists. Like cholera, it only afflicts those who are already susceptible. Pessimism does not add a single person to the ranks of the world's degenerates. Let me remind you of an important fact: during years when cholera rages, the overall number of deaths does not exceed those of other years.

Have we really become more moral? Many insist that we have, yet I find this belief itself to be grounds for skepticism. In Germany, for instance, the entire force of moral indignation—the kind that passes for morality—was directed against my idea of "Beyond Good and Evil." People argued passionately that modern moral sentiment demonstrates our progress, claiming that compared to us, a figure like Cæsar Borgia could not be seen as a "higher man" or the kind of "superman" I described him to be. One editor even congratulated me for my boldness while accusing me of aiming to abolish all decency.

A curious compliment indeed! But I pose this question in return: Have we truly become more moral?

We modern people like to imagine our heightened sensitivity and mutual consideration as evidence of moral advancement. This collective sense of care and support, this avoidance of harm or offense, seems to us a significant step forward—proof that we surpass the brutal and daring men of the Renaissance. Yet every era believes itself superior in such ways; it is inevitable.

One thing is certain: we could not survive the raw reality of the Renaissance, nor could we imagine enduring its conditions. Our nerves and constitutions are simply too frail. But this does not signify progress. It only reflects the weakened, more delicate nature of our current state, a kind of physiological aging that has given rise to a morality of tenderness and caution.

If we strip away this frailty and delicateness, our so-called morality of "humanization" loses all meaning. In such a context, it might even appear contemptible. Let us also consider how our humanitarian virtues would have seemed to Renaissance men— those accustomed to a richer, bolder, and more overflowing vitality. They would have laughed themselves to death at our modern notions of virtue. Unwittingly, we have become laughable. Our supposed "progress" in reducing suspicion and hostility is simply a byproduct of our dwindling vitality. Living in such dependency and fragility requires endless caution and cooperation. In this environment, we become a society of mutual invalids and caregivers, calling this arrangement "virtue."

To men of a fuller, more daring era, our lifestyle might be seen as cowardice, weakness, or the morality of the old and infirm. What I call our softening of morals is not progress but evidence of decline. By contrast, a harder, fiercer moral code often arises in times of surplus vitality. When life overflows with energy, people take risks, embrace challenges, and even waste their strength freely. What once added zest to life might now poison us. Even indifference—a form of strength—is beyond our reach because we are too sensitive, too frail. Our morality of pity, which I was the first to criticize, reflects the hyper- irritability that marks all decadence. Attempts to give this morality a scientific foundation, as Schopenhauer's morality of pity sought to do, are fundamentally decadent and closely aligned with Christian ethics.

Strong ages and noble cultures regarded pity, neighborly love, and self- denial as contemptible traits. They measured their worth by their positive forces, their creative tension, and their ability to stand apart. By this measure, the Renaissance stands as the last great age, while we moderns—obsessed with self- preservation, neighborly love, and cautious virtues like industry and equity— represent a weak one. Our virtues arise from our frailty. The modern idea of "equality" and the process of leveling everyone to the same standard are hallmarks of a declining culture. Strong ages celebrated the differences between people, the "pathos of distance," the instinct to distinguish oneself, and the courage to embrace hierarchy. These qualities are eroding. The gap between extremes is closing, and society is flattening into sameness.

All our political theories, including the structure of "The German Empire," reflect this decline. Even the ideals of modern science are unconsciously shaped by the forces of decadence. My critique of English and French sociology remains the same: it takes the symptoms of societal decline—its frailty and leveling instincts— and mistakes them for universal norms. Sociology today idealizes descending life, the decay of all organizing power, and the erosion of rank and distinction. This is what our socialists champion as progress. But it is not only socialists who are guilty of this error. Herbert Spencer, with his vision of altruism's triumph, was equally a decadent. To him, and to many others, this collapse of vitality appeared as an ideal to be pursued.

My Concept of Freedom.—The value of something is not always found in what it helps us achieve but often in what it demands from us—the price we must pay. Liberal institutions, for example, lose their essence of freedom the moment they become securely established. Once they are no longer contested, they turn into oppressive forces that stifle true freedom. These institutions undermine the Will to Power, promoting mediocrity as a virtue. They encourage conformity, making people timid, complacent, and fixated on comfort. Under them, the herd instinct triumphs, and humanity is reduced to a collective of obedient cattle. Liberalism, stripped of its idealism, becomes nothing more than the domestication of mankind.

However, the same liberal institutions, when fought for and not yet fully realized, can inspire the very opposite. Struggle for their creation and survival fosters freedom because it involves conflict. And it is war—war for freedom— that preserves the untamed, illiberal instincts essential for liberty. War trains individuals to be free. So, what is freedom? Freedom is the will to take responsibility for oneself. It is the capacity to maintain the distance that distinguishes you from others, to embrace hardship, endure privation, and remain indifferent even to life itself when necessary. It is the willingness to sacrifice, not only others but also yourself, for a cause you believe in. Freedom is the triumph of warrior instincts—those that revel in challenge and victory— over the instincts that crave mere comfort and happiness.

The truly free man despises the shallow comfort idolized by merchants, Christians, cattle, women, Englishmen, and democrats. For him, comfort is contemptible. The free man is a warrior. The measure of freedom, whether in individuals or nations, is determined by the resistance they have to overcome and the effort it takes to stay above it all. True freedom is greatest where the challenge is fiercest— just steps away from tyranny, on the threshold of being overpowered. Psychologically, tyranny represents the inner, powerful instincts that demand the utmost discipline to subdue. Julius Caesar is the finest example of such a free spirit, a man who mastered his instincts with an iron will. Politically, the same holds true: history shows that nations worth admiring were never formed under liberal institutions. It was great danger that shaped them into something worthy of reverence. Danger reveals our hidden strengths, awakens our virtues, and compels us to innovate and defend ourselves. It forces us to become resourceful and discover our inner genius.

The first principle of freedom is this: strength is born of necessity. Without the need to be strong, no one becomes strong. The greatest incubators of strength, the strongest individuals and societies to ever exist, emerged from aristocratic communities like Rome and Venice. These societies understood freedom as I do—not as a given, but as something that must be seized, something you either have or do not have, something you will for yourself and take by force.

A Criticism of Modernity.—We all agree on one thing: our institutions are failing. Yet the fault does not lie with these institutions themselves but with us. We no longer possess the instincts that once gave rise to institutions and sustained them. Without those instincts, the institutions themselves are crumbling and disappearing because we are no longer capable of upholding them. Democracy has always marked the decline of organizational power. I pointed this out as early as "Human,

All Too Human," where I described modern democracy, along with its half-measures like the "German Empire," as forms of a decaying State.

For institutions to exist and thrive, a particular kind of will is necessary—a will that is instinctive, commanding, and even harshly anti-liberal. This will demands allegiance to tradition, authority, and a responsibility that spans generations, stretching infinitely backward and forward in time. When such a will is present, empires with lasting power emerge, like the imperium Romanum or, in our era, Russia. Russia is the only nation today that demonstrates the endurance, strength, and patience required for genuine stability, a nation that can afford to wait, that can still promise a future. Russia stands as the antithesis of the petty- statism, fragility, and nervous exhaustion that plague Europe, particularly brought to the forefront by the foundation of the German Empire.

The modern Western world no longer harbors the instincts that produce institutions or the future. These instincts are fundamentally at odds with what is called the "modern spirit." People live recklessly in the moment, at breakneck speed, with little thought for long-term responsibility. And yet, this is celebrated and called "freedom." But all the qualities that make institutions enduring and meaningful are now despised, ridiculed, and rejected. Even the faintest whisper of authority sends people into a panic about a potential new slavery. In our politics and political parties, the instinct to value and preserve what is solid has decayed so deeply that people instinctively prefer what dissolves, what speeds up the collapse of everything.

Take modern marriage as an example. Its original rationality has vanished completely, but this is not a criticism of marriage itself— it is a criticism of modernity. Marriage once had a clear, rational foundation. It rested on the exclusive legal responsibility of the husband, which acted as a stabilizing force within the union. This stability gave marriage a weight and seriousness that countered the fleeting impulses of sentiment, passion, or momentary desires. Marriage also relied on the absolute indissolubility of the bond, which instilled it with permanence, regardless of the accidents of emotion. Additionally, the responsibility of choosing marriage partners fell to the family, which ensured a certain strategic and long-term coherence in these unions.

The increasing preference for love marriages, however, has undermined the very foundation of matrimony. No institution can ever be built upon a fleeting idiosyncrasy such as "love." Love is too transitory, too unstable to bear the weight of a lasting structure. Marriage can be based on more enduring forces: sexual desire, the instinct of property (with the wife and children seen as possessions), or the instinct of dominion. The latter is particularly vital, as it drives the creation of the smallest yet enduring unit of governance—the family. The family requires children and heirs to carry forward its acquired power, wealth, and influence, ensuring a continuity of purpose and solidarity in instincts from one generation to the next.

Marriage, as an institution, assumes a commitment to the greatest and most enduring forms of organization. It presupposes that society as a whole is willing to secure its own continuity into the distant future. Without this shared commitment, marriage loses its meaning. And this is exactly what has happened to modern marriage: it has lost its meaning, and as a result, it is gradually being abolished.

The question of the working man arises from a combination of foolishness and the underlying degenerate instincts that fuel the intellectual confusion of modern times. There are matters so basic and essential to the order of things that they should never even be questioned. This principle, rooted in instinct, serves as the foundation for survival and continuity. Yet here we are, asking what we should do about the European working class, having transformed their existence into a "question." What is expected now? These workers have been made too aware of their position, their situation framed as an issue, and their sense of entitlement has grown. They question more and more, with increasing boldness, and why wouldn't they? They know they have the numbers on their side.

There's no chance now of cultivating a humble, contented worker like the kind found in China—a course that would have been both reasonable and necessary. Instead, thoughtless and shortsighted decisions have destroyed the very instincts required for the existence of a functional and stable working class. By declaring the working man fit for military service, granting him the right to unionize, and giving him a vote, society has made his discontent inevitable. What did people expect? These concessions have led him to see his position not as a fact of life but as a moral outrage, as an injustice. And yet I ask again, what is the goal here? If people desire a certain outcome, they must also desire the means to achieve it. If society wants workers, it is madness to educate them into believing they are masters.

The kind of freedom being clamored for today is not the kind I mean when I speak of freedom. In our era, leaving individuals to their instincts only leads to chaos. These instincts often contradict and destroy one another, tearing individuals apart from within. Modern life itself can be described as a state of physiological self-contradiction. A rational system of education would seek to suppress some instincts with rigorous discipline, allowing others to grow strong and dominant. This pruning would make individuals coherent and capable. Instead, what we see today is the opposite. The loudest calls for independence, for unchecked development, and for "letting go" come from those who most desperately need restraint. This phenomenon extends to politics and even art. It is a sign of decline, another proof of our instincts faltering. The modern understanding of "freedom" is not a triumph; it is evidence of our degeneration.

When faith becomes necessary, honesty among moralists and saints becomes exceedingly rare. They may claim to value honesty; they may even believe they practice it. But when belief is more effective, more convincing, and ultimately more useful than deliberate hypocrisy, instinct makes that hypocrisy innocent. This principle is key to understanding the behavior of great saints. The same can be said for philosophers, who are their own kind of saint. Their role requires them to uphold certain truths, truths that bolster their craft and grant it public approval. To borrow from Kant, these are the truths of "practical reason." Philosophers know what they must prove. This is their pragmatism, their trade secret. They recognize one another by their shared adherence to these "essential truths." The commandment "Thou shalt not lie" is, for the philosopher, merely a warning: Do not dare, dear philosopher, to speak the entire truth.

A quiet reminder to conservatives: What we have learned—or should have learned—is that regression is impossible. Reverting to a previous state, whether biologically, culturally, or morally, is a fantasy. As physiologists, we know this for a fact. Yet priests and moralists have always believed otherwise. They have tried to bend and force humanity back into older molds of virtue, imposing the rigid standards of morality as if humanity could fit back into them. Even modern politicians mimic these moralists. Today, some political movements aim to force the world into a backward march, longing for an imagined past where everything supposedly worked. But not everyone is suited to move backward like a crab.

The truth is, humanity must move forward, even if this means deeper descent into decadence. This is how I define modern "progress": each step forward is another step further into decay. We cannot halt this trajectory entirely. At best, we might delay it, creating bottlenecks of degeneration that will only result in more violent and catastrophic outbursts later on. But we cannot turn back the tide. Progress, as we conceive of it today, is no more than the managed advance of decline.

My concept of genius begins with the idea that great men and great eras are like explosive forces, holding within them a tremendous amount of stored energy. Their very existence depends on both historical and physiological conditions. They arise only when energy has been conserved, hoarded, and preserved over long periods without any premature release. Once the tension has built to an extreme, even the slightest trigger can ignite the force, giving rise to genius, extraordinary deeds, and monumental changes in the world.

What, then, is the significance of external factors like environment, historical periods, or the so-called "spirit of the age"? Consider Napoleon as an example. Revolutionary France, and even more so the years preceding the Revolution, cultivated values and produced types of people entirely contrary to what Napoleon represented. Yet Napoleon emerged not as a product of that age, but as a legacy of a stronger, older, and more enduring civilization—a civilization whose vitality France was busy dismantling. Precisely because he was different, because he drew from a deeper reservoir of power and tradition, Napoleon became the uncontested master of his time. His strength surpassed that of his contemporaries, allowing him to dominate them.

Great individuals are essential, yet the era in which they appear is largely a matter of chance. Their near-inevitable mastery of their time stems from their greater strength, maturity, and the longer duration for which power has been stored within them. The relationship between genius and its era is like that between strength and weakness, or maturity and immaturity. A genius always towers above his age, which is comparatively youthful, feeble, indecisive, and naive.

Today, however, many people hold a different view, especially in France, where the idea that the "environment" or "zeitgeist" shapes genius has gained almost scientific credibility, even among physiologists. This belief—a sort of nervous disorder disguised as intellectual insight—is a troubling and disheartening sign. England, too, subscribes to this view, but this is hardly surprising. The English tend to interpret genius in only two ways: either through a democratic lens, as exemplified by Buckle, or through a religious perspective, as Carlyle does.

Great individuals and great ages bring with them immense danger. They exhaust what came before and often leave sterility in their wake. A great man signifies an ending, just as a great age—take the Renaissance, for instance— marks the conclusion of a long buildup of energy. Genius, in both action and creation, is inherently extravagant. Its greatness lies in its uncontainable outpouring of energy. The instinct for self-preservation is overridden in such figures; their overwhelming energy compels them to give and expend themselves completely, without restraint. This process is not calculated or deliberate—it is as inevitable as a river bursting through its dams.

People often misinterpret this self-expenditure, labeling it "self-sacrifice" or admiring it as "heroism." They speak of the genius's disregard for personal well- being, their unwavering dedication to an idea, a cause, or a nation. But these are misconceptions. A genius does not act out of deliberate self-sacrifice; they overflow naturally, consuming themselves in the process. They cannot help but give everything—they are compelled by their very nature to do so, just as a river must flow.

Humanity, having reaped countless benefits from such explosive forces, has responded with a peculiar kind of gratitude. It has attributed to these figures a higher morality, seeing in them ideals of selflessness and devotion. Yet this, too, is a misunderstanding. It is not morality that drives the genius; it is the sheer necessity of their nature. Humanity thanks its benefactors in the only way it knows— by misinterpreting them.

The criminal and those like him represent the strong man placed in conditions that do not suit him—a strong nature forced into sickness. He is a man who thrives in wild and untamed environments, where freedom and danger shape life, where the instincts of strength—his shield and sword—find their rightful place. But within society, these very virtues are outlawed. His natural instincts are immediately entangled with emotions like fear, suspicion, and shame. Such a conflict is nearly a formula for physical and psychological decline. When a person must carry out what he is best at—what he most loves—not openly but in secrecy, with constant caution, restraint, and craftiness, it saps his vitality. The repeated necessity of paying for his instincts through danger, persecution, or punishment causes him to turn against those very instincts. He comes to see them as his curse.

This process unfolds most severely in our society, which is tame, average, and emasculated. A natural man, one unshaped by civilization, coming from the mountains or the open seas, is almost certain to decay into a criminal in such an environment. Yet, not always: there are cases where the natural man is stronger than society itself. Napoleon, the Corsican, stands as the most famous example of this triumph.

To explore this further, we can turn to Dostoevsky, a witness of singular importance on this issue. Dostoevsky—incidentally the only psychologist from whom I have learned anything—was among the great discoveries of my life, even more rewarding than Stendhal. This deeply insightful man, who had every reason to hold the shallow Germans in contempt, found among the Siberian convicts he lived with for years—those utterly hopeless criminals with no chance of returning to society—a type of humanity very different from what he had anticipated. These convicts were made of the hardest and most valuable material to be found in Russian society, carved from a superior stock.

Now let us generalize the case of the criminal. Let us think of all individuals who, for whatever reason, fail to gain society's approval. These are people who know they are not seen as beneficial or respectable. They exist with the feelings of outcasts, akin to the Chandala, aware that they are not treated as equals but as untouchables, proscribed, or polluted. Their thoughts and actions are shaped by this awareness, marked by a certain shadowy, subterranean quality. Their inner world becomes dimmed compared to those who live in the sunlight of public favor.

Interestingly, many of the figures we now admire and respect once lived under such conditions. The scientist, the artist, the genius, the independent thinker, the actor, the entrepreneur, and the great adventurer—all of these lived lives that were once disdained. As long as the priest stood as the highest type of man, all others of value were diminished, seen as less worthy. However, the time is coming—this I assert with certainty—when the priest will be regarded as the lowest type of man, as our Chandala, the most dishonest and disreputable among us.

Even now, under the most lenient and humane customs ever known in Europe, any life that stands apart, that is prolonged in obscurity or strangeness, begins to resemble the criminal type. All pioneers of the spirit bear for a time the grim and fateful mark of the Chandala. It is not because they are directly seen as such by others, but because they themselves feel the enormous gulf that separates them from what is accepted and honored in tradition. Nearly every genius experiences this phase of the "Catilinarian life"—a stage filled with hatred, revenge, and rebellion against everything stagnant and established. Catiline—the early form of every future Caesar.

Here the outlook is free. When a philosopher chooses silence, it can signify the greatness of his soul; when he contradicts himself, it might stem from love; and when he lies, it may well be the courtesy of a knight of knowledge. As someone aptly remarked, "It is unworthy of great hearts to spread the turmoil they feel." Yet, it is equally true that there can be greatness in not avoiding what seems undignified. A woman in love may sacrifice her honor, a knight of knowledge who "loves" may sacrifice his humanity, and a god who loved became a Jew.

Beauty is no accident. Even the beauty of a race or family, the grace and perfection of all its movements, does not come easily. Like genius, it is the culmination of generations of effort. Great sacrifices have always been made on the altar of good taste, and much has been deliberately left undone. The 17th century in France serves as a prime example of this, a time when both action and restraint worked hand in hand to elevate aesthetics. A principle of selection was applied to everything—company, environment, clothing, and even the expression of sexual desire. Beauty was prioritized over profit, habit, public opinion, and laziness. The first rule was simple: no one should "let themselves go," not even in private.

Good things are exceedingly expensive. This is true not only in monetary terms but in the discipline required to acquire them.

Whoever possesses beauty or refinement is different from someone still striving for it. Everything good is an inheritance, something passed down and refined over time. What isn't inherited is incomplete; it is only a beginning. In ancient Athens, during Cicero's time, men and boys were more beautiful than women. But this was the result of centuries of rigorous effort and self-discipline devoted to male beauty. Let us not be deceived: refining feelings and thoughts alone is insufficient. This is the great failing of German culture, which emphasizes abstract ideals but neglects the body.

The body must be persuaded first. Maintaining a refined and tasteful demeanor, associating only with others who do the same, shapes one's entire being over a few generations. The destiny of a people or humanity is determined by where they begin their cultural efforts. The starting point must be the body, behavior, diet, and physiology—not the "soul," as priests and moralists insist. The Greeks understood this foundational truth and acted upon it, which is why they remain the first true creators of culture. Christianity, with its disdain for the body, has been the greatest misfortune to ever befall humanity.

Progress, as I see it, is not about returning to a primal state but ascending into a more profound and untamed naturalness. It is about reaching a height where one can grapple with grand challenges, even play with them. Take Napoleon as an example of what I mean by a "return to nature." In his tactics and strategy, he exemplified this ascent. But Rousseau? Where did he wish to return? Rousseau, that first modern man, was both an idealist and a scoundrel. Needing moral dignity to endure his own reflection, he was a creature of vanity and self-loathing. He camped on the threshold of modernity, calling for a "return to nature." But what kind of nature did he envision? I detest Rousseau even in the Revolution. The Revolution's bloody spectacle does not disturb me as much as its Rousseau-inspired morality. It was the morality of mediocrity masquerading as justice.

The doctrine of equality is the deadliest poison of all, for it pretends to speak in the name of justice while veiling true justice. Justice would say, "To equals, equality; to unequals, inequality." Never should unequal things be made equal. The horrors and bloodshed associated with this doctrine have granted it an undeserved aura of sanctity. The Revolution, as a drama, has deceived even noble minds. Only Goethe, as far as I can see, viewed it as it should be seen— with utter disdain.

Goethe was not merely a German figure but a European one. He was a bold attempt to overcome the 18th century by reclaiming the naturalness of the Renaissance. In Goethe, the instincts of his century—its sentimentality, its idolization of nature, and its anti-historical spirit—were transformed. He was a realist who embraced life rather than shrinking from it. Goethe sought wholeness, uniting reason, feeling, sensuality, and will, in opposition to the fragmented doctrines of Kant. He disciplined himself into a harmonious whole and became a master of himself.

Goethe dreamed of a complete human being: cultured, physically skilled, self-respecting, and capable of indulging in life's richness without being destroyed by it. He was tolerant not from weakness but from strength, turning adversity to his advantage.

He embodied a cheerful fatalism, embracing the universe with confidence. Such faith, the highest of all, is what I have called Dionysian—a celebration of life that affirms all existence.

In some ways, the 19th century aspired to Goethe's ideals: broad understanding, bold realism, and reverence for life's facts. Yet, the result was chaos, fatigue, and a retreat into the sentimental mediocrity of the 18th century—romanticism, socialism, and altruism. This century, especially in its later years, became an intensified version of its predecessor: a period of decline. Goethe, despite his greatness, was merely an episode—a magnificent but futile effort.

Great men should not be judged by their immediate utility. Humanity often misunderstands its benefactors, attributing to them motives they never had. Goethe is the last German I respect. He understood the cross, as I understand it, and shared my disdain for what it symbolizes. People often ask why I write in German when I am so little read in Germany. My aim is not immediate recognition but to create works that time itself cannot erode. Both in form and content, I strive for a degree of immortality. The aphorism and the concise sentence, forms in which I am a master, are eternal. My ambition is to say in ten sentences what others cannot say in a whole book.

With Thus Spoke Zarathustra, I have given humanity its deepest book.

Soon, I will give it its most independent one.

Chapter 10
Things I owe to The Ancients

In conclusion, I want to say a few words about that world to which I have sought new ways of access and for which I may have discovered a new passage—the ancient world. My taste, which is perhaps the opposite of tolerant, does not wholeheartedly embrace even this world. In general, I am not eager to say Yes to things. I would rather say No, or, better yet, say nothing at all. This is true of entire cultures; it is true of books; and it is true of places and landscapes.

To be honest, there are very few ancient books that hold a special place in my life, and the most famous ones are not included among them.

My sense of style, particularly for the epigram as a form of expression, seemed to awaken almost instantly when I first encountered Sallust. I still recall the astonishment of my respected teacher Corssen when he was compelled to give his worst Latin student the highest marks. Suddenly, and all at once, I understood everything there was to learn. The condensed and austere language, packed with meaning and with an almost mischievous indifference to "beautiful words" and "beautiful feelings"—in these I found my own inclination. In my writings leading up to Thus Spoke Zarathustra, you will notice a serious effort to achieve a Roman style—a style that aspires to the permanence of "more enduring than bronze."

The same thing occurred when I first read Horace. No poet, even to this day, has given me the same intense artistic pleasure as an ode by Horace did from the very beginning. In some languages, it would be ridiculous to even attempt what Horace achieves. His writing is like a mosaic where every word radiates its influence both to the left and the right. Its placement, sound, and meaning all work together to create an extraordinary effect. This economy of words—where the least amount of signs produces the maximum energy—is distinctly Roman. And, if you trust my judgment, it is the very definition of noble excellence. Compared to this, all other poetry seems almost crude, like meaningless, sentimental rambling.

I cannot say that I owe the Greeks anything resembling the profound impressions I have received from the Romans. To be frank, the Greeks can never hold the same significance for us as the Romans do. The Greeks are not teachers in the same way. Their style is too peculiar, too fluid, to impose itself as a model or to attain the weight of a true classic. Who has ever truly learned how to write from a Greek? It is impossible to imagine anyone mastering writing without the Romans. They are our true instructors. And do not suggest Plato to me—I remain fundamentally skeptical of him. I have never been able to align myself with the tradition among scholars of admiring Plato as an artist.

Even in antiquity, the most refined critics of taste were not taken by Plato as we are led to believe. To my mind, Plato jumbles all the forms of style into a chaotic mix. In this sense, he is one of the earliest examples of stylistic decadence. He shares this fault with the Cynics, who created the satura Menippea. The Platonic dialogue—a smug, almost juvenile form of dialectics—could only charm someone who has never read good French writers, such as Fontenelle. Plato, I must confess, bores me. At heart, my distrust of him is fundamental. I see him as profoundly removed from the essential instincts of the Hellenes, steeped in moral prejudices, and, in some respects, as a precursor to Christianity. For Plato, the idea of "good" is already the supreme value—a concept that foreshadows the Christian morality to come. If I had to give Plato's philosophy a blunt name, I might call it "lofty nonsense," or, if preferred, "idealism."

Humanity has paid a high price for this Athenian's education among the Egyptians—or perhaps among the Jews in Egypt? Plato, with his double-edged charm—the so-called "ideal"— became the bridge by which the nobler spirits of antiquity were led to misunderstand themselves and cross into the ideology that culminated in the Christian cross. And even now, how much Plato remains entrenched in the concepts of the "church," in its architecture, its system, and its practices!

For me, the cure, the antidote, and the reprieve from all this Platonism has always been Thucydides. His work represents my ideal of clarity and realism.

Perhaps Machiavelli's The Prince is his closest relative in spirit. Both refuse to delude themselves. They seek reason in reality, not in abstract rationality or morality. Thucydides is the antithesis of the sugary, romanticised vision of the Greeks that modern "classical education" instills in young minds. His writings should be read with great care, each line scrutinised, and his unspoken ideas considered just as seriously as his explicit words. Few thinkers possess so much depth in what they leave unsaid.

Thucydides is the consummate expression of the Sophist tradition, that movement grounded in realism which resisted the idealistic pretensions and moral posturing of Socratic thought as it spread in all directions. For me, Greek philosophy represents the decline of Greek instincts, whereas Thucydides encapsulates the unflinching, rigorous realism of the ancient Hellene.

The distinction between Thucydides and Plato is ultimately one of courage versus fear. Thucydides confronts reality with bravery and clarity, while Plato shrinks from it, retreating into the comforting arms of ideals. Thucydides is a master of his own mind and therefore a master of life. Plato, on the other hand, flees from life into the shadows of abstract ideals. This makes Thucydides not just a historian, but a thinker of unyielding power and strength, unmatched in his affirmation of reality.

To unearth examples of "beautiful souls," "golden means," or other supposed perfections among the Greeks, to admire their serene grandeur, their so-called ideal attitudes, or their exalted simplicity—this "exalted simplicity," which in truth is nothing more than a piece of German naivety, was something from which my inner psychologist always saved me. What I saw instead was their most powerful instinct: the relentless Will to Power. I saw them driven by the fierce and untamed force of this will, trembling with its violence. I recognized that their institutions were not built on harmony but on strategies of containment, created to protect every individual from the volatile, explosive energy simmering within their neighbor.

This immense internal tension found its outlet in violent and ruthless aggression directed outward, toward other states. Their cities tore at one another in brutal conflict, each striving to maintain peace within by externalizing the chaos. Strength became an absolute necessity in this environment, for danger was constant and ever-present, lurking at every corner. The extraordinary grace and flexibility of their bodies, the bold realism, and even the characteristic amorality of the Hellenes—these were not innate attributes but rather survival mechanisms. These traits were forged under the pressures of their circumstances, not gifts they were born with.

Even their festivals and artistic achievements were not mere expressions of joy or creativity but instruments of self-assertion and self-glorification. These were deliberate efforts to heighten their sense of superiority, to project it outward, and sometimes to inspire terror in those who observed them. Imagine judging the Greeks through a lens shaped by German interpretations—seeing them through the narrow focus of their philosophers. Worse yet, imagine using the staid, suburban respectability of the Socratic schools as the key to understanding the essence of what is truly Hellenic!

The truth is that the philosophers were the decadent offshoots of Hellas, a counter-movement that ran against the grain of their original and noble values. They opposed the agonal instinct, the competitive drive that defined the Hellenic spirit; they rejected the spirit of the polis, the pride in racial excellence, and the authority of deep-rooted traditions. Socratic virtues were only preached to the Greeks because the Greeks had already begun to lose their virtue. Irritable, cowardly, unsteady, and increasingly prone to theatricality, they were a people in decline, desperate for the moral sermons directed at them.

But these moral prescriptions did not save them. They could not. Instead, these grand gestures and lofty words were little more than adornments for a society in decay. Decadents are always drawn to such displays, for they cling to the illusion of greatness even as it slips further from their grasp. Morality, as the Greeks came to know it through their philosophers, was not a cure but a symptom—a symptom of a people who had already lost their way.

I was the first to take the phenomenon of Dionysus seriously in order to understand the ancient, vibrant, and abundantly rich Hellenic instinct. This phenomenon, remarkable in its essence, can only be interpreted as an expression of overflowing energy. Whoever has studied the Greeks as profoundly as Jakob Burckhardt of Basel, one of the finest connoisseurs of their culture, would immediately recognize that this interpretation opened a new path of understanding. In his Cultur der Griechen, Burckhardt even dedicated a special chapter to this subject, acknowledging its significance. On the other hand, consider the almost laughable deficiency of instinct displayed by German philologists when they approach the question of Dionysus. The famous Lobeck, for example, burrowed into this mysterious realm with the assuredness of a dried-up bookworm, convinced he was being scientific when, in truth, his approach was painfully superficial and immature.

With all the pomp of erudition, Lobeck reduced the mysteries to trivialities, suggesting that the orgies merely taught participants banal facts like how wine stirs desire or that plants bloom and fade with the seasons. He explained away the immense wealth of rites, symbols, and myths rooted in these rituals—which permeate the entirety of antiquity—with the dismissive notion that the Greeks merely invented festivals and myths as idle diversions. His conclusion, that celebratory behaviors like laughing, weeping, and dancing formed the basis of elaborate traditions, is nothing short of absurd. This reductionist nonsense, presented as scholarship, deserves no serious consideration.

Contrast this with the more profound vision of the Greeks as seen by figures like Winckelmann and Goethe. Yet even they misunderstood something essential. Their idealized image of the Greeks—one of calm grandeur, rational simplicity, and harmonious beauty—could not accommodate the Dionysian essence. Goethe, for instance, likely dismissed the ecstatic fervor of Dionysian rites, failing to recognize that these mysteries revealed the core of the Greek soul. This core was their "will to life," expressed most powerfully in the Dionysian state. Through these mysteries, the Greeks secured for themselves a profound connection to life eternal, embracing its cyclical nature and celebrating the continuity of existence through procreation and renewal.

To the Greeks, the mysteries of sexuality symbolized the sacred foundation of life itself. Every aspect of birth, creation, and renewal was steeped in reverence and seen as divine. Even pain, particularly the pain of childbirth, was sanctified, as it was inseparable from creation and growth. This sanctification of pain carried a deeper message: to ensure the endless joy of creation, the "pains of childbirth" must be eternal. Such is the symbolism of Dionysus, the affirmation of life in all its fullness, including its suffering, its ecstasy, and its inexhaustible capacity for renewal.

Christianity later distorted this profound connection, branding sexuality as impure and casting filth upon the very foundation of existence. In doing so, it severed humanity from the instinctual reverence for life that the Greeks held sacred. Yet it was the psychology of orgiasm—this experience of overwhelming vitality, where even pain becomes a stimulant—that gave me the key to understanding the concept of tragic feeling. Aristotle and the pessimists misunderstood tragedy entirely. Far from being an expression of Greek pessimism, as Schopenhauer claimed, tragedy represents the ultimate rejection of such a worldview. It is a triumphant affirmation of life, embracing even its most perplexing and terrifying aspects.

The essence of tragedy lies in its exultation of life's inexhaustible energy, even in the sacrifice of its highest forms. This is the Dionysian spirit, the bridge to the psychology of the tragic poet. It does not aim to escape terror and pity or to purge dangerous passions through catharsis, as Aristotle supposed. Instead, it transcends terror and pity, rejoicing in the eternal cycle of creation and destruction, the endless becoming that is life itself. This lust for life, which includes a love for destruction as part of creation, is at the heart of the Dionysian worldview.

With this understanding, I return to the foundation of my philosophy, to the starting point of my intellectual journey. The Birth of Tragedy was my first attempt to reevaluate all values, and here, once again, I stand upon the same ground from which my will and power originate. I am the last disciple of the philosopher Dionysus, the prophet of eternal recurrence.

The End

Thank You for Reading

Dear Reader,

We hope this timeless classic has sparked your imagination and enriched your literary journey. Now that you've turned the final page, we want to share a vision for the future of reading—one where every classic you've ever wanted to explore is at your fingertips, in a format that best suits your life.

We'd like to invite you to gain immediate, unlimited digital & audiobook access to hundreds of the most treasured literary classics ever written—along with the option to secure deluxe paperback, hardcover & box set editions at printing cost. Together, we can spark a new global literary renaissance alongside our small, independent publishing house called "The Library of Alexandria."

Thousands of years ago, the Library of Alexandria stood as a beacon of knowledge—until it was lost to history. We aim to reignite that spirit of preservation and discovery right now, in the modern age—only this time, it's accessible to all, in every language and every format.

Picture a world where every timeless classic, novel, poem, or philosophical treatise is not only available to read but also updated for today's readers—modernized, translated into any language or dialect, and ready to enjoy in any format you choose, whether that is in an eBook, audiobook, paperback, or deluxe hardcover & box set version a printing cost.

By joining our movement to rebuild the modern Library of Alexandria, you become part of an unprecedented mission to offer:

* **Unlimited Audiobook & eBook Access to the Greatest Classics of All Time**

  Instantly explore thousands of legendary works, from Plato and Shakespeare to Jane Austen and Leo Tolstoy. All are instantly ready to read or listen to, giving you a complete literary universe at your fingertips.

- **Paperback & Deluxe Editions at Printing Costs:**

  Purchase any title in a paperback, deluxe hardbound, or deluxe boxset edition at printing costs, shipped right to your doorstep. Curate your personal library of Alexandria with editions worthy of display—crafted to last, designed to captivate, and delivered straight to your door.

- **Modern translations for Contemporary Readers in all languages and dialects**

  Discover a vast selection of classics reimagined in clear, current language—no more struggling with outdated phrases or obscure references. Next to the original versions, we aim to offer translations in as many languages and dialects as possible.

  As we continue our translation efforts and add new languages, readers everywhere can connect with these works as if they were written today. By bridging linguistic divides, you're contributing to ensuring that these timeless stories become more meaningful, accessible, and inspiring for people across the globe.

- **Your Personal Library of Alexandria:**

  Over the months and years, you'll curate a unique physical archive of classics—each volume a testament to your taste, curiosity, and love of knowledge. It's not just about owning books—it's about curating a cultural legacy you'll cherish and pass down for generations to come.

- **Join a Global Literary Renaissance:**

  Your support fuels an ongoing mission: allowing us to reinvest in offering deluxe print editions (including special boxsets) at their true cost, broaden the range of available formats and translations, and extend the reach of these works to new audiences worldwide. By joining today, you're not just preserving a legacy of masterpieces; you set in motion a powerful wave of literary accessibility.

We are more than a publisher—we're a movement, and we can't do it alone. Your support lets us scale our mission, preserving and reimagining history's greatest works for tomorrow's readers.

Become a Torchbearer of knowledge.

Thank you for picking up this book and allowing us into your literary journey. As you turn the pages, know that you're part of something larger: a global effort to keep these stories alive, share their wisdom across borders and generations, and spark a true cultural revival for the modern era.

If this resonates with you—please consider taking the next step by visiting:

www.libraryofalexandria.com

With gratitude and a shared love of knowledge,

The Modern Library of Alexandria Team

Visit:

www.libraryofalexandria.com

Or scan the code below: